MIHACK

...LEOPATRA
IN SPACE

BOOK THREE
...T OF THE TIME TABLETS

ace.
ret of t

7
7

graphix
AN IMPRINT OF
SCHOLASTIC

Copyright © 2016 by Mike Maihack

All rights reserved. Published by Graphix, an imprint of Scholastic Inc.,
Publishers since 1920. SCHOLASTIC, GRAPHIX, and associated logos are
trademarks and/or registered trademarks of Scholastic Inc.

The publisher does not have any control over and does not assume any
responsibility for author or third-party websites or their content.

No part of this publication may be reproduced, stored in a retrieval system,
or transmitted in any form or by any means, electronic, mechanical,
photocopying, recording, or otherwise, without written permission of the
publisher. For information regarding permission, write to Scholastic Inc.,
Attention: Permissions Department, 557 Broadway, New York, NY 10012.

This book is a work of fiction. Names, characters, places, and incidents
are either the product of the author's imagination or are used fictitiously,
and any resemblance to actual persons, living or dead, business
establishments, events, or locales is entirely coincidental.

Library of Congress Control Number: 2015946169

ISBN 978-0-545-83868-9 (hardcover)
ISBN 978-0-545-83867-2 (paperback)

10 9 8 7 6 5 4 3 2 1   16 17 18 19 20

Printed in China   62
First edition, May 2016
Color flatting by Dan Conner and Kate Carleton
Edited by Cassandra Pelham
Book design by Phil Falco
Creative Director: David Saylor

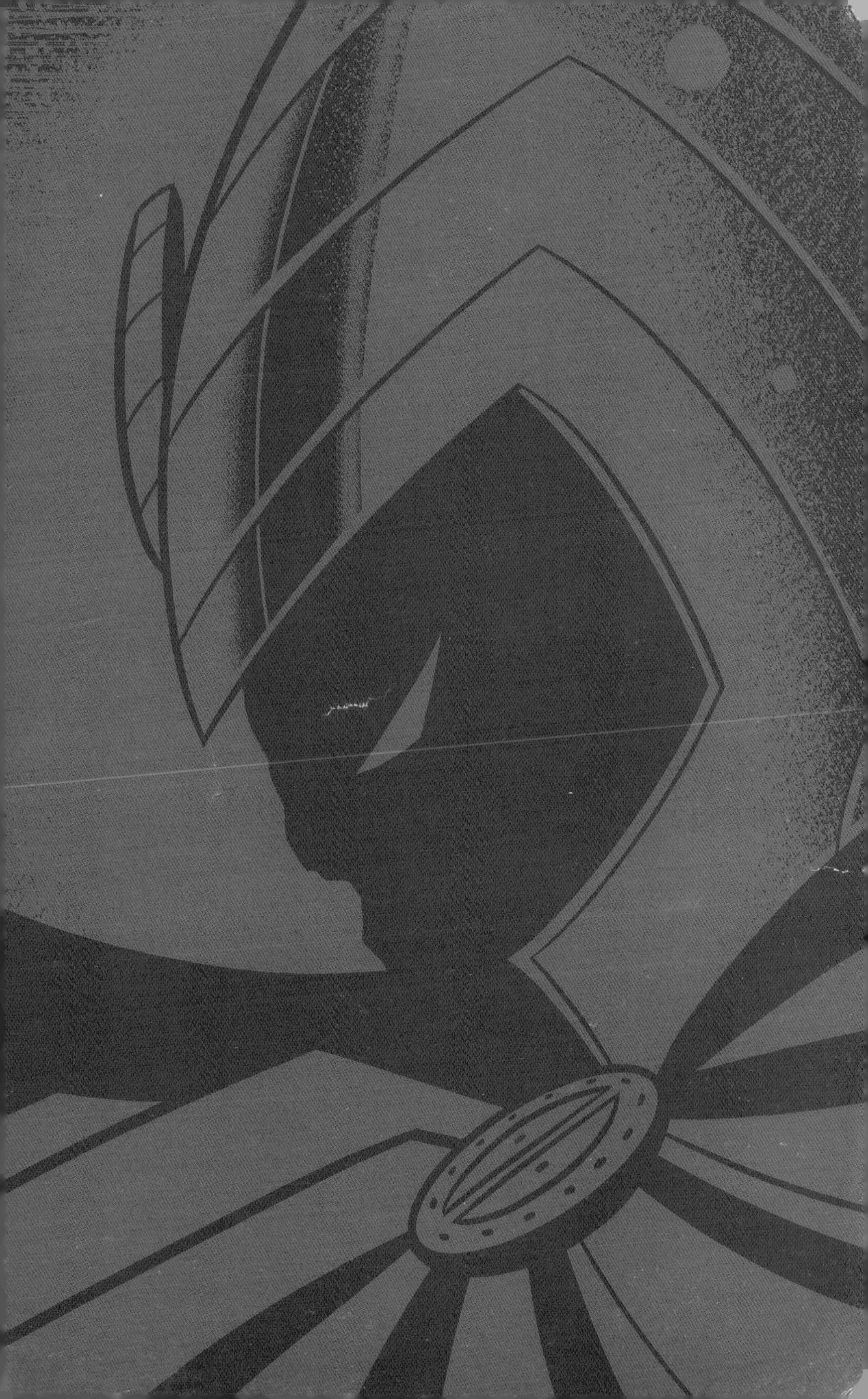

CHAPTER ONE

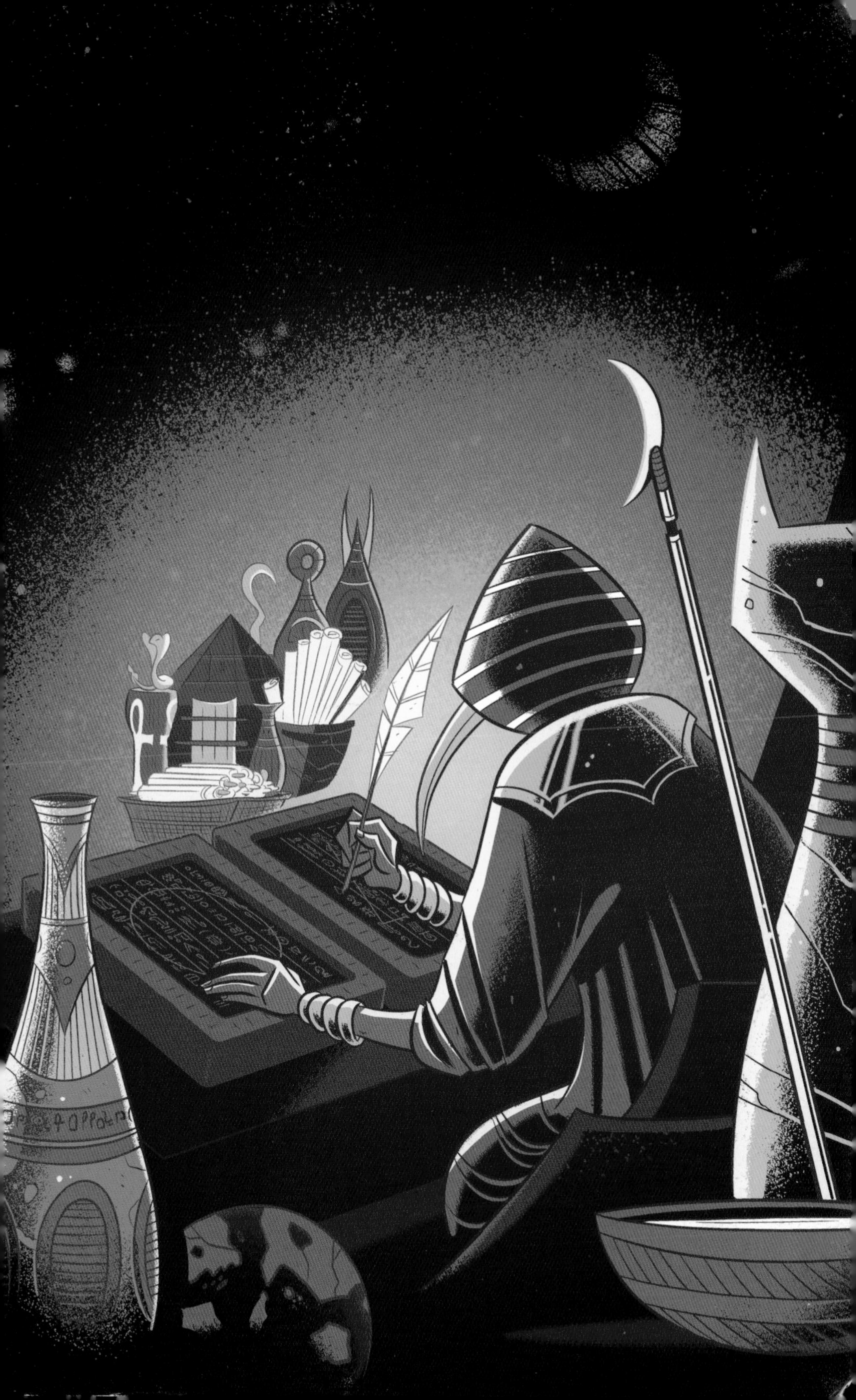

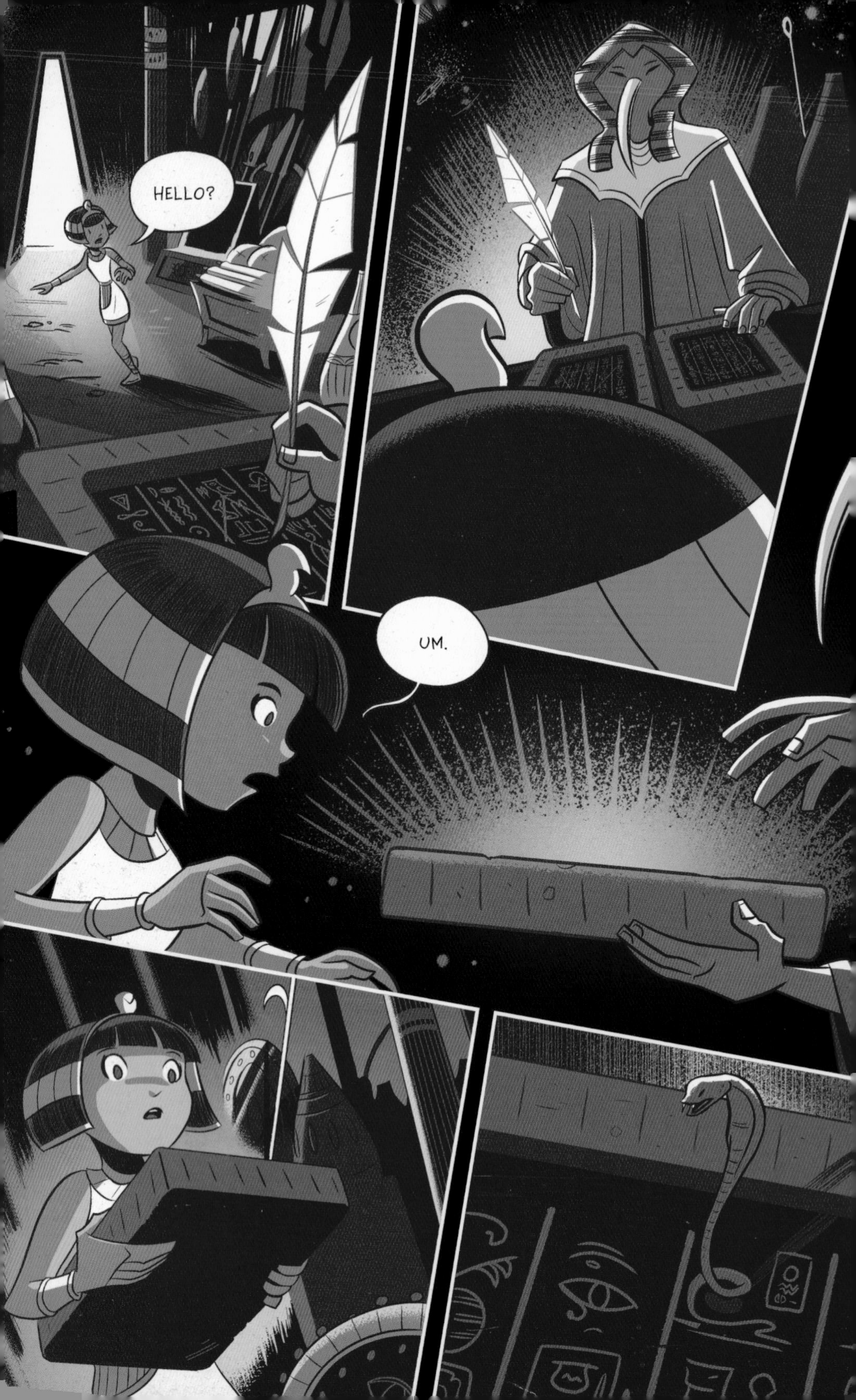
HELLO?
UM.

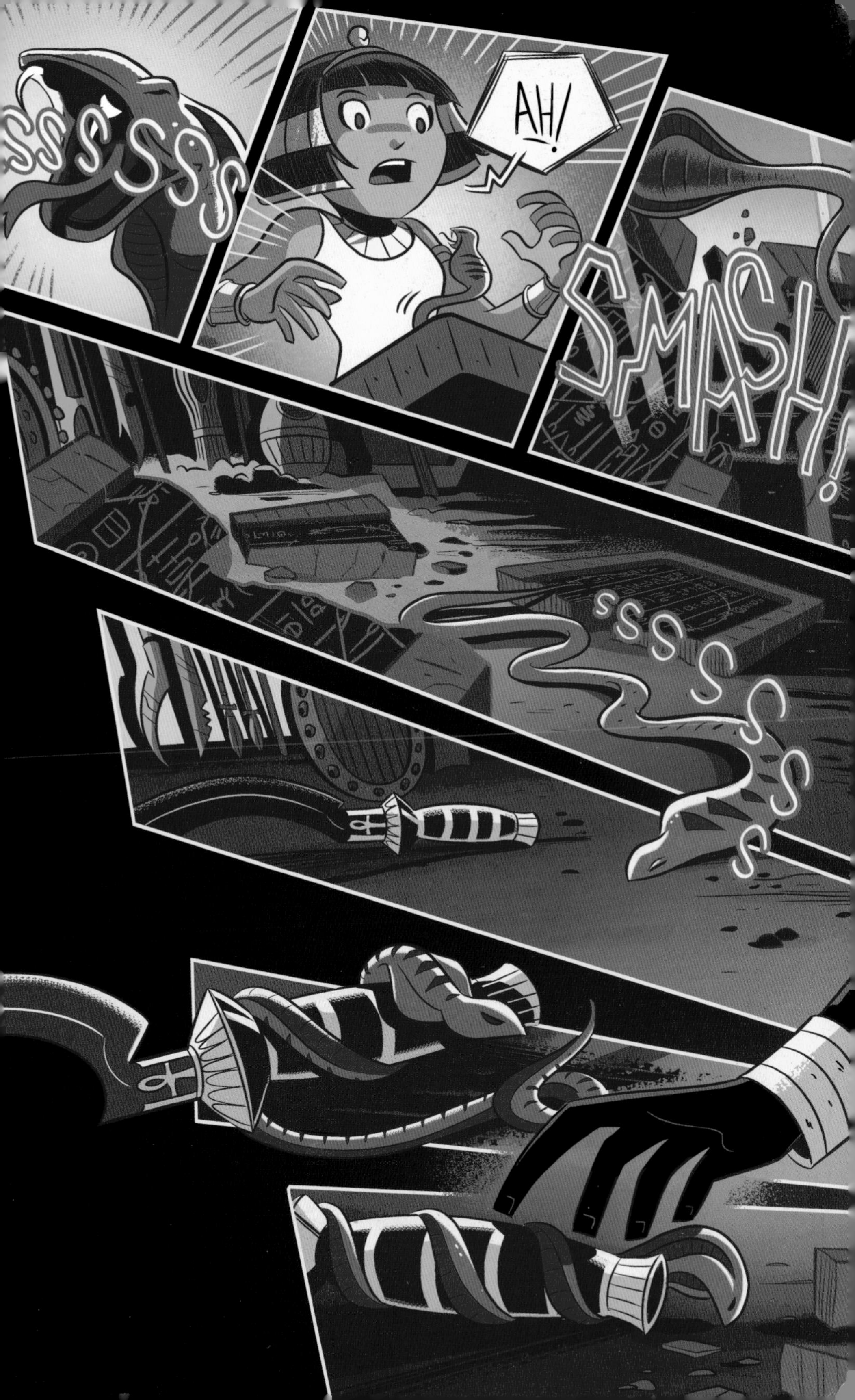
SSSSSS
AH!
SMASH!
SSSSSSSSS

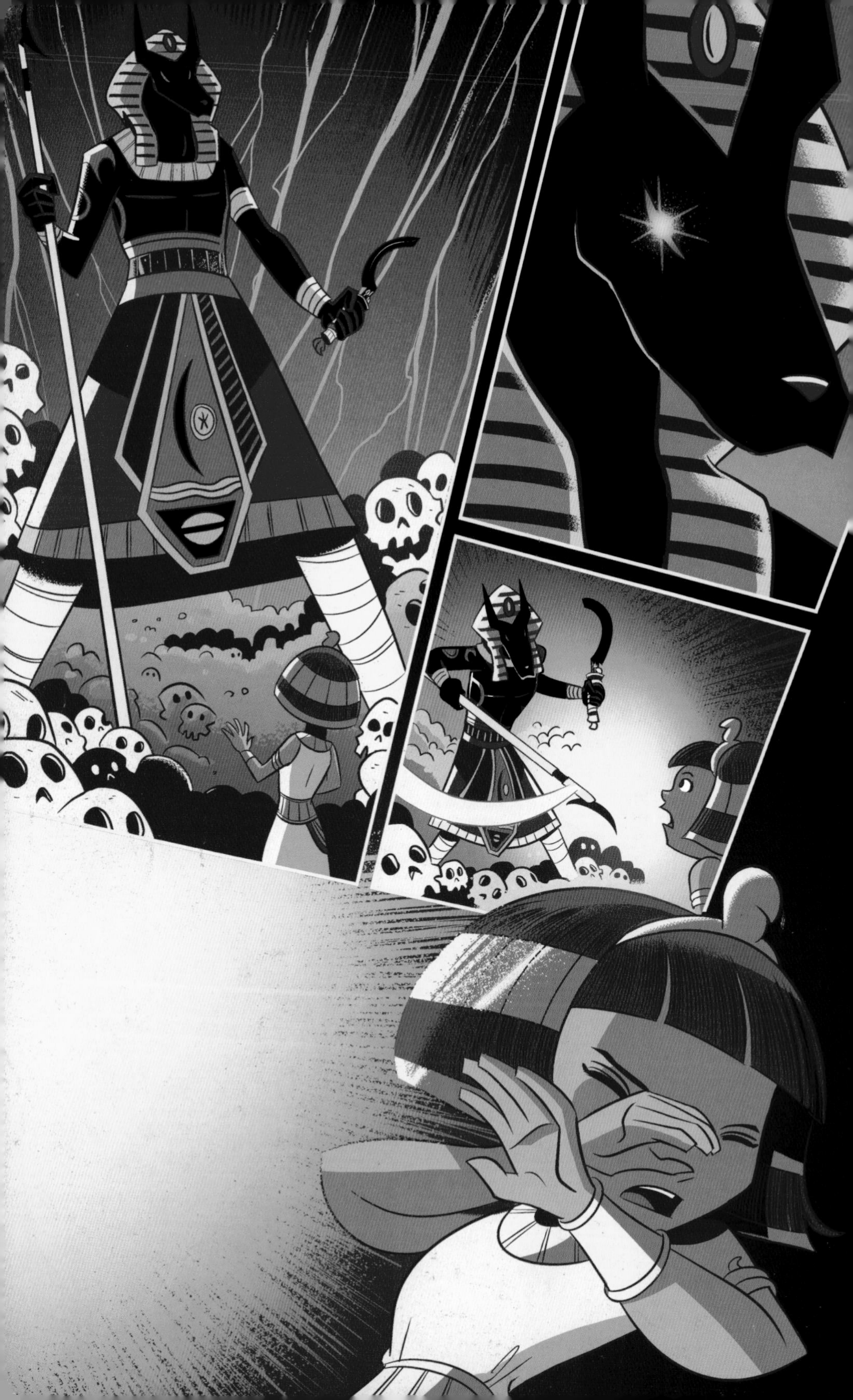

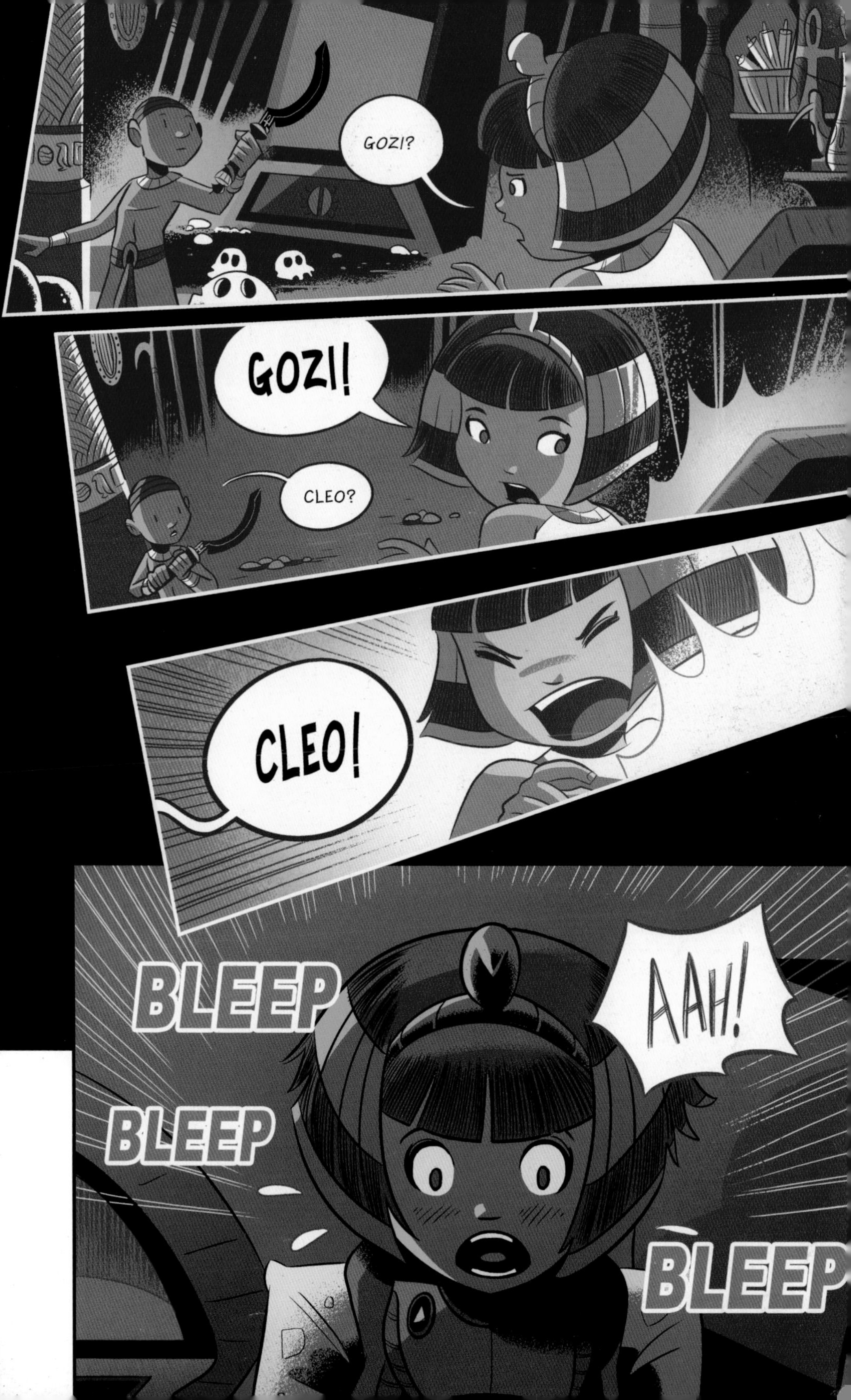
GOZI?
GOZI!
CLEO?
CLEO!
BLEEP
AAH!
BLEEP
BLEEP

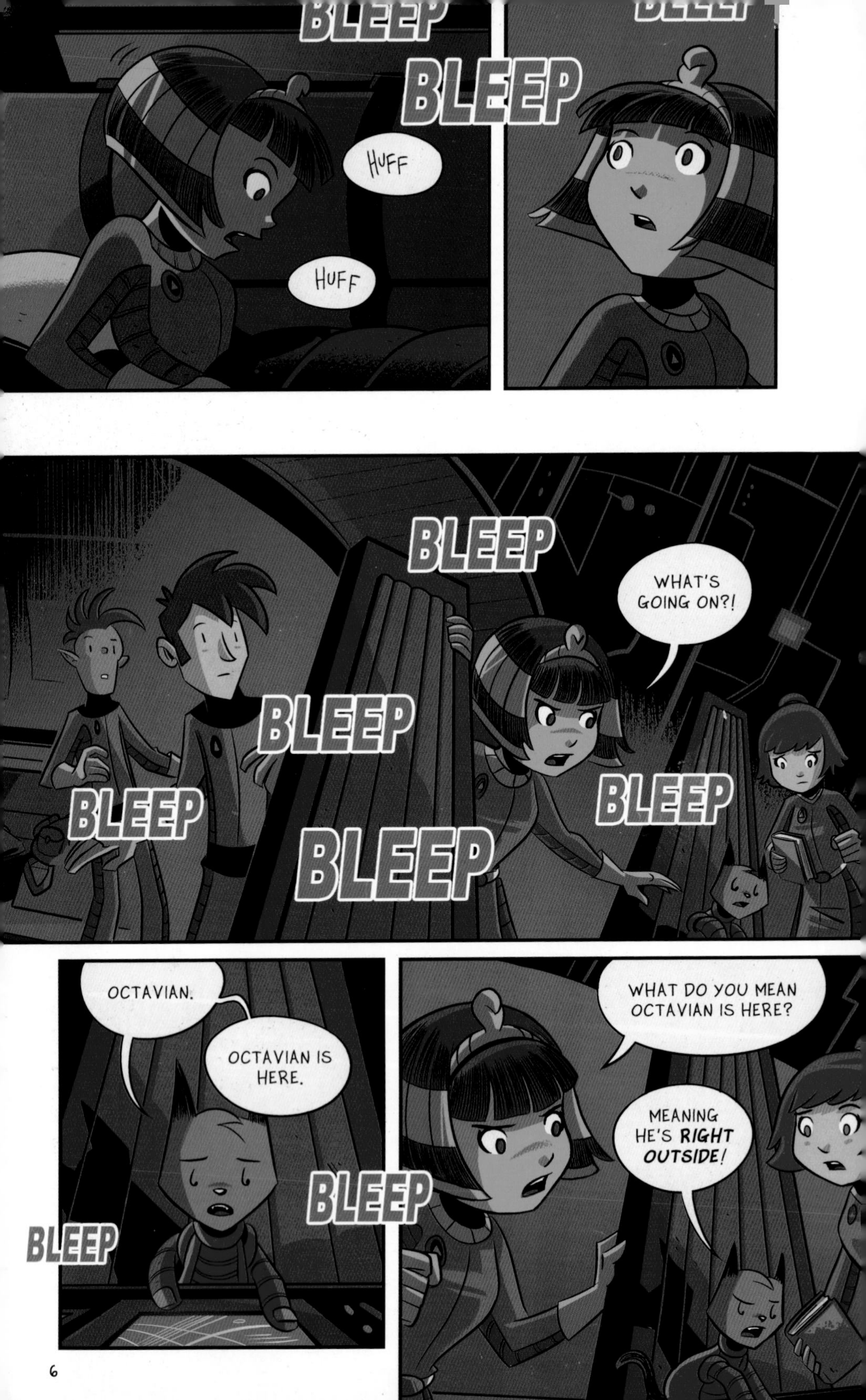
BLEEP
BLEEP
HUFF
HUFF
BLEEP
WHAT'S GOING ON?!
BLEEP
BLEEP
BLEEP
BLEEP
OCTAVIAN.
OCTAVIAN IS HERE.
BLEEP
BLEEP
WHAT DO YOU MEAN OCTAVIAN IS HERE?
MEANING HE'S **RIGHT OUTSIDE**!

AN ENTIRE XERX FLEET HAS US SURROUNDED.

KEEP THEM FROM ESCAPING.

DO NOT FIRE AT THEIR SHIP UNLESS YOU HEAR THE ORDER FROM ME.

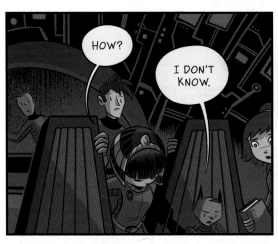

HOW?

I DON'T KNOW.

BUT HE SOMEHOW LOCKED OUR CONTROLS SO WE AREN'T GOING ANYWHERE.

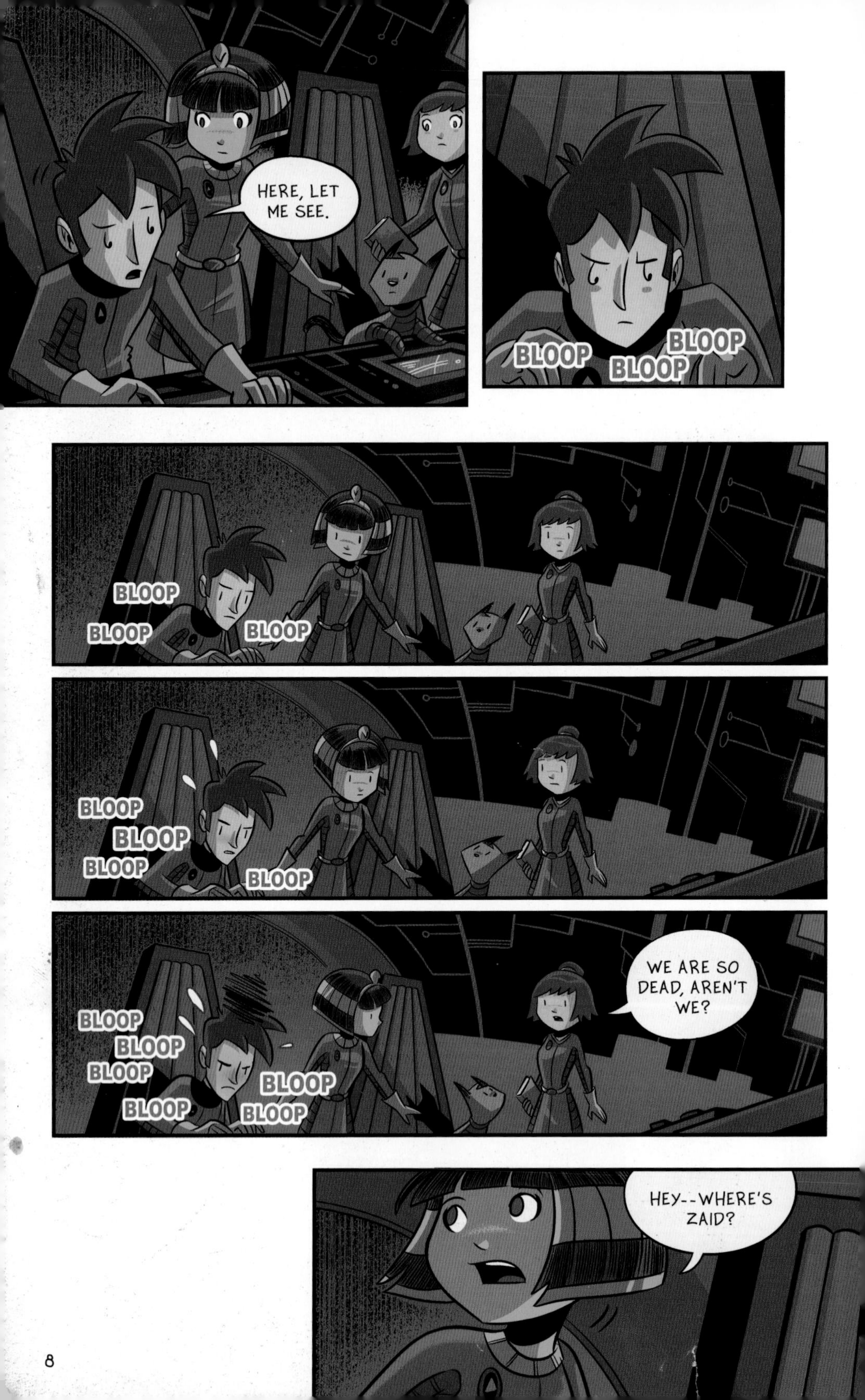
HERE, LET ME SEE.
BLOOP
BLOOP
BLOOP
BLOOP
BLOOP
BLOOP
BLOOP
BLOOP
BLOOP
BLOOP
WE ARE SO DEAD, AREN'T WE?
BLOOP
BLOOP
BLOOP
BLOOP
BLOOP
BLOOP
HEY--WHERE'S ZAID?

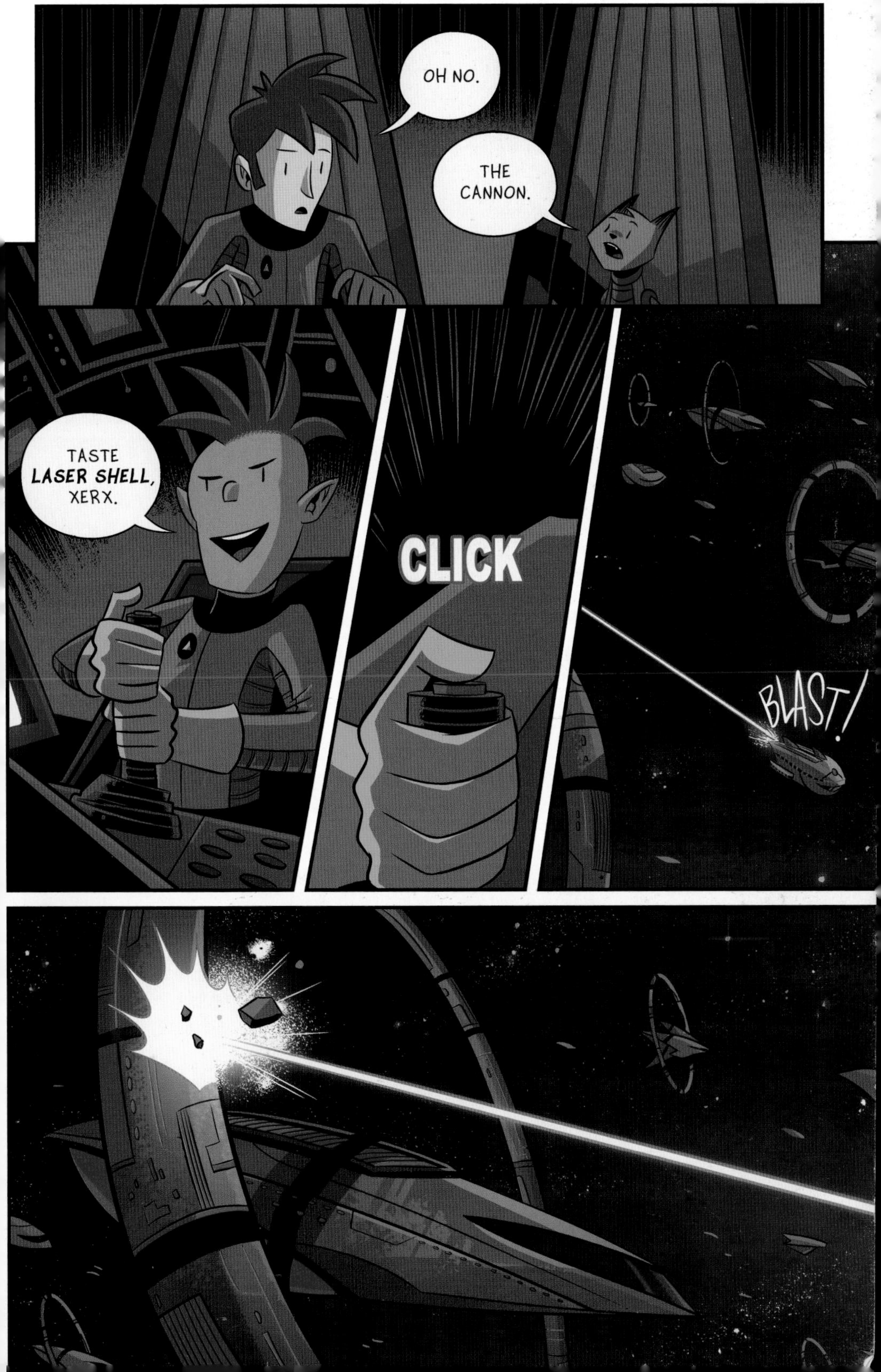
OH NO.
THE CANNON.
TASTE **LASER SHELL,** XERX.
CLICK
BLAST!

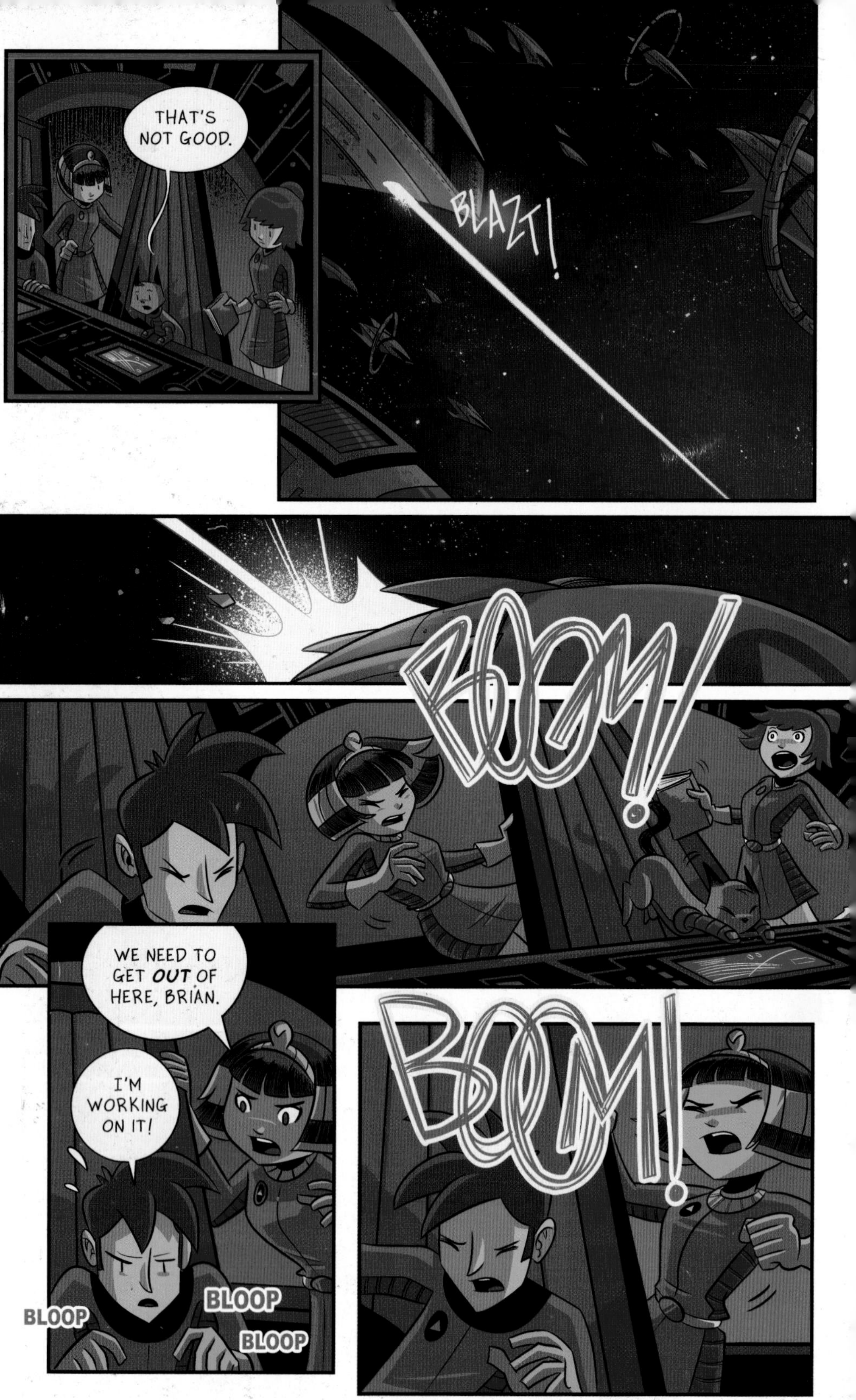
THAT'S NOT GOOD.
BLAZT!
BOOM!
WE NEED TO GET OUT OF HERE, BRIAN.
I'M WORKING ON IT!
BLOOP
BLOOP
BLOOP
BOOM!

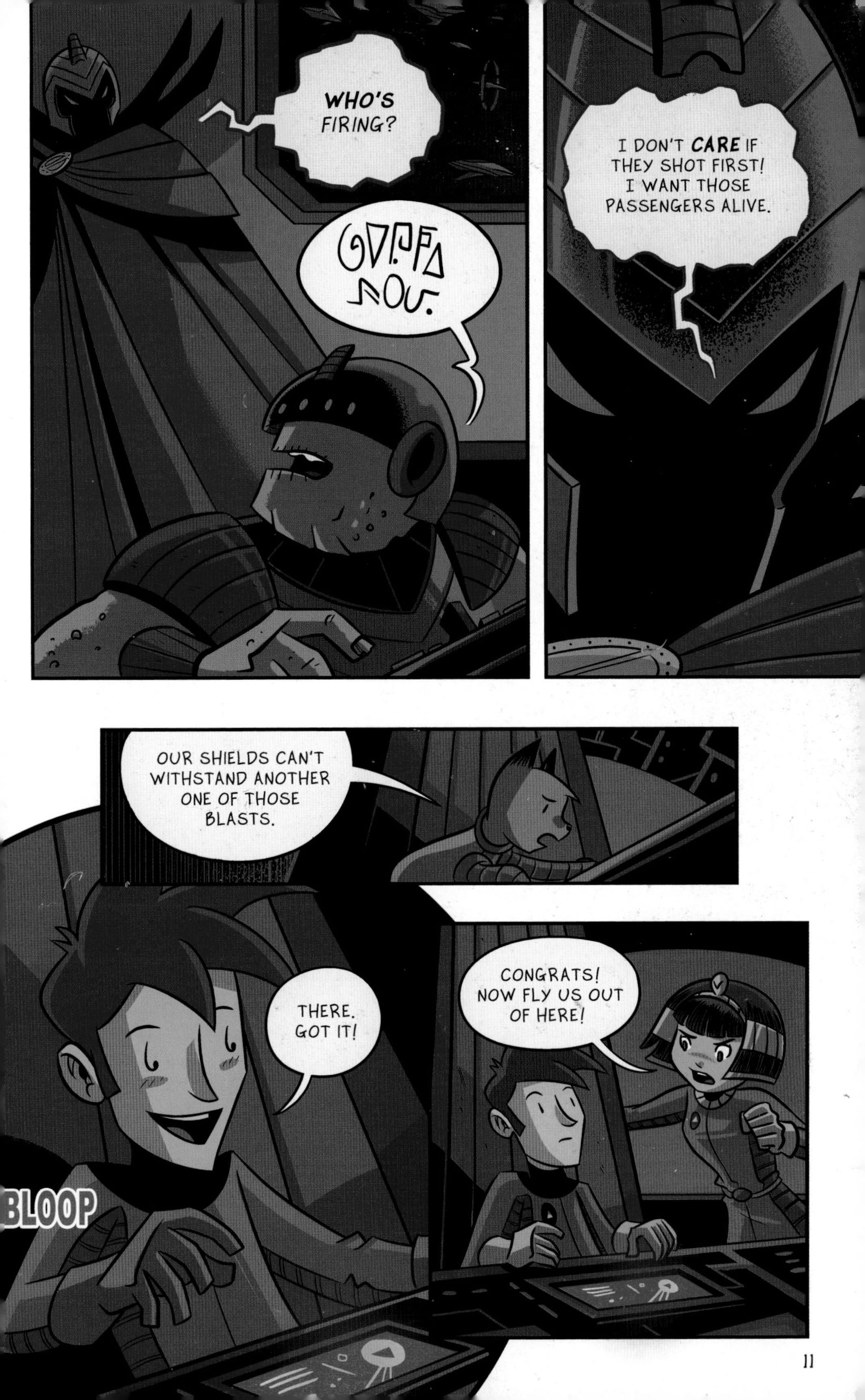

WHO'S FIRING?
I DON'T CARE IF THEY SHOT FIRST! I WANT THOSE PASSENGERS ALIVE.
OUR SHIELDS CAN'T WITHSTAND ANOTHER ONE OF THOSE BLASTS.
BLOOP
THERE. GOT IT!
CONGRATS! NOW FLY US OUT OF HERE!

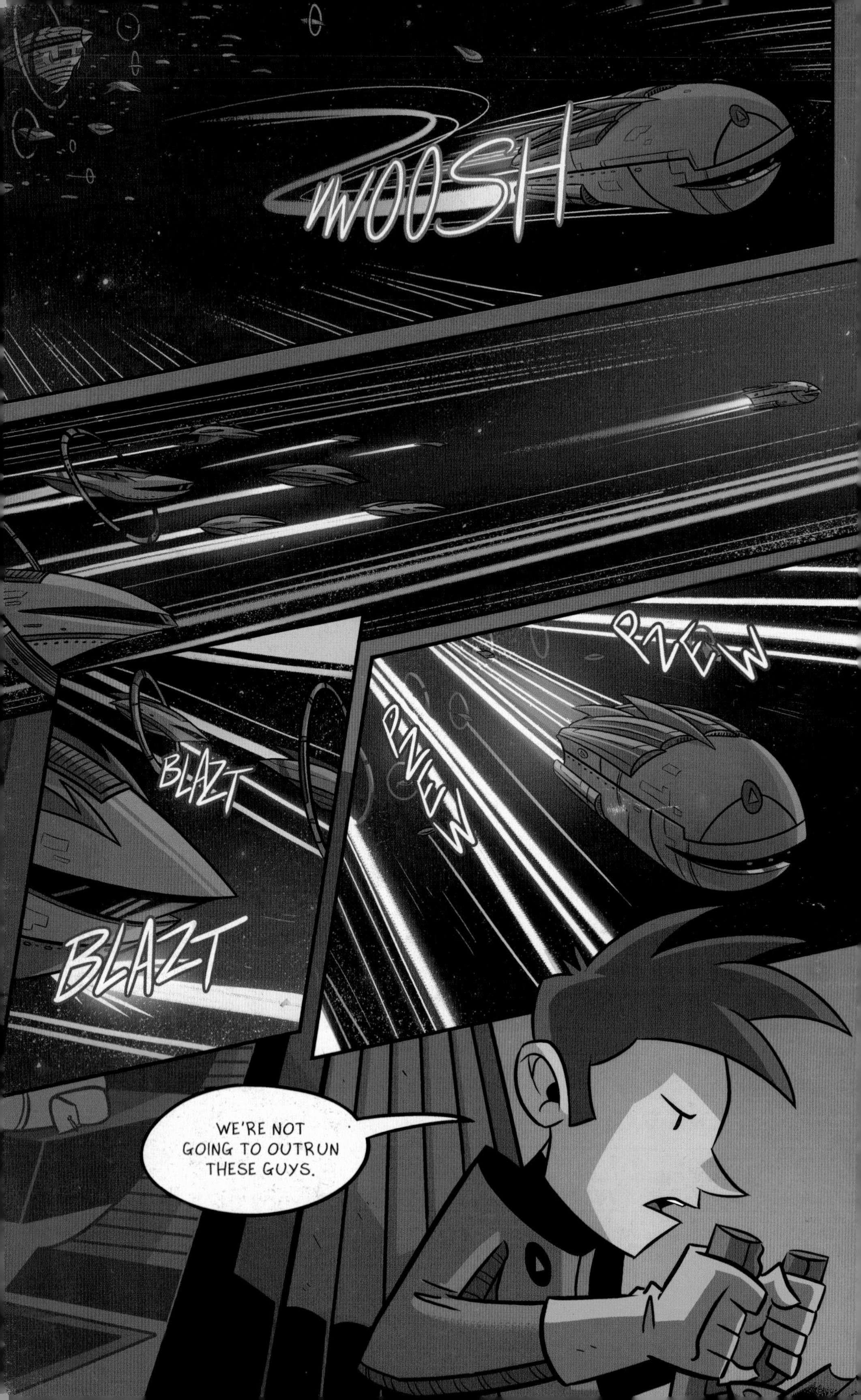
WOOSH
BLAZT
BLAZT
PNEW
PNEW
WE'RE NOT GOING TO OUTRUN THESE GUYS.

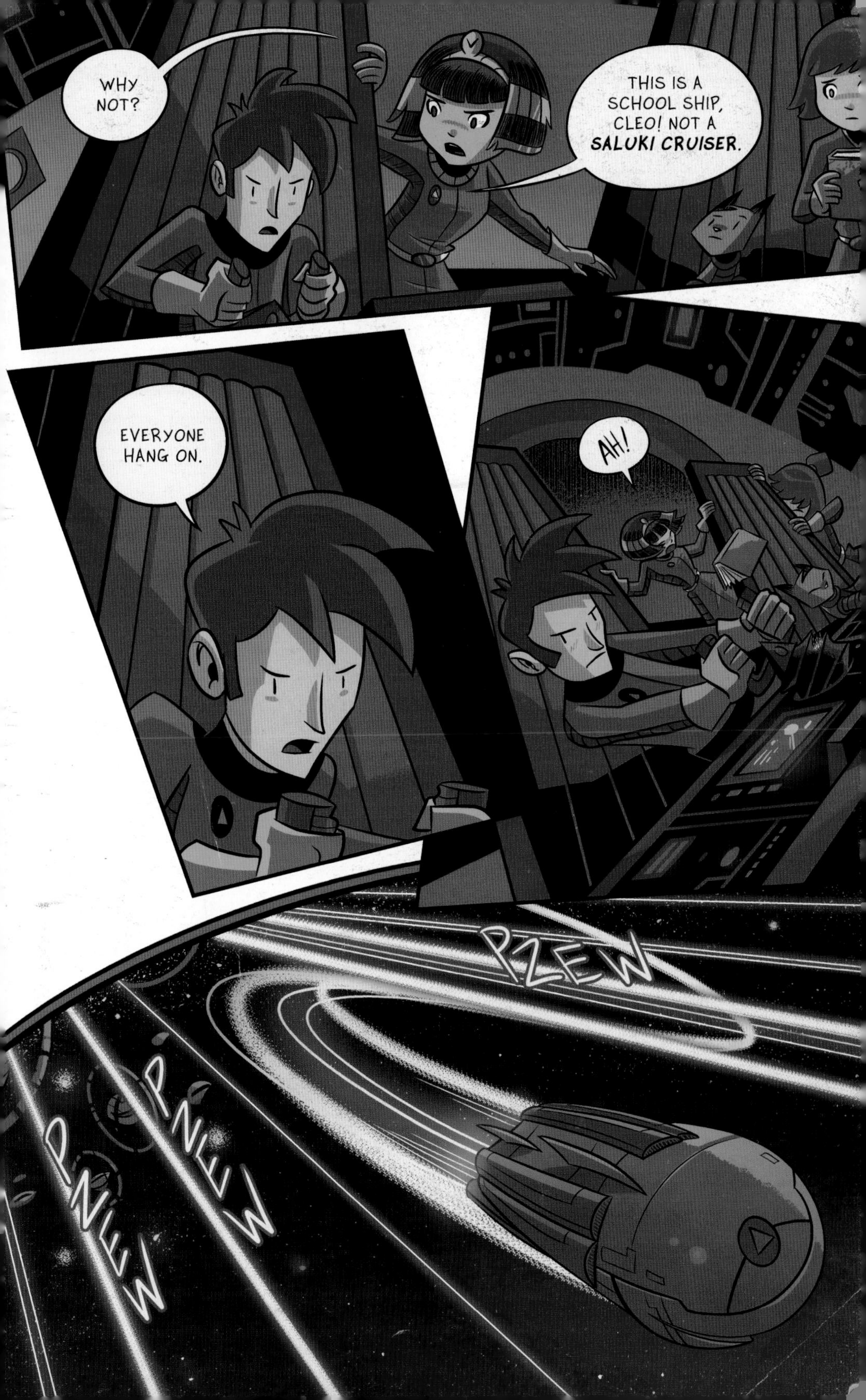
WHY NOT?
THIS IS A SCHOOL SHIP, CLEO! NOT A **SALUKI CRUISER.**
EVERYONE HANG ON.
AH!
PZEW
PNEW
PNEW

BRIAN'S RIGHT.

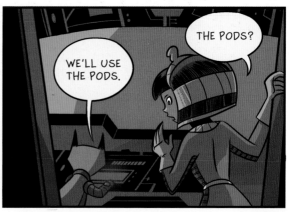

WE'LL USE THE PODS.

THE PODS?

THE SHIP IS EQUIPPED WITH ESCAPE PODS--IN CASE OF AN EMERGENCY. THEY'RE SMALL, AND IF WE CAN DISTRACT THE XERX USING THE SHIP, THEY SHOULD DEPLOY UNDETECTED.

THAT'S A BIG **IF**.

IT'S OUR BEST CHANCE. CAN YOU GIVE US ONE LAST THRUST TO PUSH US AHEAD OF THE XERX?

IT'LL DRAIN THE LAST OF OUR FUEL.

WE WON'T NEED IT.

VWOOSH

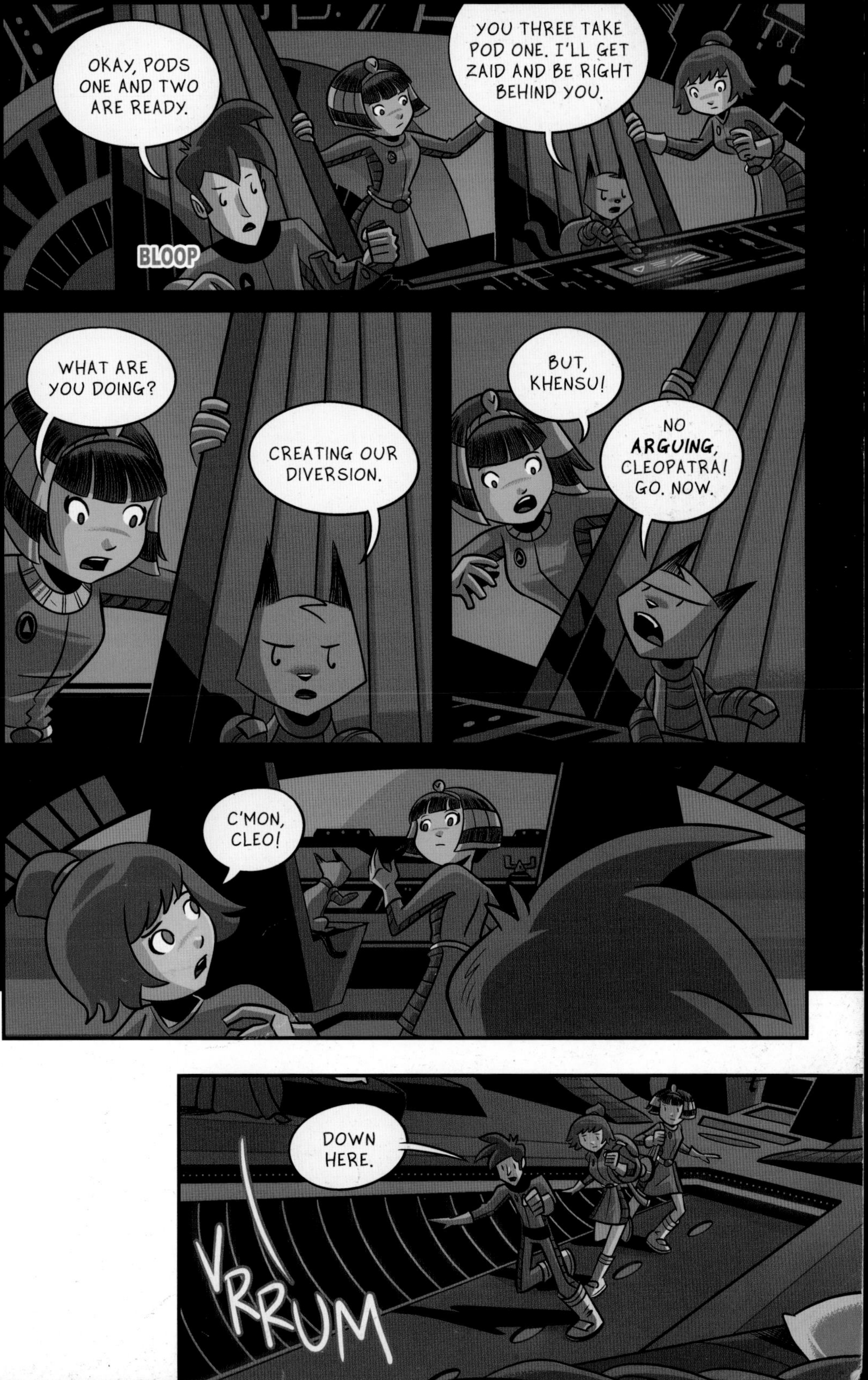
OKAY, PODS ONE AND TWO ARE READY.
BLOOP
YOU THREE TAKE POD ONE. I'LL GET ZAID AND BE RIGHT BEHIND YOU.
WHAT ARE YOU DOING?
CREATING OUR DIVERSION.
BUT, KHENSU!
NO **ARGUING**, CLEOPATRA! GO. NOW.
C'MON, CLEO!
DOWN HERE.
VRRRUM

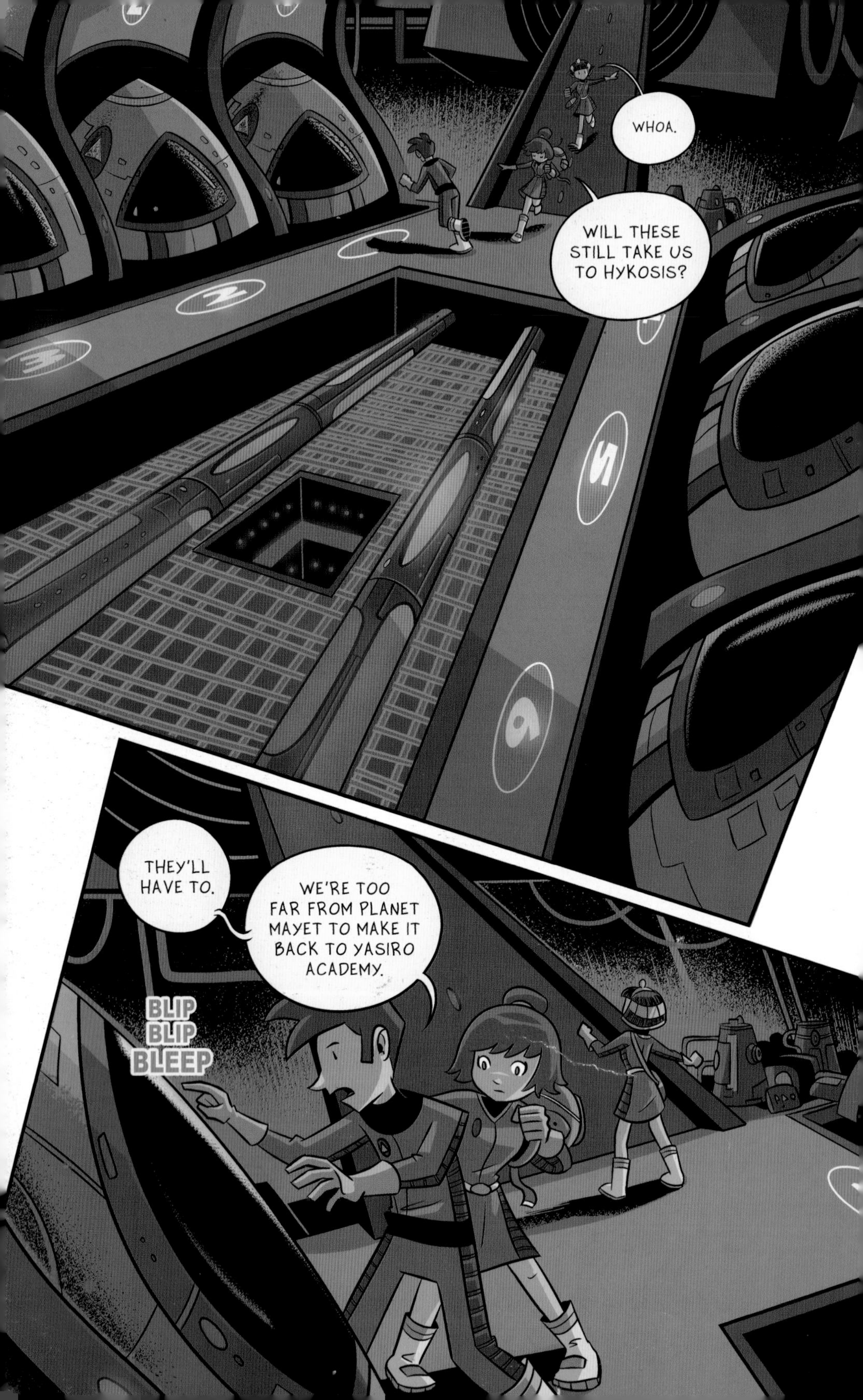
WHOA.
WILL THESE STILL TAKE US TO HYKOSIS?
THEY'LL HAVE TO.
WE'RE TOO FAR FROM PLANET MAYET TO MAKE IT BACK TO YASIRO ACADEMY.
BLIP BLIP BLEEP

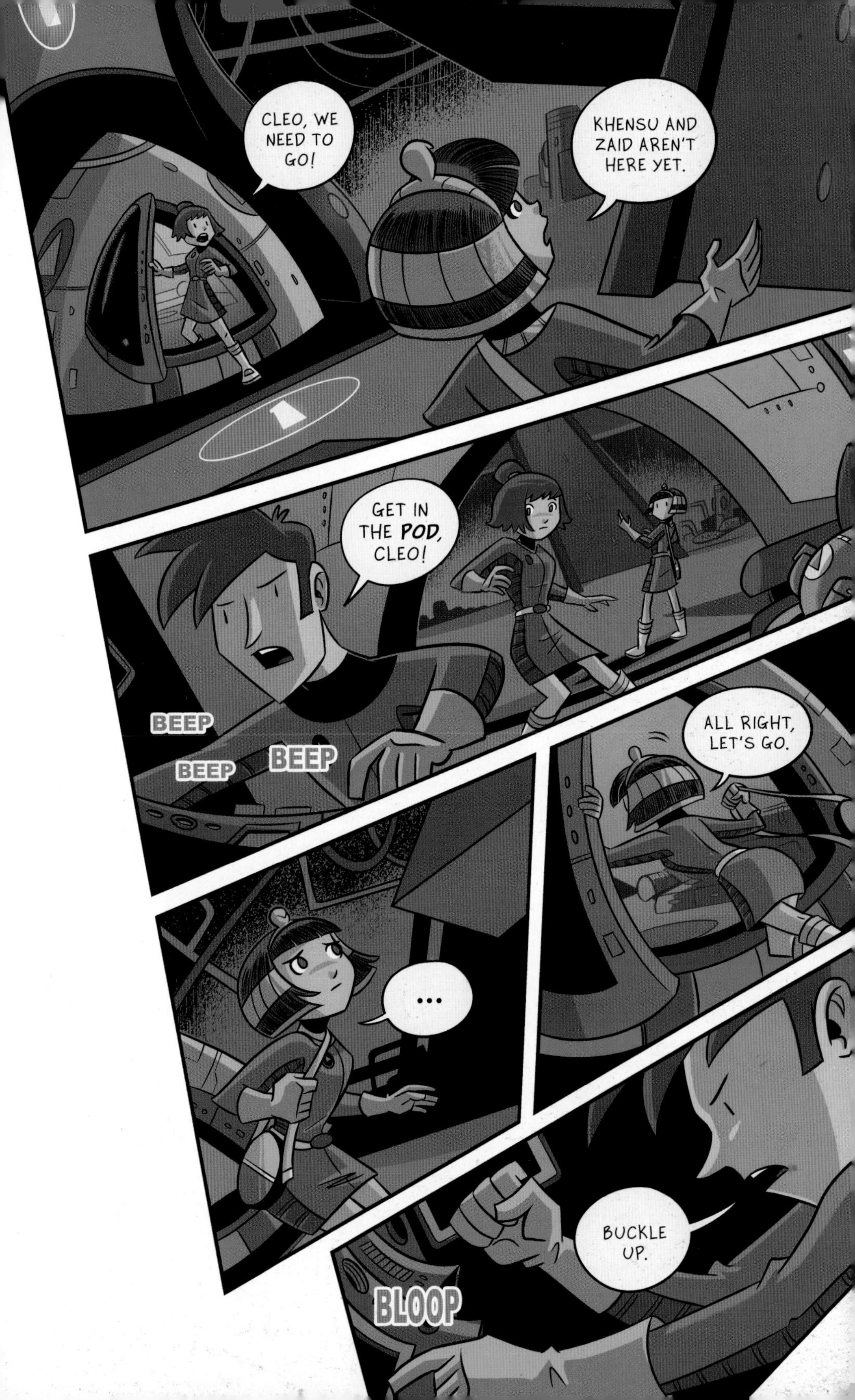

CLEO, WE NEED TO GO!
KHENSU AND ZAID AREN'T HERE YET.
GET IN THE **POD**, CLEO!
BEEP
BEEP
BEEP
ALL RIGHT, LET'S GO.
...
BUCKLE UP.
BLOOP

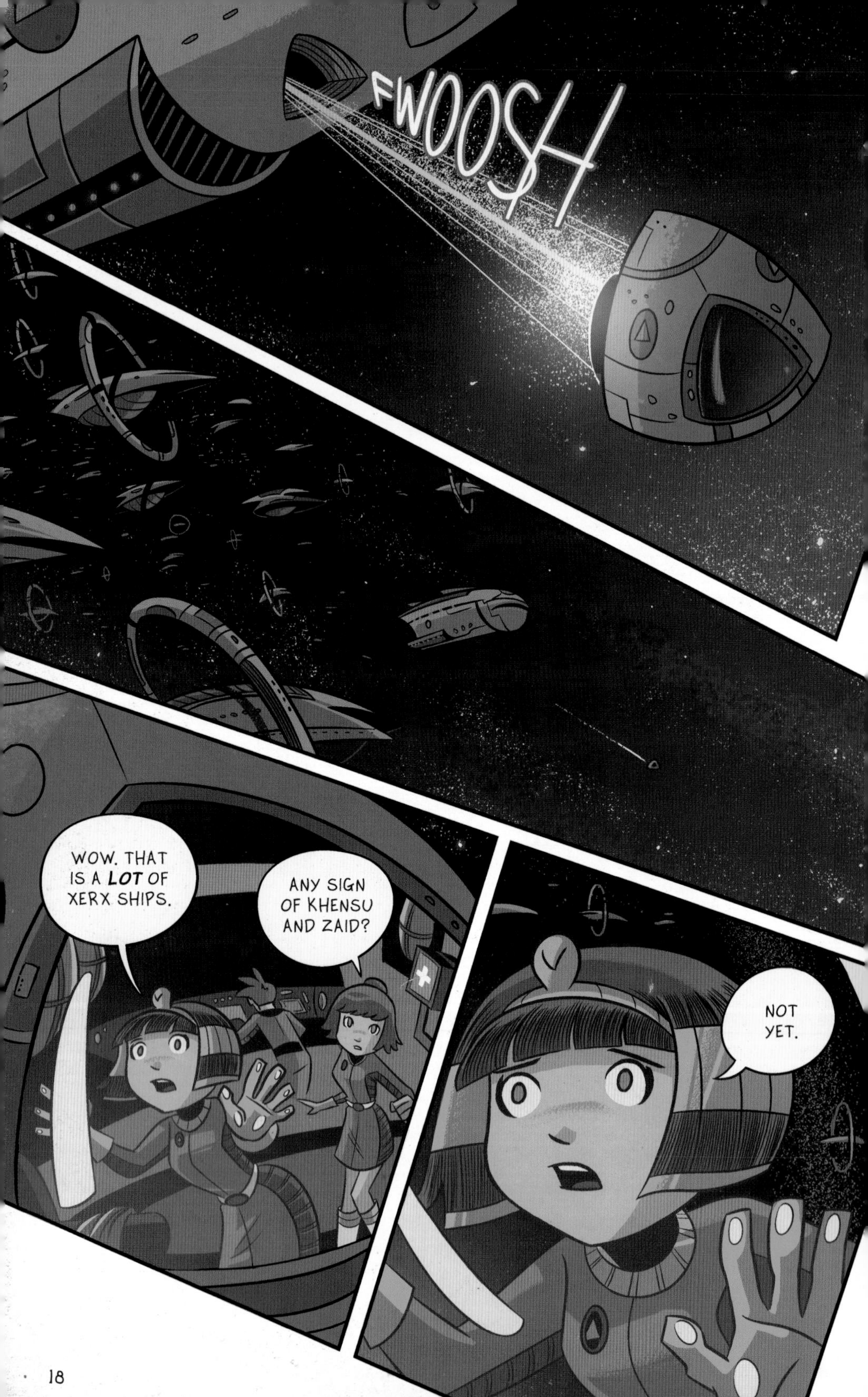
FWOOSH
WOW. THAT IS A **LOT** OF XERX SHIPS.
ANY SIGN OF KHENSU AND ZAID?
NOT YET.

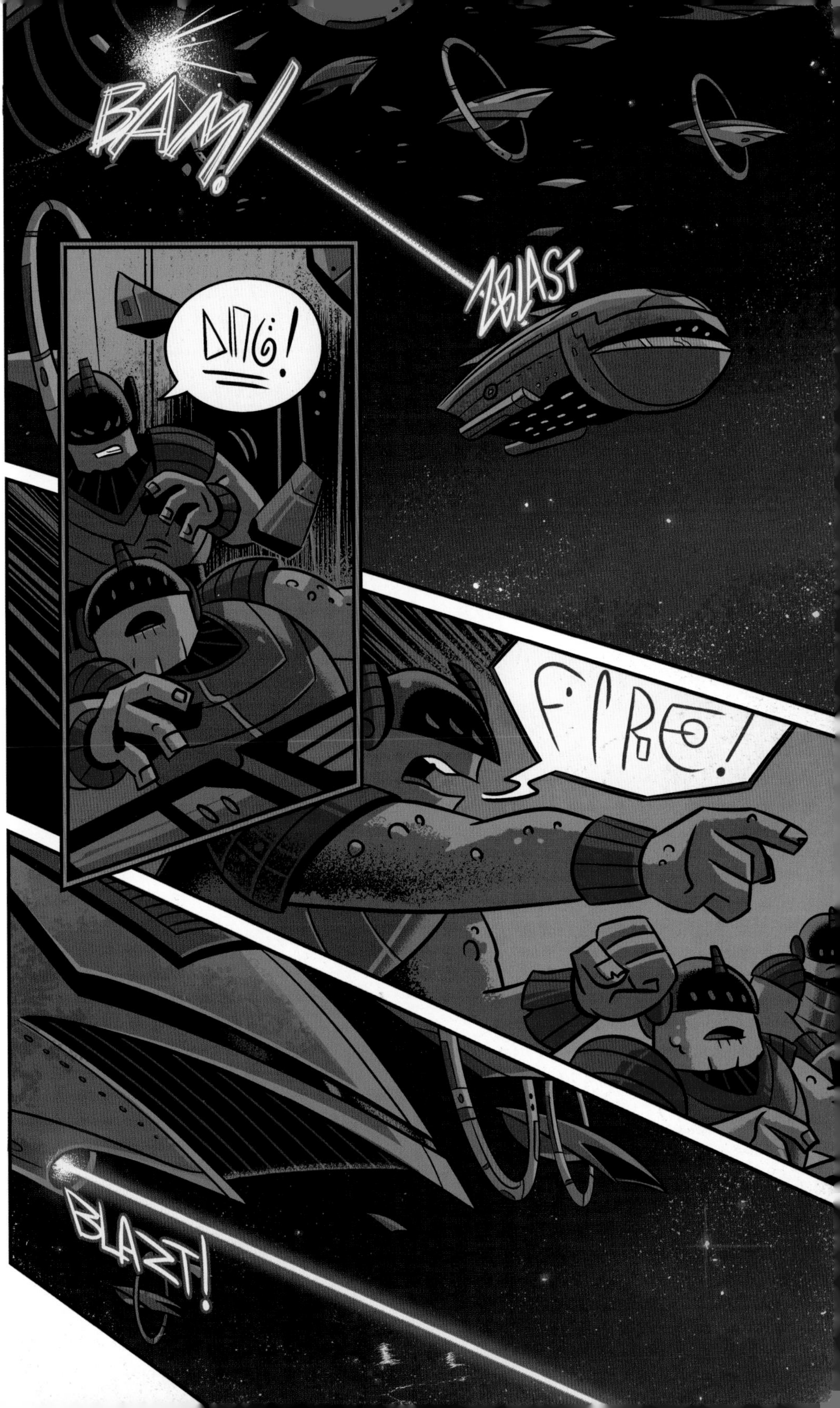
BAM!
ZBLAST
DING!
FIRE!
BLAZT!

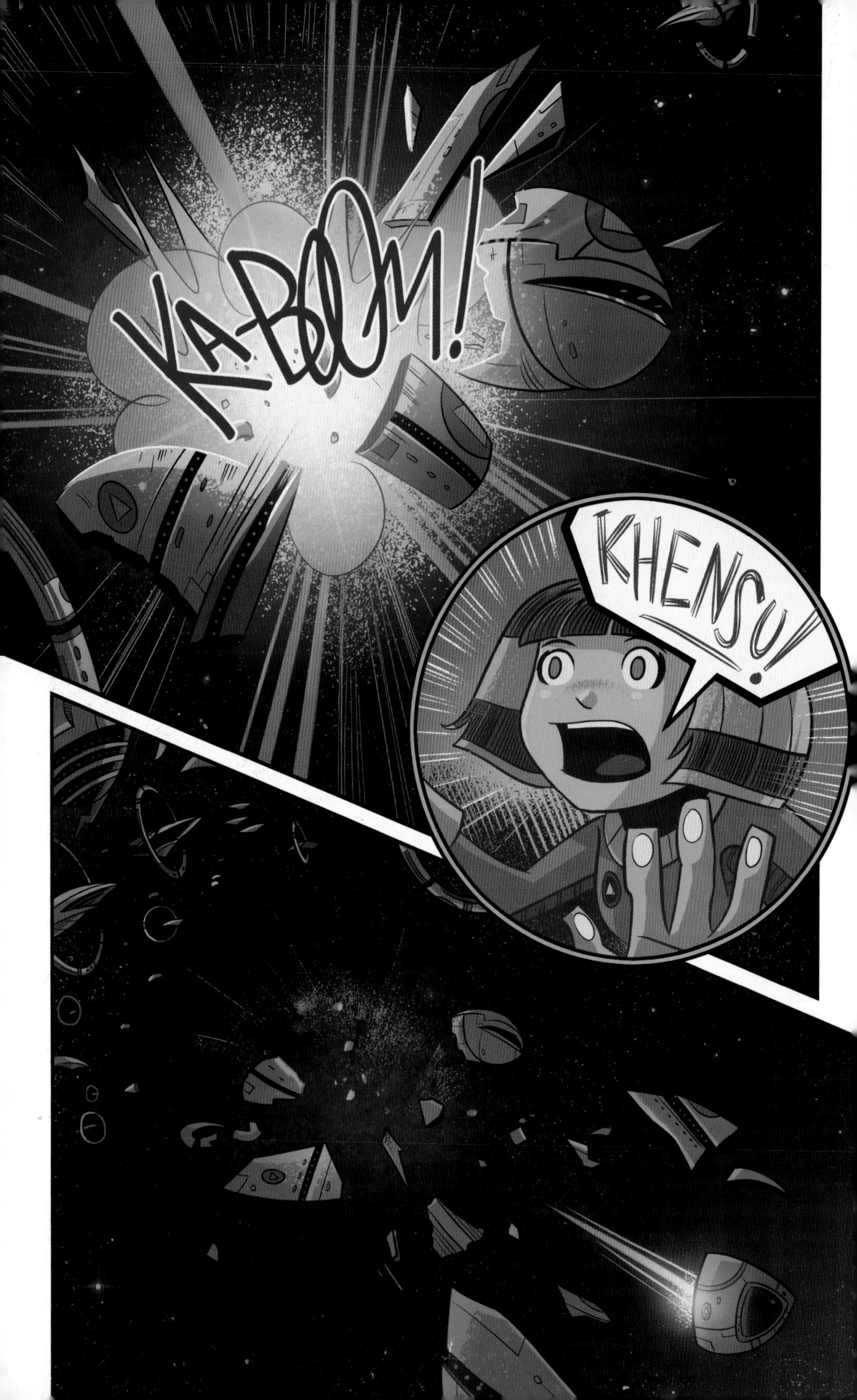
KA-BOOM!
KHENSU!

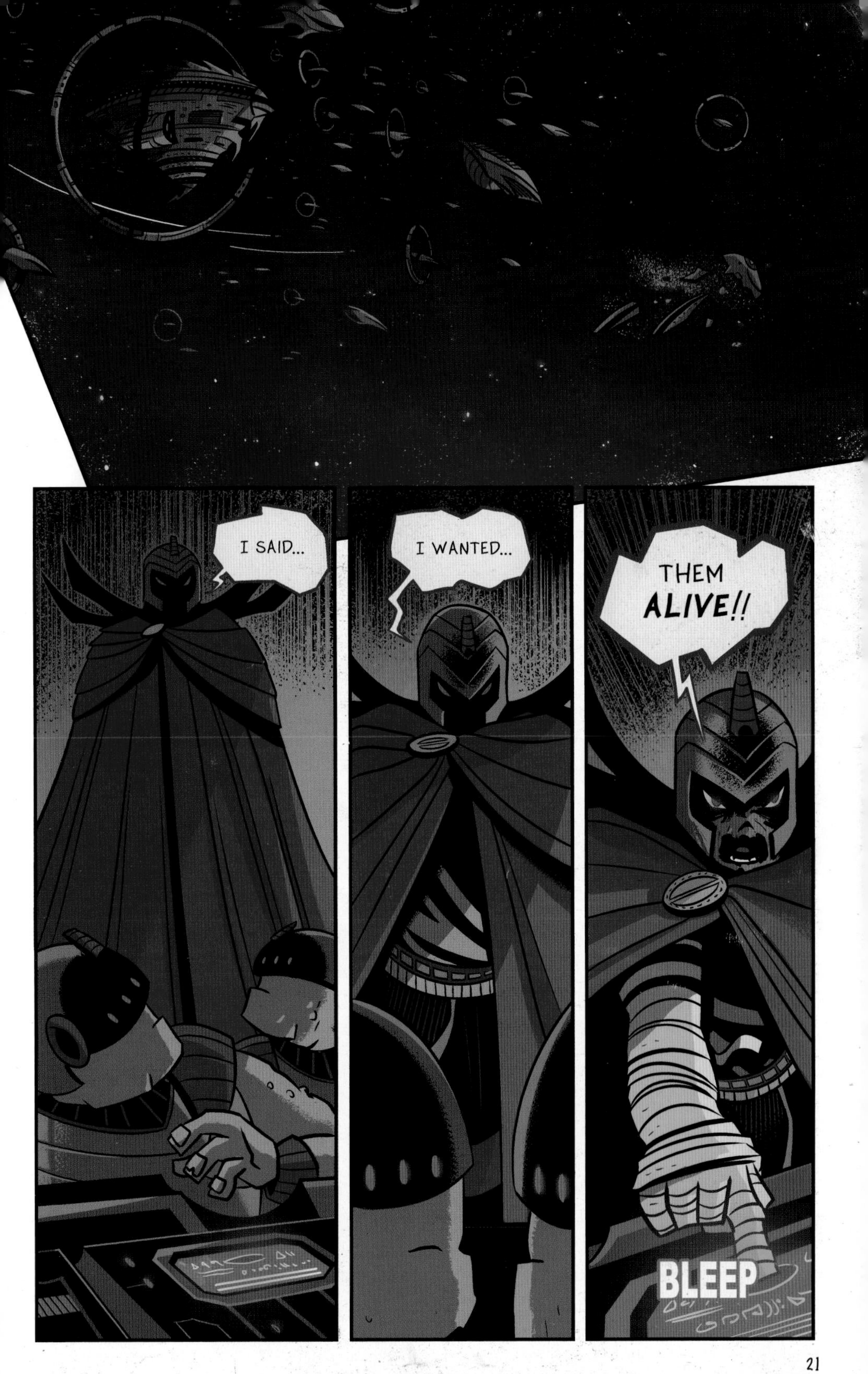
I SAID...
I WANTED...
THEM ALIVE!!
BLEEP

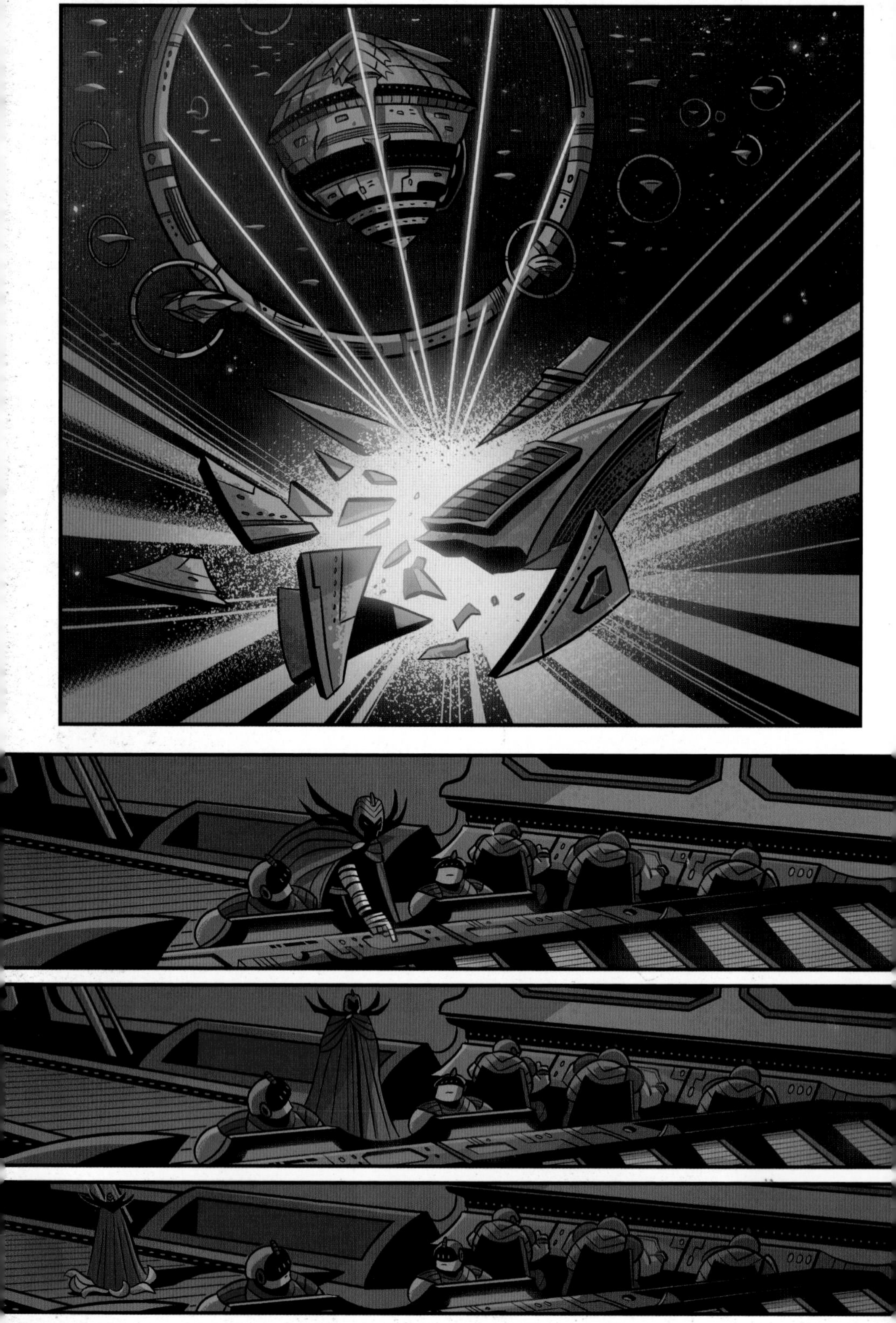

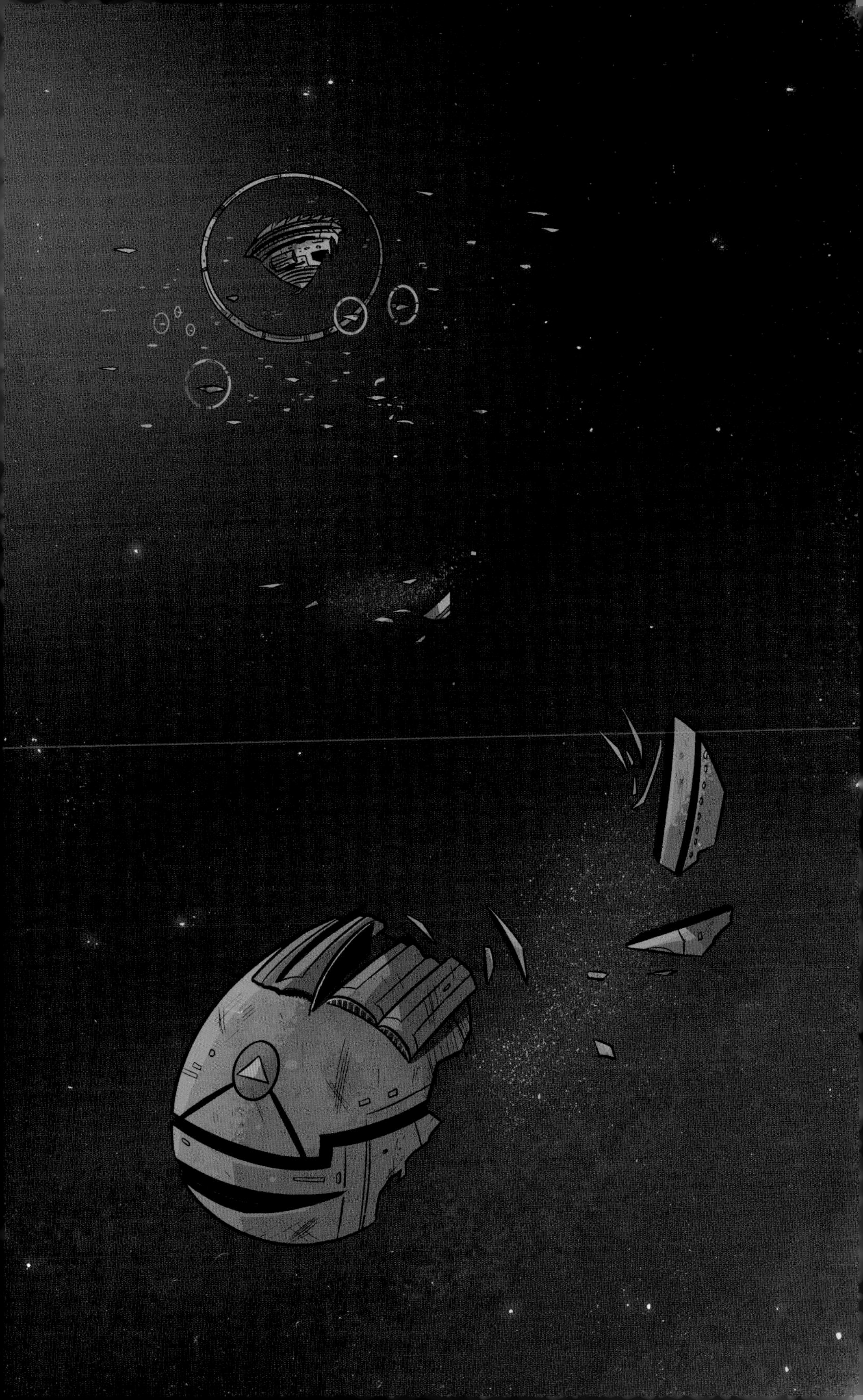

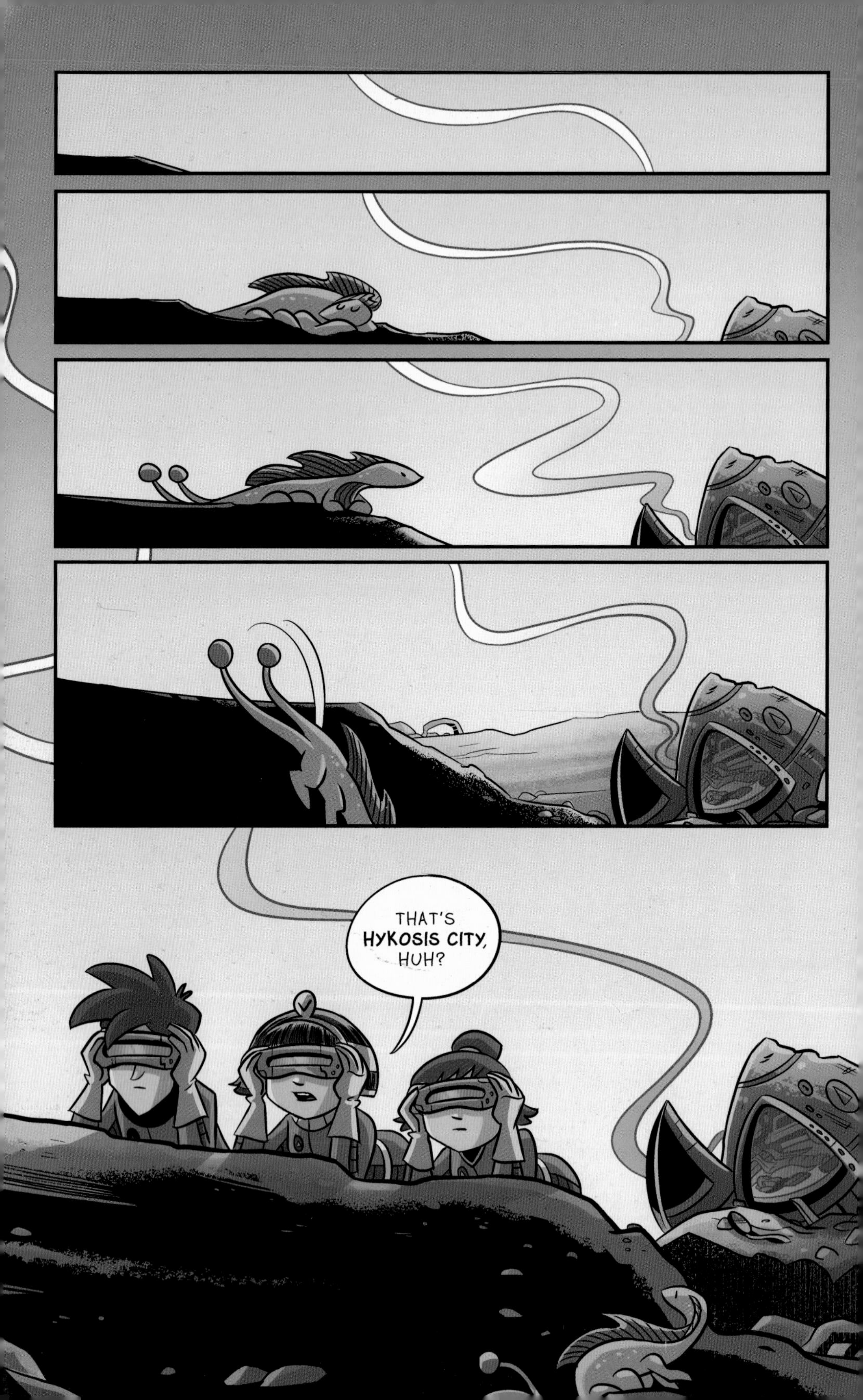
THAT'S HYKOSIS CITY, HUH?

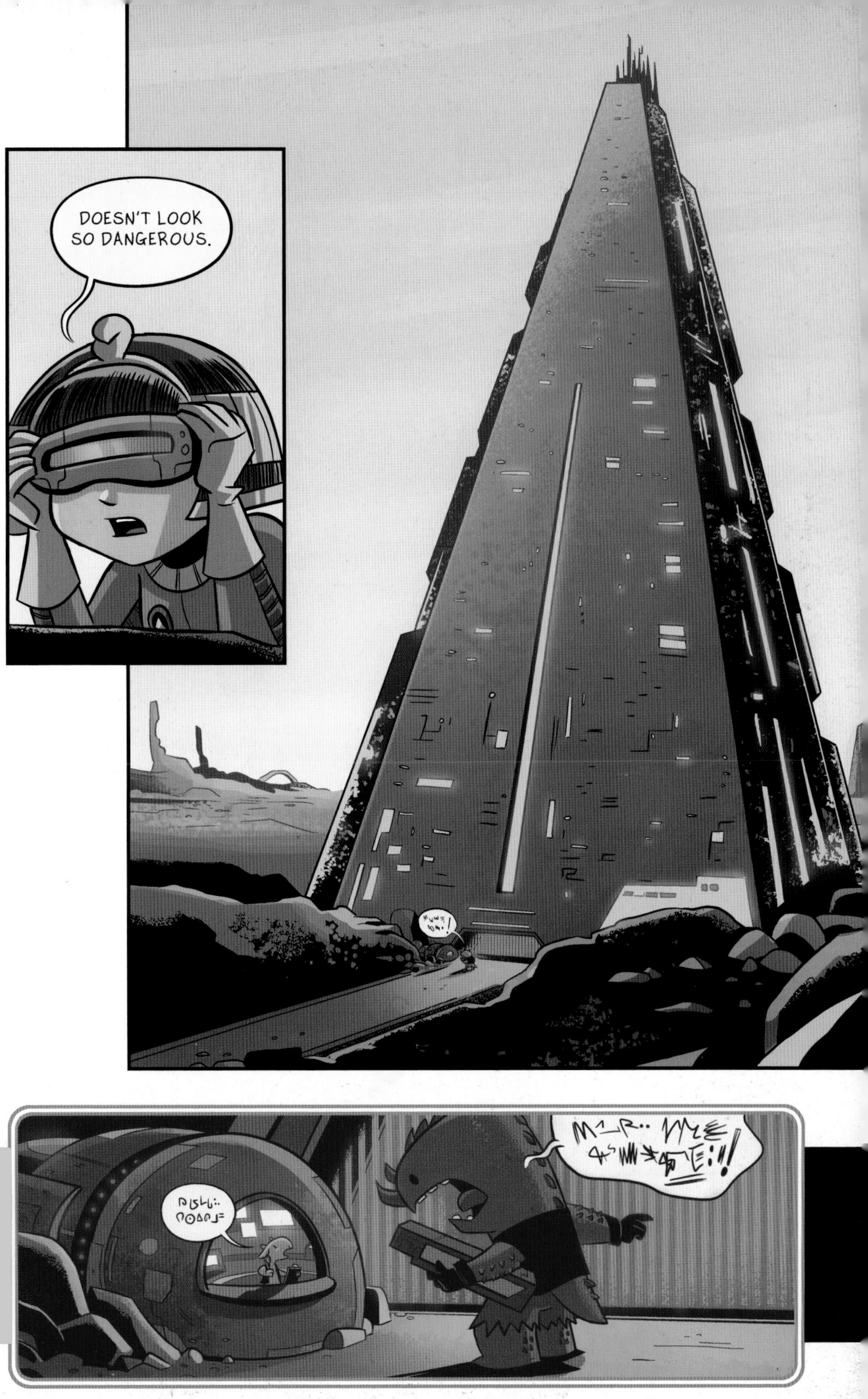
DOESN'T LOOK SO DANGEROUS.

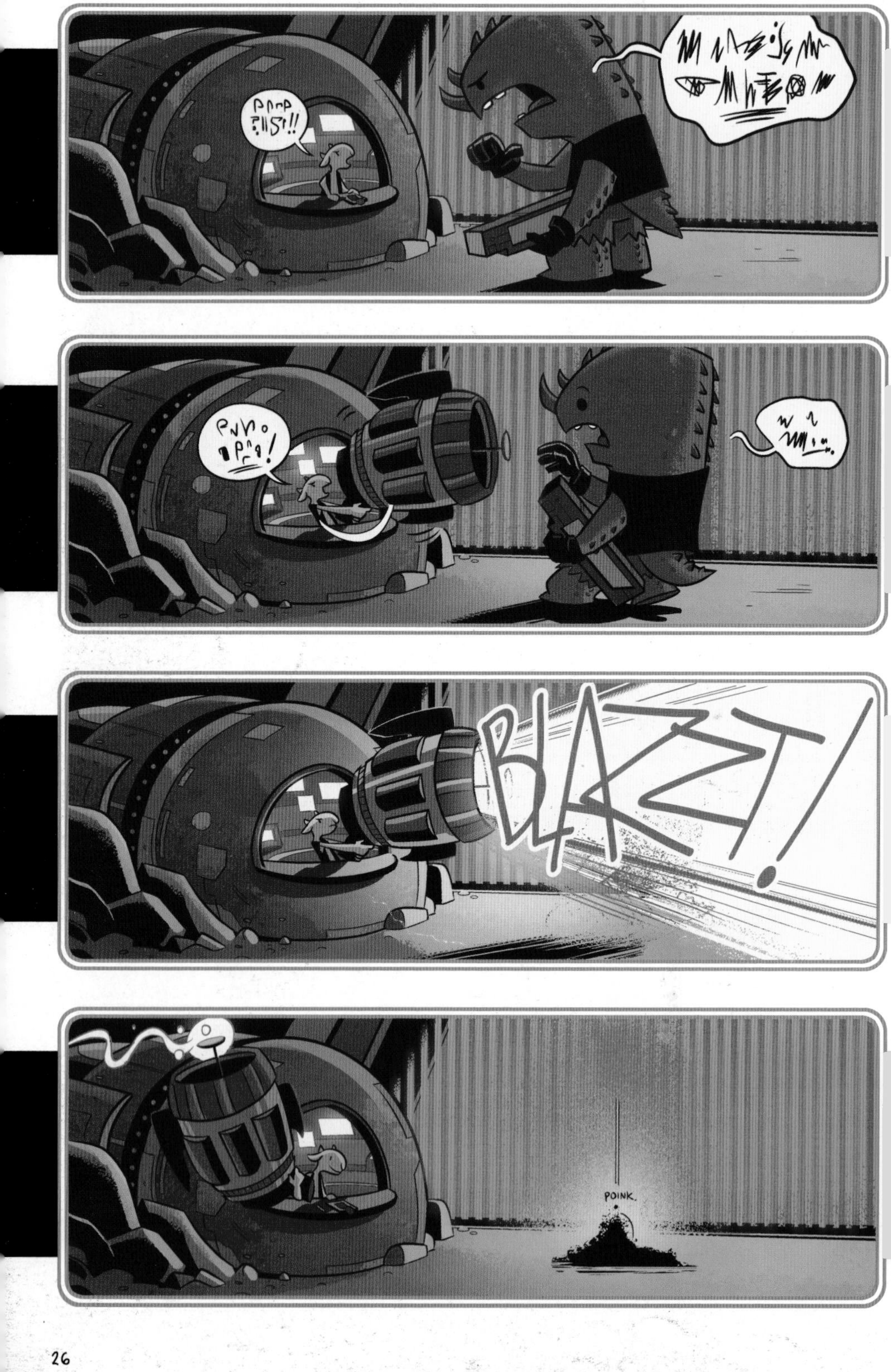
BLAZT!
POINK.

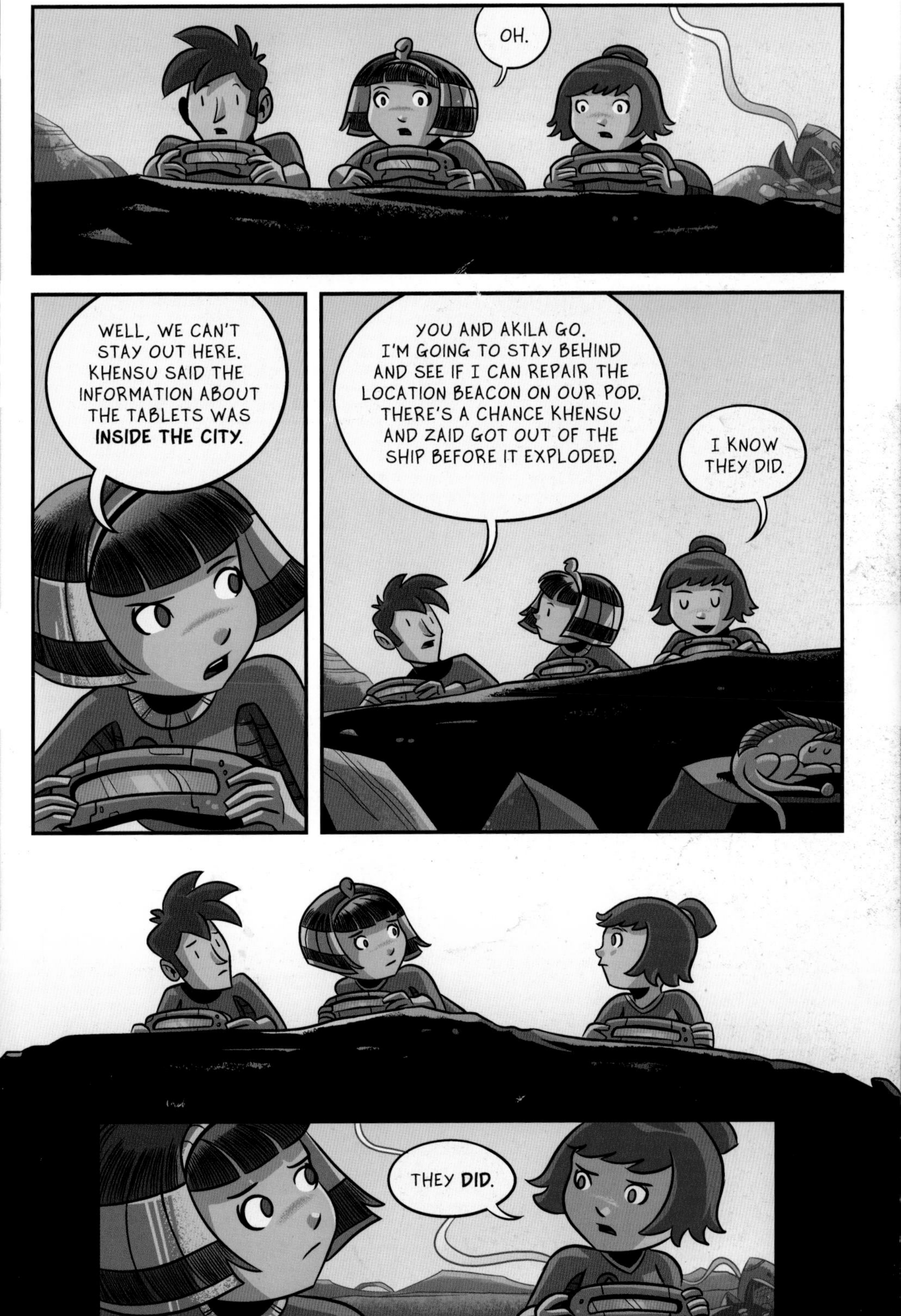
OH.
WELL, WE CAN'T STAY OUT HERE. KHENSU SAID THE INFORMATION ABOUT THE TABLETS WAS **INSIDE THE CITY**.
YOU AND AKILA GO. I'M GOING TO STAY BEHIND AND SEE IF I CAN REPAIR THE LOCATION BEACON ON OUR POD. THERE'S A CHANCE KHENSU AND ZAID GOT OUT OF THE SHIP BEFORE IT EXPLODED.
I KNOW THEY DID.
THEY **DID**.

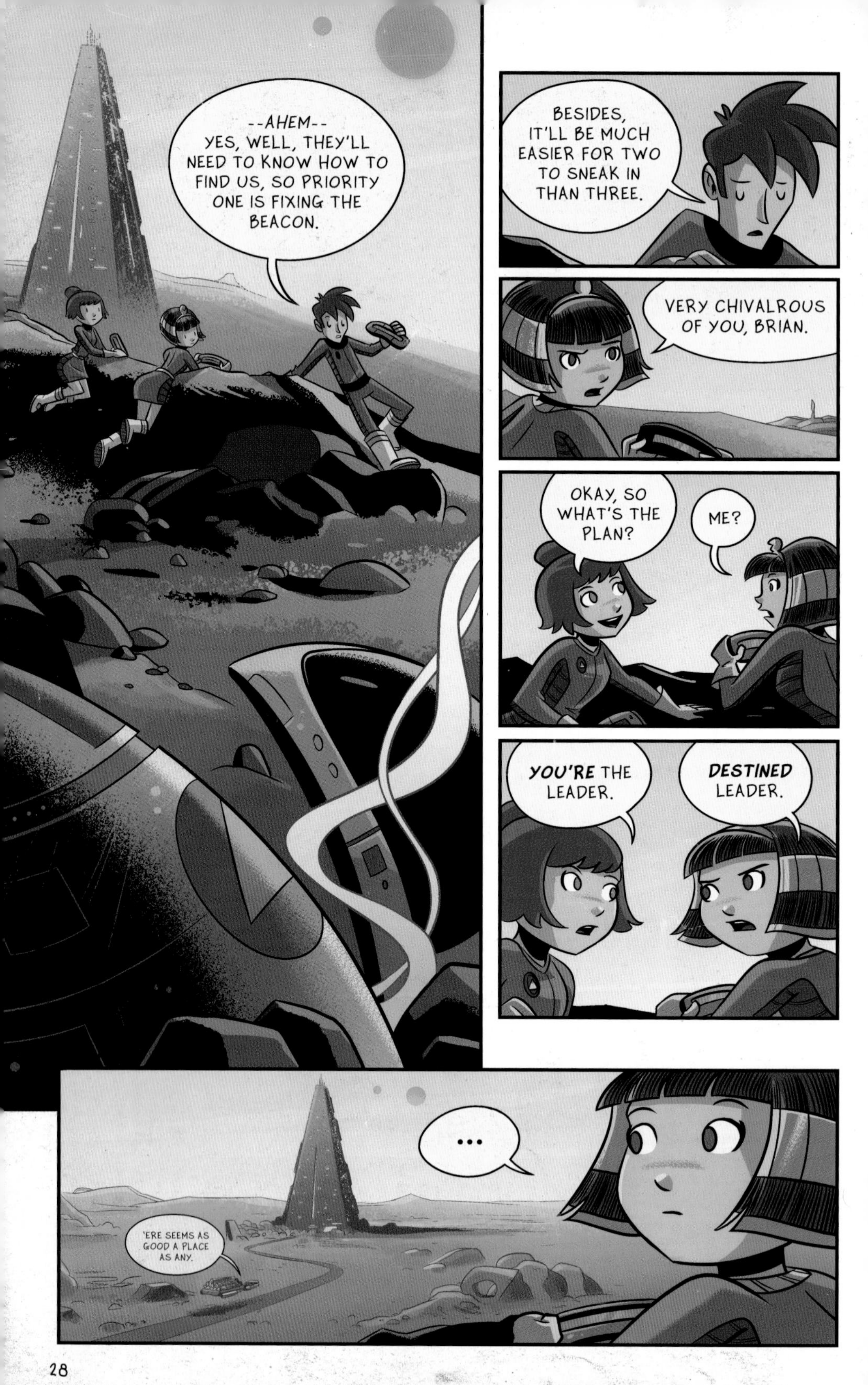
--AHEM-- YES, WELL, THEY'LL NEED TO KNOW HOW TO FIND US, SO PRIORITY ONE IS FIXING THE BEACON.
BESIDES, IT'LL BE MUCH EASIER FOR TWO TO SNEAK IN THAN THREE.
VERY CHIVALROUS OF YOU, BRIAN.
OKAY, SO WHAT'S THE PLAN?
ME?
YOU'RE THE LEADER.
DESTINED LEADER.
...
'ERE SEEMS AS GOOD A PLACE AS ANY.

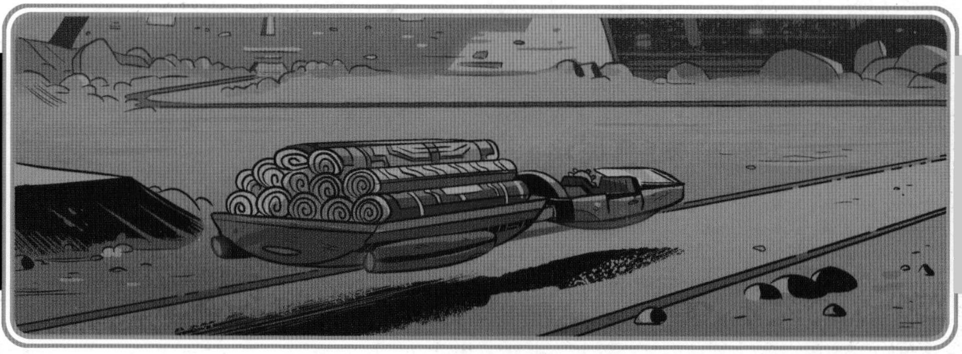

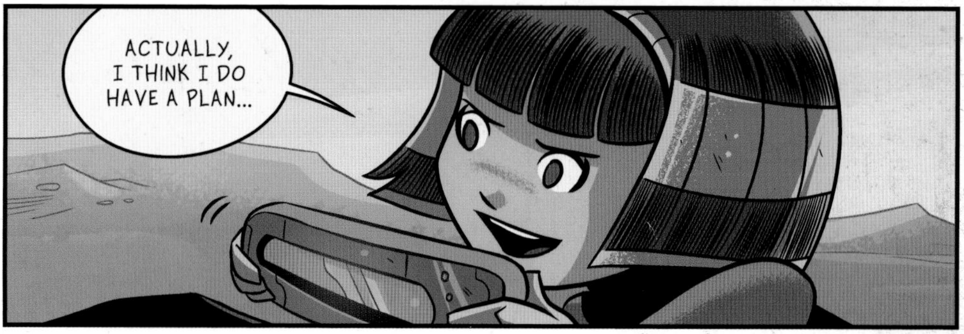
ACTUALLY, I THINK I DO HAVE A PLAN...

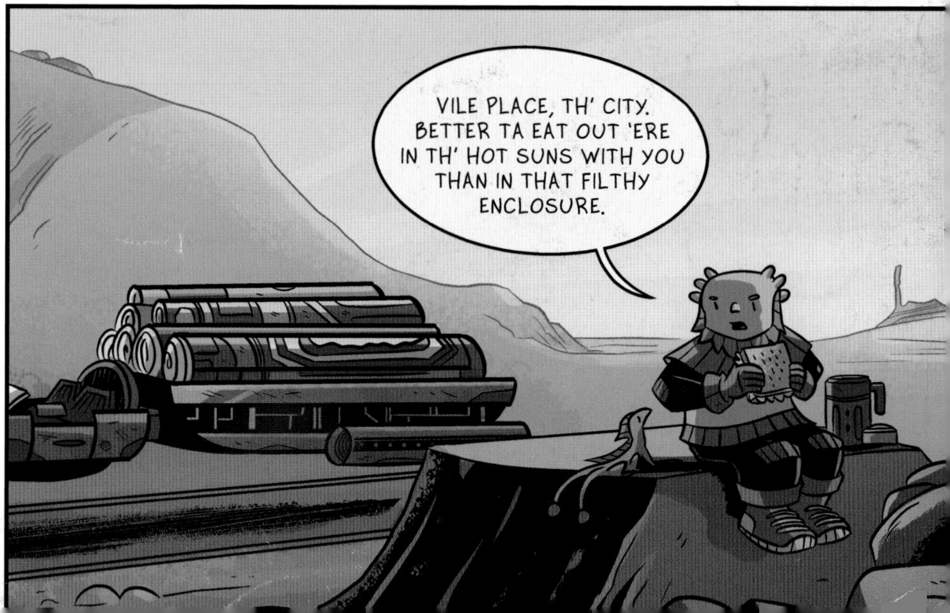
VILE PLACE, TH' CITY. BETTER TA EAT OUT 'ERE IN TH' HOT SUNS WITH YOU THAN IN THAT FILTHY ENCLOSURE.

GOTTA MAKE A LIVIN' THOUGH, AH SUPPOSE.

SHOULD BE GRATEFUL THIEVES AND THUGS STILL MAINTAIN AN APPRECIATION FOR INTERIOR DECORATIN'.

'ERE'S TH' LAST BITE OF MAH SANDWICH. SORRY ABOUT IT BEIN' A BIT STALE.

OH, SURE. EAT AN' RUN.

EVEN TH' LIZARDS ON THIS PLANET ARE RUDE.

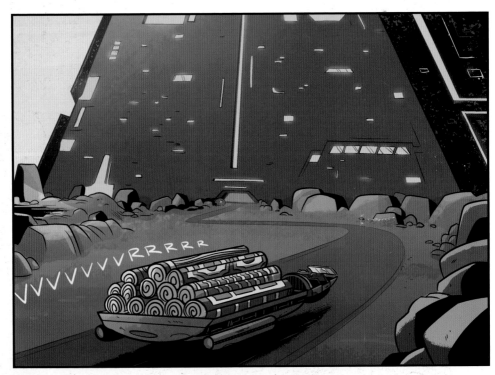

VVVVVVVRRRRR

PULL:: OODr:E.

YEAH, YEAH. KEEP YER BLASTER HOLSTERED.

AH GOT MAH PAPERS RIGHT 'ERE.

FINNIAS FARSH. PEDDLER OF FINE CARPETS AN' TAPESTRIES.

WON'T FIND A FINER RUG IN ALL TH' NILE.

ᴘᴘᴏ= ‖·ᴘᴏ:.

BEEP

ᴘRᴀᴘːᴏᴏᴏ ᴢᴘ‖‖ᴏ!

VVVUUMM

ENJOY HYKOSIS CITY?

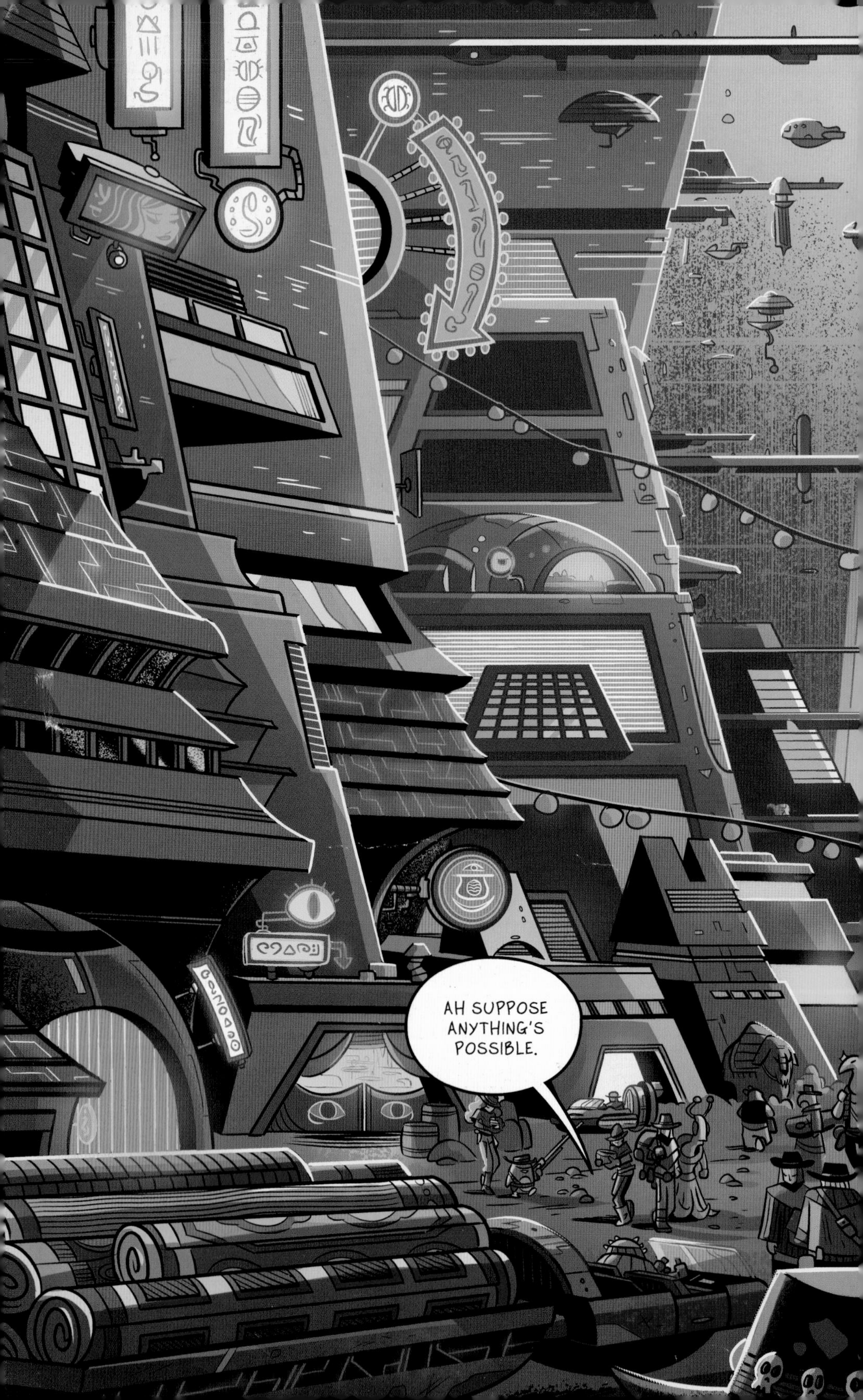
AH SUPPOSE ANYTHING'S POSSIBLE.

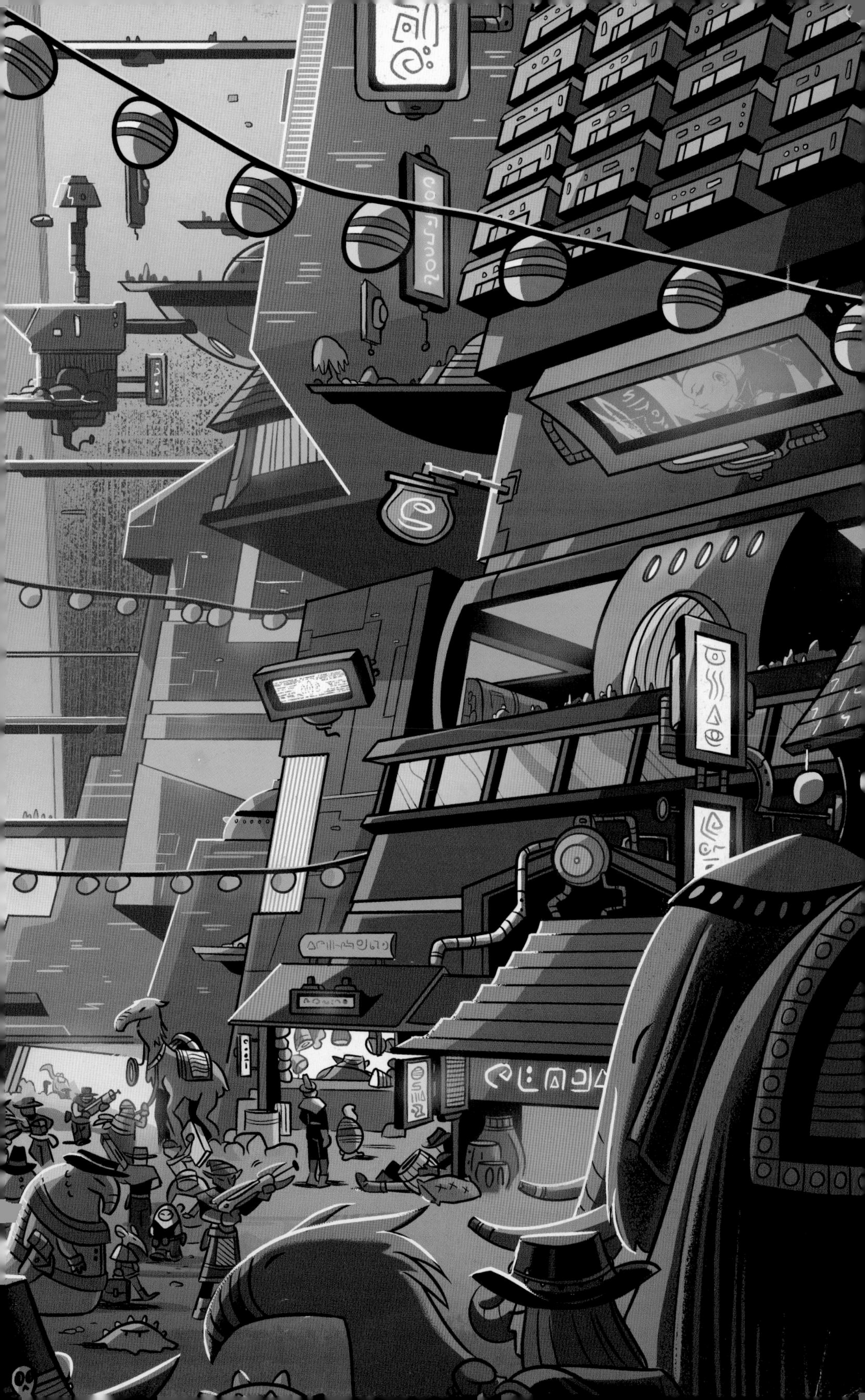

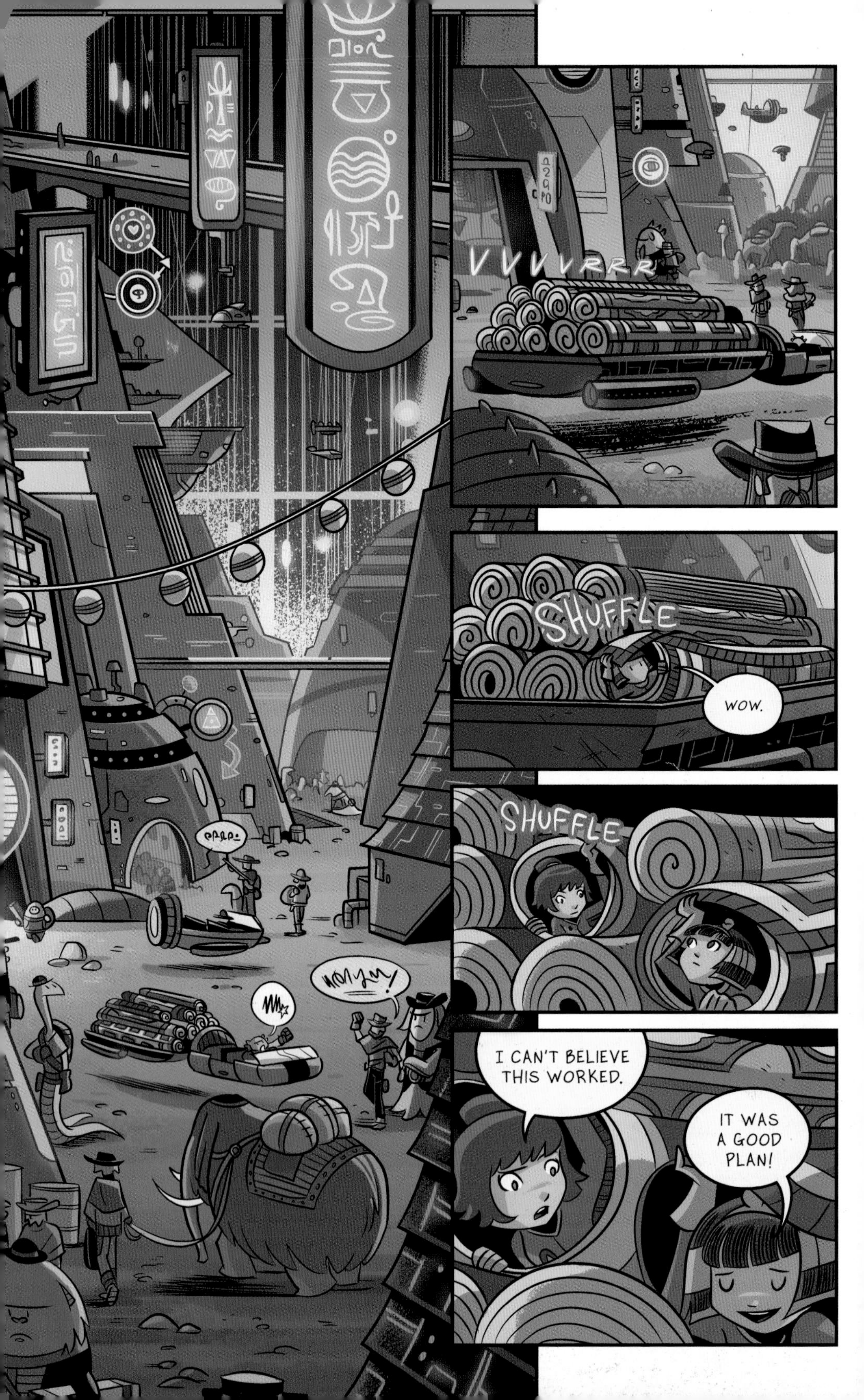
VVVVVRRRR
SHUFFLE
WOW.
SHUFFLE
I CAN'T BELIEVE THIS WORKED.
IT WAS A GOOD PLAN!

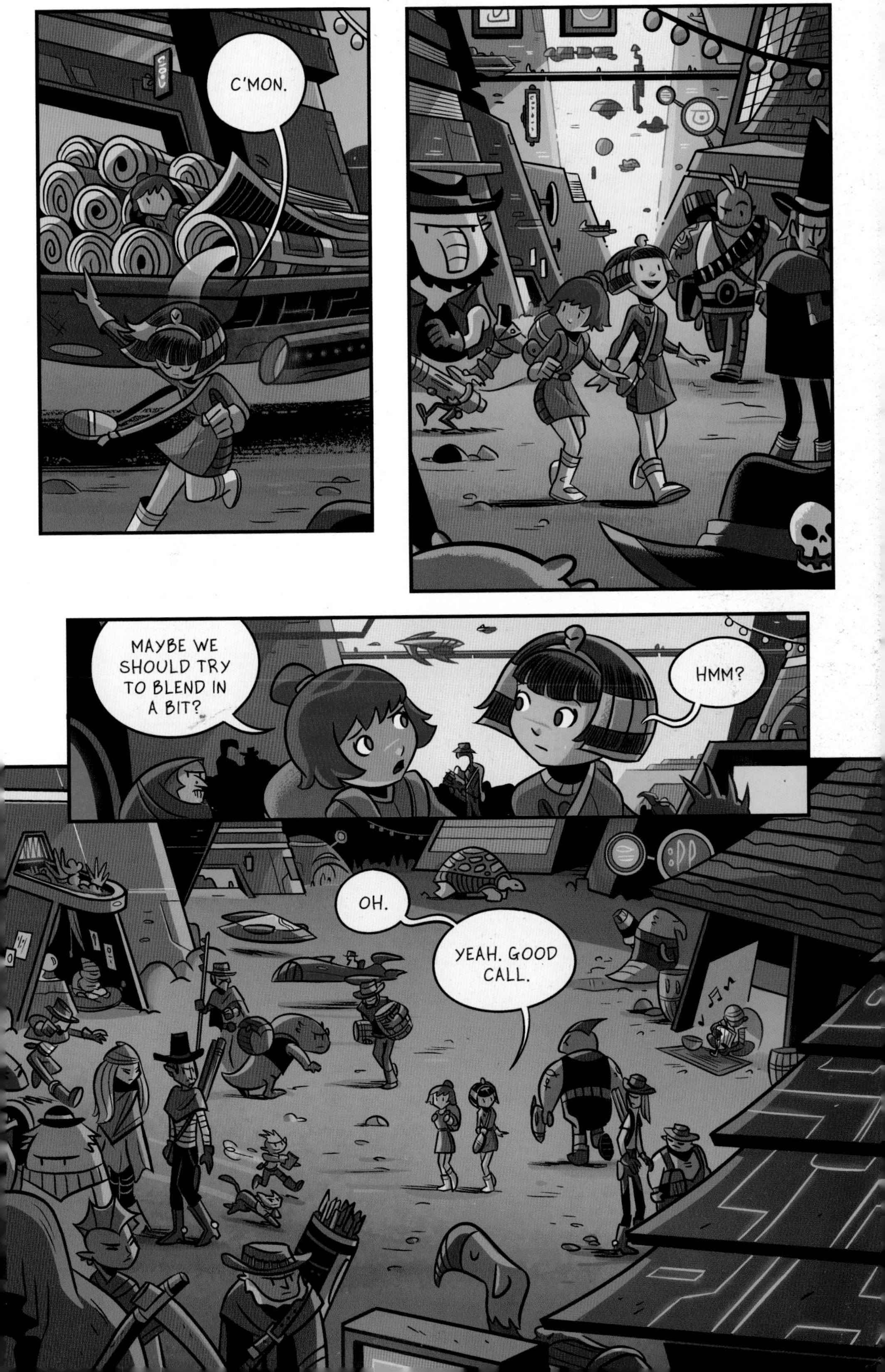
C'MON.
MAYBE WE SHOULD TRY TO BLEND IN A BIT?
HMM?
OH.
YEAH. GOOD CALL.

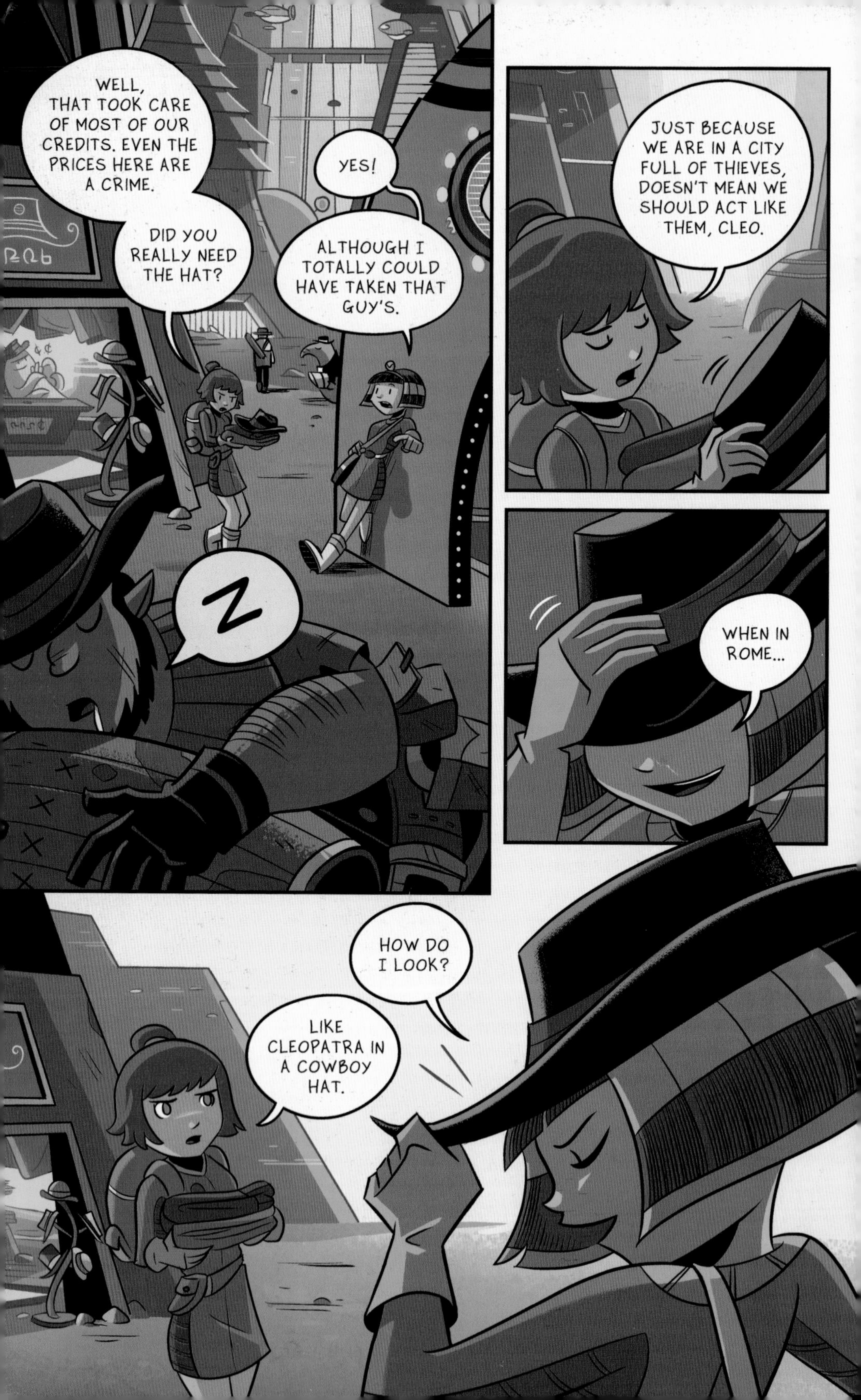
WELL, THAT TOOK CARE OF MOST OF OUR CREDITS. EVEN THE PRICES HERE ARE A CRIME.
YES!
DID YOU REALLY NEED THE HAT?
ALTHOUGH I TOTALLY COULD HAVE TAKEN THAT GUY'S.
Z
JUST BECAUSE WE ARE IN A CITY FULL OF THIEVES, DOESN'T MEAN WE SHOULD ACT LIKE THEM, CLEO.
WHEN IN ROME...
HOW DO I LOOK?
LIKE CLEOPATRA IN A COWBOY HAT.

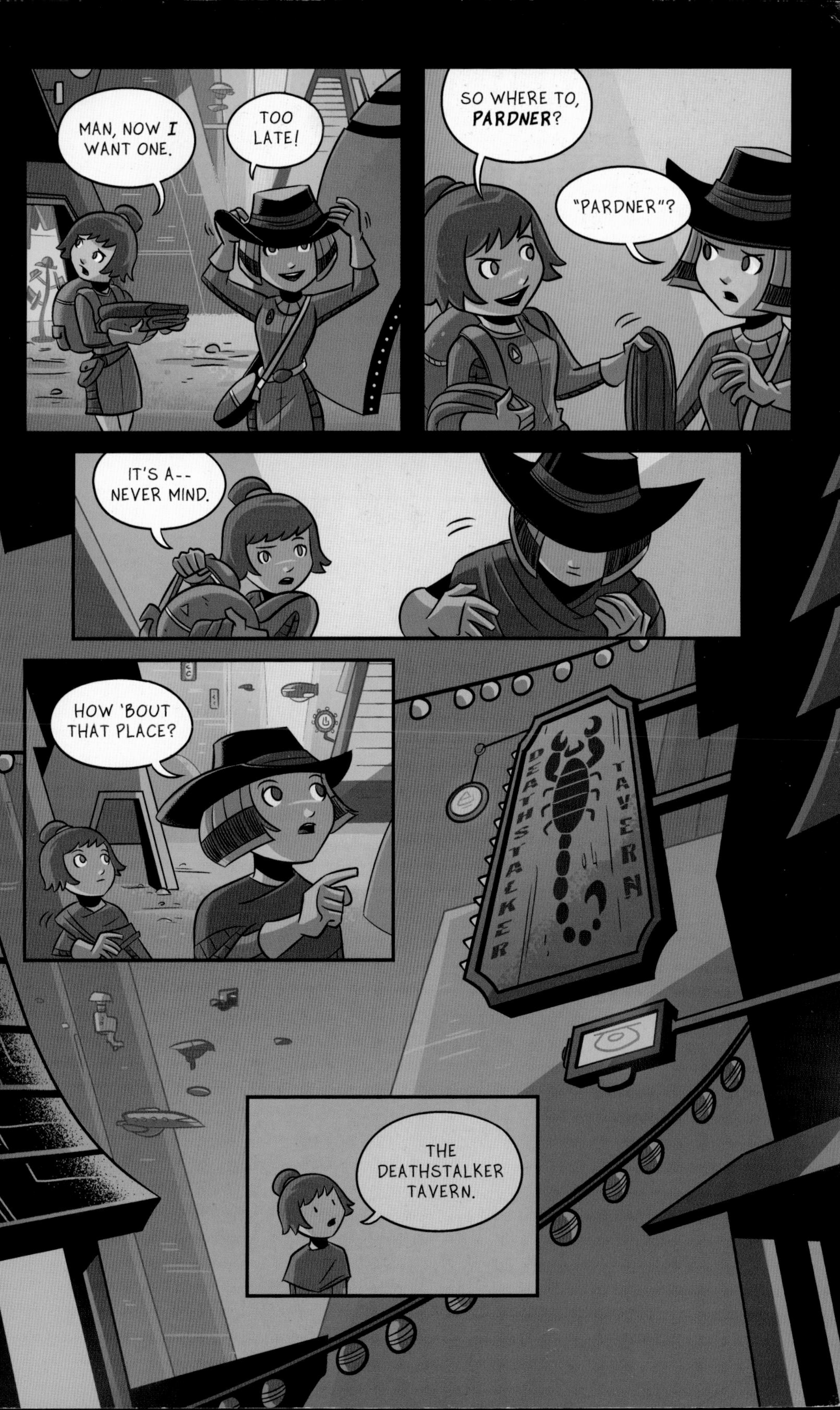
MAN, NOW **I** WANT ONE.
TOO LATE!
SO WHERE TO, **PARDNER**?
"PARDNER"?
IT'S A-- NEVER MIND.
HOW 'BOUT THAT PLACE?
DEATHSTALKER TAVERN
THE DEATHSTALKER TAVERN.

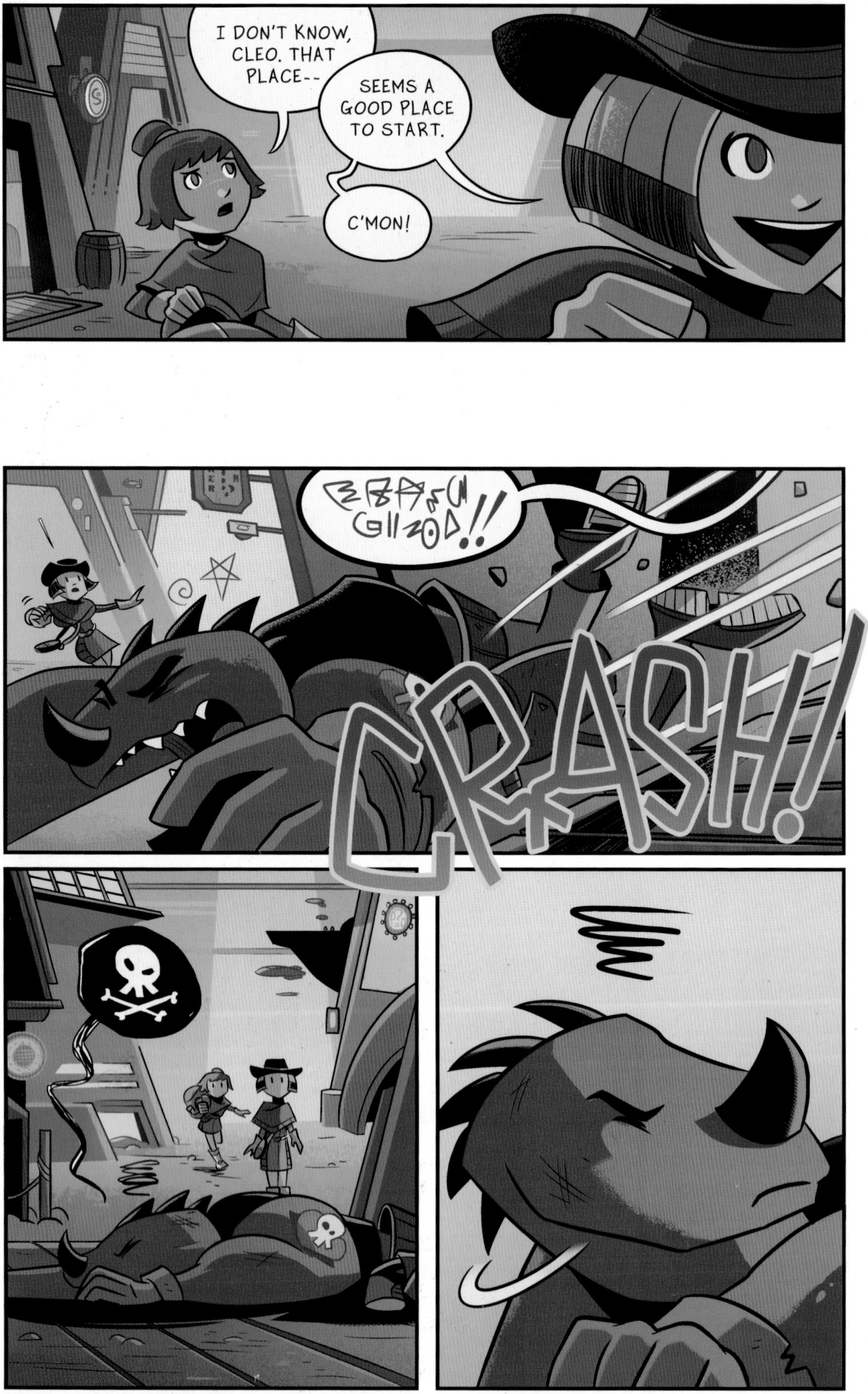
I DON'T KNOW, CLEO. THAT PLACE--
SEEMS A GOOD PLACE TO START.
C'MON!
CRASH!

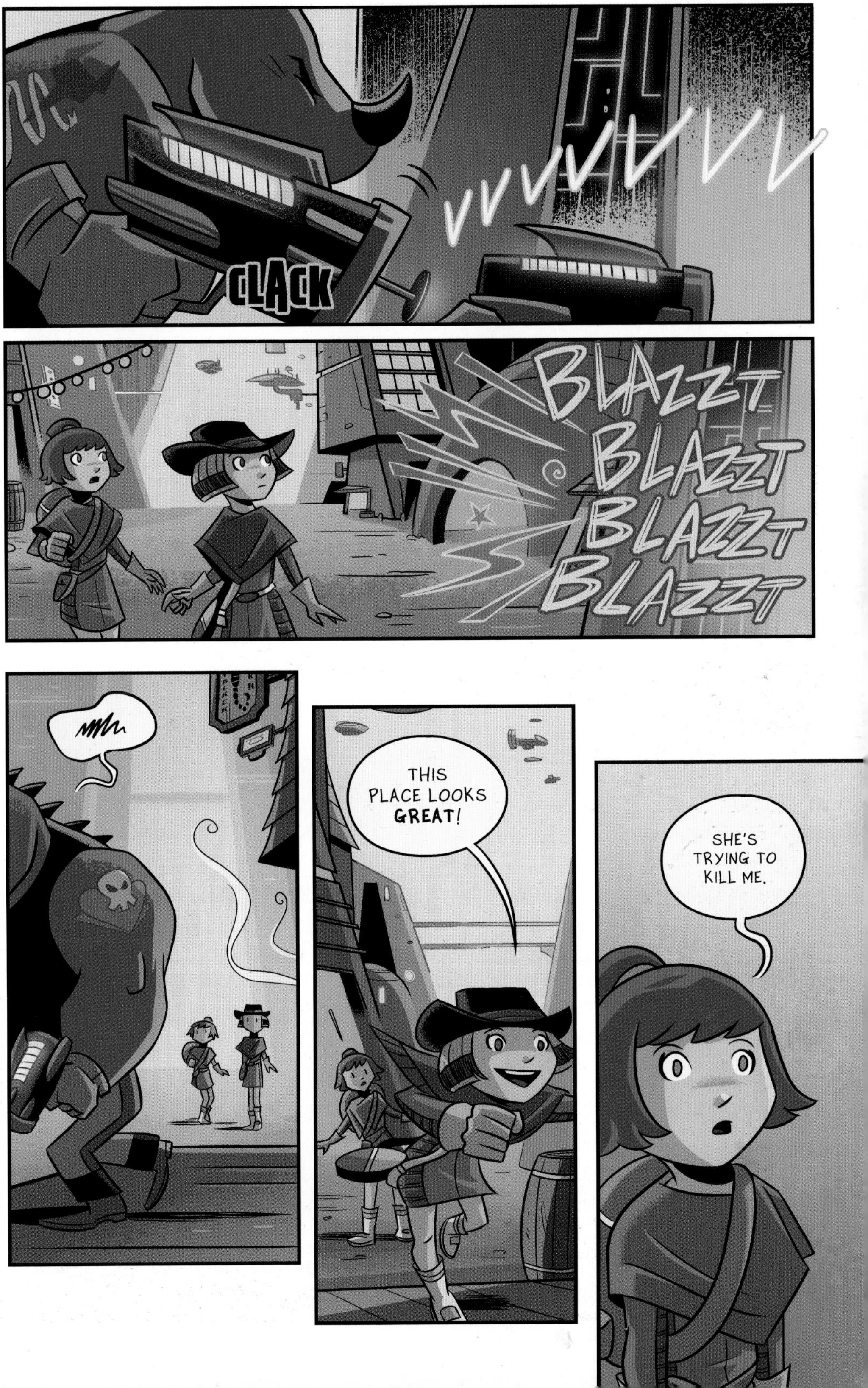
VVVVVVVVVV
CLACK
BLAZZT
BLAZZT
BLAZZT
BLAZZT
THIS PLACE LOOKS GREAT!
SHE'S TRYING TO KILL ME.

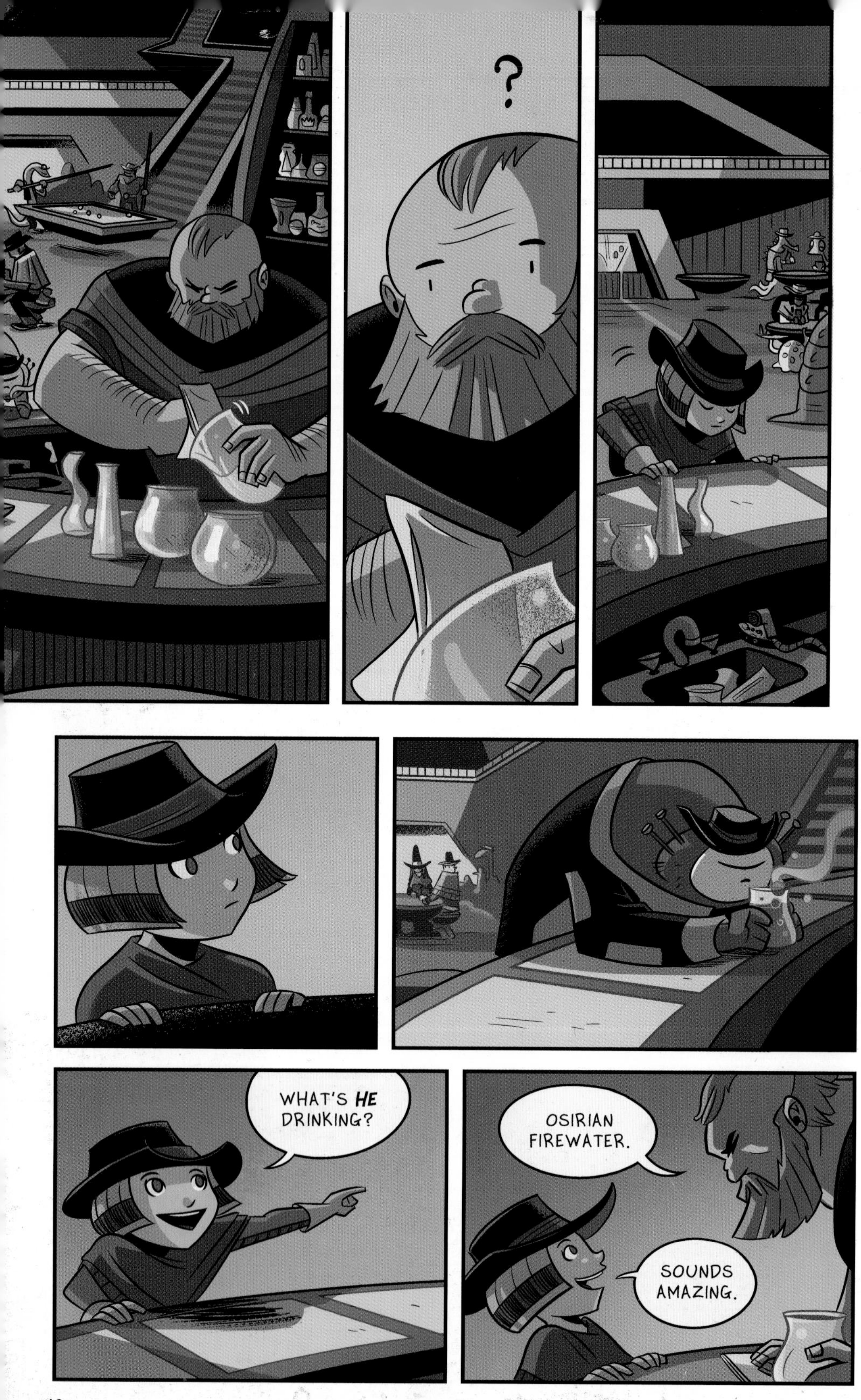
?
WHAT'S **HE** DRINKING?
OSIRIAN FIREWATER.
SOUNDS AMAZING.

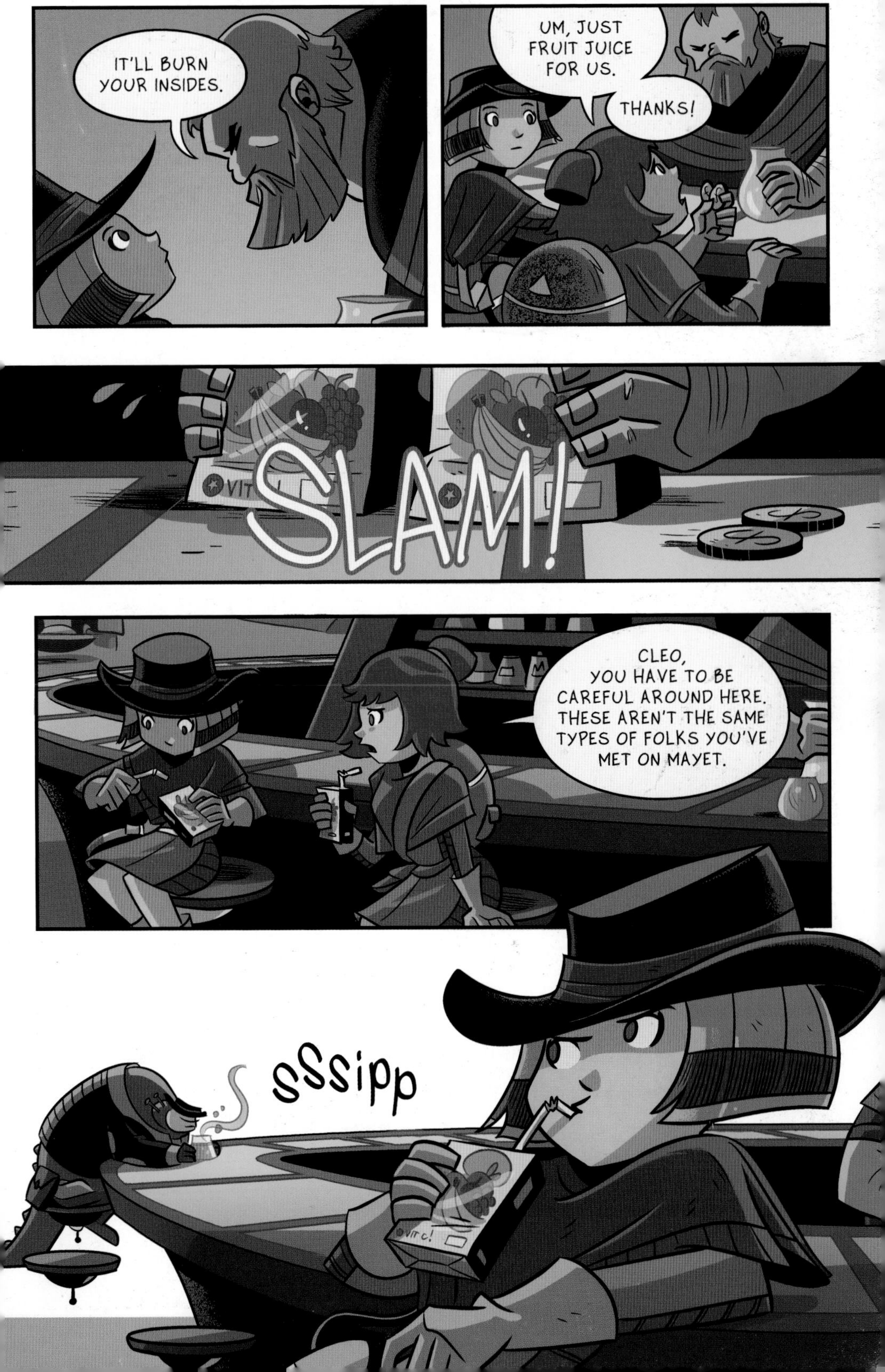
IT'LL BURN YOUR INSIDES.
UM, JUST FRUIT JUICE FOR US.
THANKS!
SLAM!
CLEO, YOU HAVE TO BE CAREFUL AROUND HERE. THESE AREN'T THE SAME TYPES OF FOLKS YOU'VE MET ON MAYET.
sSsipp

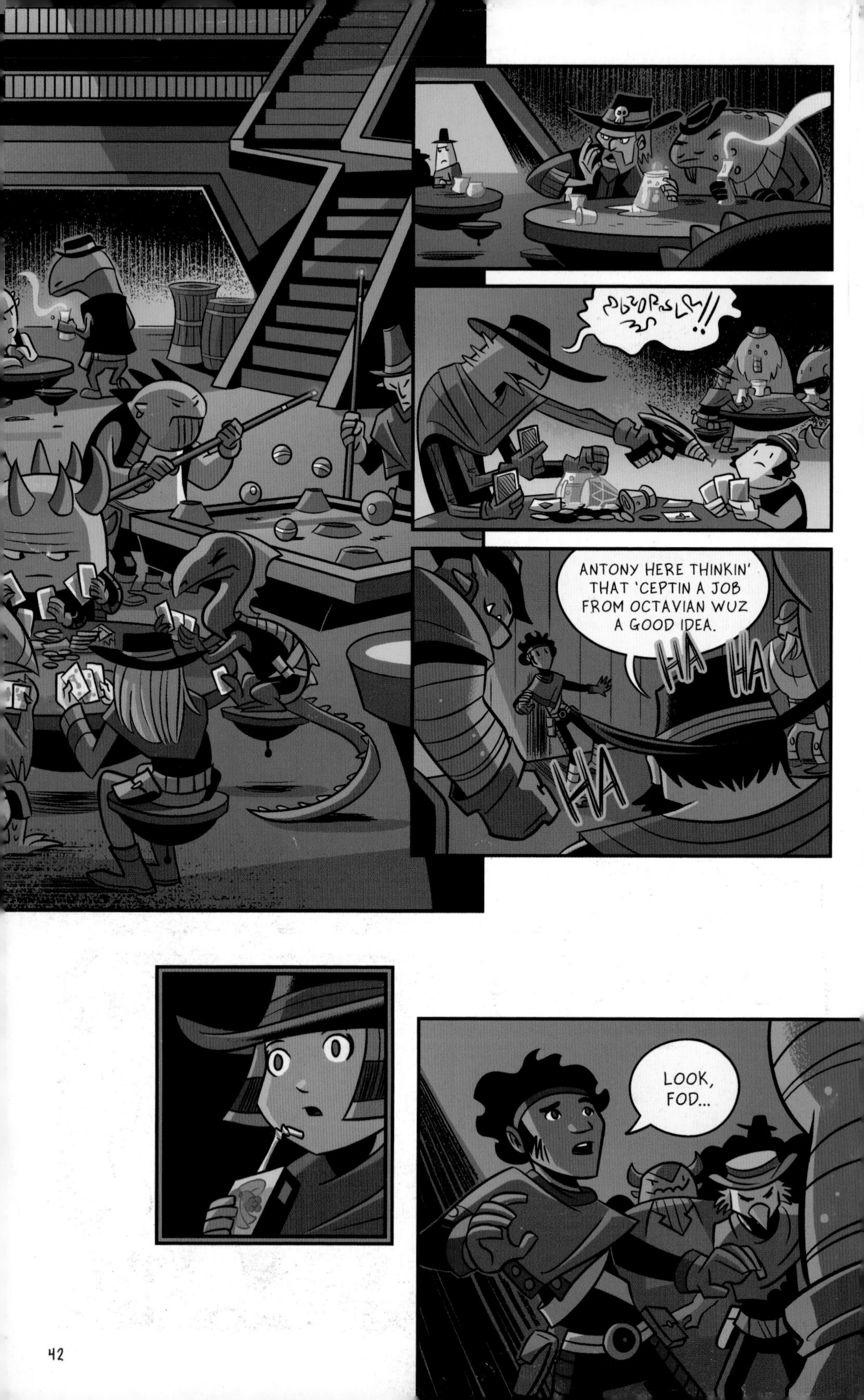

ANTONY HERE THINKIN' THAT 'CEPTIN A JOB FROM OCTAVIAN WUZ A GOOD IDEA.
HA HA
HA
LOOK, FOD...

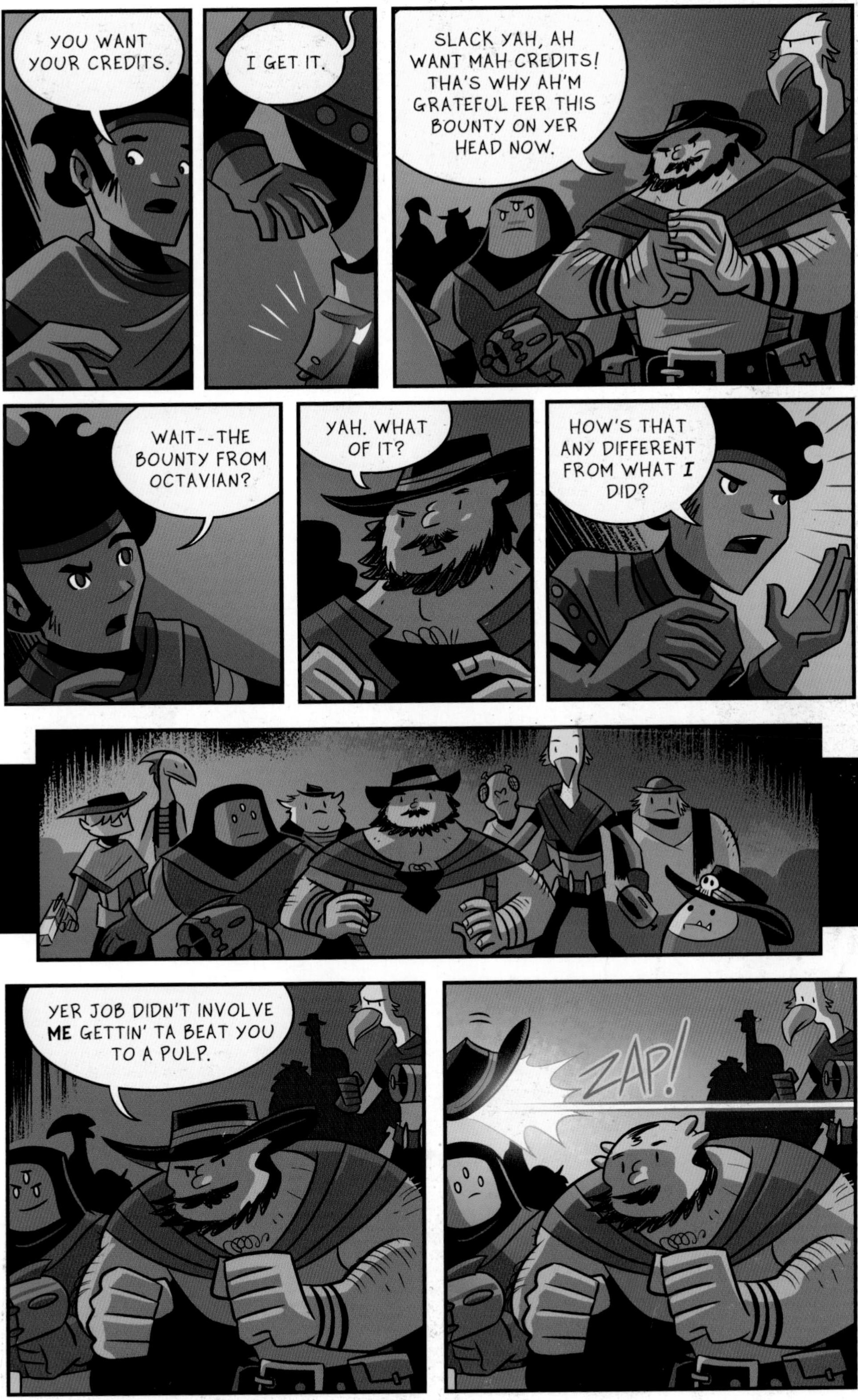
YOU WANT YOUR CREDITS.
I GET IT.
SLACK YAH, AH WANT MAH CREDITS! THA'S WHY AH'M GRATEFUL FER THIS BOUNTY ON YER HEAD NOW.
WAIT--THE BOUNTY FROM OCTAVIAN?
YAH. WHAT OF IT?
HOW'S THAT ANY DIFFERENT FROM WHAT **I** DID?
YER JOB DIDN'T INVOLVE **ME** GETTIN' TA BEAT YOU TO A PULP.
ZAP!

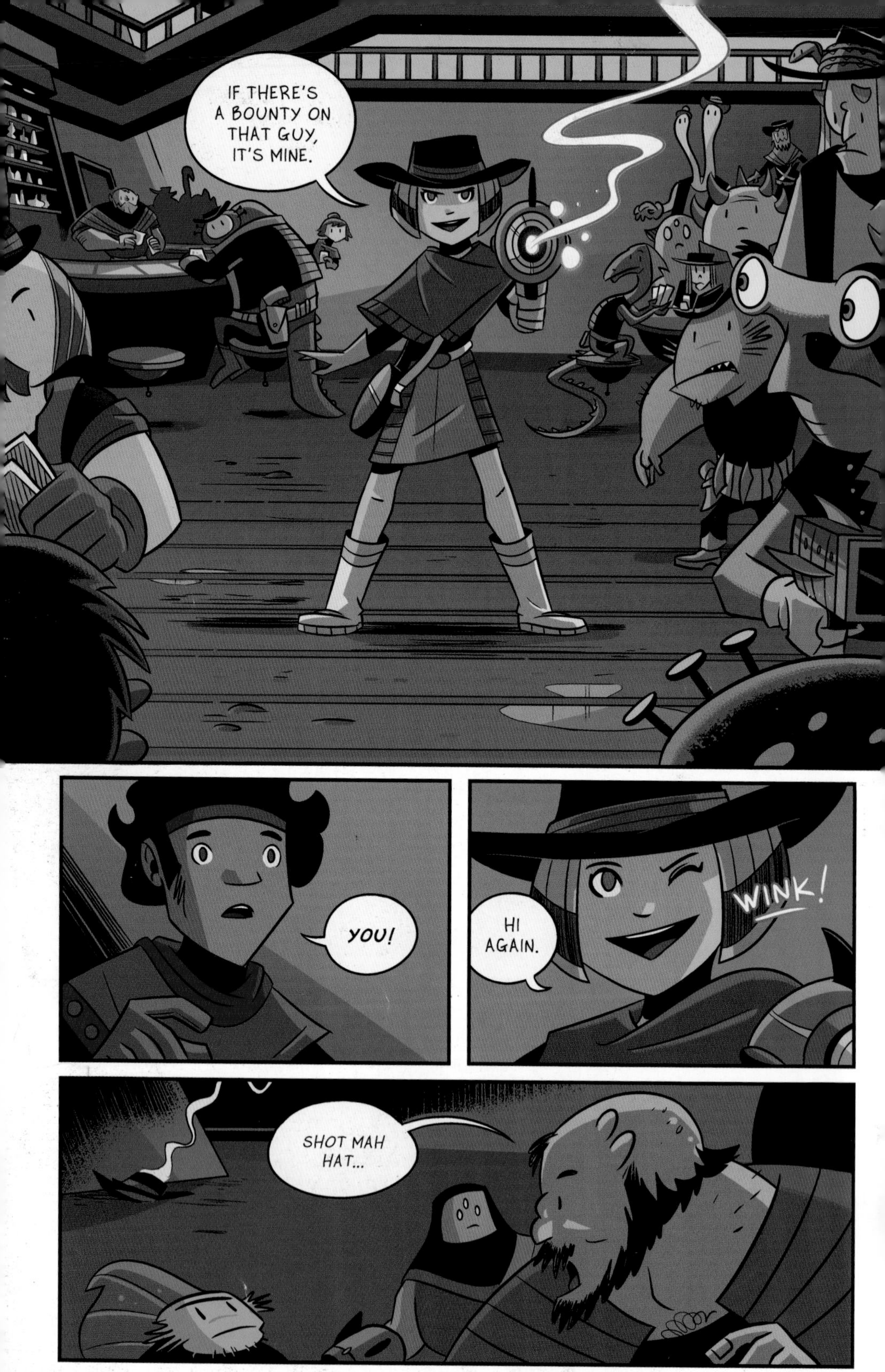
IF THERE'S A BOUNTY ON THAT GUY, IT'S MINE.
YOU!
HI AGAIN.
WINK!
SHOT MAH HAT...

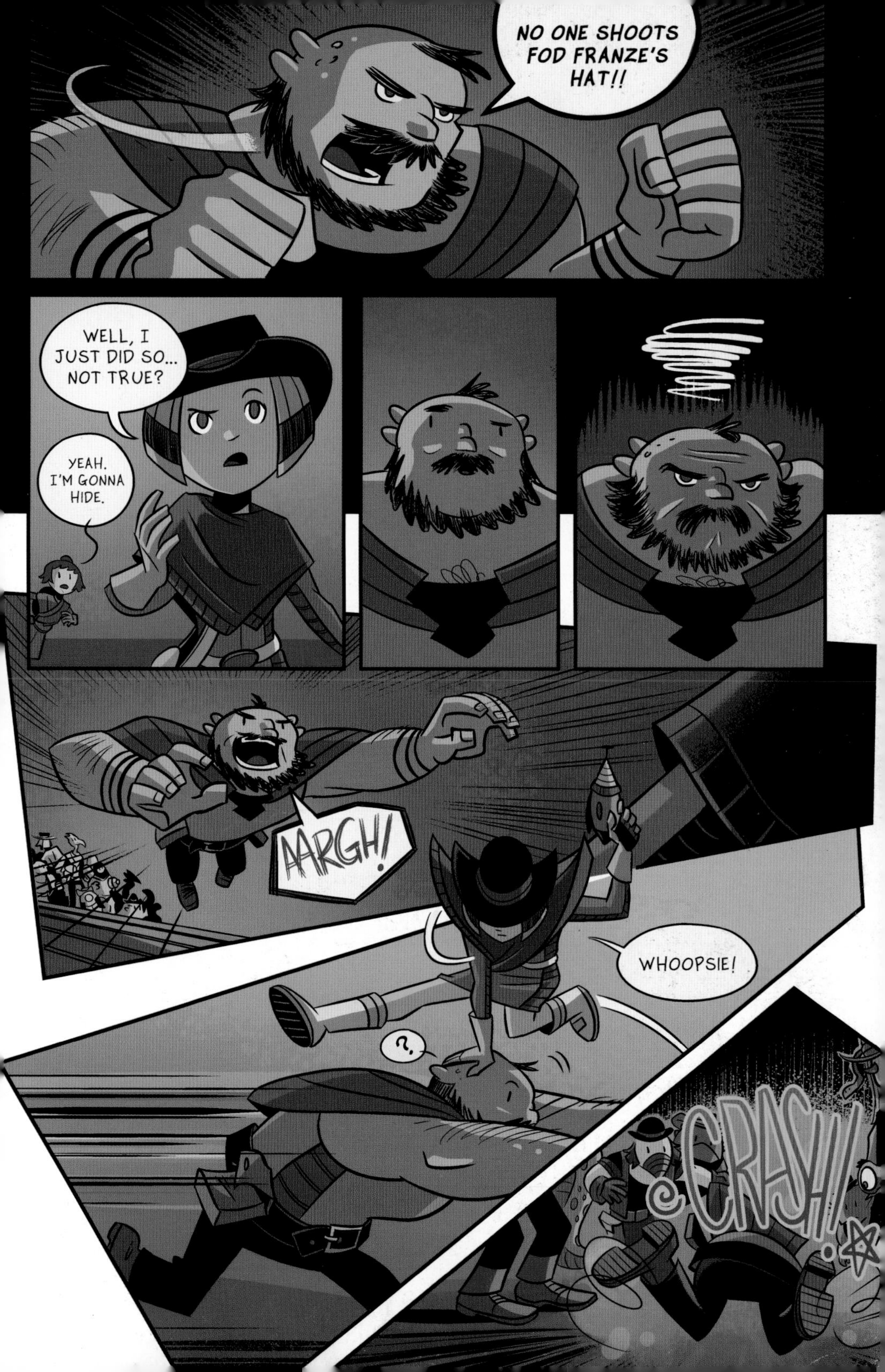
NO ONE SHOOTS FOD FRANZE'S HAT!!
WELL, I JUST DID SO... NOT TRUE?
YEAH. I'M GONNA HIDE.
AARGH!
WHOOPSIE!
?.
CRASH!!

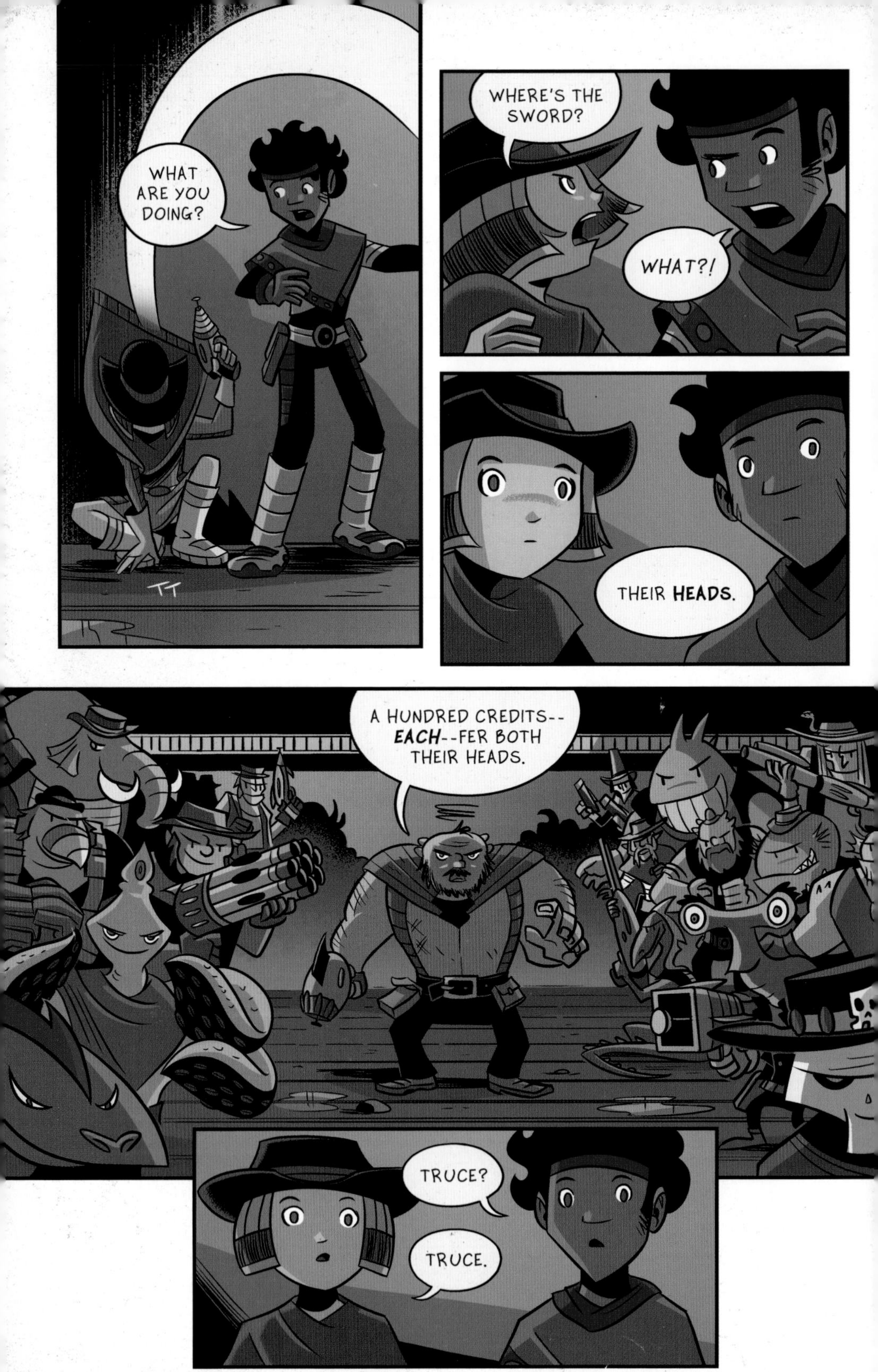
WHAT ARE YOU DOING?
TT
WHERE'S THE SWORD?
WHAT?!
THEIR **HEADS**.
A HUNDRED CREDITS-- **EACH**--FER BOTH THEIR HEADS.
TRUCE?
TRUCE.

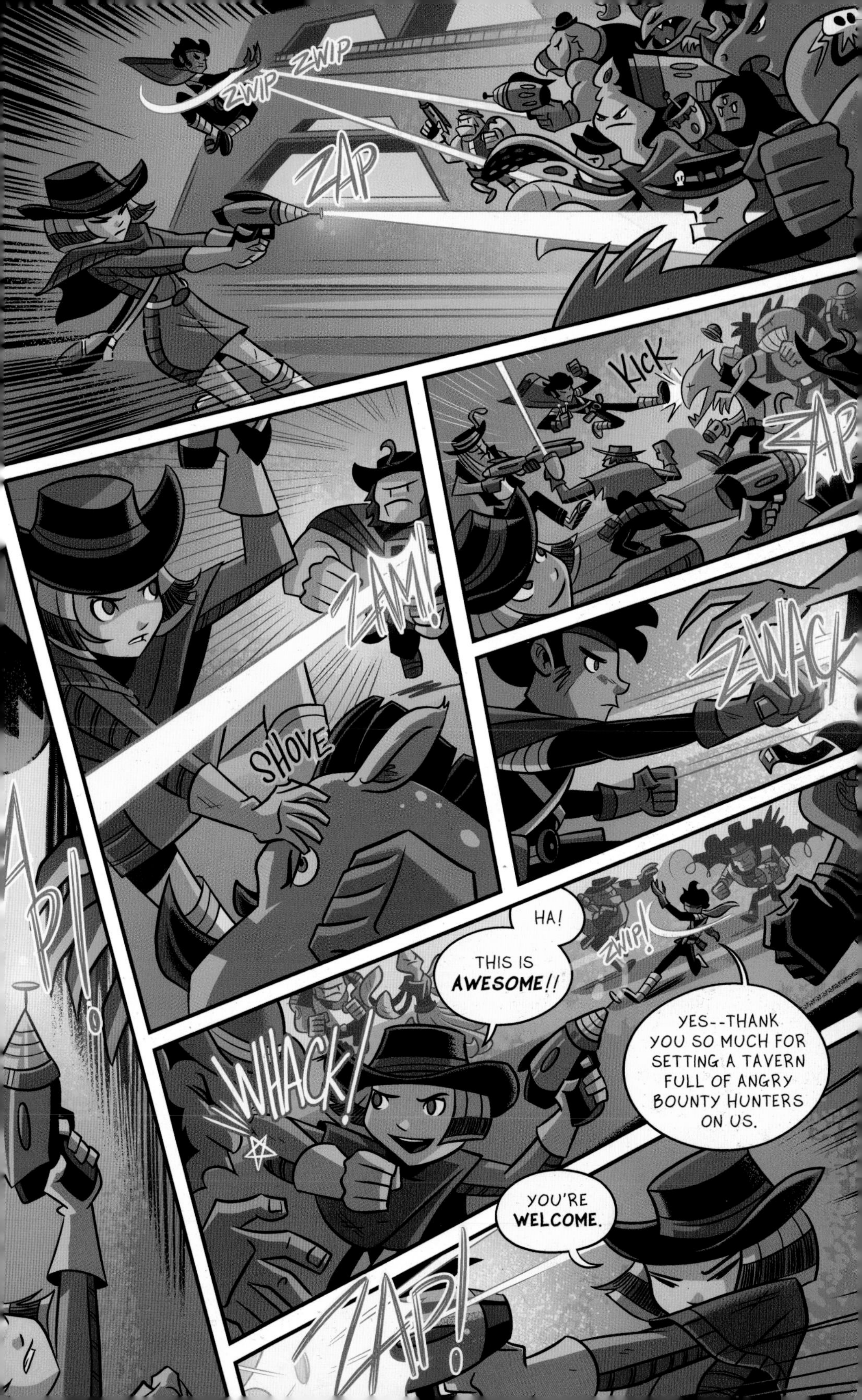
ZWIP
ZWIP
ZAP
KICK
ZAP
ZAM!
SHOVE
ZWACK
ZAP!
HA!
THIS IS **AWESOME**!!
ZWIP!
WHACK!
YES--THANK YOU SO MUCH FOR SETTING A TAVERN FULL OF ANGRY BOUNTY HUNTERS ON US.
YOU'RE **WELCOME**.
ZAP!

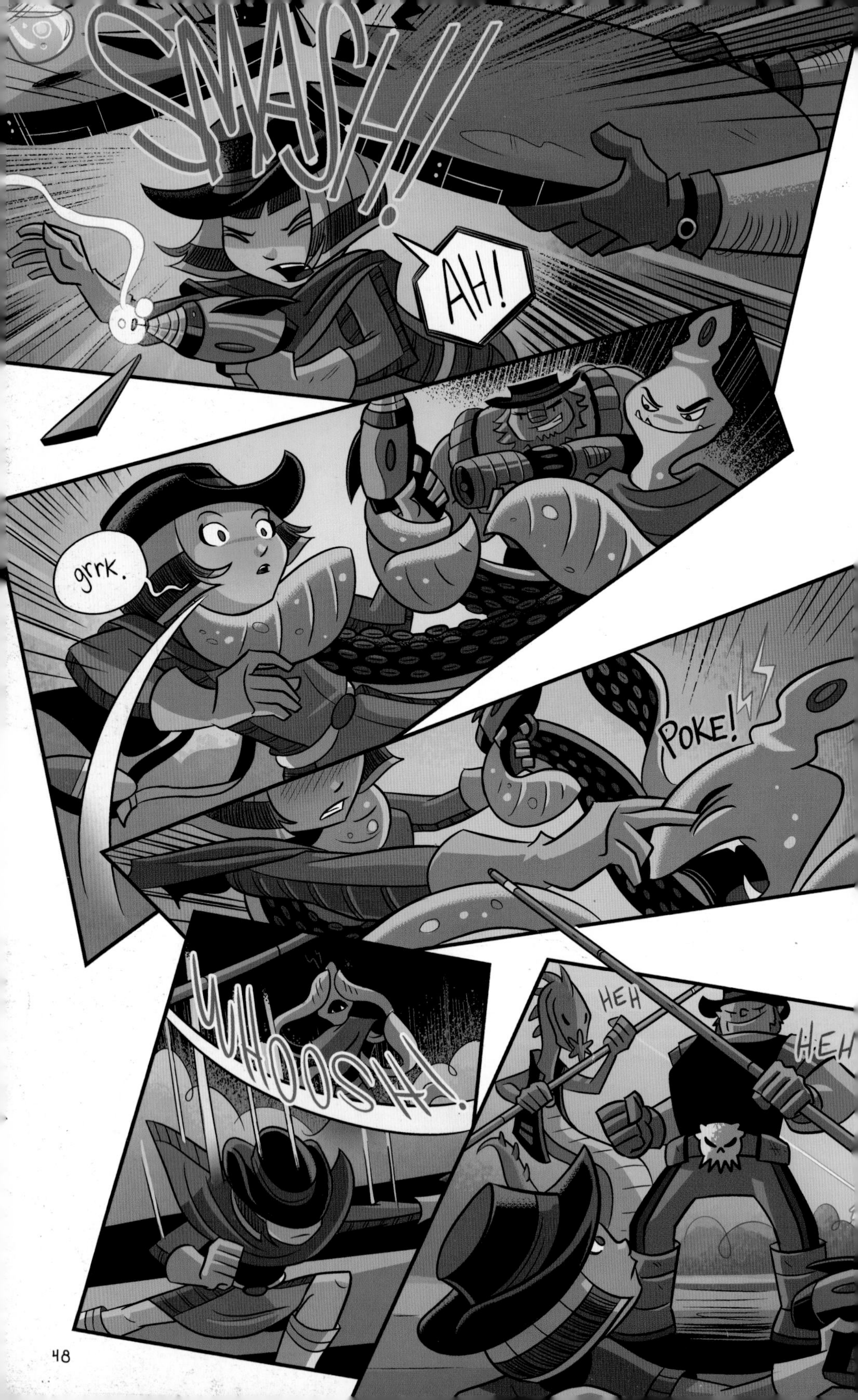
SMASH!!
AH!
grrk.
POKE!
WHOOSH!
HEH
HEH

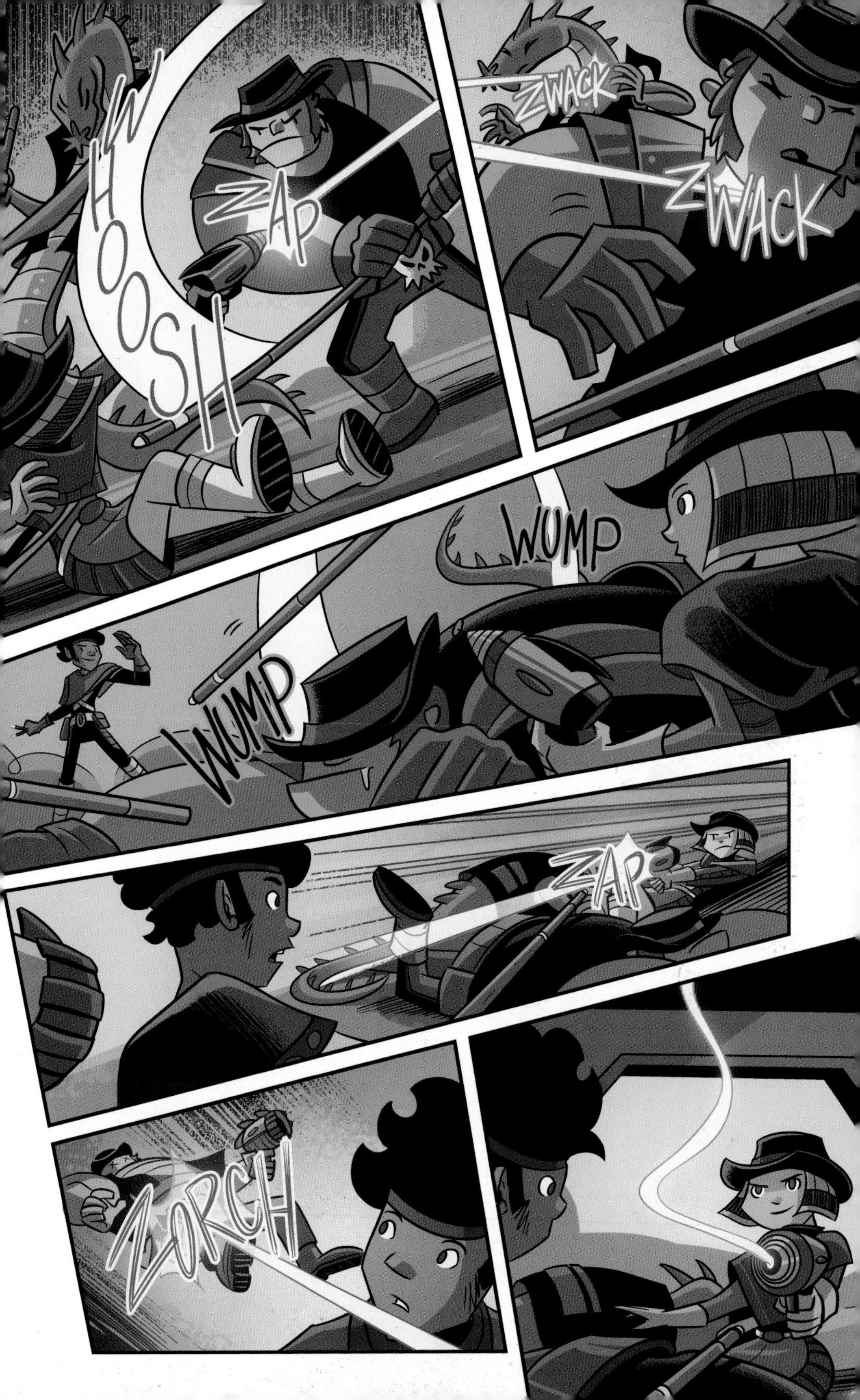
WHOOSH
ZAP
ZWACK
ZWACK
WUMP
WUMP
ZAP
ZORCH

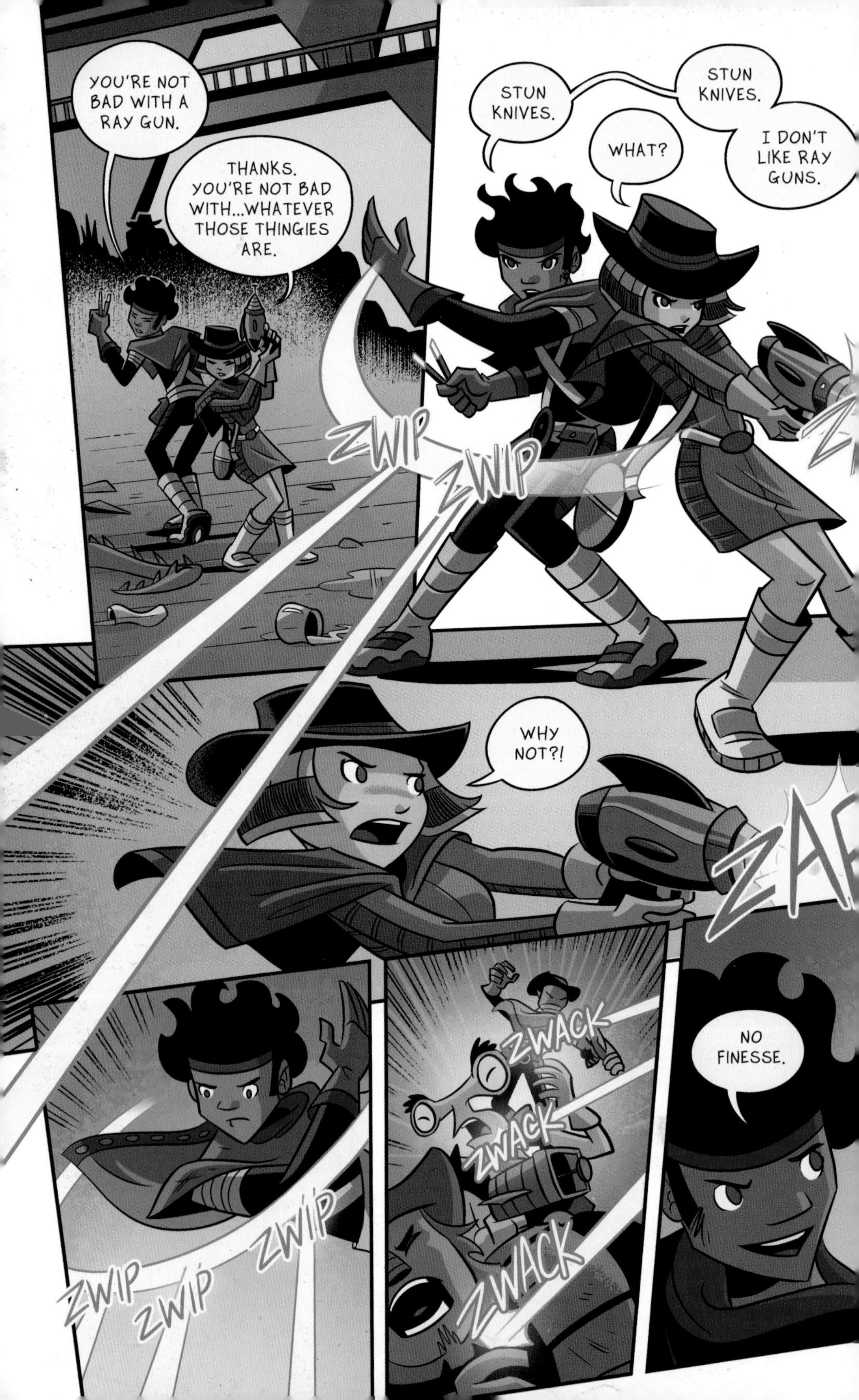
YOU'RE NOT BAD WITH A RAY GUN.
THANKS. YOU'RE NOT BAD WITH...WHATEVER THOSE THINGIES ARE.
STUN KNIVES.
WHAT?
STUN KNIVES.
I DON'T LIKE RAY GUNS.
ZWIP
ZWIP
WHY NOT?!
ZWIP
ZWIP
ZWIP
ZWACK
ZWACK
ZWACK
NO FINESSE.

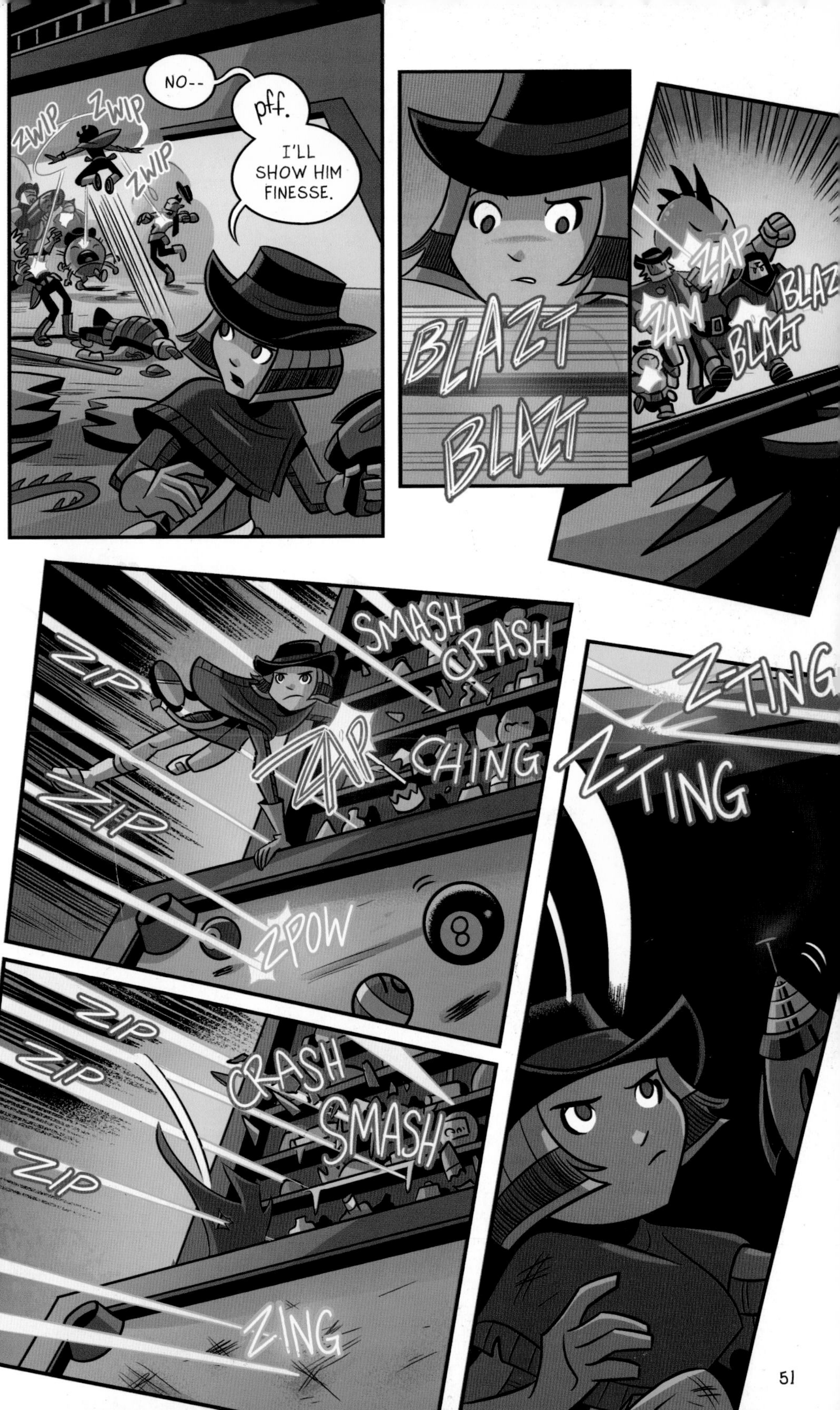

NO--
ZWIP
ZWIP
ZWIP
pff.
I'LL SHOW HIM FINESSE.
BLAZT
BLAZT
ZAP
ZAM
BLAZ
BLAZT
SMASH
CRASH
ZIP
ZIP
ZAP
CHING
Z-TING
Z-TING
ZPOW
ZIP
ZIP
CRASH
SMASH
ZIP
ZING

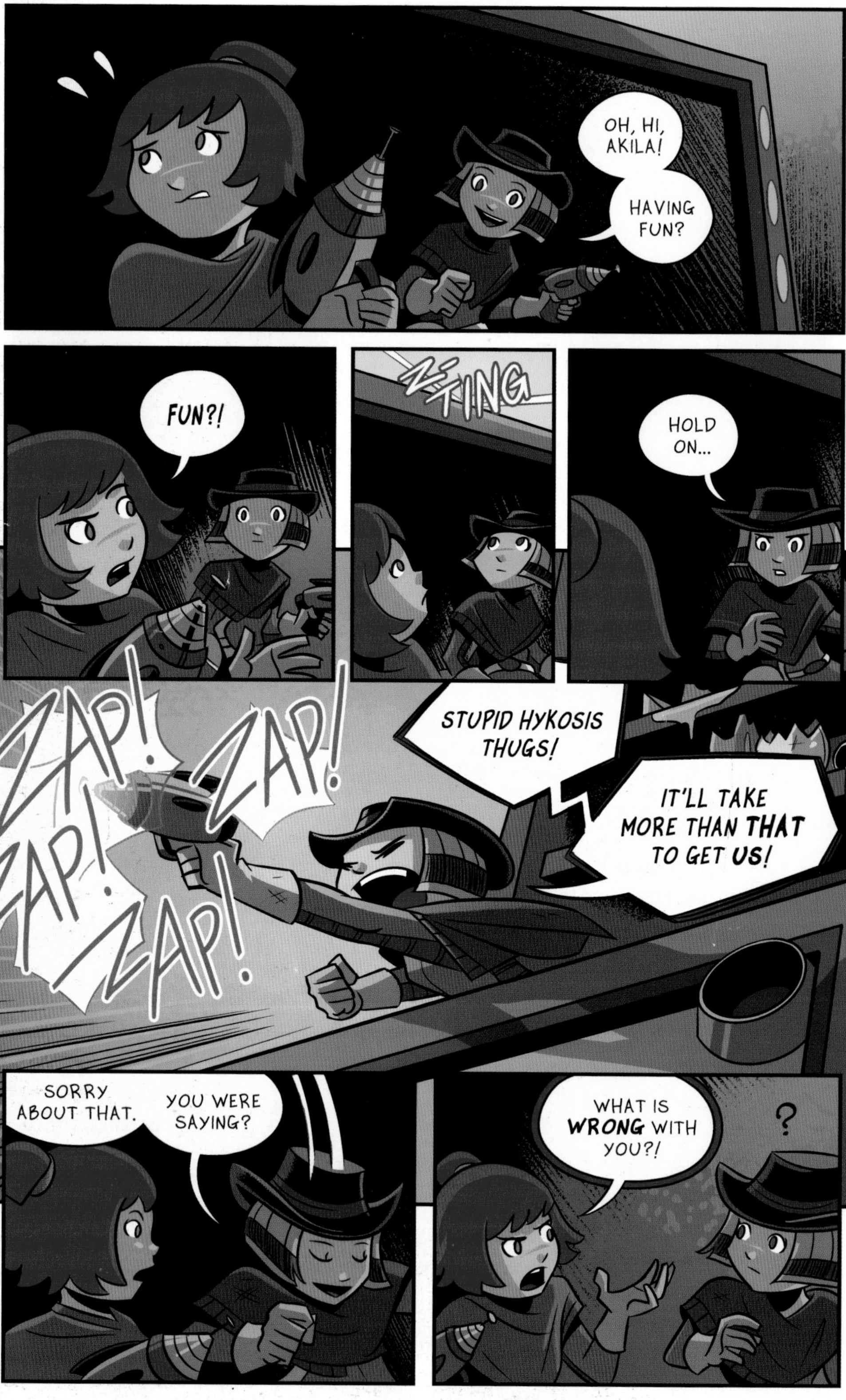
OH, HI, AKILA!
HAVING FUN?
FUN?!
ZZTING
HOLD ON...
ZAP! ZAP! ZAP! ZAP!
STUPID HYKOSIS THUGS!
IT'LL TAKE MORE THAN THAT TO GET US!
SORRY ABOUT THAT.
YOU WERE SAYING?
WHAT IS WRONG WITH YOU?!
?

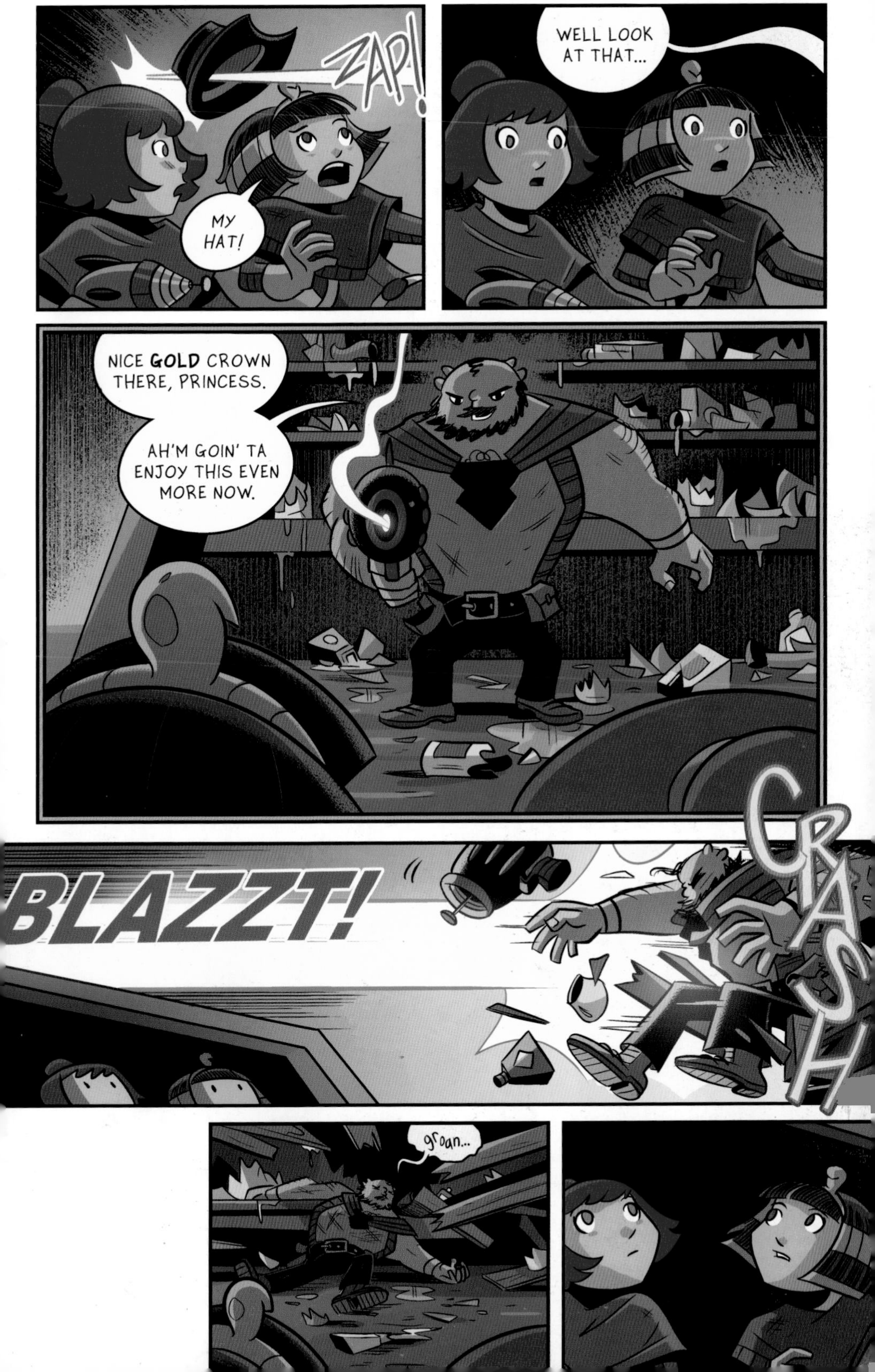
ZAP!
MY HAT!
WELL LOOK AT THAT...
NICE GOLD CROWN THERE, PRINCESS.
AH'M GOIN' TA ENJOY THIS EVEN MORE NOW.
BLAZZT!
CRASH
groan...

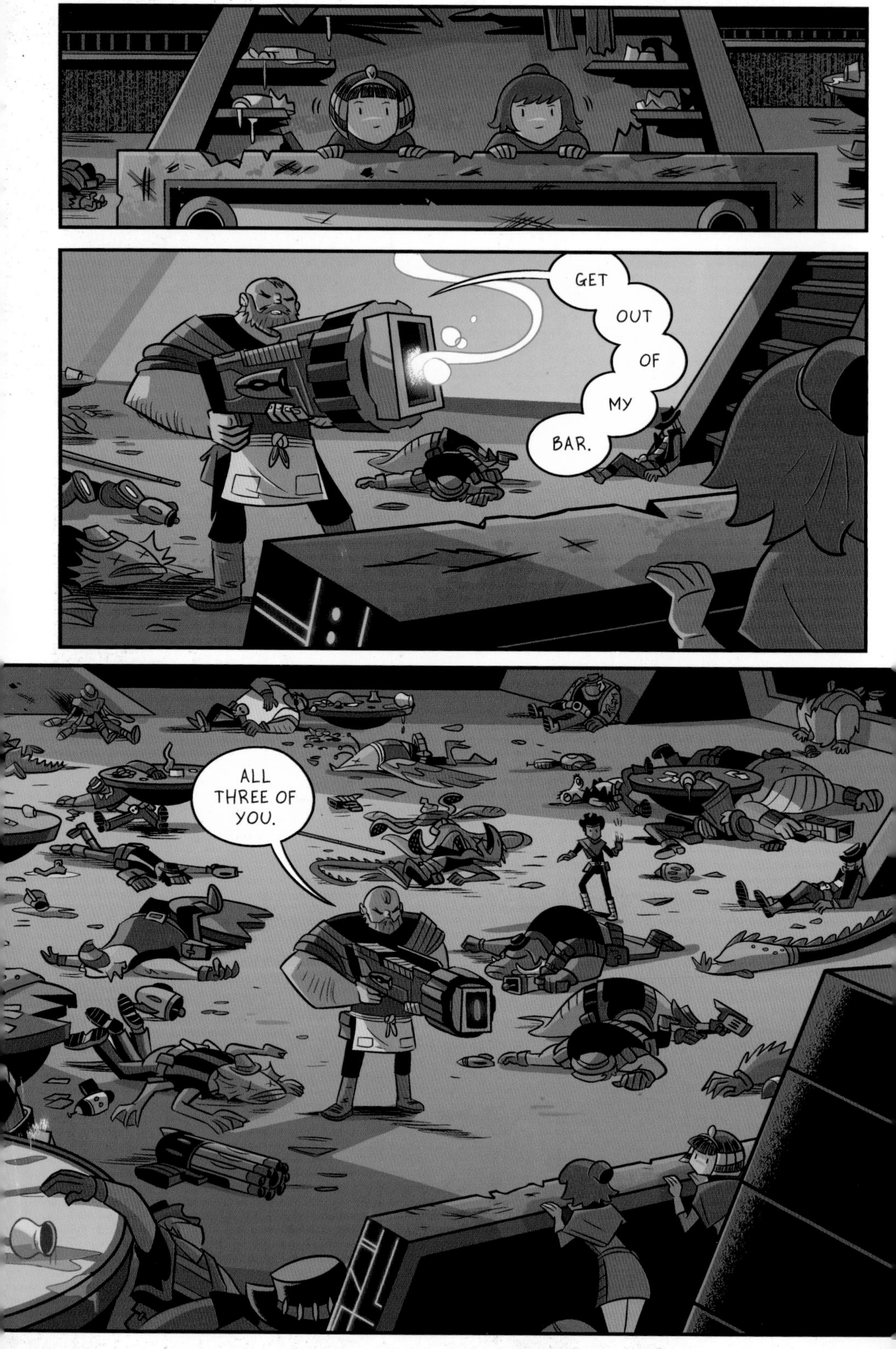
GET OUT OF MY BAR.
ALL THREE OF YOU.

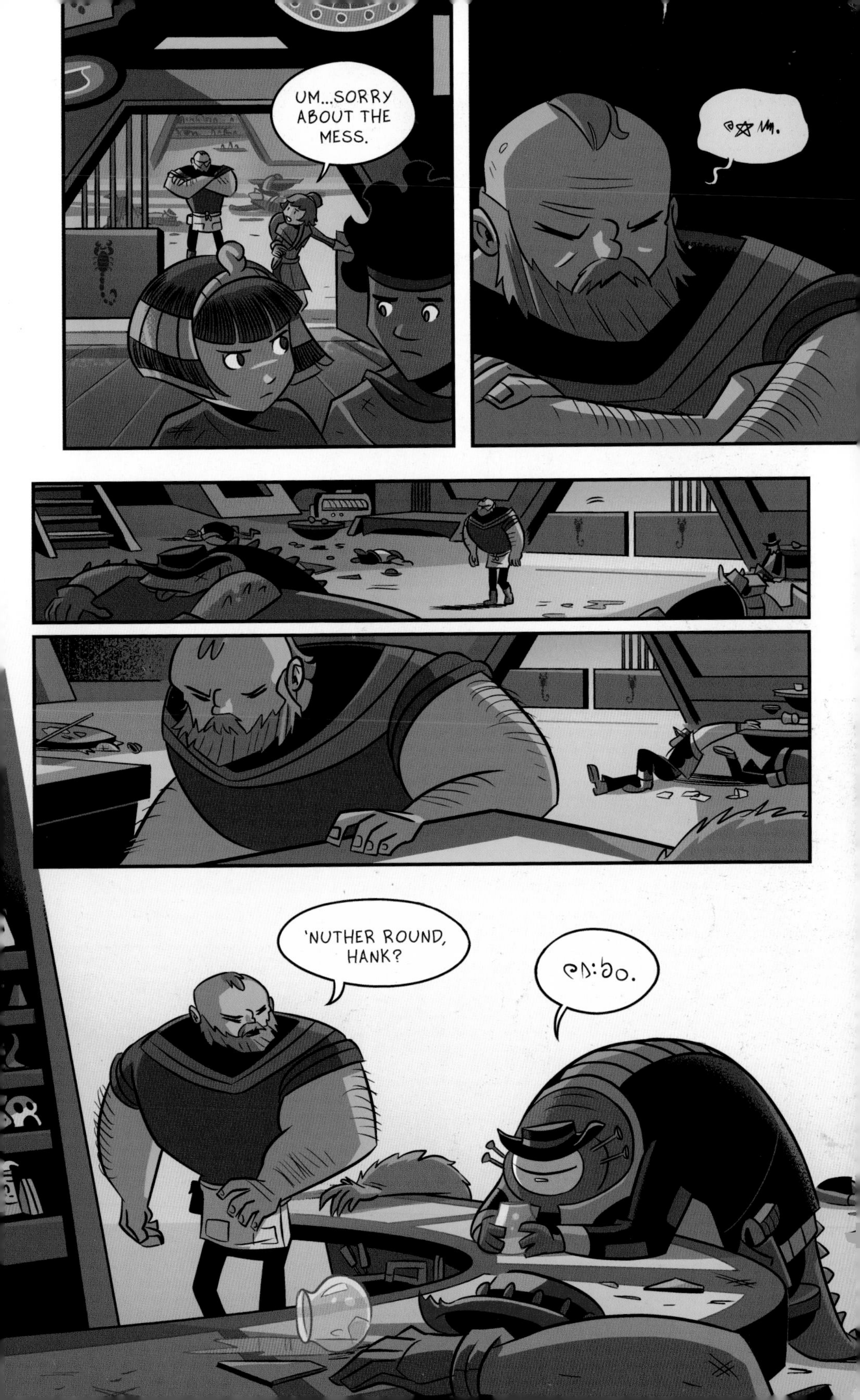
UM...SORRY ABOUT THE MESS.
'NUTHER ROUND, HANK?

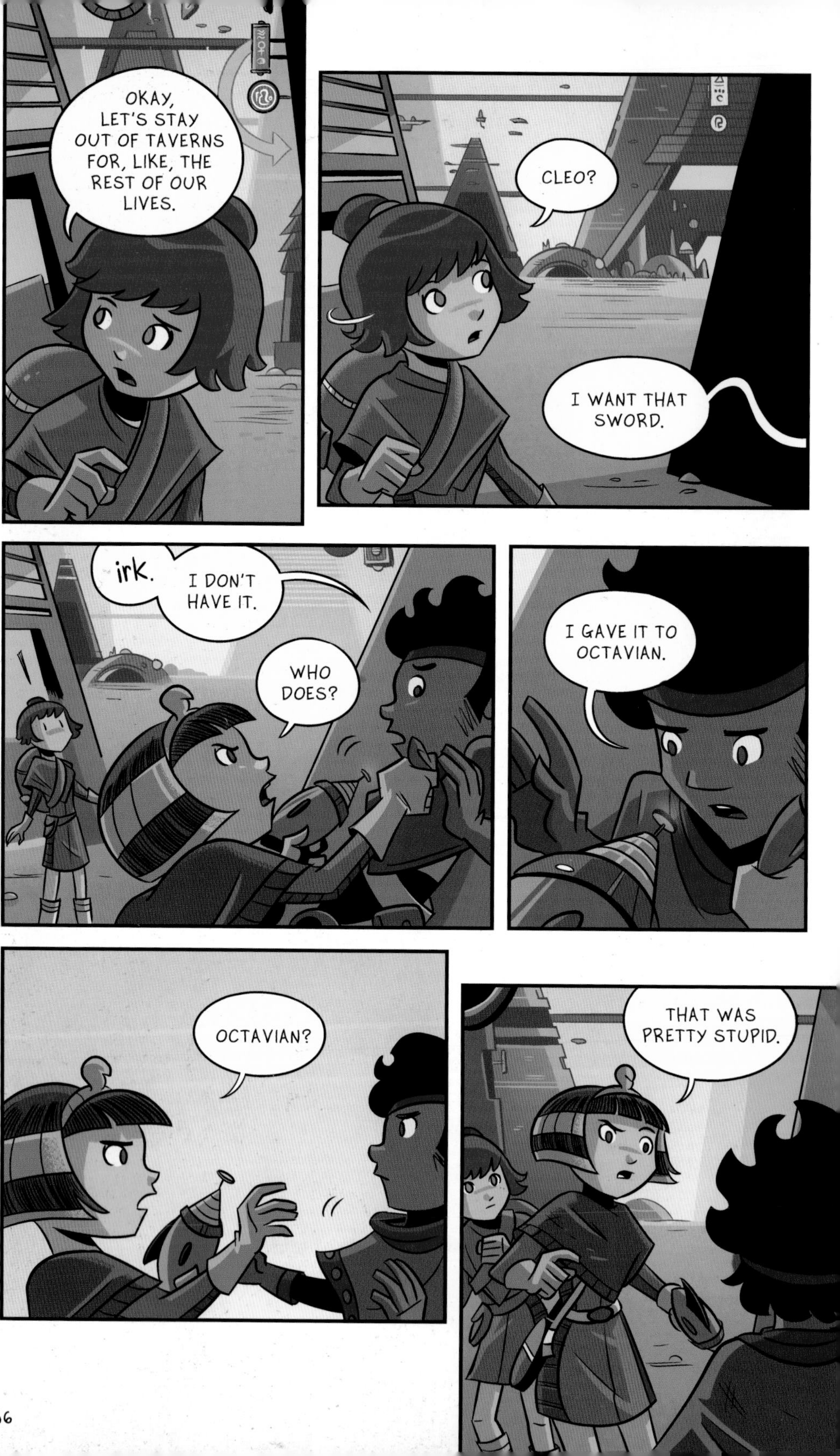
OKAY, LET'S STAY OUT OF TAVERNS FOR, LIKE, THE REST OF OUR LIVES.
CLEO?
I WANT THAT SWORD.
irk.
I DON'T HAVE IT.
WHO DOES?
I GAVE IT TO OCTAVIAN.
OCTAVIAN?
THAT WAS PRETTY STUPID.

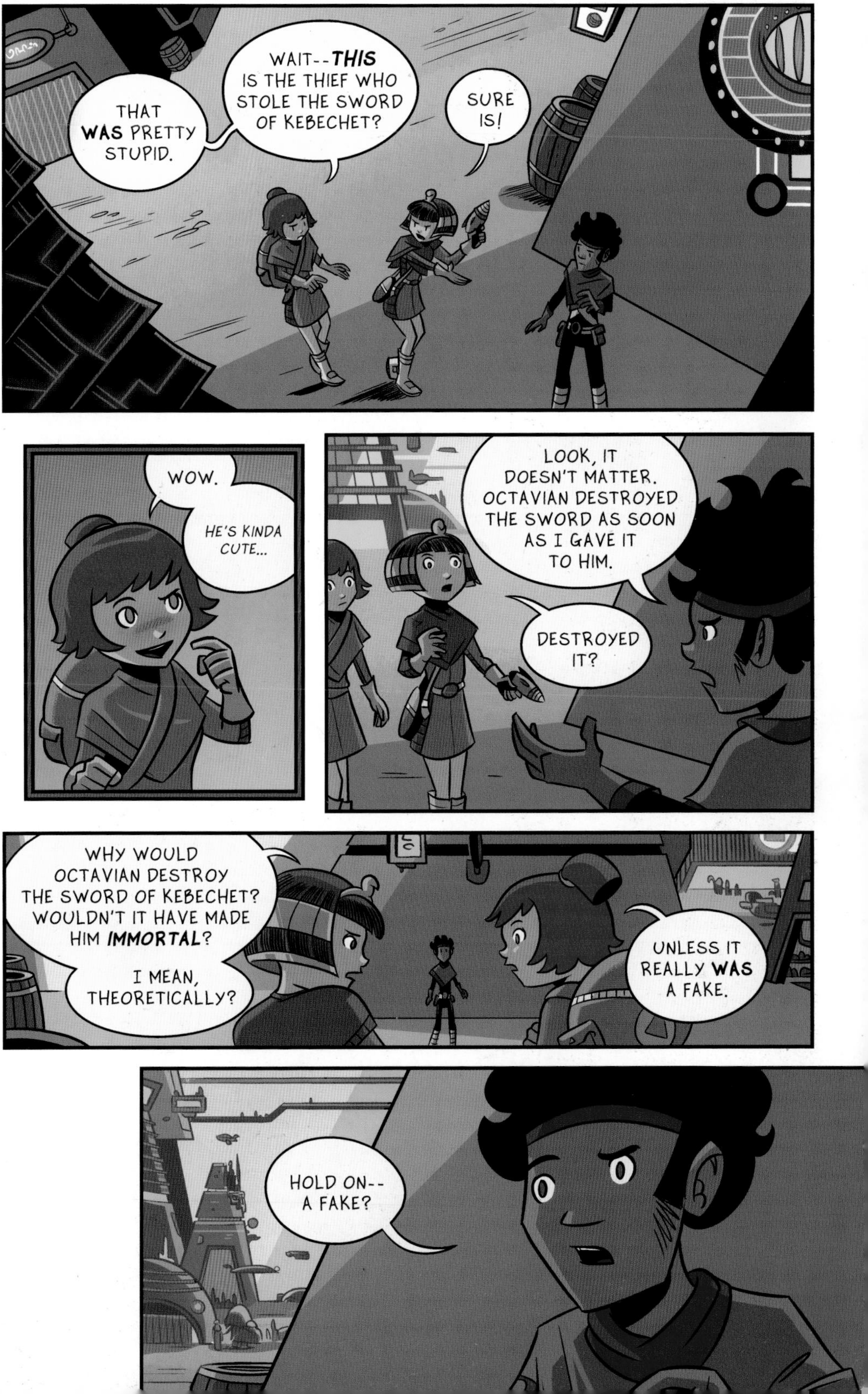

THAT WAS PRETTY STUPID.
WAIT--THIS IS THE THIEF WHO STOLE THE SWORD OF KEBECHET?
SURE IS!
WOW.
HE'S KINDA CUTE...
LOOK, IT DOESN'T MATTER. OCTAVIAN DESTROYED THE SWORD AS SOON AS I GAVE IT TO HIM.
DESTROYED IT?
WHY WOULD OCTAVIAN DESTROY THE SWORD OF KEBECHET? WOULDN'T IT HAVE MADE HIM IMMORTAL?
I MEAN, THEORETICALLY?
UNLESS IT REALLY WAS A FAKE.
HOLD ON-- A FAKE?

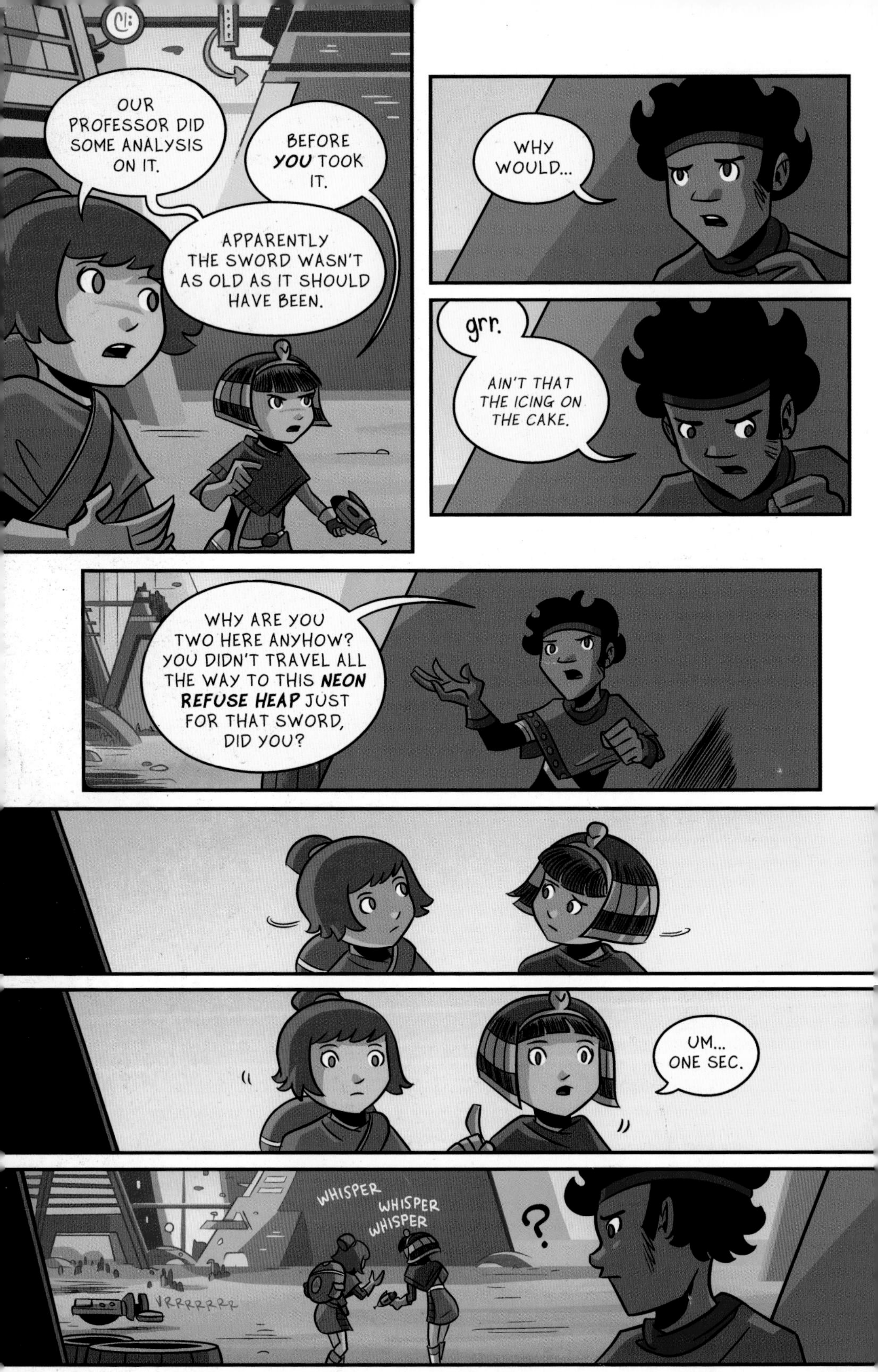
OUR PROFESSOR DID SOME ANALYSIS ON IT.
BEFORE YOU TOOK IT.
APPARENTLY THE SWORD WASN'T AS OLD AS IT SHOULD HAVE BEEN.
WHY WOULD...
grr.
AIN'T THAT THE ICING ON THE CAKE.
WHY ARE YOU TWO HERE ANYHOW? YOU DIDN'T TRAVEL ALL THE WAY TO THIS NEON REFUSE HEAP JUST FOR THAT SWORD, DID YOU?
UM... ONE SEC.
WHISPER
WHISPER
WHISPER
?
VRRRRRRR

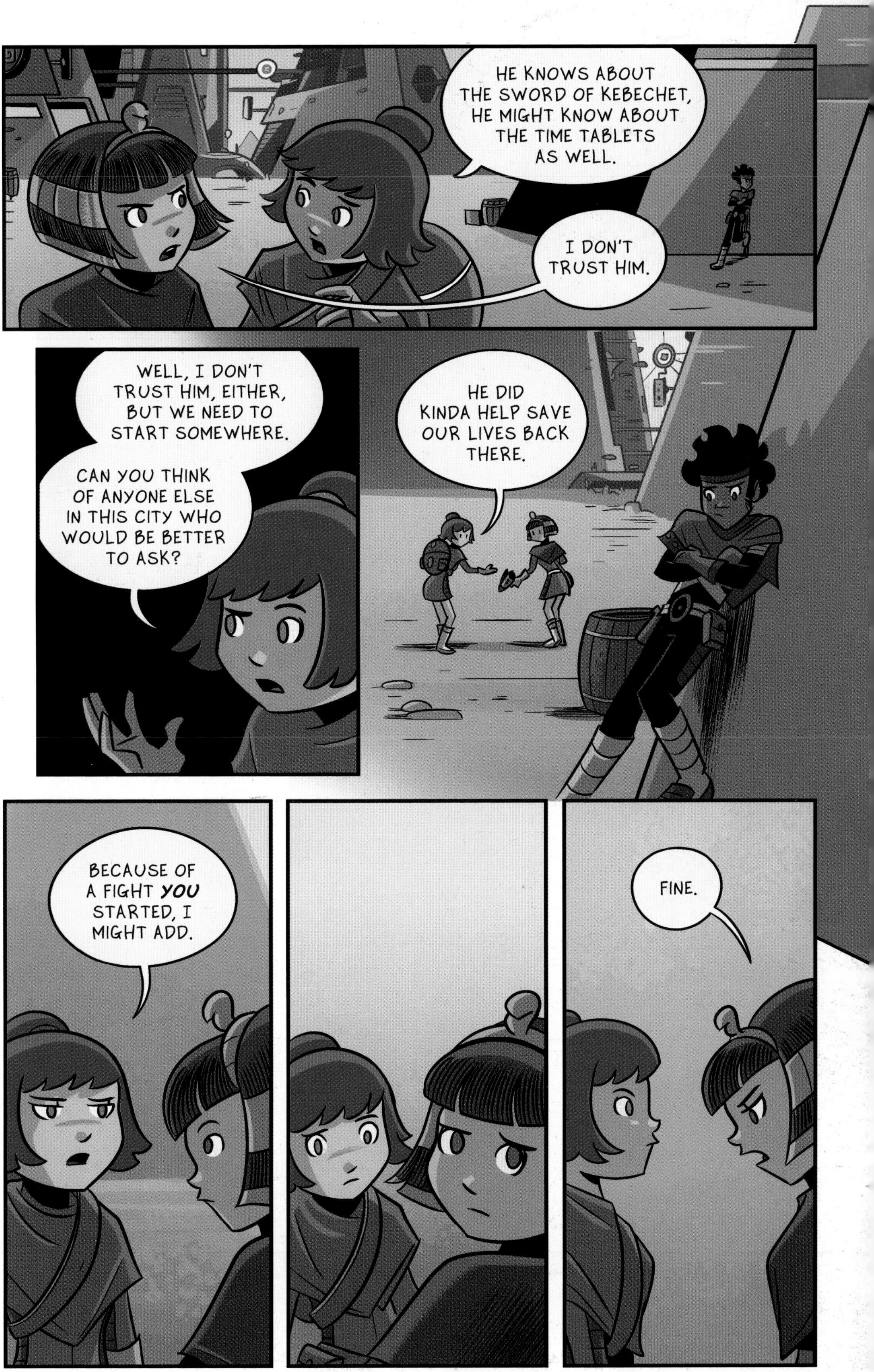
HE KNOWS ABOUT THE SWORD OF KEBECHET, HE MIGHT KNOW ABOUT THE TIME TABLETS AS WELL.
I DON'T TRUST HIM.
WELL, I DON'T TRUST HIM, EITHER, BUT WE NEED TO START SOMEWHERE.
CAN YOU THINK OF ANYONE ELSE IN THIS CITY WHO WOULD BE BETTER TO ASK?
HE DID KINDA HELP SAVE OUR LIVES BACK THERE.
BECAUSE OF A FIGHT *YOU* STARTED, I MIGHT ADD.
FINE.

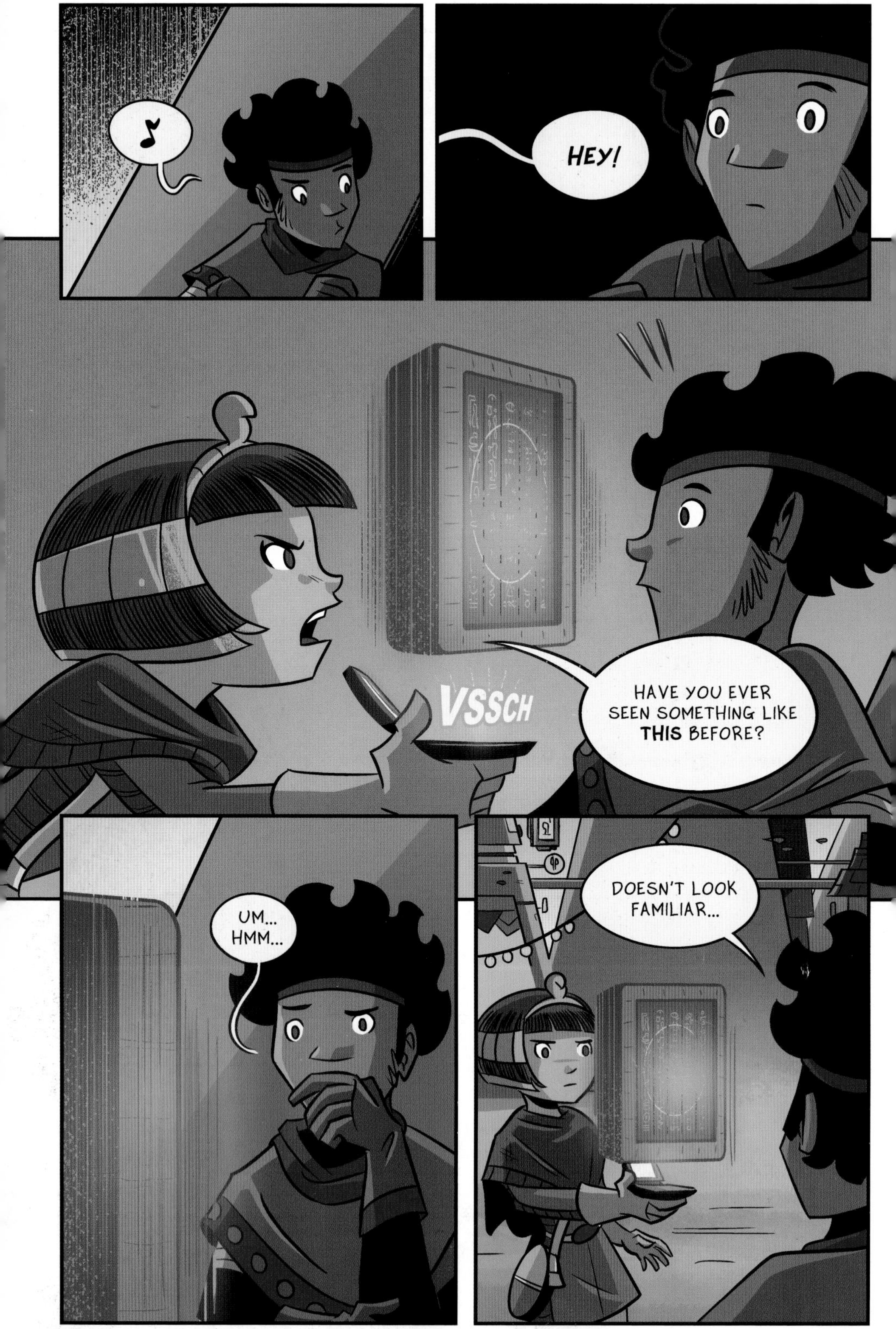
♪
HEY!
VSSCH
HAVE YOU EVER SEEN SOMETHING LIKE **THIS** BEFORE?
UM... HMM...
DOESN'T LOOK FAMILIAR...

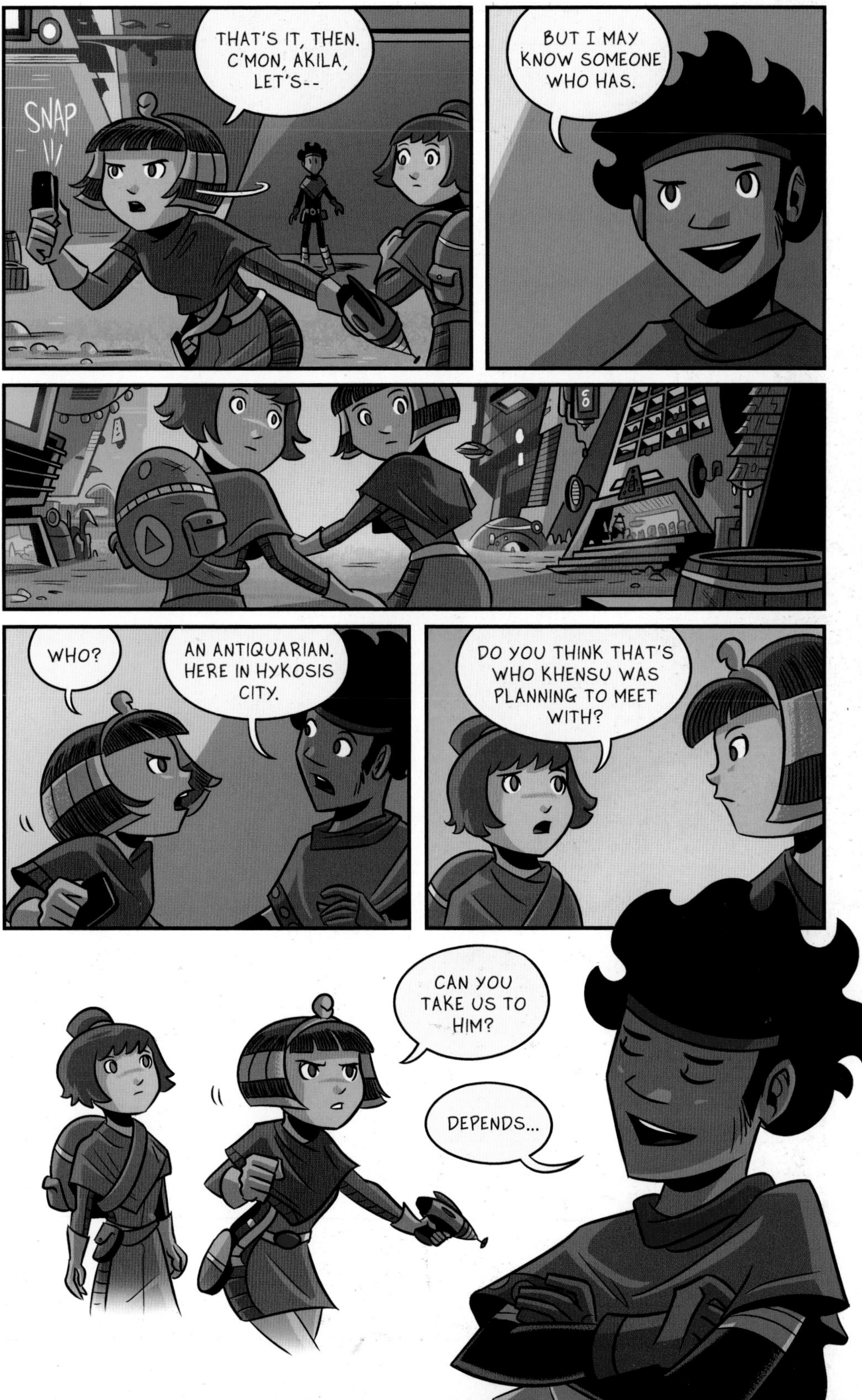
THAT'S IT, THEN. C'MON, AKILA, LET'S--
SNAP
BUT I MAY KNOW SOMEONE WHO HAS.
WHO?
AN ANTIQUARIAN. HERE IN HYKOSIS CITY.
DO YOU THINK THAT'S WHO KHENSU WAS PLANNING TO MEET WITH?
CAN YOU TAKE US TO HIM?
DEPENDS...

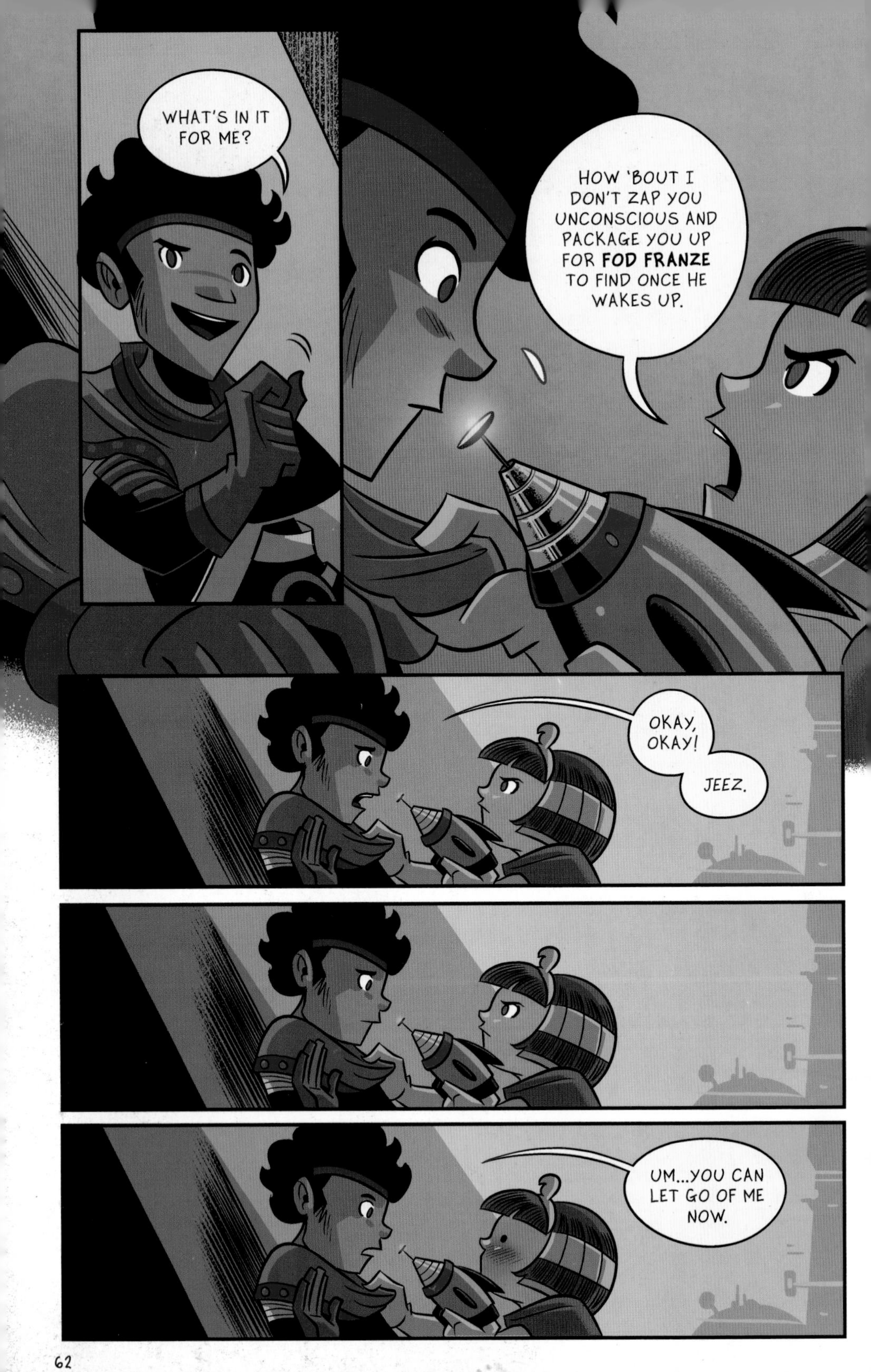
WHAT'S IN IT FOR ME?
HOW 'BOUT I DON'T ZAP YOU UNCONSCIOUS AND PACKAGE YOU UP FOR **FOD FRANZE** TO FIND ONCE HE WAKES UP.
OKAY, OKAY!
JEEZ.
UM...YOU CAN LET GO OF ME NOW.

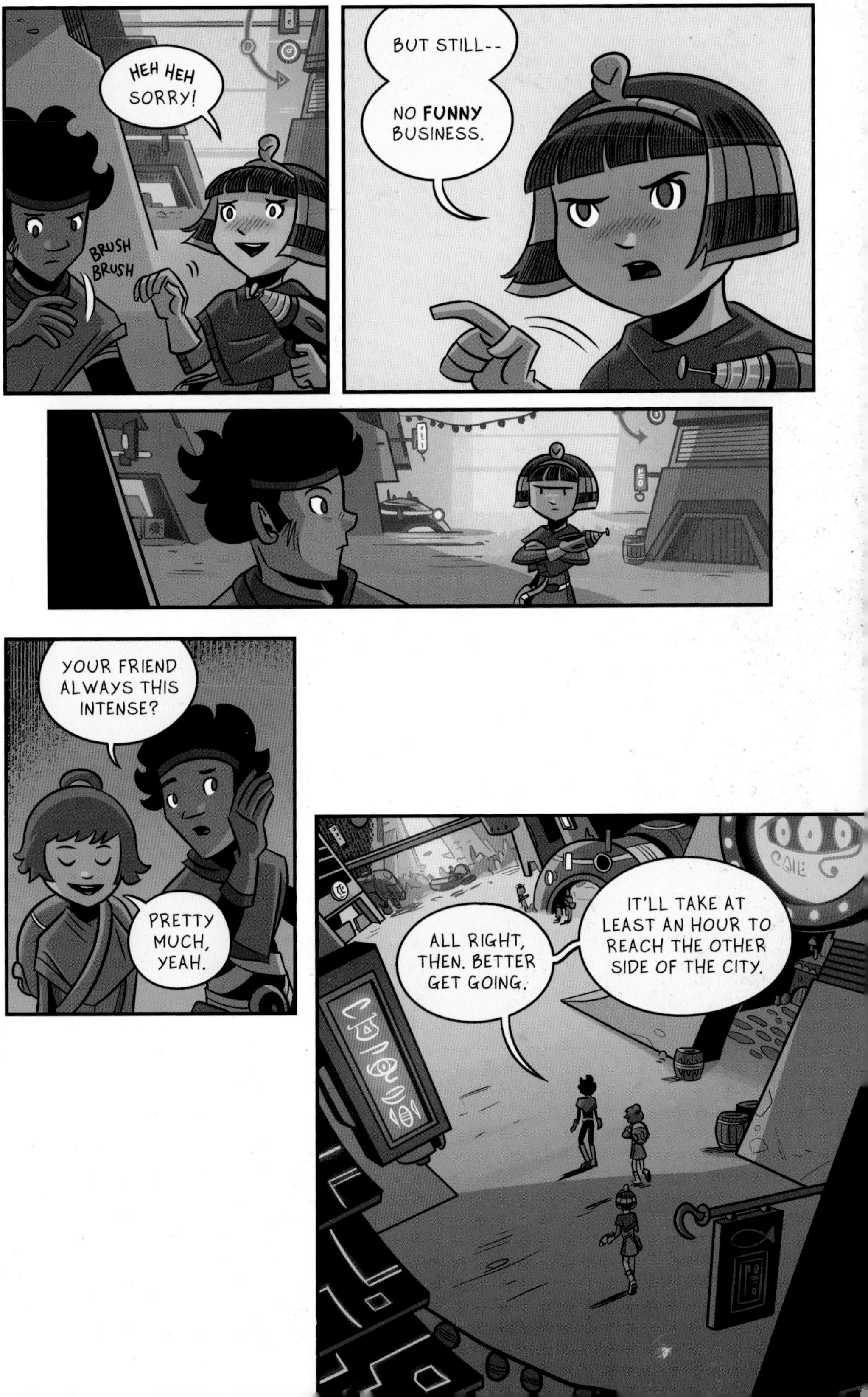
HEH HEH SORRY!
BRUSH BRUSH
BUT STILL--
NO FUNNY BUSINESS.
YOUR FRIEND ALWAYS THIS INTENSE?
PRETTY MUCH, YEAH.
ALL RIGHT, THEN. BETTER GET GOING.
IT'LL TAKE AT LEAST AN HOUR TO REACH THE OTHER SIDE OF THE CITY.

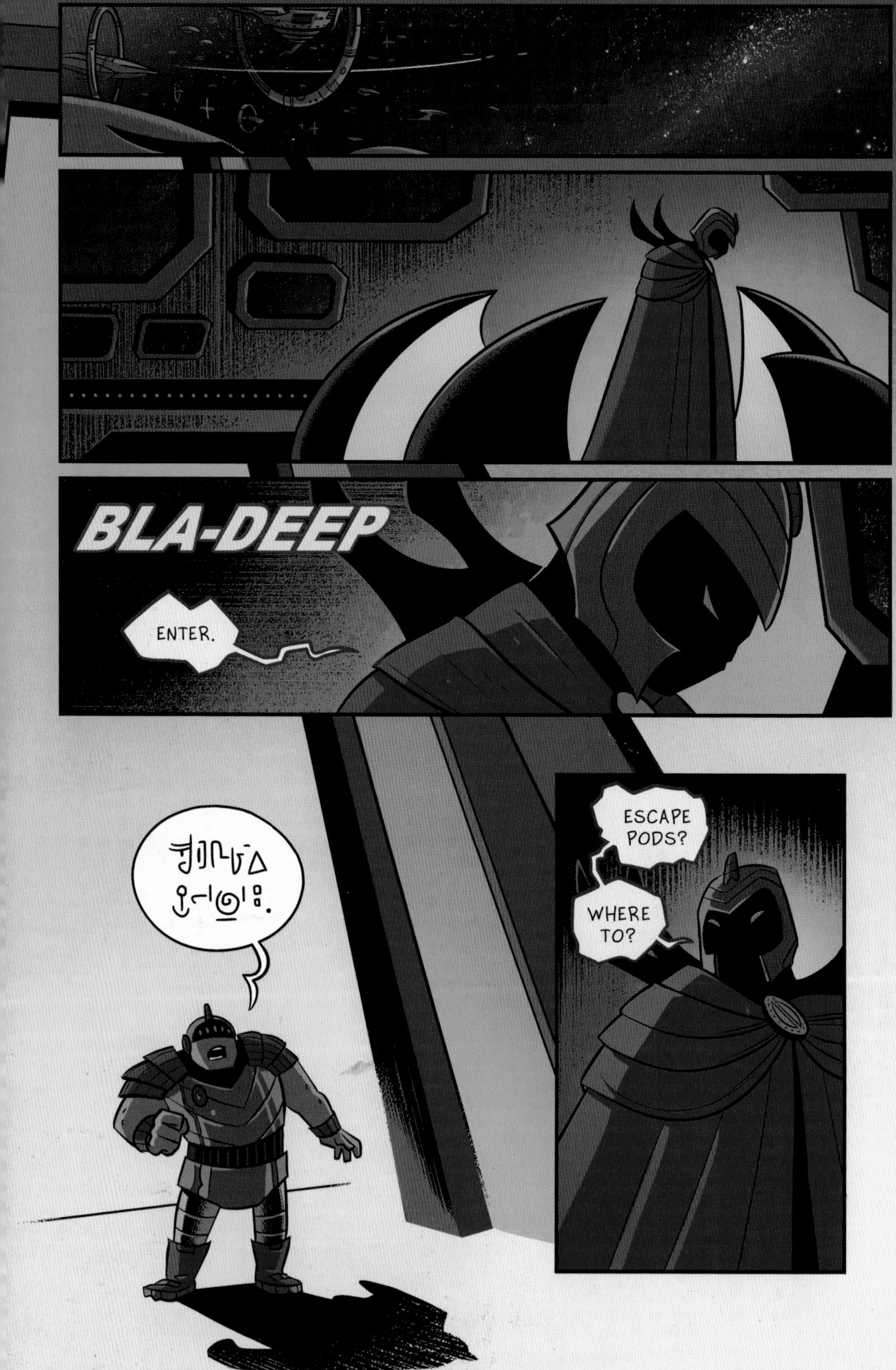
BLA-DEEP
ENTER.
ESCAPE PODS?
WHERE TO?

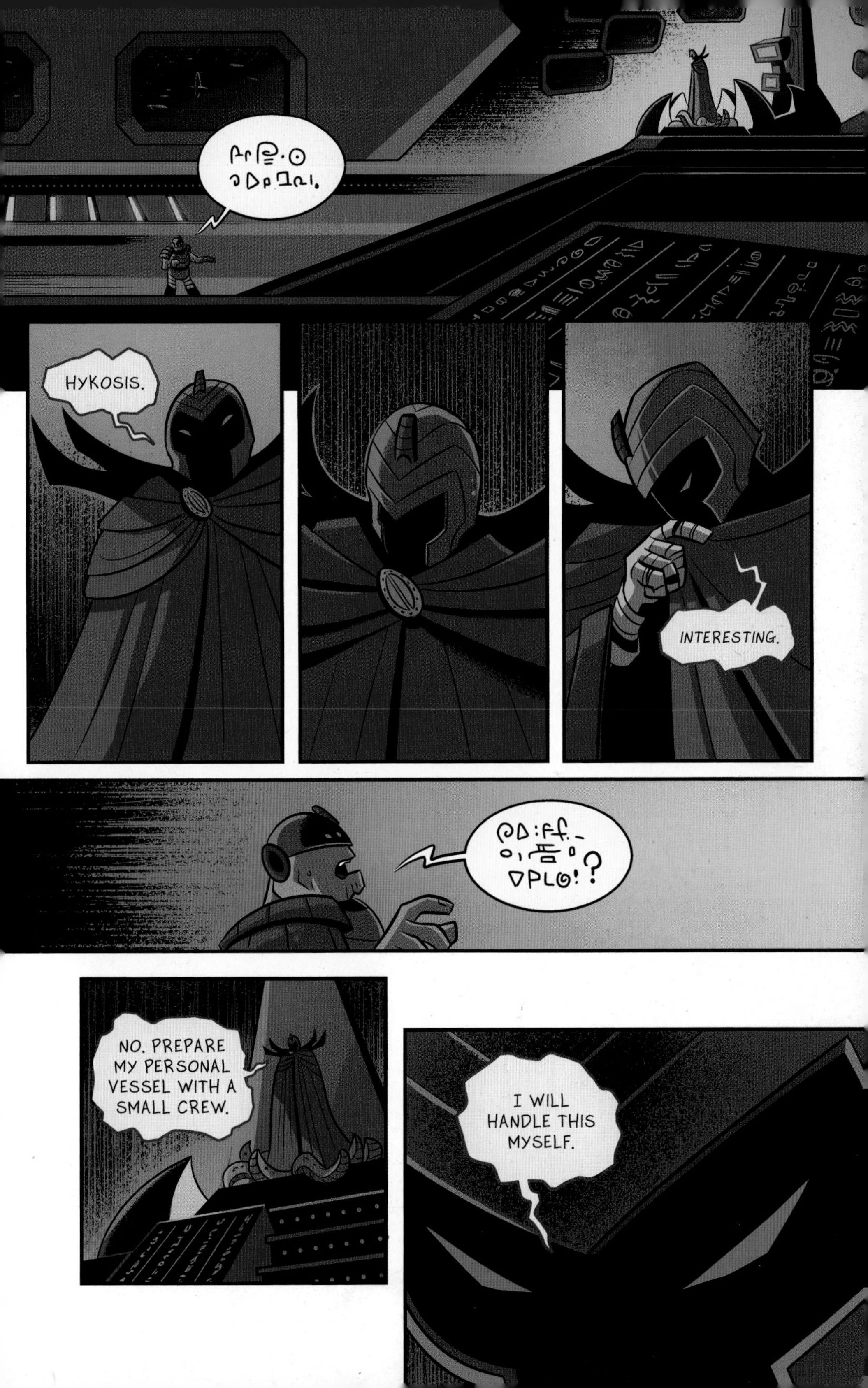
HYKOSIS.
INTERESTING.
NO. PREPARE MY PERSONAL VESSEL WITH A SMALL CREW.
I WILL HANDLE THIS MYSELF.

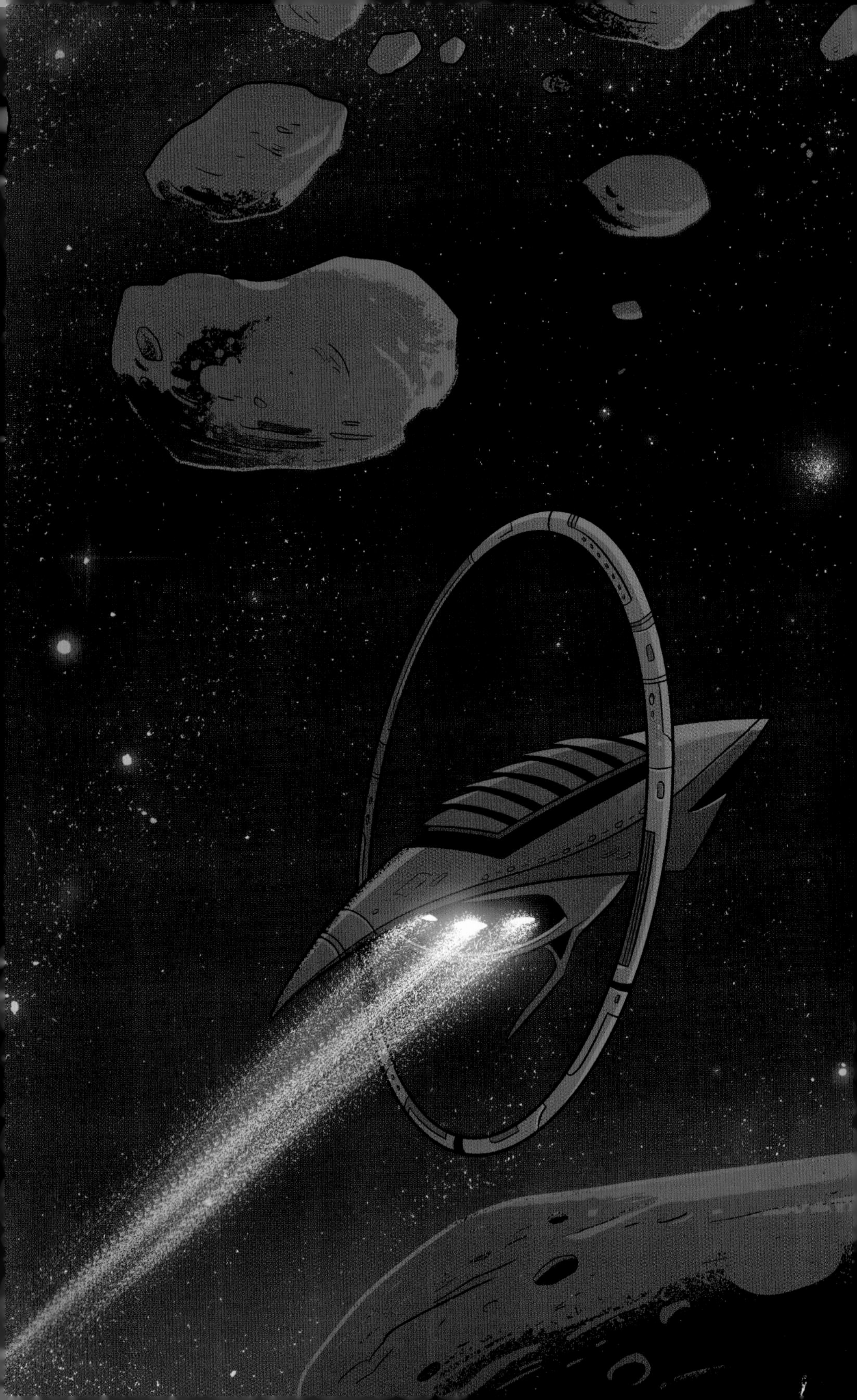

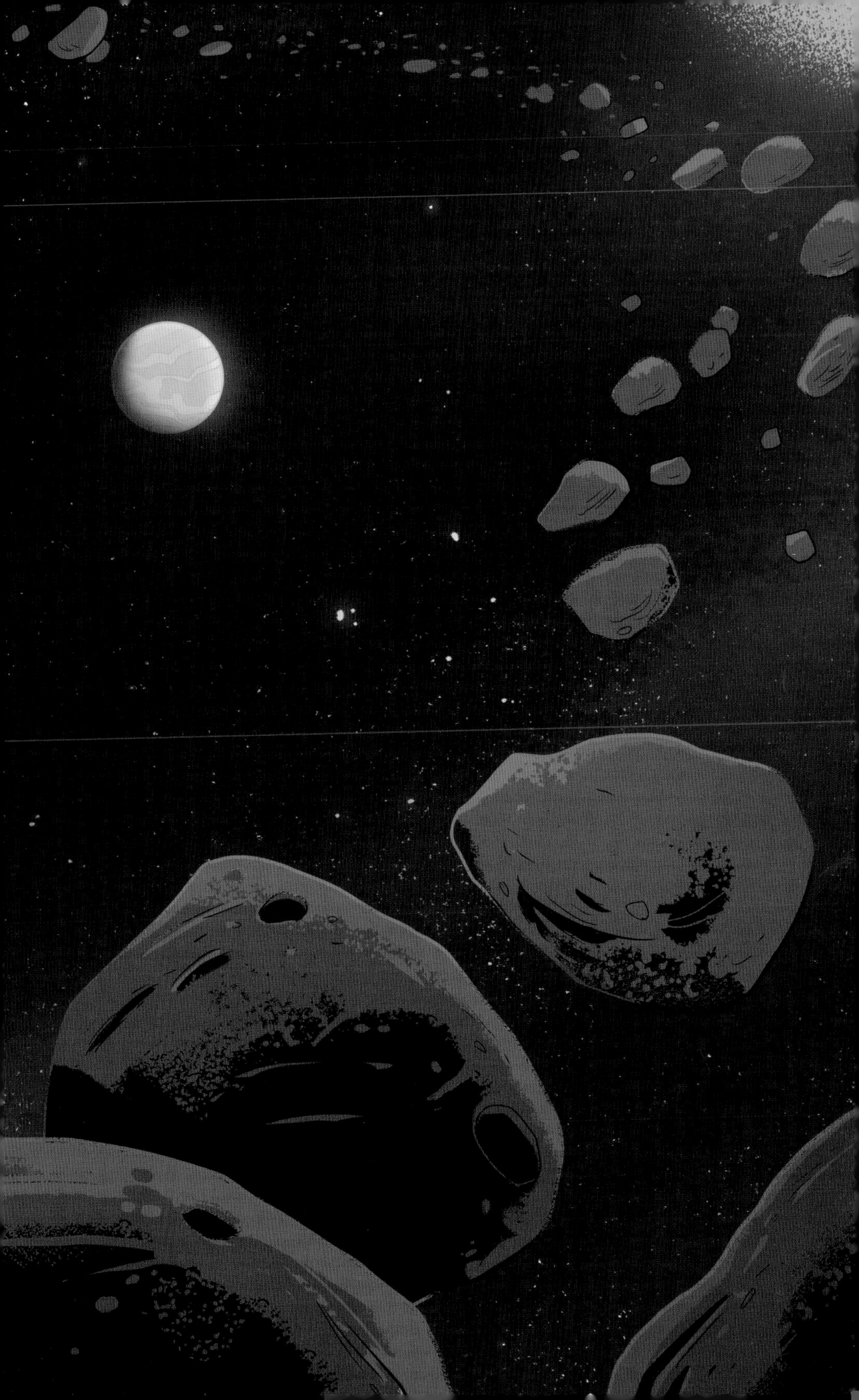

CHAPTER TWO

WHAT A DEPRESSING HEAP OF ROCK.
SHOULDN'T WE BE LOOKING FOR OUR RELUCTANT SAVIOR OF THE GALAXY INSTEAD OF TRYING TO FIND SOME **SECRET DOOR**?
THEIR POD HAD THE SAME TRAJECTORY AS OURS.
KNOWING CLEO, SHE'S LIKELY ALREADY IN THE CITY SOMEHOW INSTEAD OF WAITING PATIENTLY FOR US TO FIND HER.
OR UNCONSCIOUS SOMEWHERE.

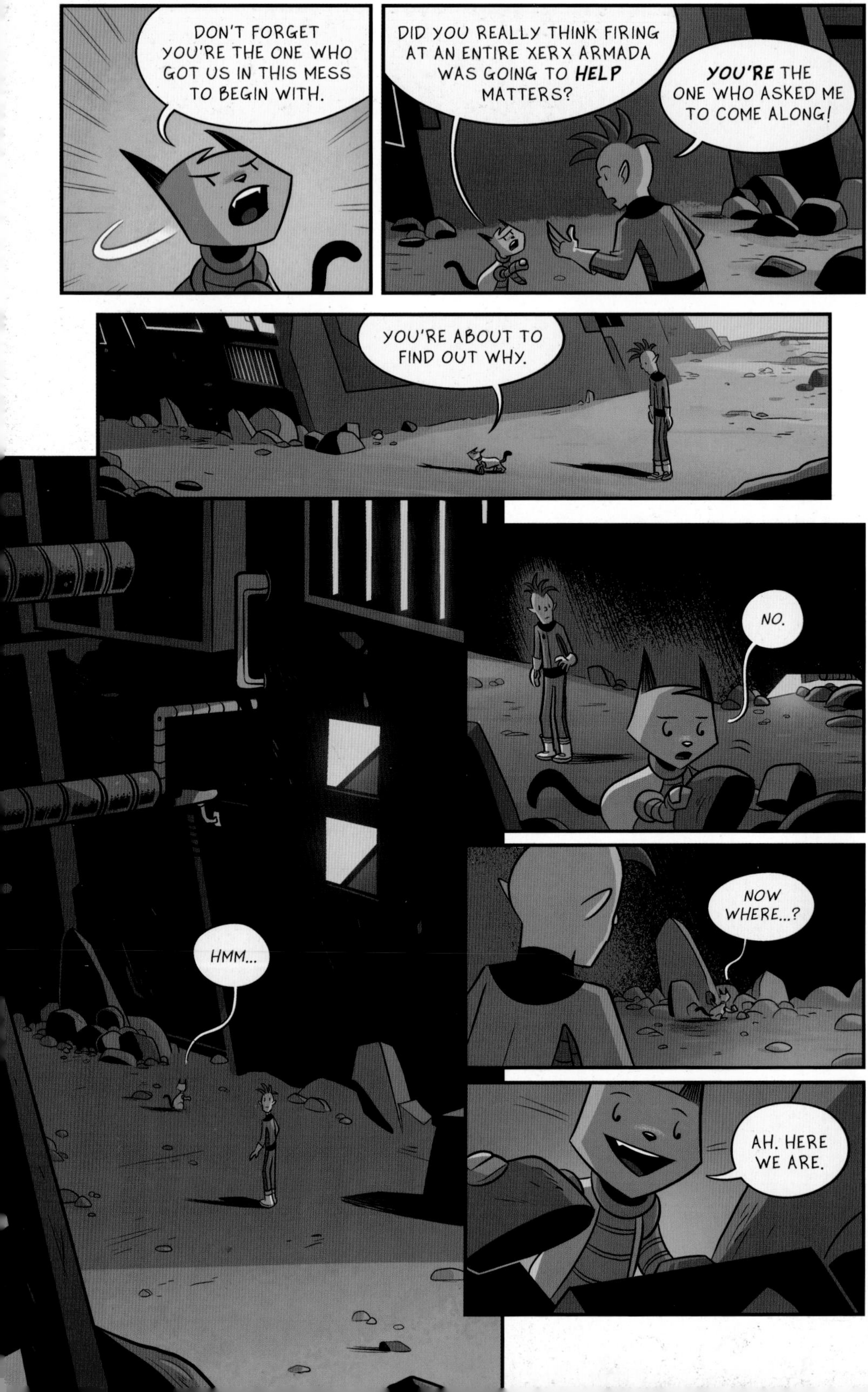
DON'T FORGET YOU'RE THE ONE WHO GOT US IN THIS MESS TO BEGIN WITH.
DID YOU REALLY THINK FIRING AT AN ENTIRE XERX ARMADA WAS GOING TO **HELP** MATTERS?
YOU'RE THE ONE WHO ASKED ME TO COME ALONG!
YOU'RE ABOUT TO FIND OUT WHY.
HMM...
NO.
NOW WHERE...?
AH. HERE WE ARE.

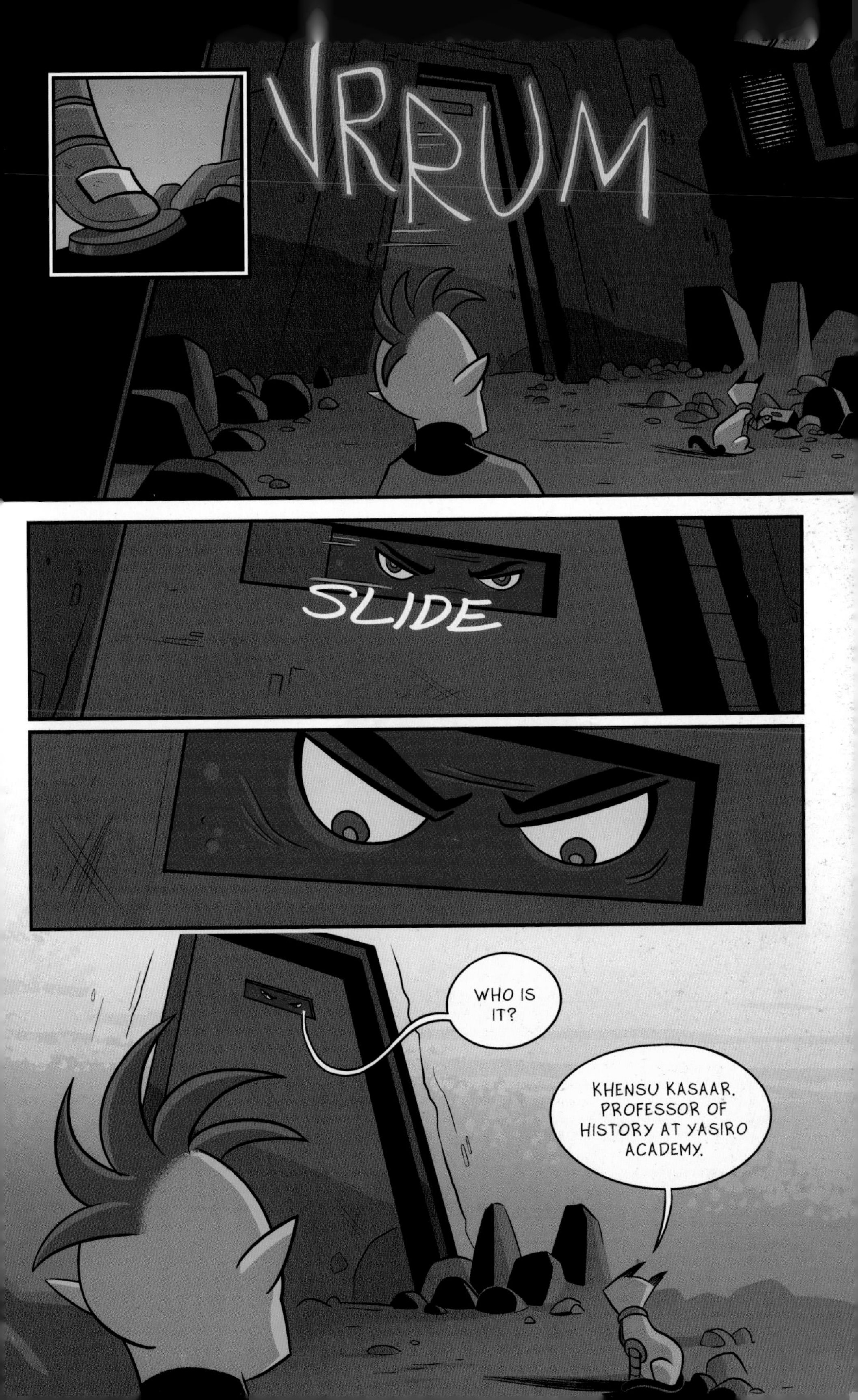
VRRUM
SLIDE
WHO IS IT?
KHENSU KASAAR. PROFESSOR OF HISTORY AT YASIRO ACADEMY.

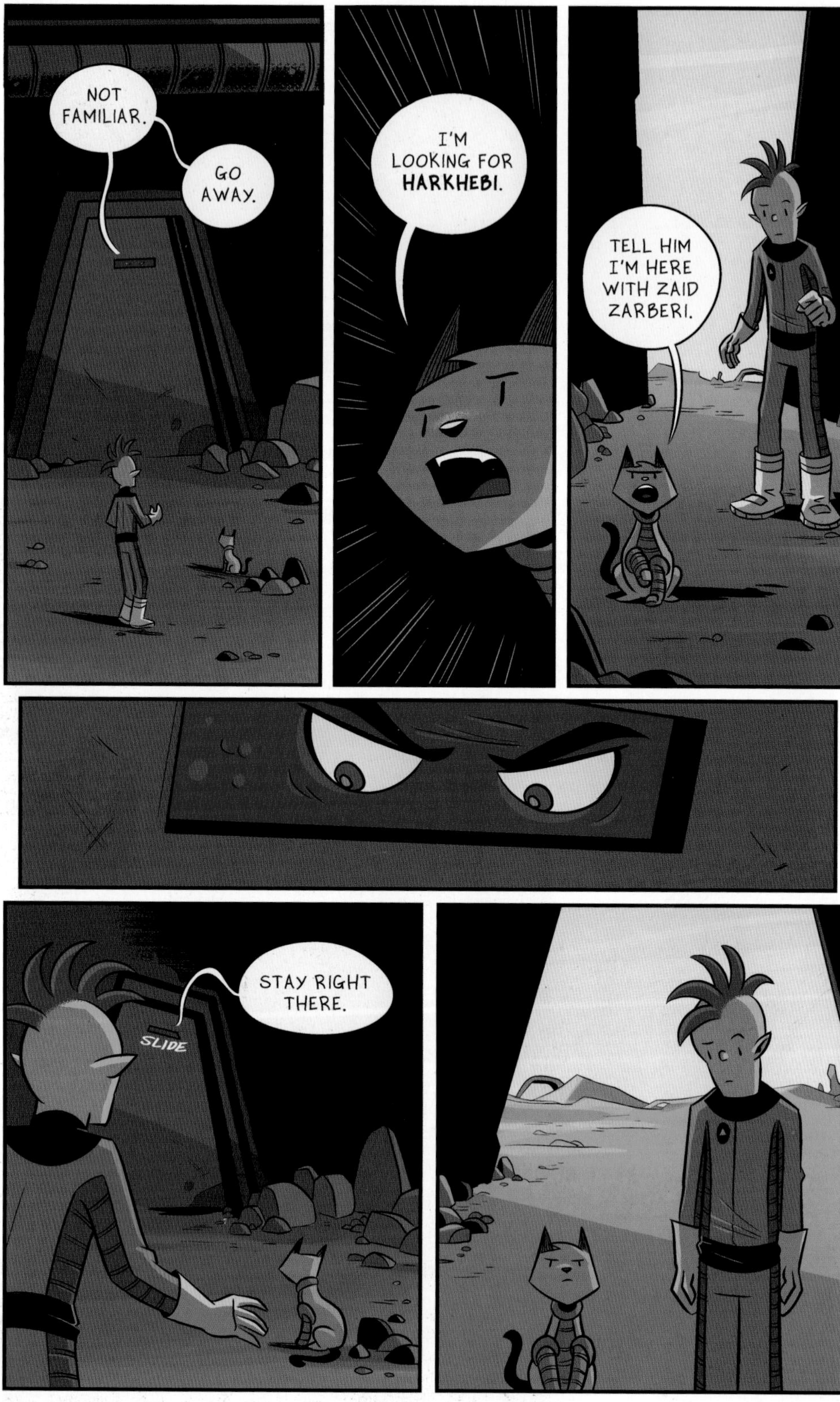
NOT FAMILIAR.
GO AWAY.
I'M LOOKING FOR **HARKHEBI.**
TELL HIM I'M HERE WITH ZAID ZARBERI.
STAY RIGHT THERE.
SLIDE

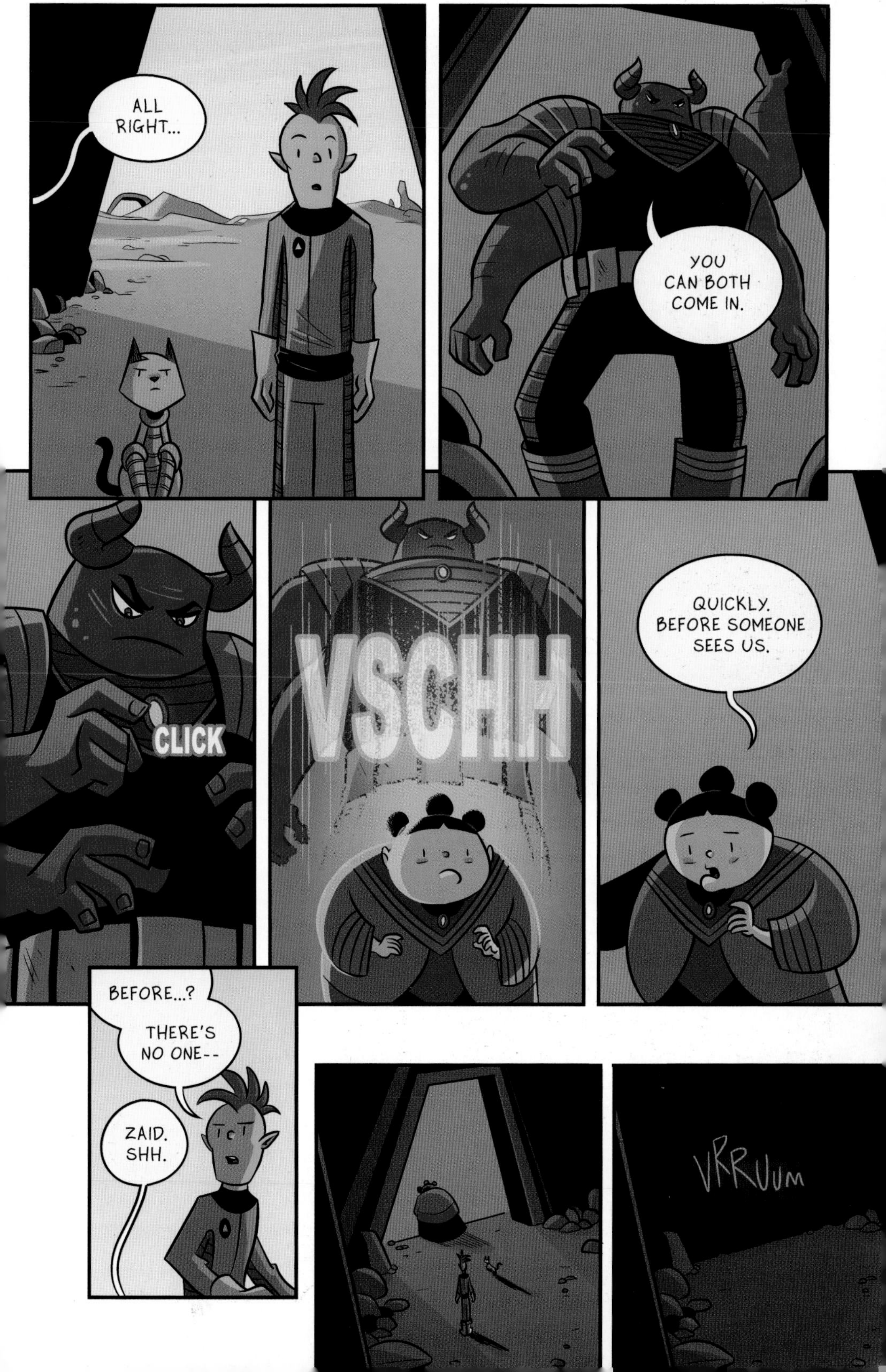
ALL RIGHT...
YOU CAN BOTH COME IN.
CLICK
VSCHH
QUICKLY. BEFORE SOMEONE SEES US.
BEFORE...?
THERE'S NO ONE--
ZAID. SHH.
VRRUUM

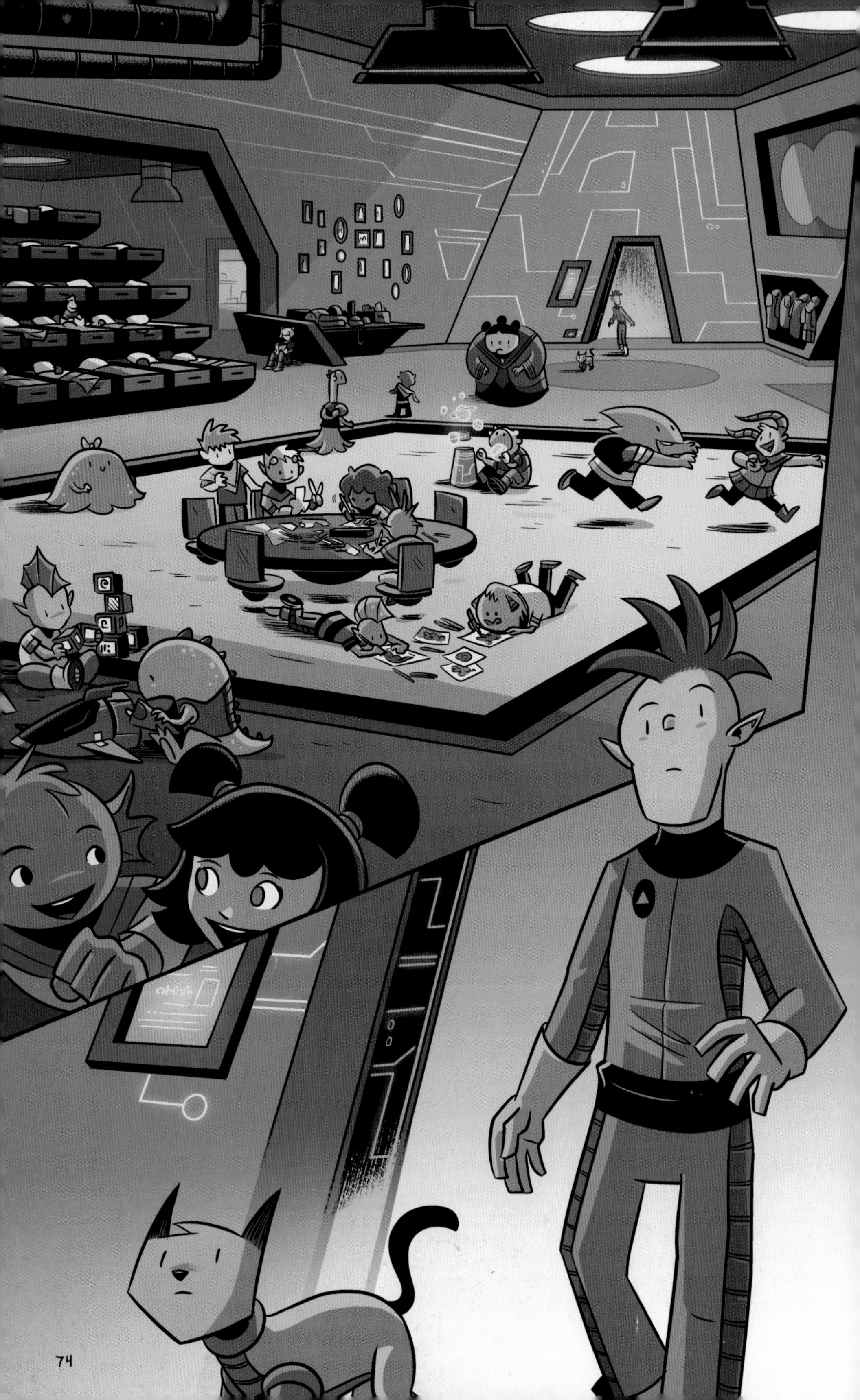

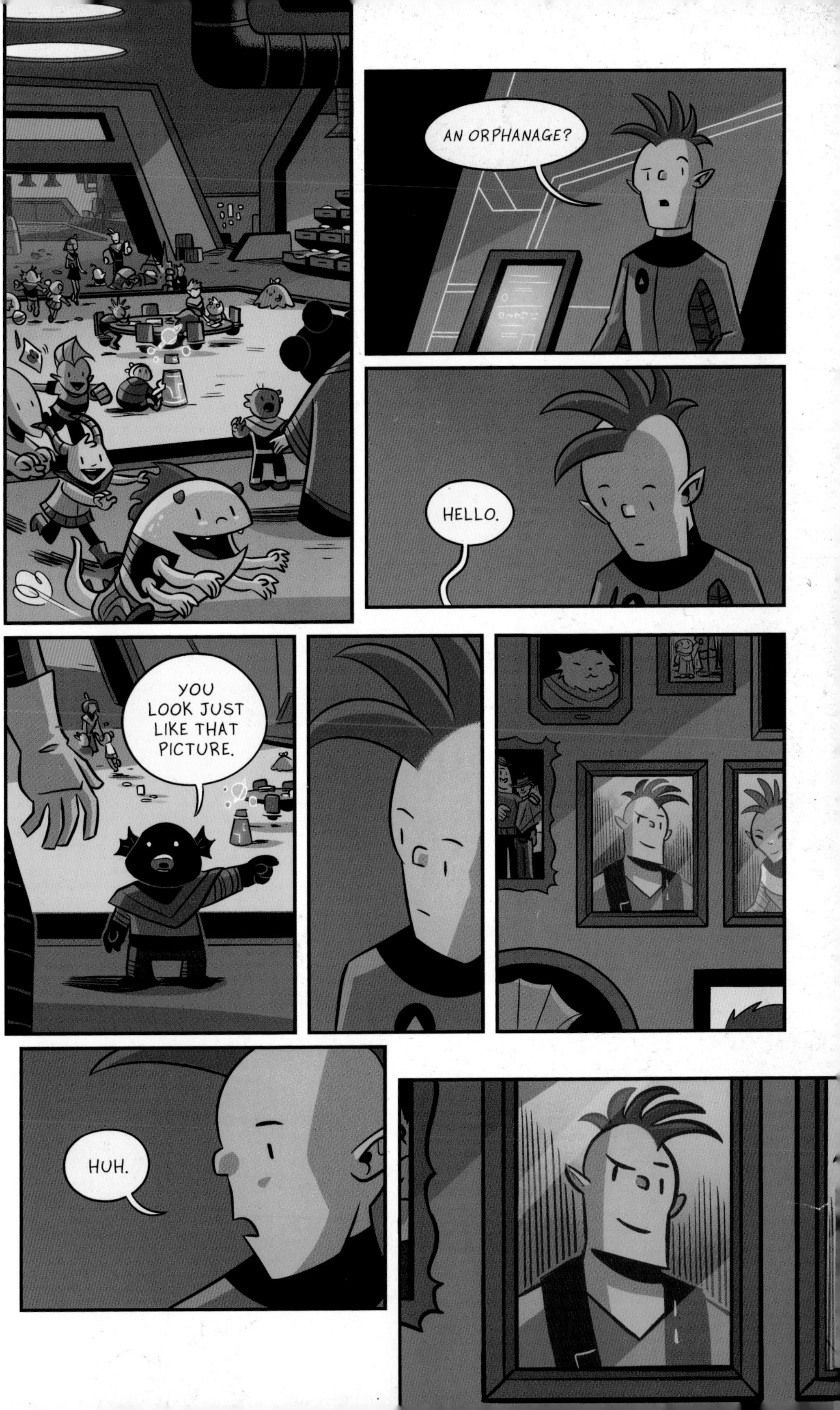
AN ORPHANAGE?
HELLO.
YOU LOOK JUST LIKE THAT PICTURE.
HUH.

HYKOSIS SEEMS LIKE A PRETTY LOUSY PLACE FOR AN ORPHANAGE.

ON THE CONTRARY, IT'S ONE OF THE BEST.

purrr

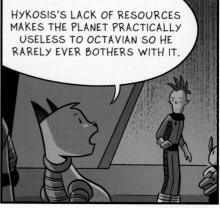

HYKOSIS'S LACK OF RESOURCES MAKES THE PLANET PRACTICALLY USELESS TO OCTAVIAN SO HE RARELY EVER BOTHERS WITH IT.

YES, THE FARTHER THESE KIDS ARE FROM THAT MONSTER, THE BETTER.

PLUS, THE PARENTING ABILITIES IN THIS CITY ARE **ATROCIOUS.**

HARKHEBI AND I ARE CONSTANTLY FINDING KIDS ON THE STREET IN NEED OF BETTER HOMES.

WHERE **IS** HARKHEBI?

IN HIS OFFICE. YOU TWO MUST GO BACK A WAYS. IT'S BEEN YEARS SINCE I'VE SEEN HIM PERK UP THAT MUCH AT THE MENTION OF SOMEONE'S NAME.

HERE. I'LL SHOW YOU IN.

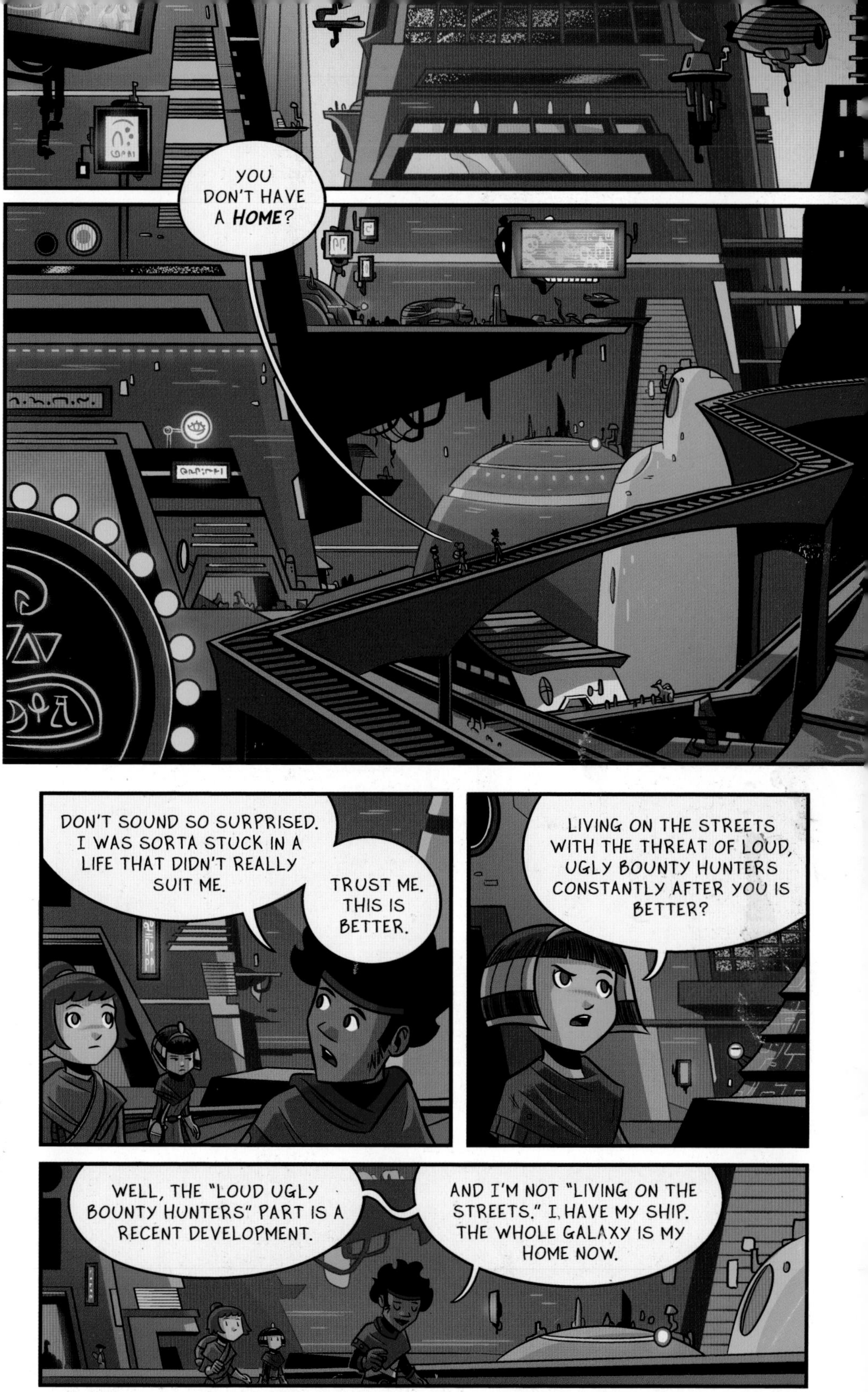
YOU DON'T HAVE A **HOME**?
DON'T SOUND SO SURPRISED. I WAS SORTA STUCK IN A LIFE THAT DIDN'T REALLY SUIT ME.
TRUST ME. THIS IS BETTER.
LIVING ON THE STREETS WITH THE THREAT OF LOUD, UGLY BOUNTY HUNTERS CONSTANTLY AFTER YOU IS BETTER?
WELL, THE "LOUD UGLY BOUNTY HUNTERS" PART IS A RECENT DEVELOPMENT.
AND I'M NOT "LIVING ON THE STREETS." I HAVE MY SHIP. THE WHOLE GALAXY IS MY HOME NOW.

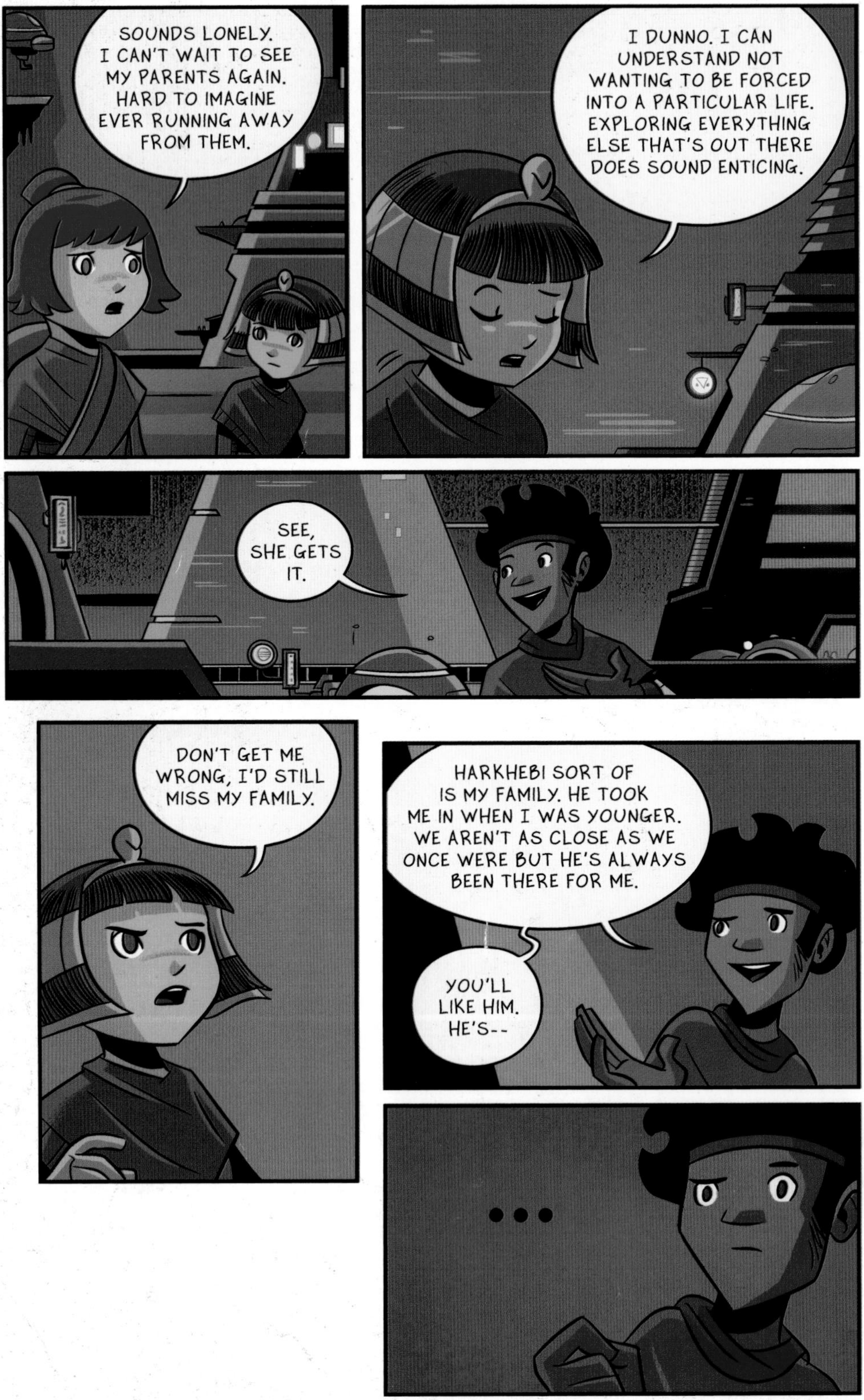
SOUNDS LONELY. I CAN'T WAIT TO SEE MY PARENTS AGAIN. HARD TO IMAGINE EVER RUNNING AWAY FROM THEM.
I DUNNO. I CAN UNDERSTAND NOT WANTING TO BE FORCED INTO A PARTICULAR LIFE. EXPLORING EVERYTHING ELSE THAT'S OUT THERE DOES SOUND ENTICING.
SEE, SHE GETS IT.
DON'T GET ME WRONG, I'D STILL MISS MY FAMILY.
HARKHEBI SORT OF IS MY FAMILY. HE TOOK ME IN WHEN I WAS YOUNGER. WE AREN'T AS CLOSE AS WE ONCE WERE BUT HE'S ALWAYS BEEN THERE FOR ME.
YOU'LL LIKE HIM. HE'S--
...

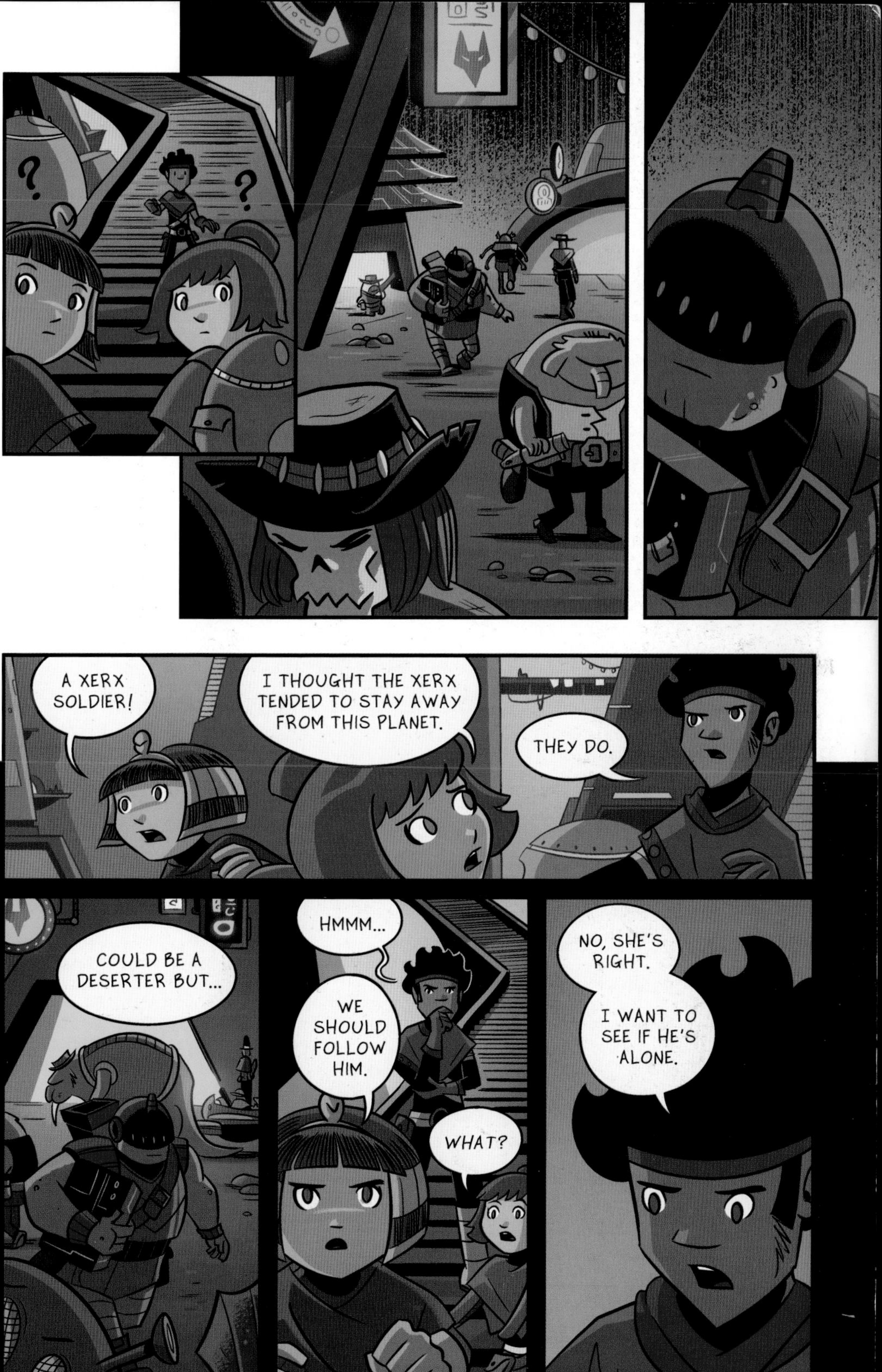
?
?
A XERX SOLDIER!
I THOUGHT THE XERX TENDED TO STAY AWAY FROM THIS PLANET.
THEY DO.
COULD BE A DESERTER BUT...
HMMM...
WE SHOULD FOLLOW HIM.
WHAT?
NO, SHE'S RIGHT.
I WANT TO SEE IF HE'S ALONE.

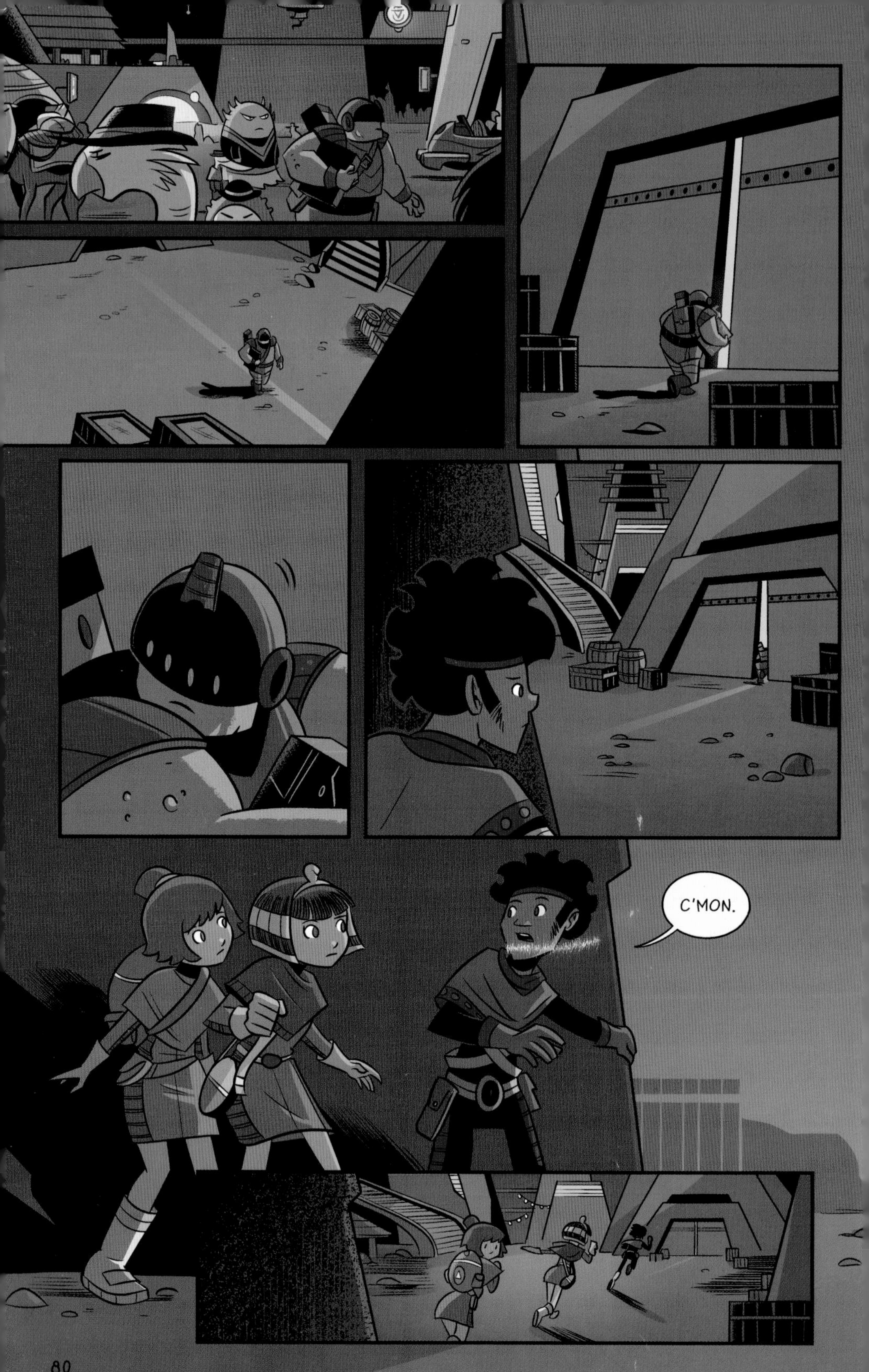
C'MON.

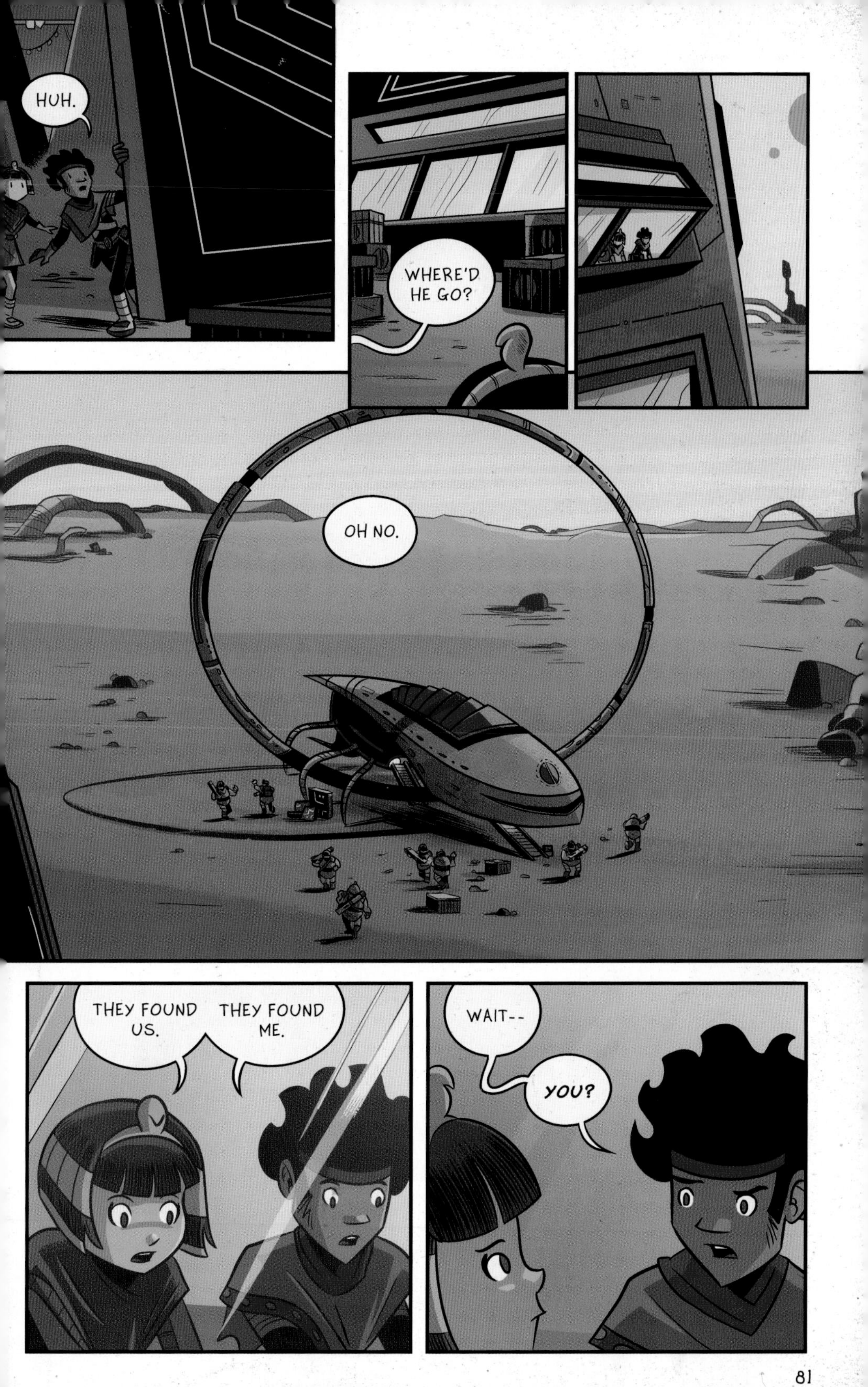
HUH.
WHERE'D HE GO?
OH NO.
THEY FOUND US.
THEY FOUND ME.
WAIT--
YOU?

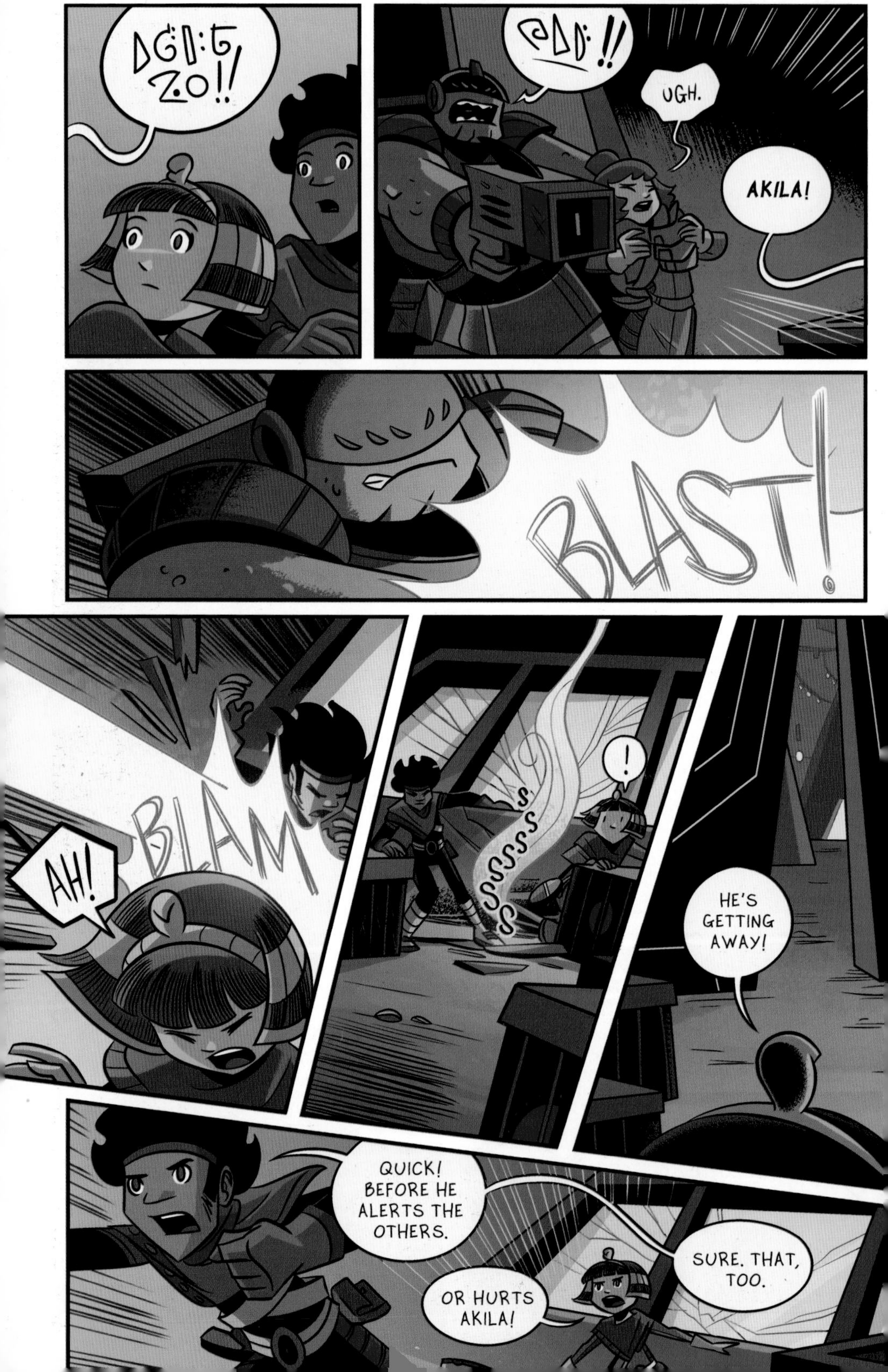

UGH.
AKILA!
BLAST!
BLAM
AH!
!
SSSSSSSS
HE'S GETTING AWAY!
QUICK! BEFORE HE ALERTS THE OTHERS.
OR HURTS AKILA!
SURE. THAT, TOO.

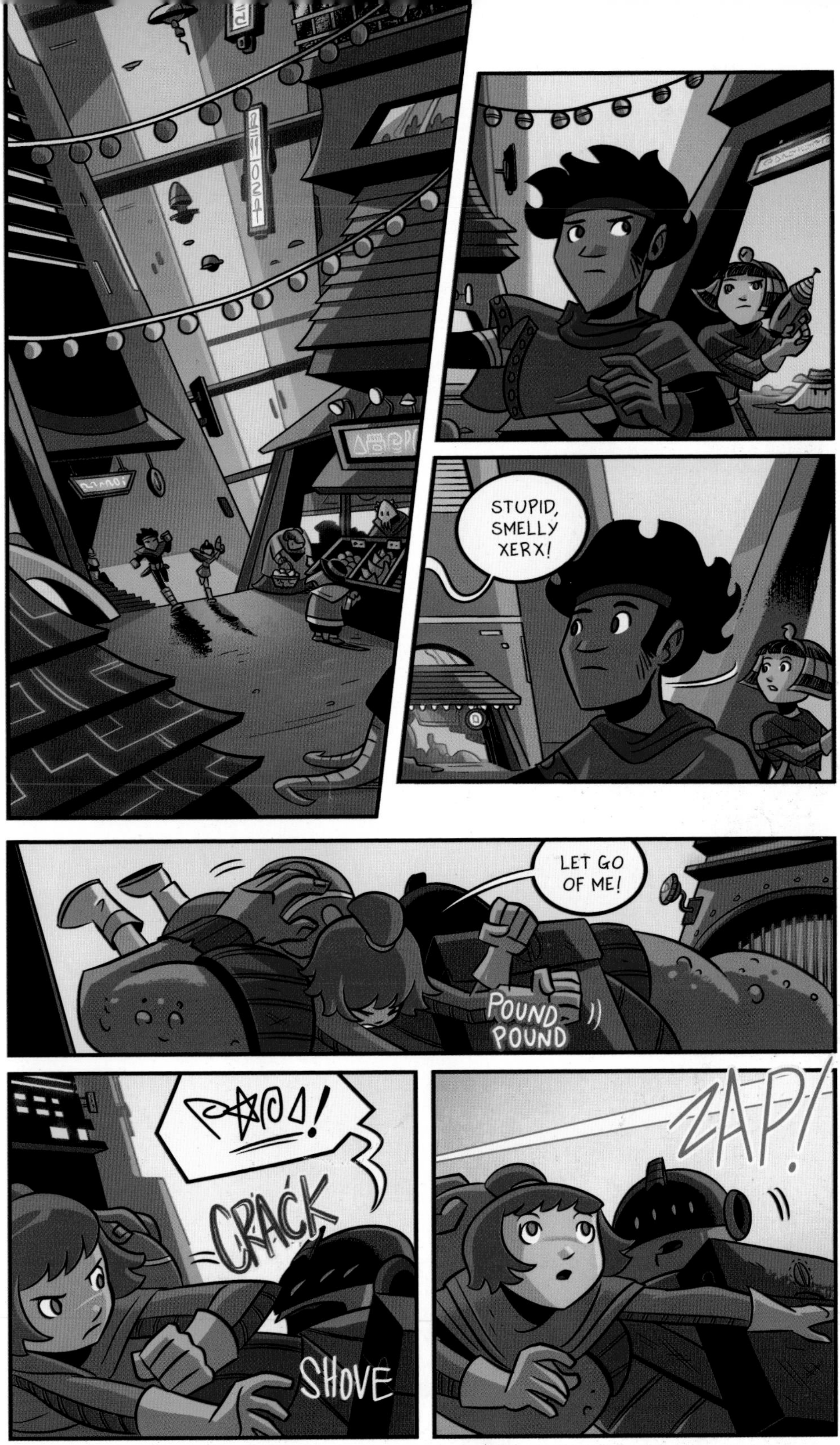
STUPID, SMELLY XERX!
LET GO OF ME!
POUND POUND
CRACK
SHOVE
ZAP!

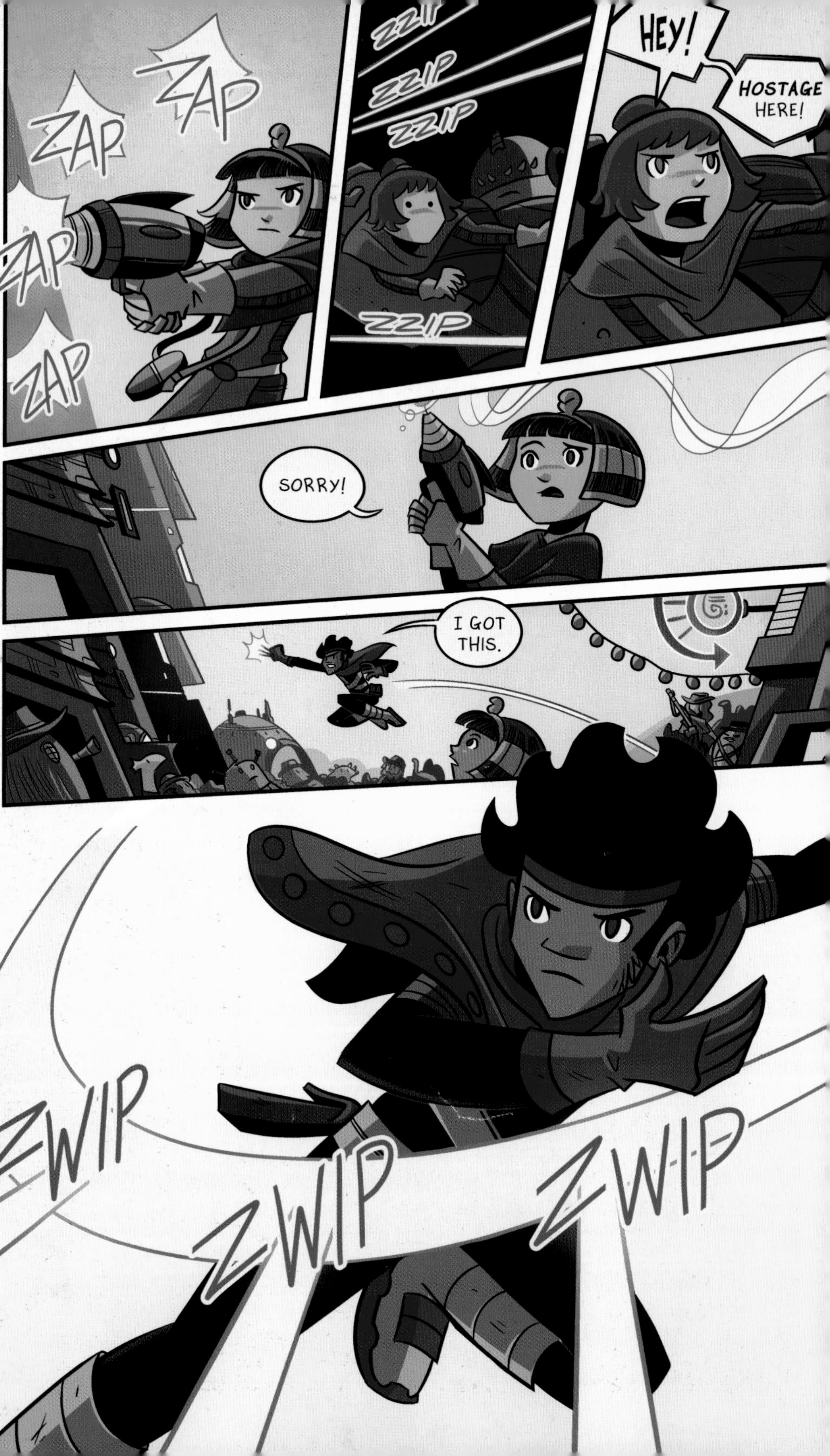
ZAP
ZAP
ZAP
ZAP
ZZIP
ZZIP
ZZIP
ZZIP
HEY!
HOSTAGE HERE!
SORRY!
I GOT THIS.
ZWIP
ZWIP
ZWIP

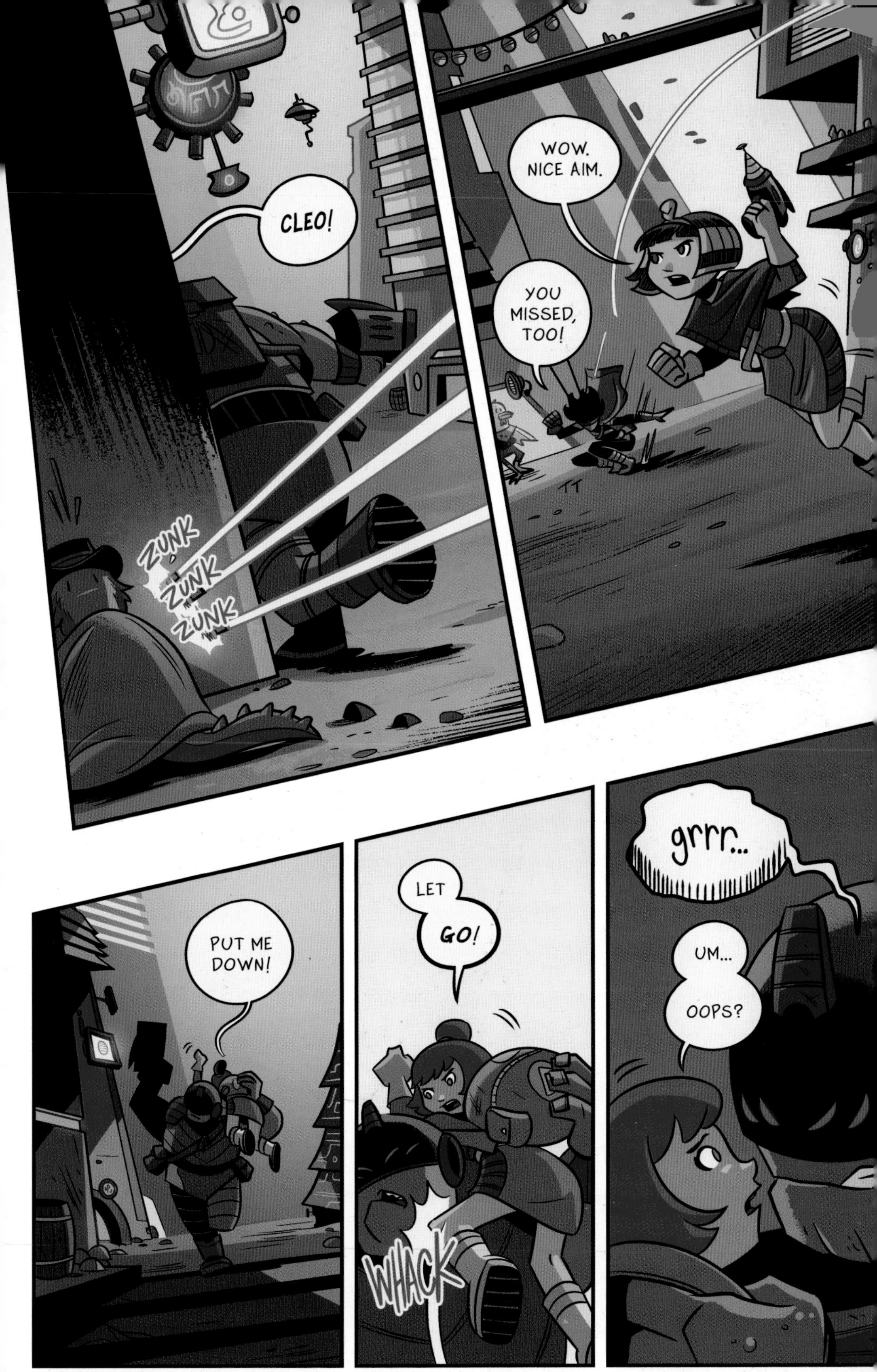

CLEO!
ZUNK
ZUNK
ZUNK
WOW. NICE AIM.
YOU MISSED, TOO!
PUT ME DOWN!
LET
GO!
WHACK
grrr...
UM...
OOPS?

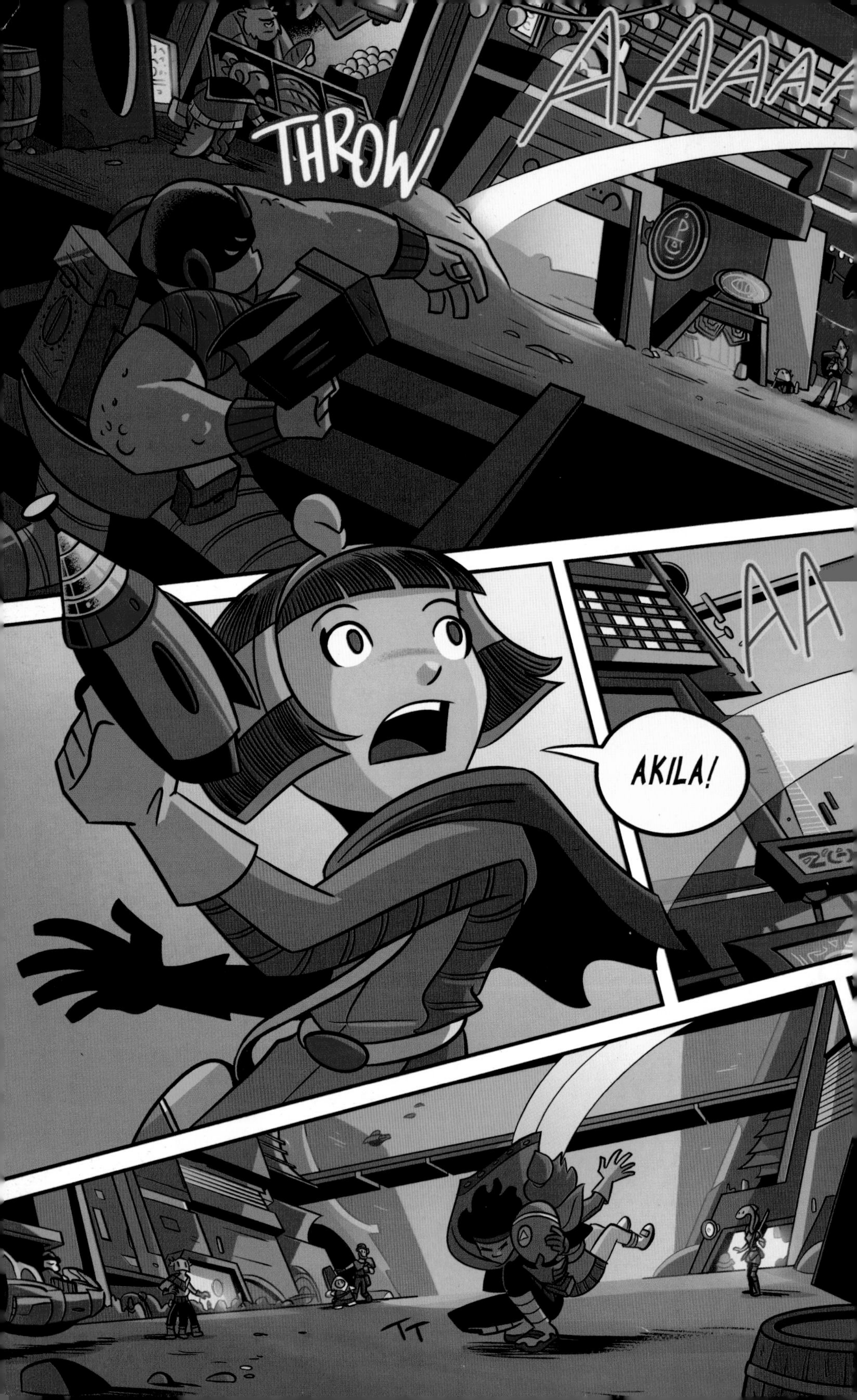
THROW
AAAAA
AA
AKILA!
TT

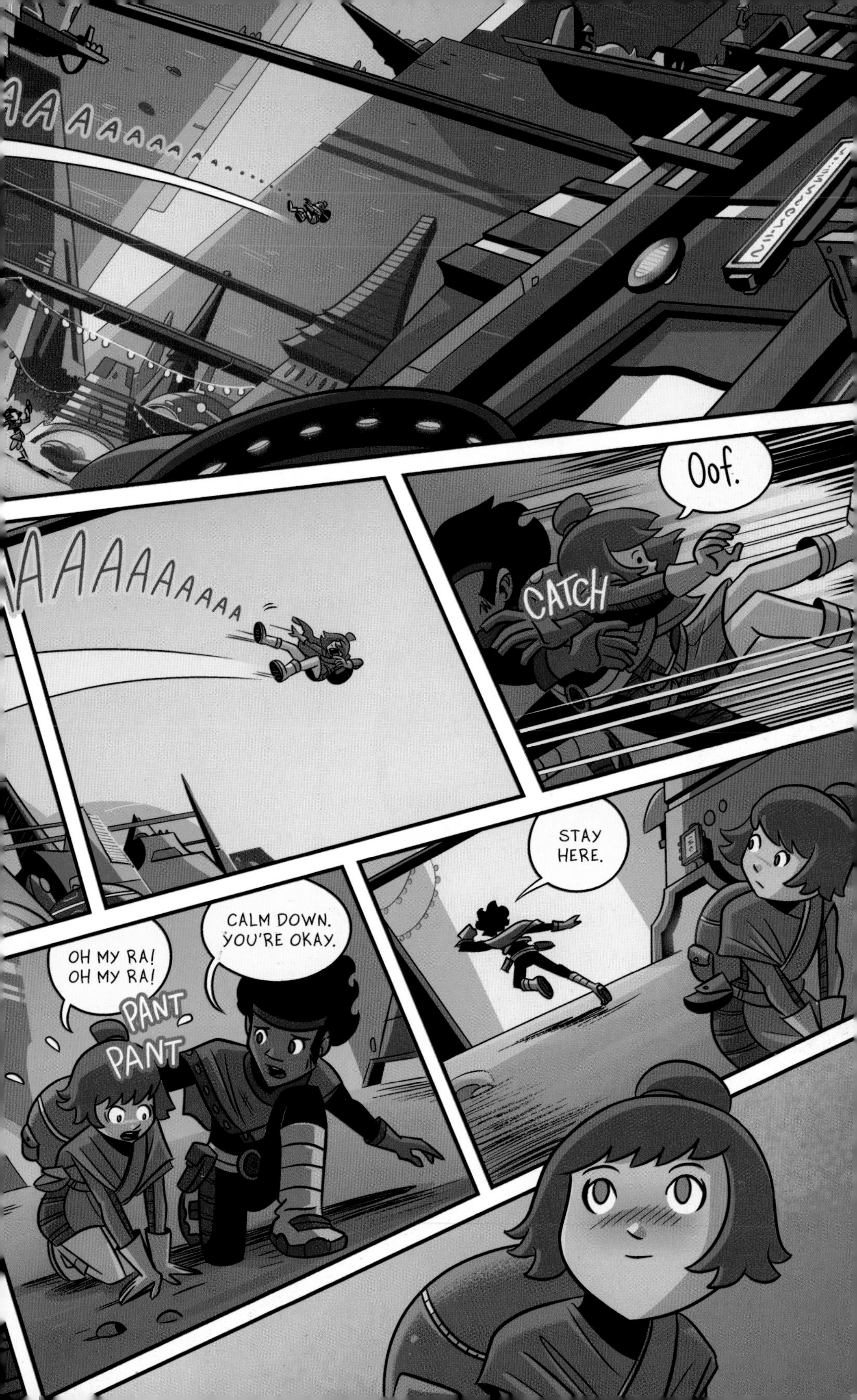
AAAAAAAAAAA.........
AAAAAAAAAAA
Oof.
CATCH
STAY HERE.
CALM DOWN. YOU'RE OKAY.
OH MY RA! OH MY RA!
PANT PANT

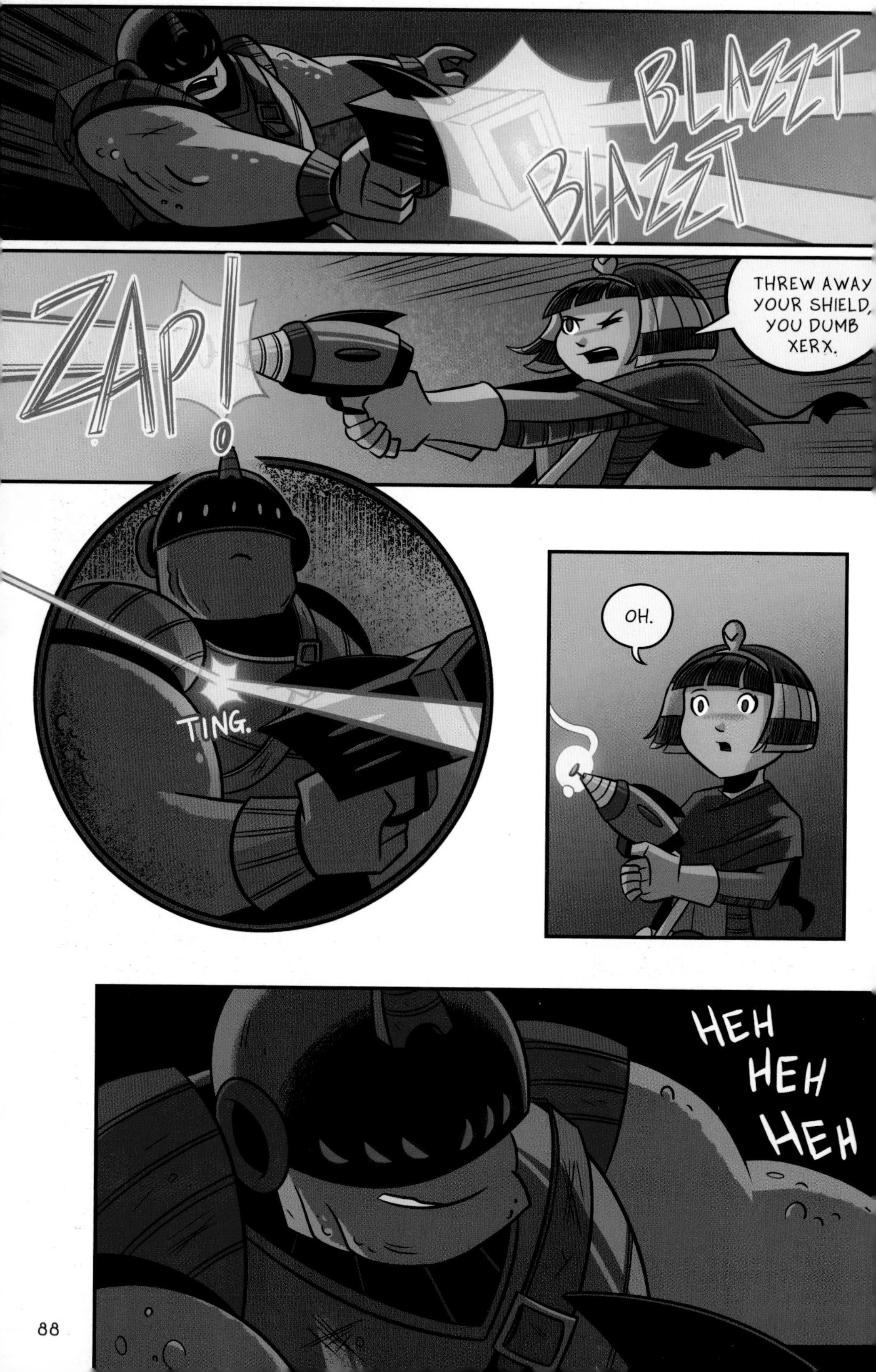
BLAZZT
BLAZZT
ZAP!
THREW AWAY YOUR SHIELD, YOU DUMB XERX.
TING.
OH.
HEH HEH HEH

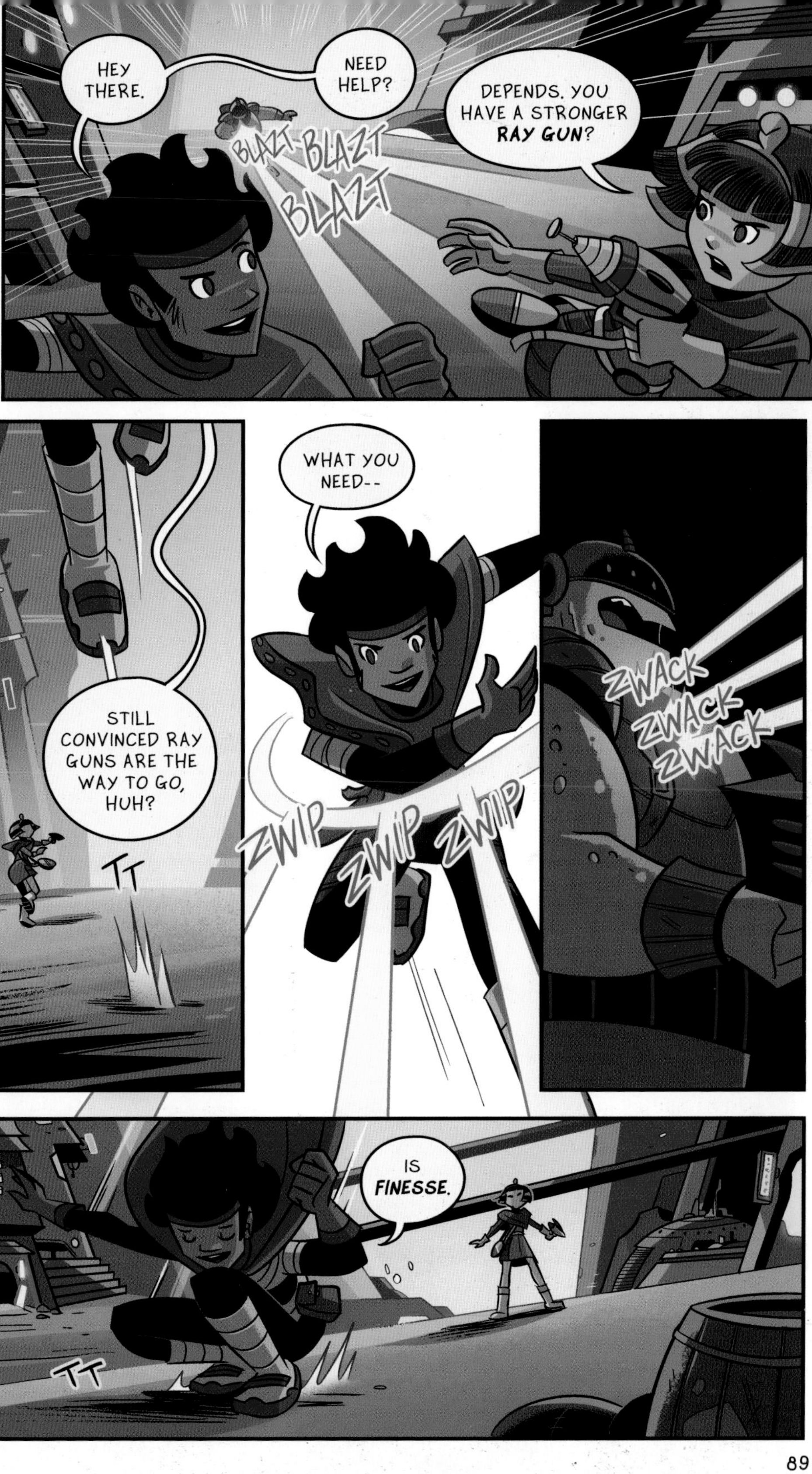
HEY THERE.
NEED HELP?
BLAZT BLAZT BLAZT
DEPENDS. YOU HAVE A STRONGER **RAY GUN**?
STILL CONVINCED RAY GUNS ARE THE WAY TO GO, HUH?
TT
WHAT YOU NEED--
ZWIP ZWIP ZWIP
ZWACK ZWACK ZWACK
IS **FINESSE.**
TT

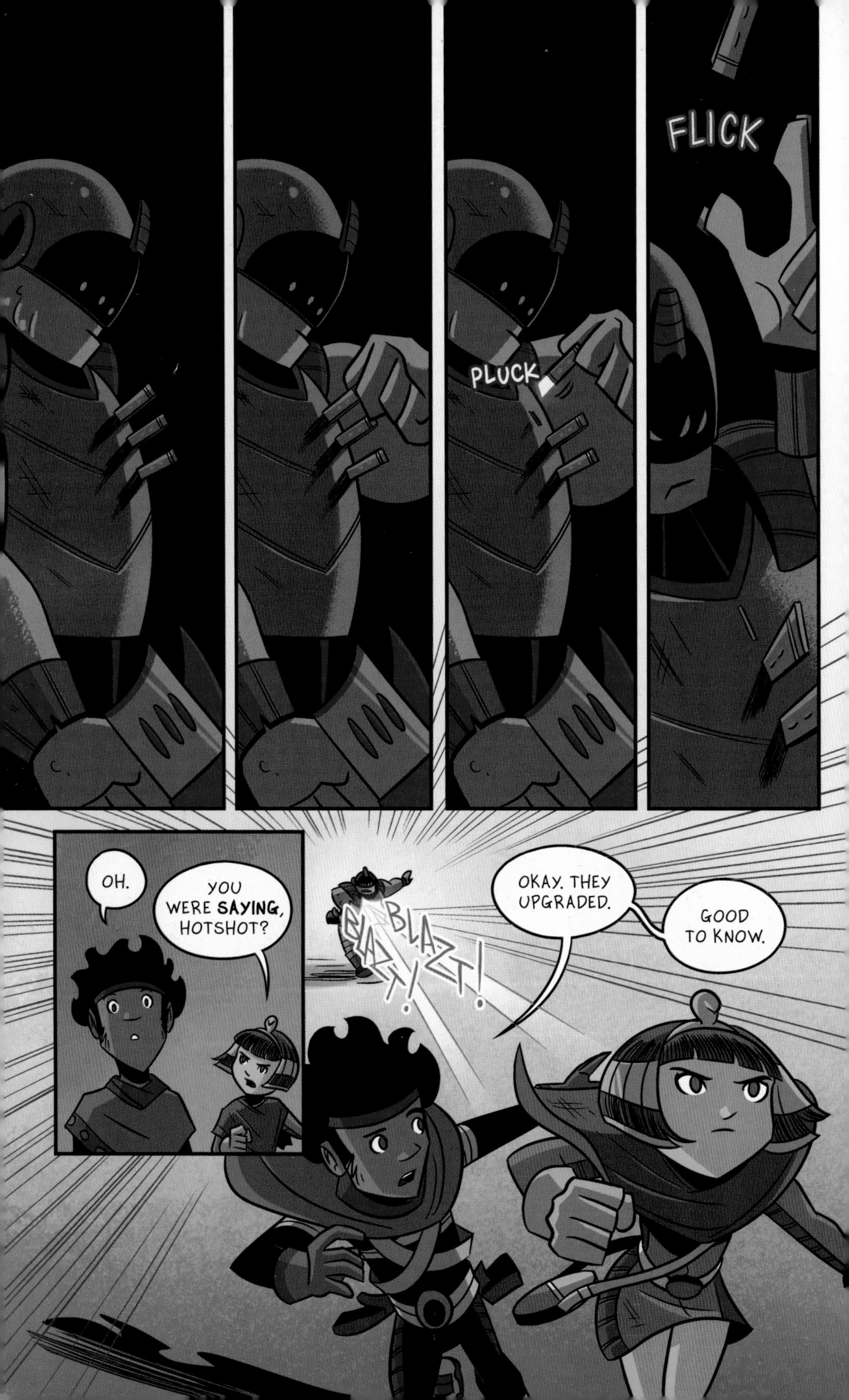
FLICK
PLUCK
OH.
YOU WERE SAYING, HOTSHOT?
BLAZT!
BLAZT!
OKAY. THEY UPGRADED.
GOOD TO KNOW.

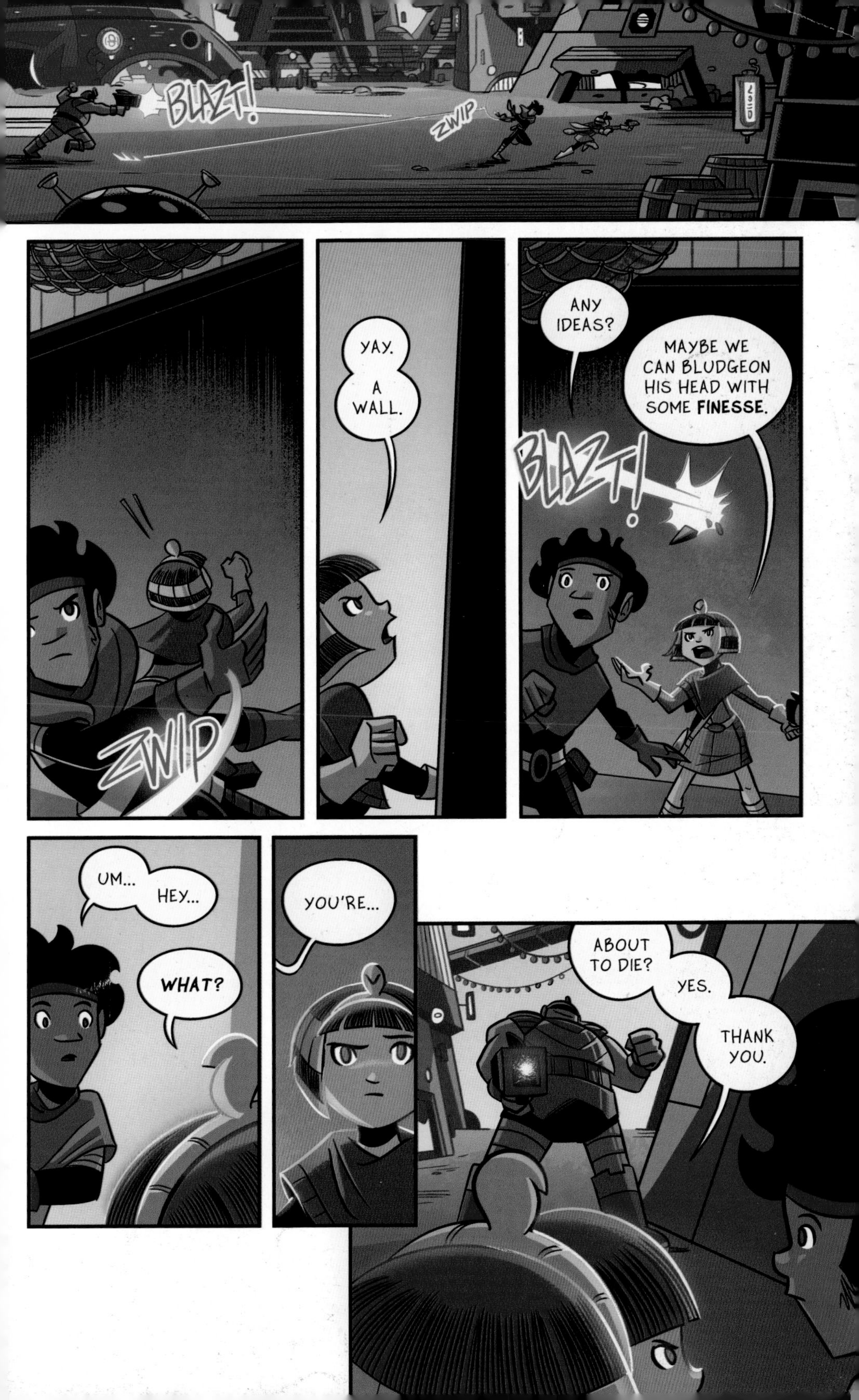
BLAZT!
ZWIP
ZWIP
YAY.
A WALL.
ANY IDEAS?
MAYBE WE CAN BLUDGEON HIS HEAD WITH SOME **FINESSE**.
BLAZT!
UM...
HEY...
WHAT?
YOU'RE...
ABOUT TO DIE?
YES.
THANK YOU.

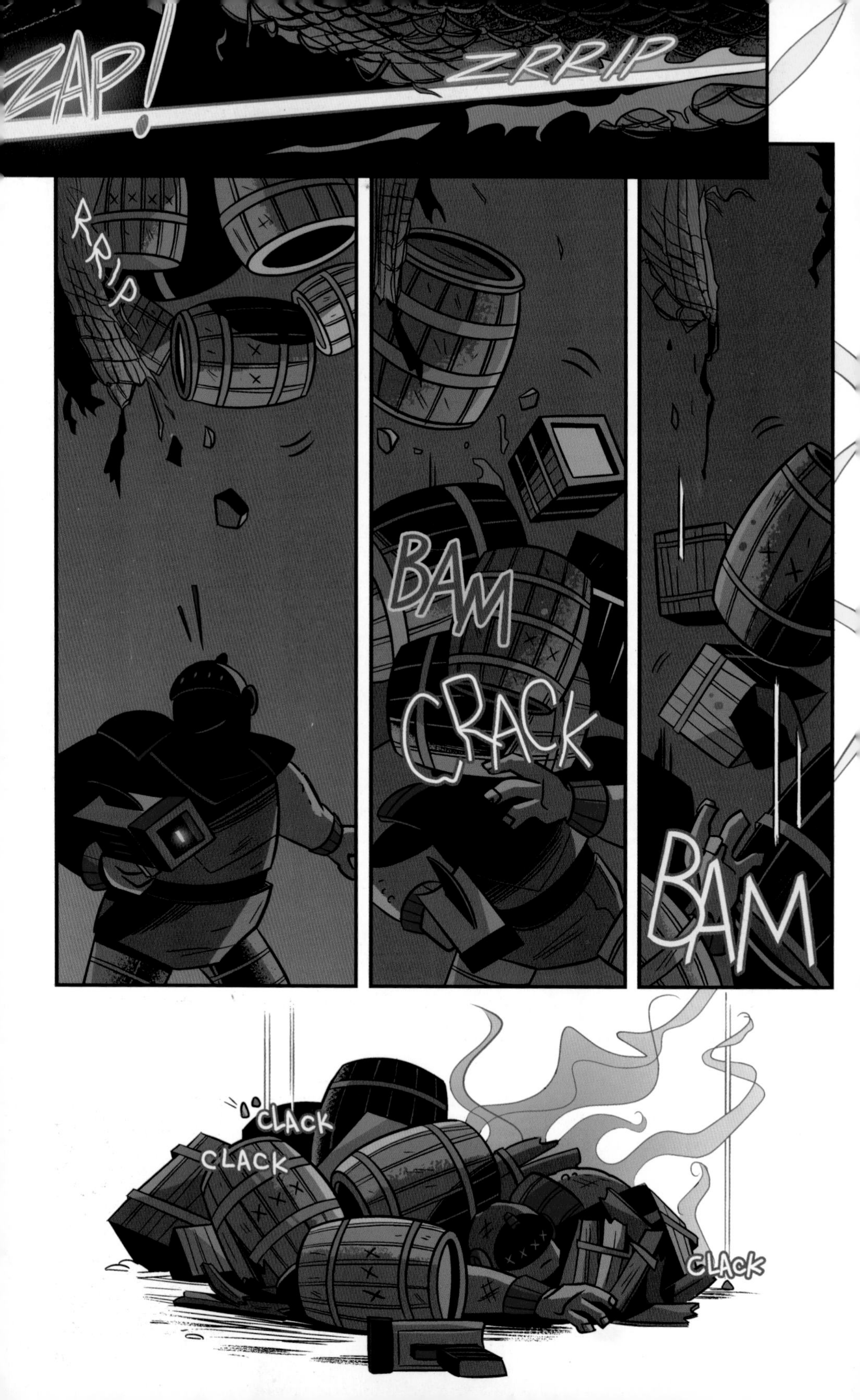
ZAP!
ZRRIP
RRRIP
BAM
CRACK
BAM
CLACK
CLACK
CLACK

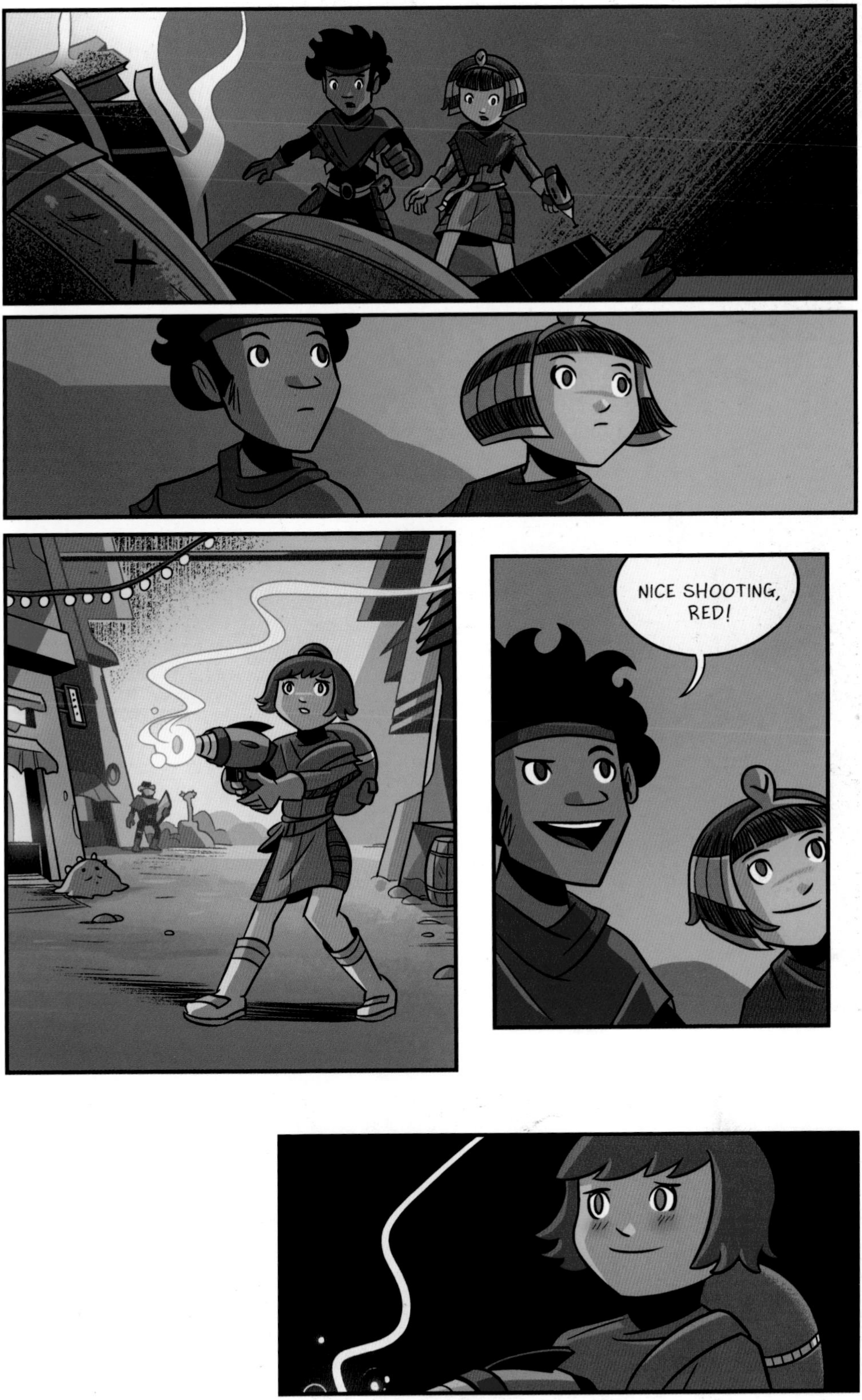
NICE SHOOTING, RED!

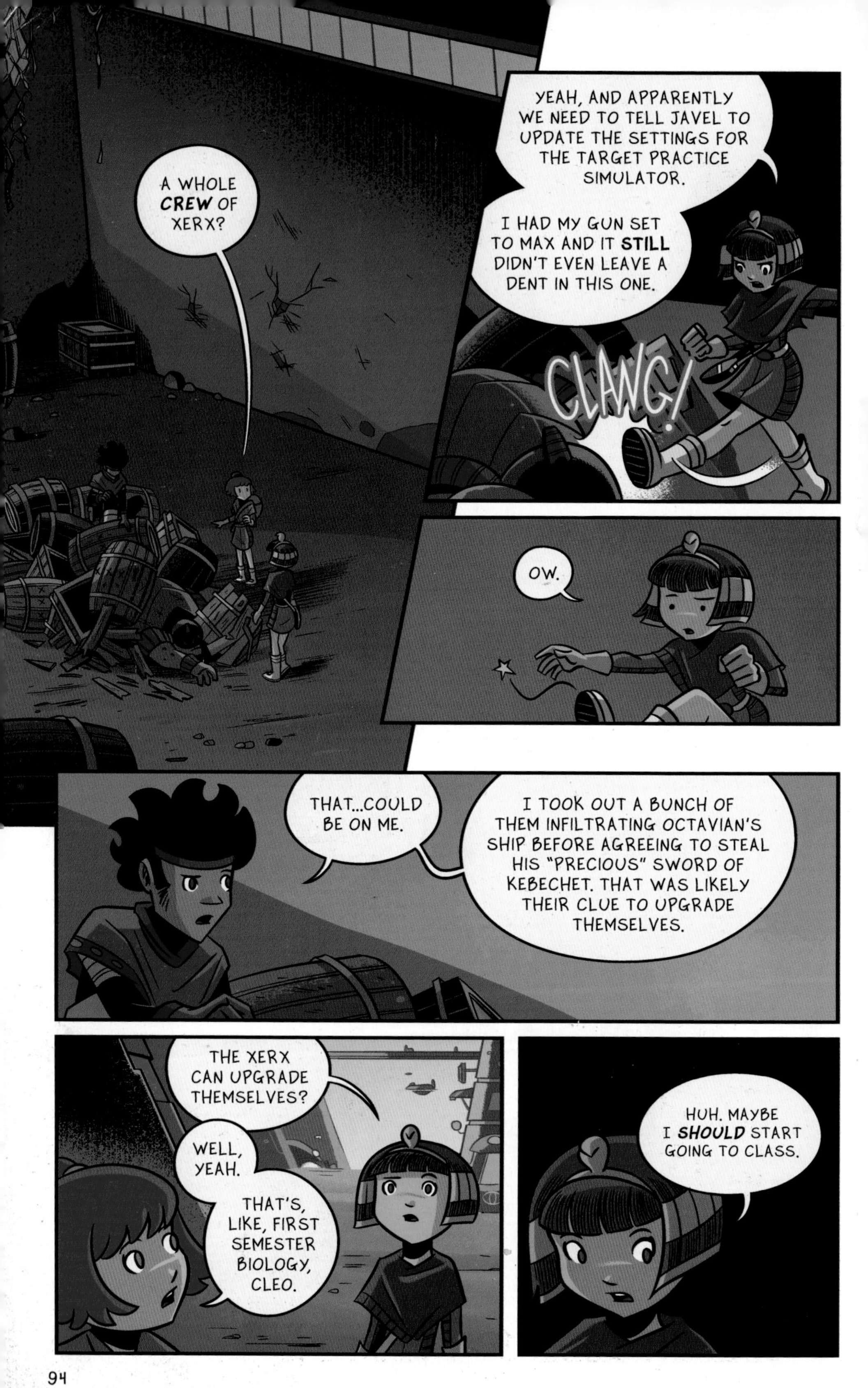
A WHOLE CREW OF XERX?
YEAH, AND APPARENTLY WE NEED TO TELL JAVEL TO UPDATE THE SETTINGS FOR THE TARGET PRACTICE SIMULATOR.
I HAD MY GUN SET TO MAX AND IT STILL DIDN'T EVEN LEAVE A DENT IN THIS ONE.
CLANG!
OW.
THAT...COULD BE ON ME.
I TOOK OUT A BUNCH OF THEM INFILTRATING OCTAVIAN'S SHIP BEFORE AGREEING TO STEAL HIS "PRECIOUS" SWORD OF KEBECHET. THAT WAS LIKELY THEIR CLUE TO UPGRADE THEMSELVES.
THE XERX CAN UPGRADE THEMSELVES?
WELL, YEAH.
THAT'S, LIKE, FIRST SEMESTER BIOLOGY, CLEO.
HUH. MAYBE I SHOULD START GOING TO CLASS.

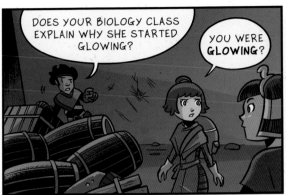

DOES YOUR BIOLOGY CLASS EXPLAIN WHY SHE STARTED GLOWING?

YOU WERE **GLOWING**?

WHAT ARE YOU TALKING ABOUT?

BEFORE YOUR FRIEND SAVED OUR BUTTS. YOU... I DON'T KNOW...JUST STARTED GLOWING.

PINK.

I WAS GLOWING PINK.

UM, YEAH.

ARE YOU OKAY?

I'M NOT MAKING THIS--

HOLD ON.

"CLEO"?

YYYYES?

THAT'S SHORT FOR **CLEOPATRA**, ISN'T IT?

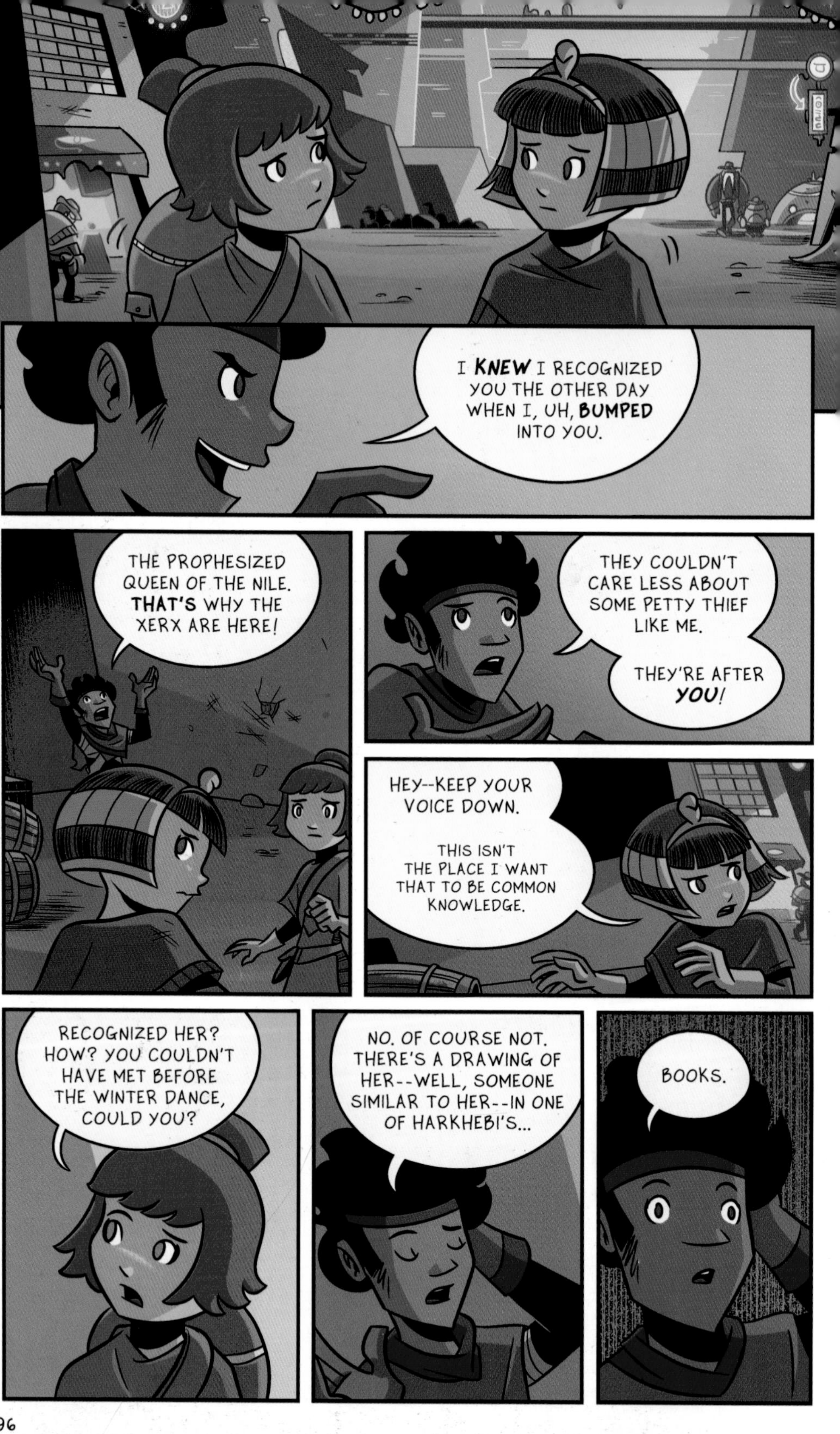

I KNEW I RECOGNIZED YOU THE OTHER DAY WHEN I, UH, BUMPED INTO YOU.
THE PROPHESIZED QUEEN OF THE NILE. THAT'S WHY THE XERX ARE HERE!
THEY COULDN'T CARE LESS ABOUT SOME PETTY THIEF LIKE ME.
THEY'RE AFTER YOU!
HEY--KEEP YOUR VOICE DOWN.
THIS ISN'T THE PLACE I WANT THAT TO BE COMMON KNOWLEDGE.
RECOGNIZED HER? HOW? YOU COULDN'T HAVE MET BEFORE THE WINTER DANCE, COULD YOU?
NO. OF COURSE NOT. THERE'S A DRAWING OF HER--WELL, SOMEONE SIMILAR TO HER--IN ONE OF HARKHEBI'S...
BOOKS.

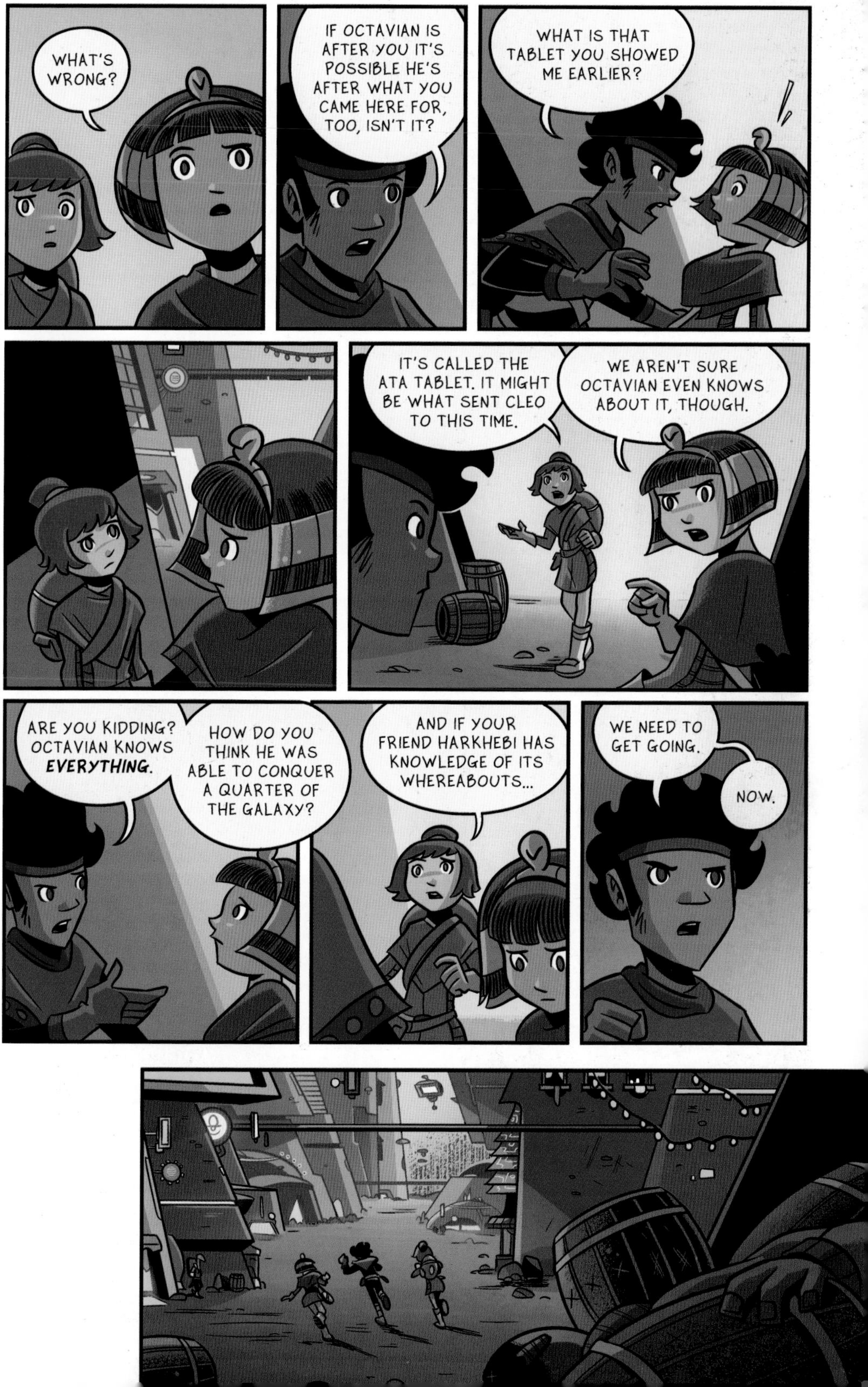
WHAT'S WRONG?
IF OCTAVIAN IS AFTER YOU IT'S POSSIBLE HE'S AFTER WHAT YOU CAME HERE FOR, TOO, ISN'T IT?
WHAT IS THAT TABLET YOU SHOWED ME EARLIER?
IT'S CALLED THE ATA TABLET. IT MIGHT BE WHAT SENT CLEO TO THIS TIME.
WE AREN'T SURE OCTAVIAN EVEN KNOWS ABOUT IT, THOUGH.
ARE YOU KIDDING? OCTAVIAN KNOWS **EVERYTHING**.
HOW DO YOU THINK HE WAS ABLE TO CONQUER A QUARTER OF THE GALAXY?
AND IF YOUR FRIEND HARKHEBI HAS KNOWLEDGE OF ITS WHEREABOUTS...
WE NEED TO GET GOING.
NOW.

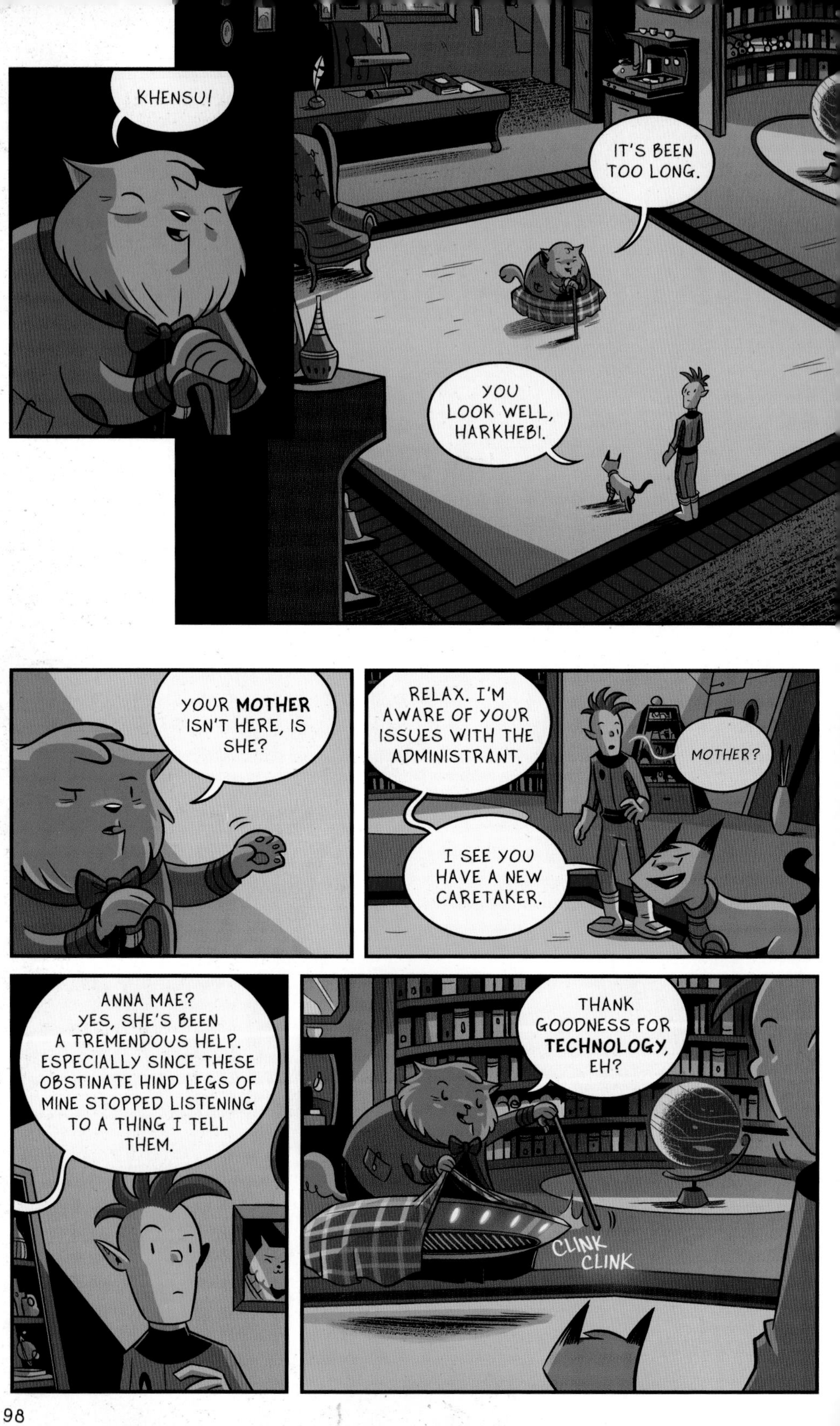
KHENSU!
IT'S BEEN TOO LONG.
YOU LOOK WELL, HARKHEBI.
YOUR **MOTHER** ISN'T HERE, IS SHE?
RELAX. I'M AWARE OF YOUR ISSUES WITH THE ADMINISTRANT.
MOTHER?
I SEE YOU HAVE A NEW CARETAKER.
ANNA MAE? YES, SHE'S BEEN A TREMENDOUS HELP. ESPECIALLY SINCE THESE OBSTINATE HIND LEGS OF MINE STOPPED LISTENING TO A THING I TELL THEM.
THANK GOODNESS FOR **TECHNOLOGY**, EH?
CLINK
CLINK

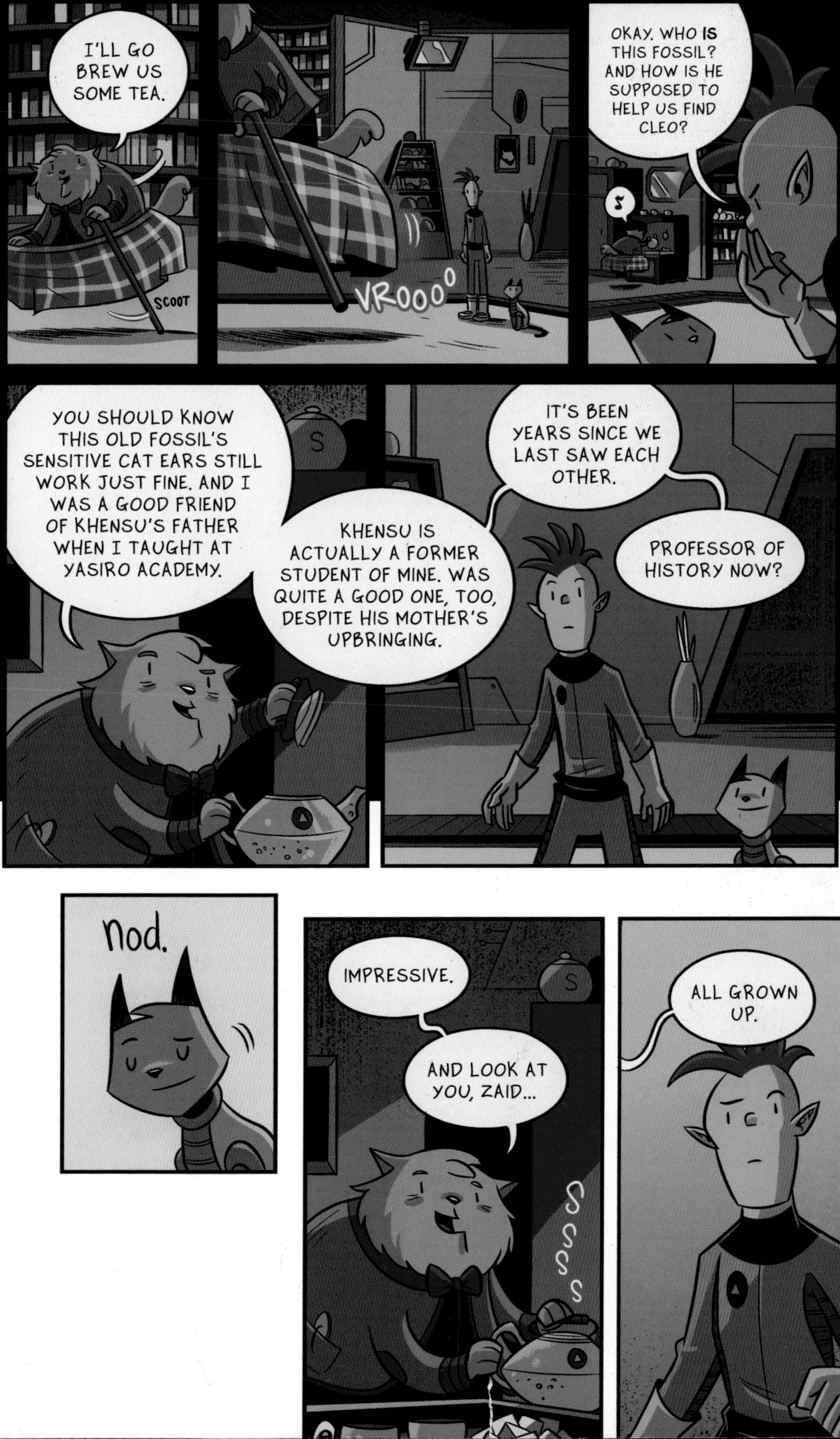
I'LL GO BREW US SOME TEA.
SCOOT
VROOOO
OKAY. WHO IS THIS FOSSIL? AND HOW IS HE SUPPOSED TO HELP US FIND CLEO?
YOU SHOULD KNOW THIS OLD FOSSIL'S SENSITIVE CAT EARS STILL WORK JUST FINE. AND I WAS A GOOD FRIEND OF KHENSU'S FATHER WHEN I TAUGHT AT YASIRO ACADEMY.
KHENSU IS ACTUALLY A FORMER STUDENT OF MINE. WAS QUITE A GOOD ONE, TOO, DESPITE HIS MOTHER'S UPBRINGING.
IT'S BEEN YEARS SINCE WE LAST SAW EACH OTHER.
PROFESSOR OF HISTORY NOW?
nod.
IMPRESSIVE.
AND LOOK AT YOU, ZAID...
SSSS
ALL GROWN UP.

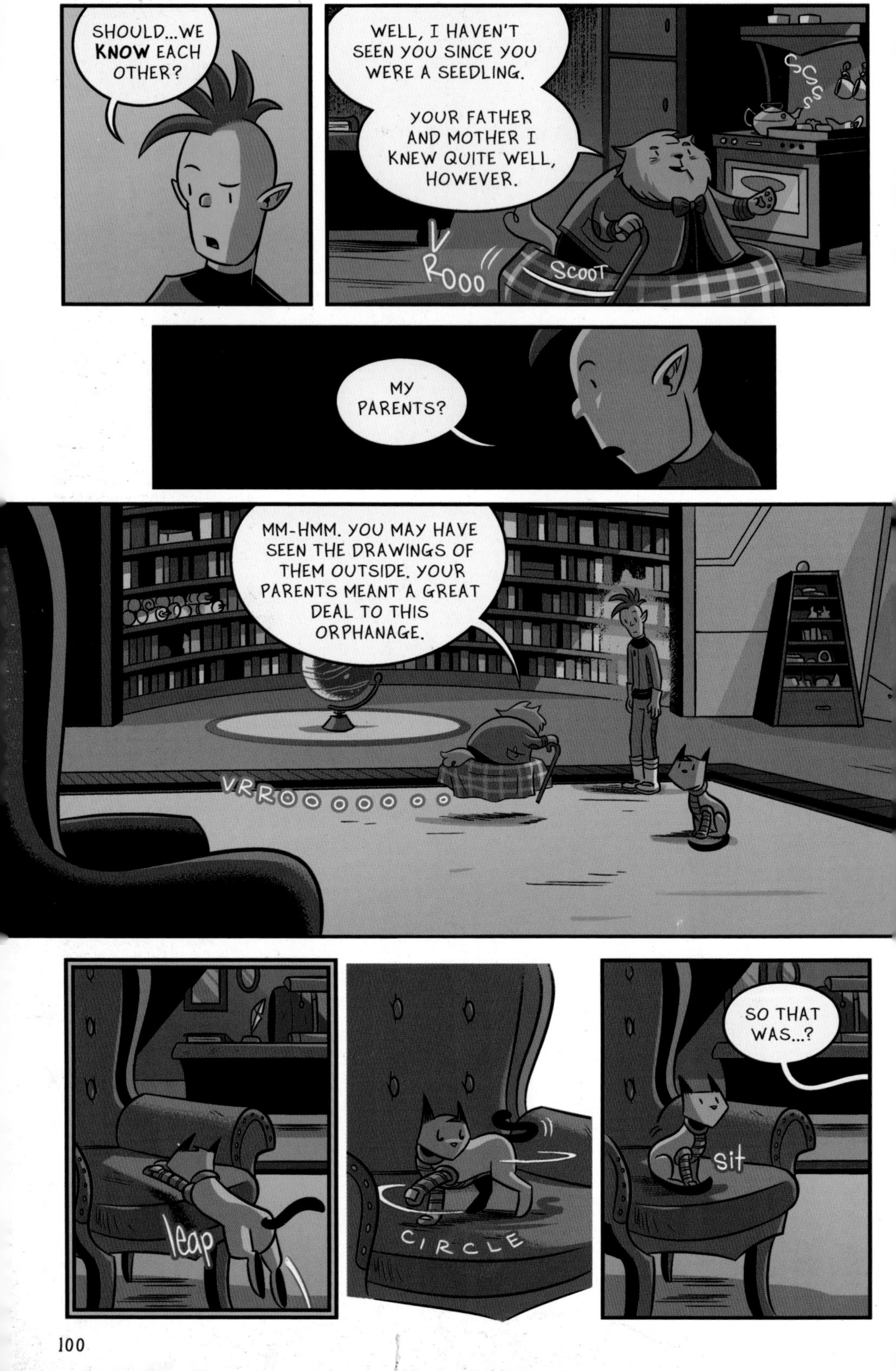
SHOULD...WE KNOW EACH OTHER?
WELL, I HAVEN'T SEEN YOU SINCE YOU WERE A SEEDLING.
YOUR FATHER AND MOTHER I KNEW QUITE WELL, HOWEVER.
SSSS
VROOO
SCOOT
MY PARENTS?
MM-HMM. YOU MAY HAVE SEEN THE DRAWINGS OF THEM OUTSIDE. YOUR PARENTS MEANT A GREAT DEAL TO THIS ORPHANAGE.
VRROOOOOOO OO
leap
CIRCLE
SO THAT WAS...?
sit

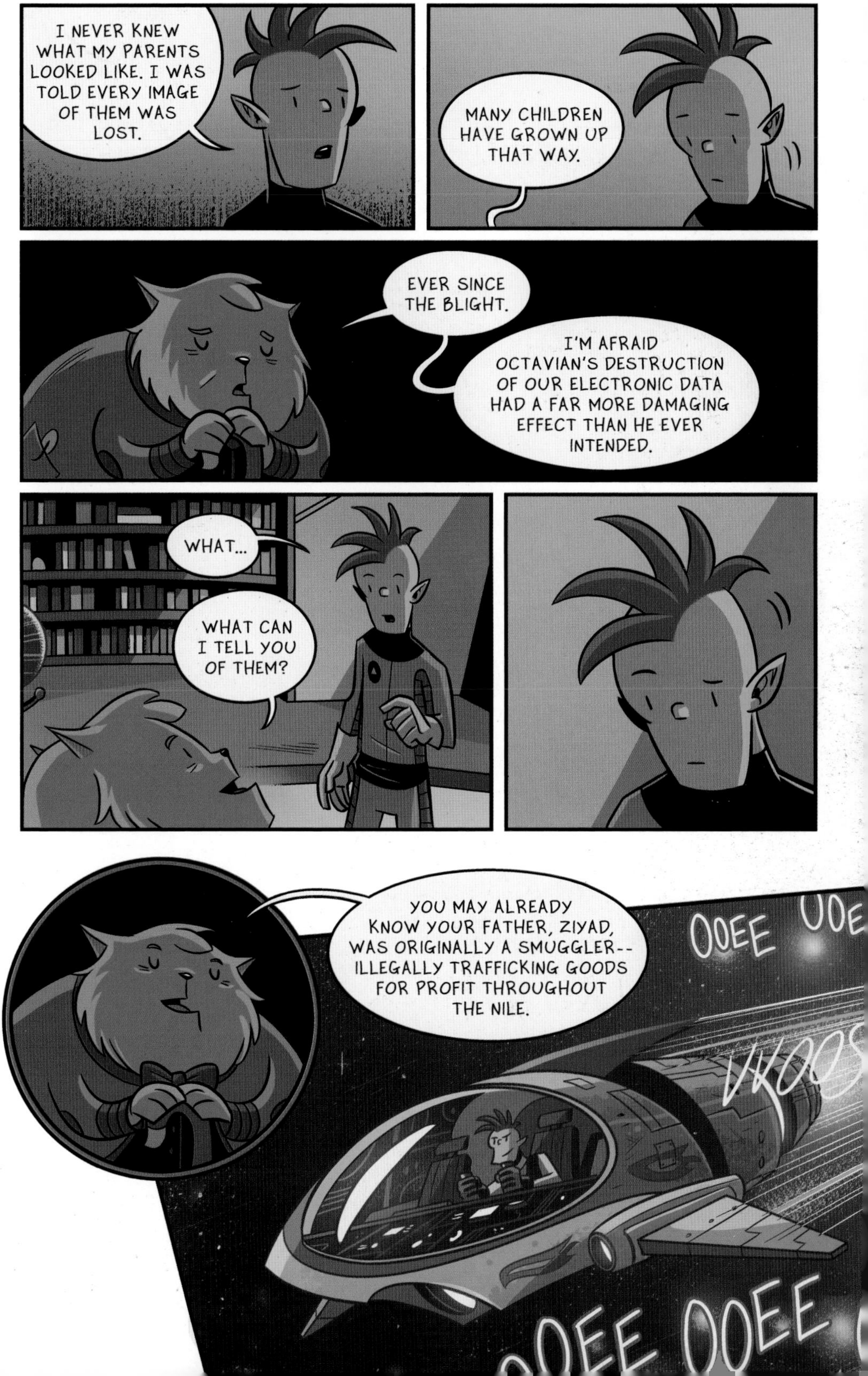
I NEVER KNEW WHAT MY PARENTS LOOKED LIKE. I WAS TOLD EVERY IMAGE OF THEM WAS LOST.
MANY CHILDREN HAVE GROWN UP THAT WAY.
EVER SINCE THE BLIGHT.
I'M AFRAID OCTAVIAN'S DESTRUCTION OF OUR ELECTRONIC DATA HAD A FAR MORE DAMAGING EFFECT THAN HE EVER INTENDED.
WHAT...
WHAT CAN I TELL YOU OF THEM?
YOU MAY ALREADY KNOW YOUR FATHER, ZIYAD, WAS ORIGINALLY A SMUGGLER-- ILLEGALLY TRAFFICKING GOODS FOR PROFIT THROUGHOUT THE NILE.
OOEE
OOEE OOEE

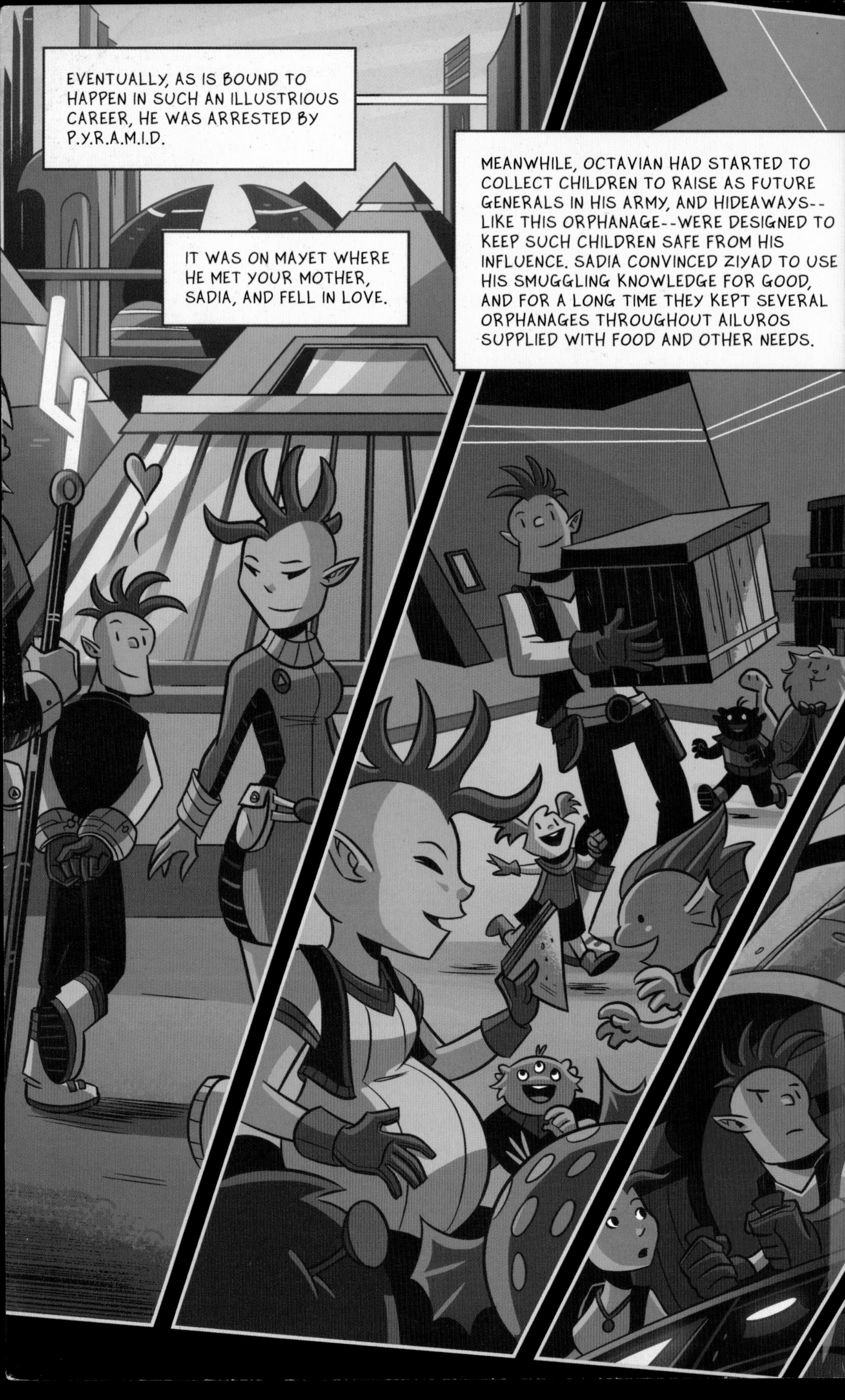
EVENTUALLY, AS IS BOUND TO HAPPEN IN SUCH AN ILLUSTRIOUS CAREER, HE WAS ARRESTED BY P.Y.R.A.M.I.D.
IT WAS ON MAYET WHERE HE MET YOUR MOTHER, SADIA, AND FELL IN LOVE.
MEANWHILE, OCTAVIAN HAD STARTED TO COLLECT CHILDREN TO RAISE AS FUTURE GENERALS IN HIS ARMY, AND HIDEAWAYS--LIKE THIS ORPHANAGE--WERE DESIGNED TO KEEP SUCH CHILDREN SAFE FROM HIS INFLUENCE. SADIA CONVINCED ZIYAD TO USE HIS SMUGGLING KNOWLEDGE FOR GOOD, AND FOR A LONG TIME THEY KEPT SEVERAL ORPHANAGES THROUGHOUT AILUROS SUPPLIED WITH FOOD AND OTHER NEEDS.

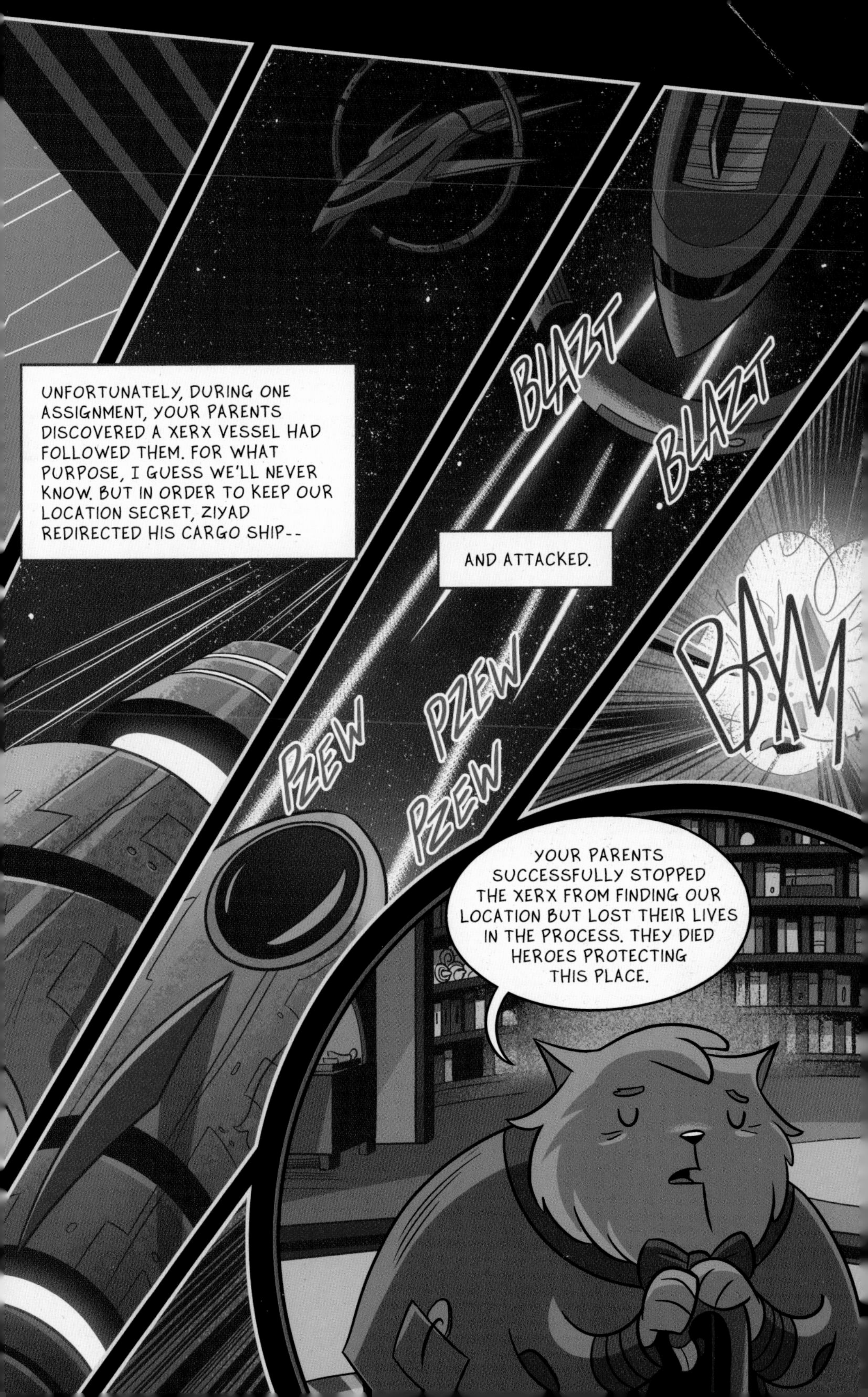
UNFORTUNATELY, DURING ONE ASSIGNMENT, YOUR PARENTS DISCOVERED A XERX VESSEL HAD FOLLOWED THEM. FOR WHAT PURPOSE, I GUESS WE'LL NEVER KNOW. BUT IN ORDER TO KEEP OUR LOCATION SECRET, ZIYAD REDIRECTED HIS CARGO SHIP--
BLAZT
BLAZT
AND ATTACKED.
PZEW
PZEW
PZEW
BAM
YOUR PARENTS SUCCESSFULLY STOPPED THE XERX FROM FINDING OUR LOCATION BUT LOST THEIR LIVES IN THE PROCESS. THEY DIED HEROES PROTECTING THIS PLACE.

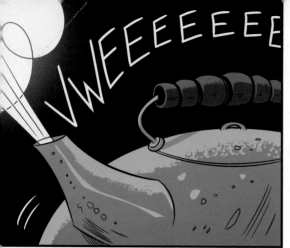

VWEEEEEEE

OH, THE TEA!

HEROES...

VROoo

MY UNCLE NEVER TOLD ME ANY OF THIS.

YES, HE ALWAYS DID SIDE MORE WITH YOUR FATHER'S CRIMINAL TENDENCIES. I'M NOT SURE HE EVER APPROVED OF HIS RELATIONSHIP WITH YOUR MOTHER, EITHER.

HOW IS YOUR UNCLE?

HE'S DEAD.

OH.

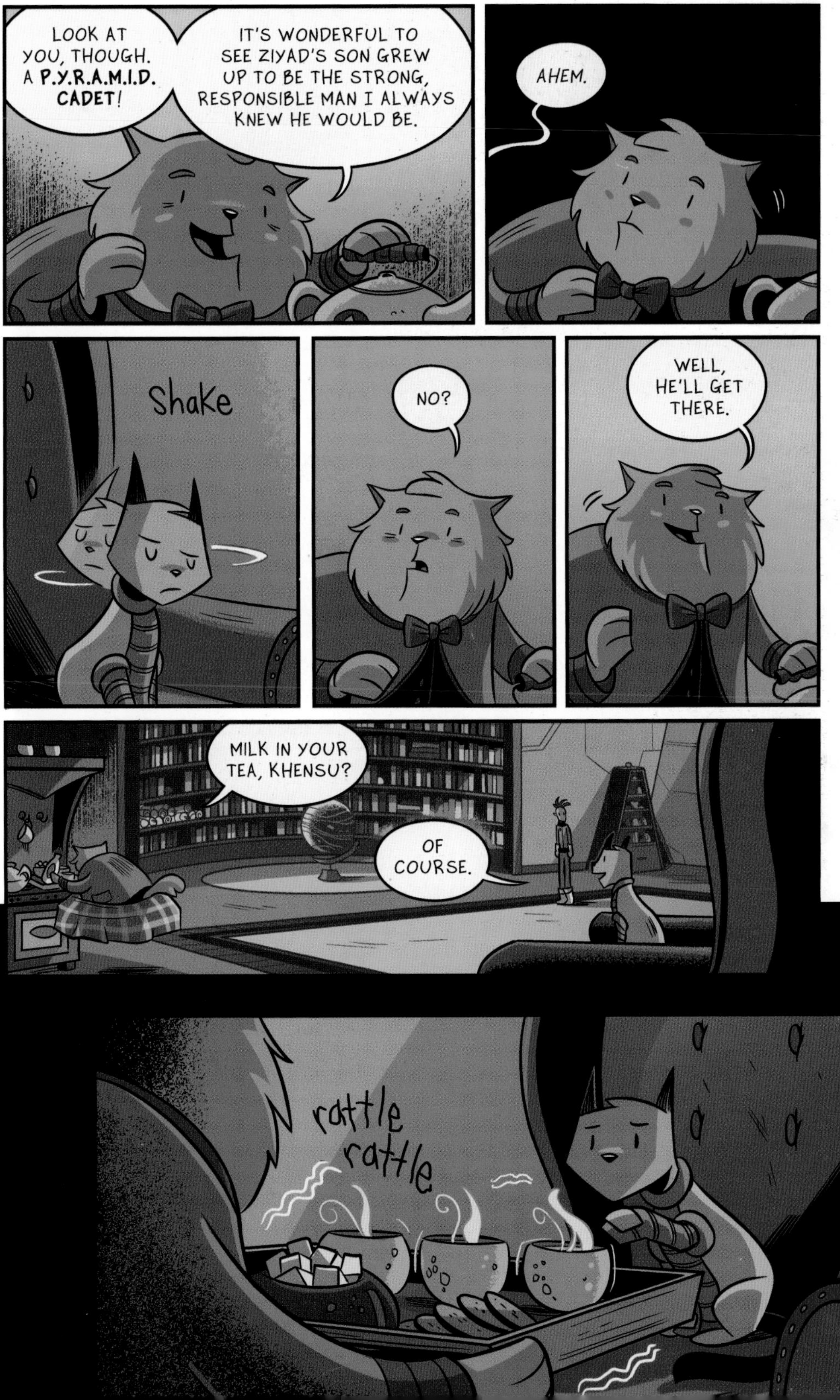
LOOK AT YOU, THOUGH. A P.Y.R.A.M.I.D. CADET!
IT'S WONDERFUL TO SEE ZIYAD'S SON GREW UP TO BE THE STRONG, RESPONSIBLE MAN I ALWAYS KNEW HE WOULD BE.
AHEM.
Shake
NO?
WELL, HE'LL GET THERE.
MILK IN YOUR TEA, KHENSU?
OF COURSE.
rattle rattle

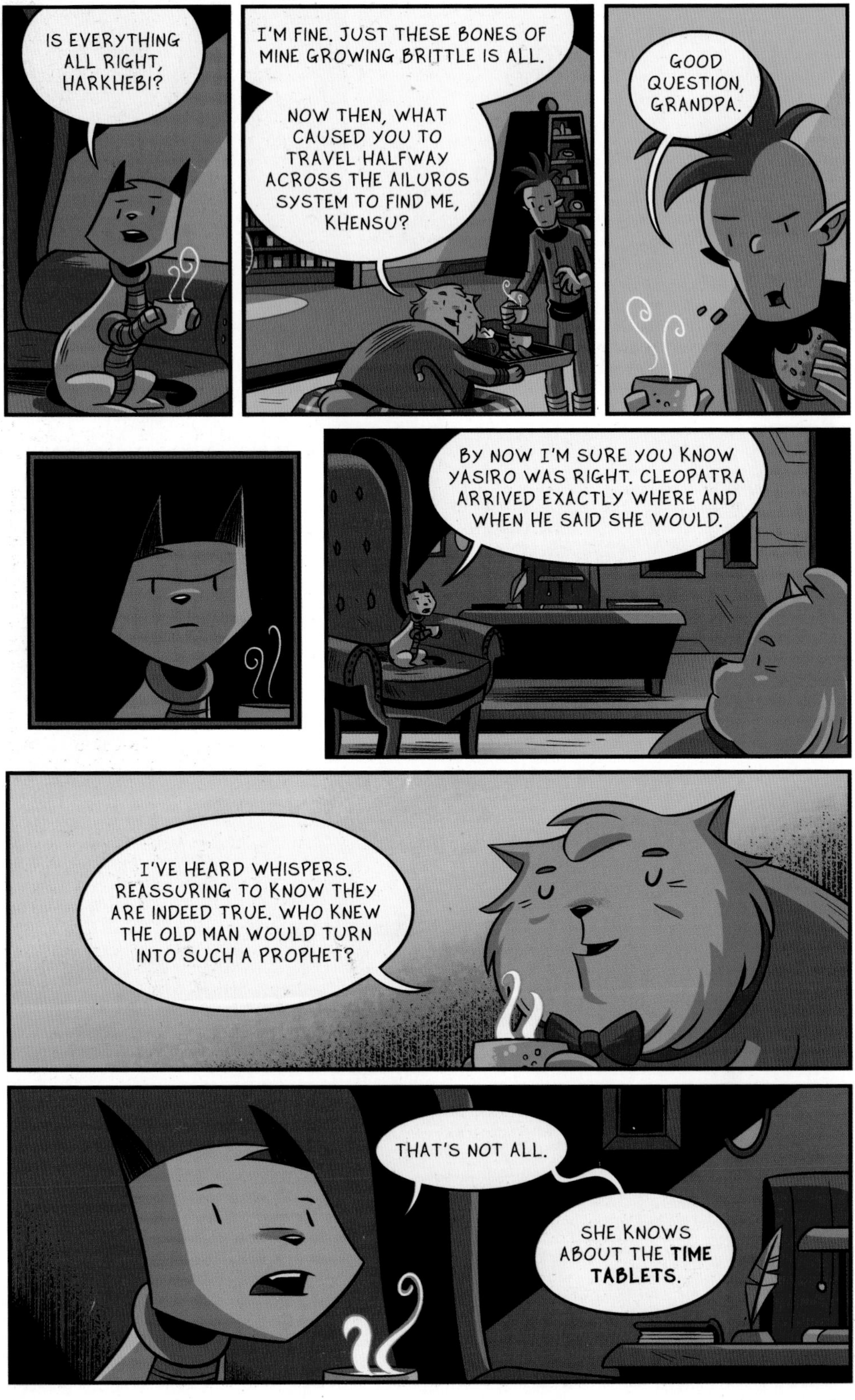
IS EVERYTHING ALL RIGHT, HARKHEBI?
I'M FINE. JUST THESE BONES OF MINE GROWING BRITTLE IS ALL.
NOW THEN, WHAT CAUSED YOU TO TRAVEL HALFWAY ACROSS THE AILUROS SYSTEM TO FIND ME, KHENSU?
GOOD QUESTION, GRANDPA.
BY NOW I'M SURE YOU KNOW YASIRO WAS RIGHT. CLEOPATRA ARRIVED EXACTLY WHERE AND WHEN HE SAID SHE WOULD.
I'VE HEARD WHISPERS. REASSURING TO KNOW THEY ARE INDEED TRUE. WHO KNEW THE OLD MAN WOULD TURN INTO SUCH A PROPHET?
THAT'S NOT ALL.
SHE KNOWS ABOUT THE **TIME TABLETS**.

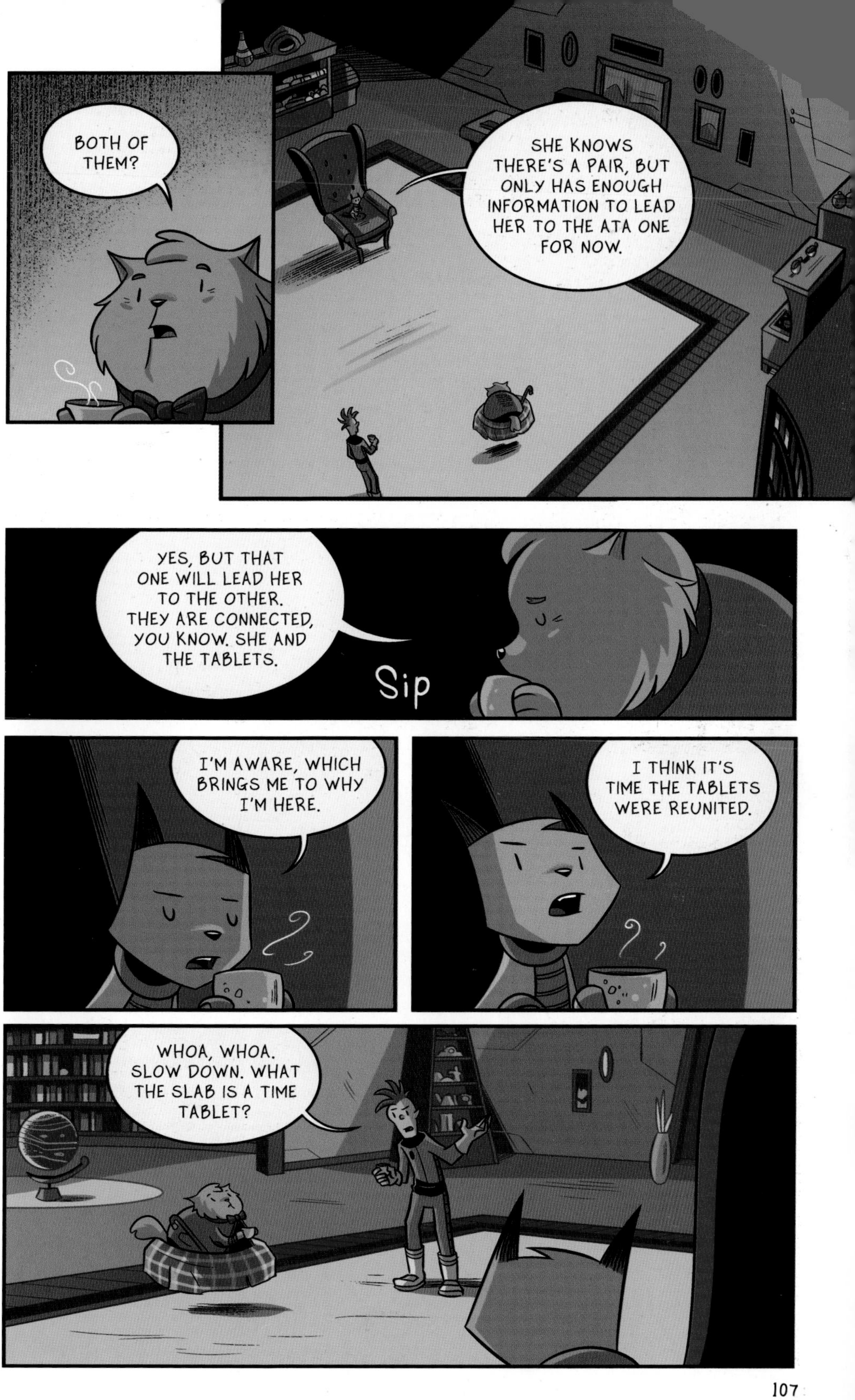
BOTH OF THEM?
SHE KNOWS THERE'S A PAIR, BUT ONLY HAS ENOUGH INFORMATION TO LEAD HER TO THE ATA ONE FOR NOW.
YES, BUT THAT ONE WILL LEAD HER TO THE OTHER. THEY ARE CONNECTED, YOU KNOW. SHE AND THE TABLETS.
Sip
I'M AWARE, WHICH BRINGS ME TO WHY I'M HERE.
I THINK IT'S TIME THE TABLETS WERE REUNITED.
WHOA, WHOA. SLOW DOWN. WHAT THE SLAB IS A TIME TABLET?

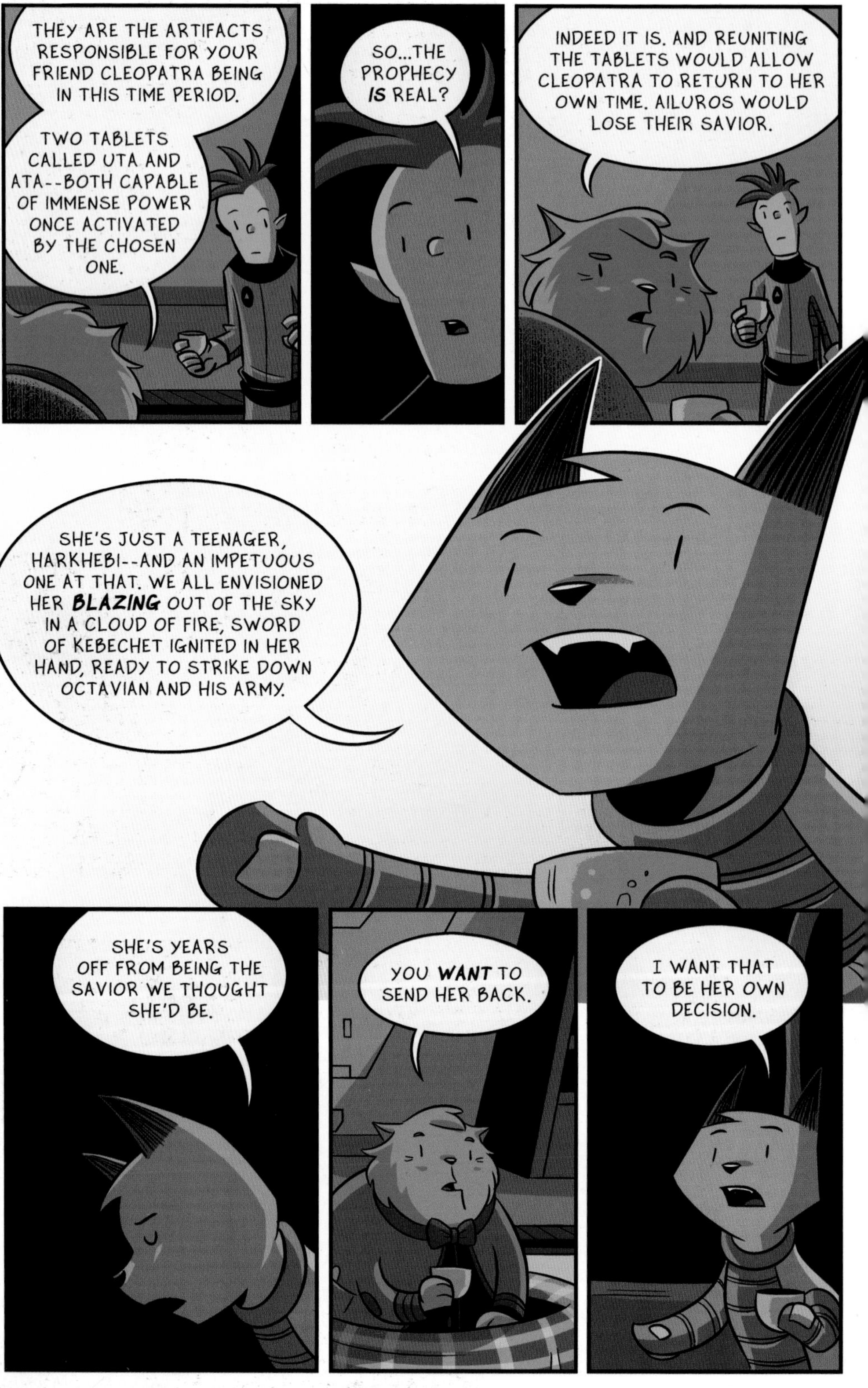
THEY ARE THE ARTIFACTS RESPONSIBLE FOR YOUR FRIEND CLEOPATRA BEING IN THIS TIME PERIOD.
TWO TABLETS CALLED UTA AND ATA--BOTH CAPABLE OF IMMENSE POWER ONCE ACTIVATED BY THE CHOSEN ONE.
SO...THE PROPHECY **IS** REAL?
INDEED IT IS. AND REUNITING THE TABLETS WOULD ALLOW CLEOPATRA TO RETURN TO HER OWN TIME. AILUROS WOULD LOSE THEIR SAVIOR.
SHE'S JUST A TEENAGER, HARKHEBI--AND AN IMPETUOUS ONE AT THAT. WE ALL ENVISIONED HER **BLAZING** OUT OF THE SKY IN A CLOUD OF FIRE, SWORD OF KEBECHET IGNITED IN HER HAND, READY TO STRIKE DOWN OCTAVIAN AND HIS ARMY.
SHE'S YEARS OFF FROM BEING THE SAVIOR WE THOUGHT SHE'D BE.
YOU **WANT** TO SEND HER BACK.
I WANT THAT TO BE HER OWN DECISION.

Sigh.

I SUSPECT YOU'RE RIGHT. I NEVER THOUGHT IT WISE TO TRY TO CHART THE DIRECTION OF HER LIFE. ONLY TO PROTECT AILUROS.

YOU REALIZE I'LL BE BETRAYING YOUR FATHER'S TRUST IF I GIVE YOU THE ATA TABLET'S LOCATION?

YOU'LL ALSO BE PROVIDING **ME** WITH INTEL THE COUNCIL HAS BEEN TRYING TO GET AHOLD OF FOR YEARS.

HAHA!

TRUE.

VROOOO SCOOT

SPIN

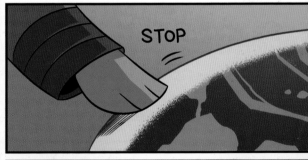

STOP

BLOOP

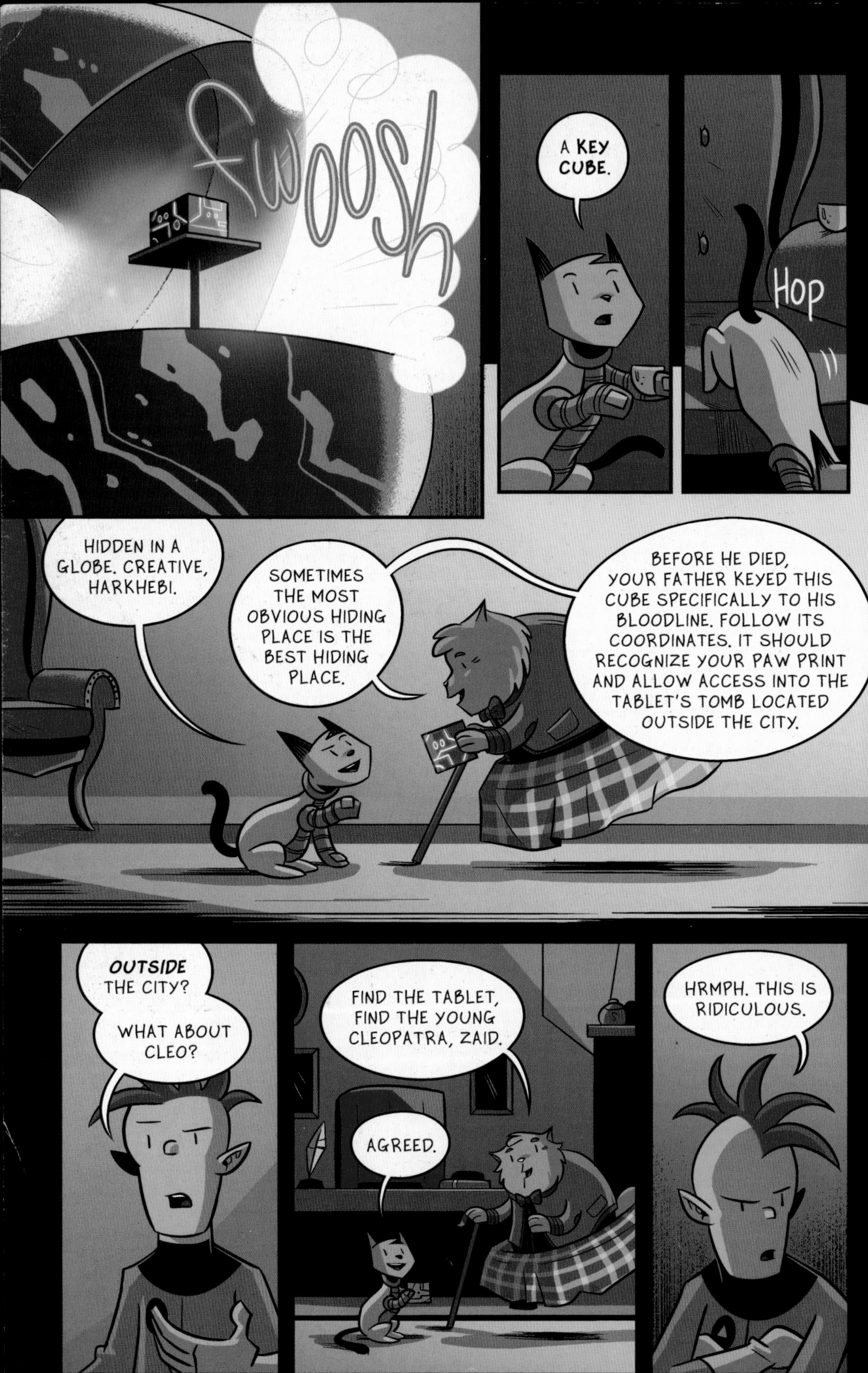
FWOOSH
A KEY CUBE.
HOP
HIDDEN IN A GLOBE. CREATIVE, HARKHEBI.
SOMETIMES THE MOST OBVIOUS HIDING PLACE IS THE BEST HIDING PLACE.
BEFORE HE DIED, YOUR FATHER KEYED THIS CUBE SPECIFICALLY TO HIS BLOODLINE. FOLLOW ITS COORDINATES. IT SHOULD RECOGNIZE YOUR PAW PRINT AND ALLOW ACCESS INTO THE TABLET'S TOMB LOCATED OUTSIDE THE CITY.
OUTSIDE THE CITY?
WHAT ABOUT CLEO?
FIND THE TABLET, FIND THE YOUNG CLEOPATRA, ZAID.
AGREED.
HRMPH. THIS IS RIDICULOUS.

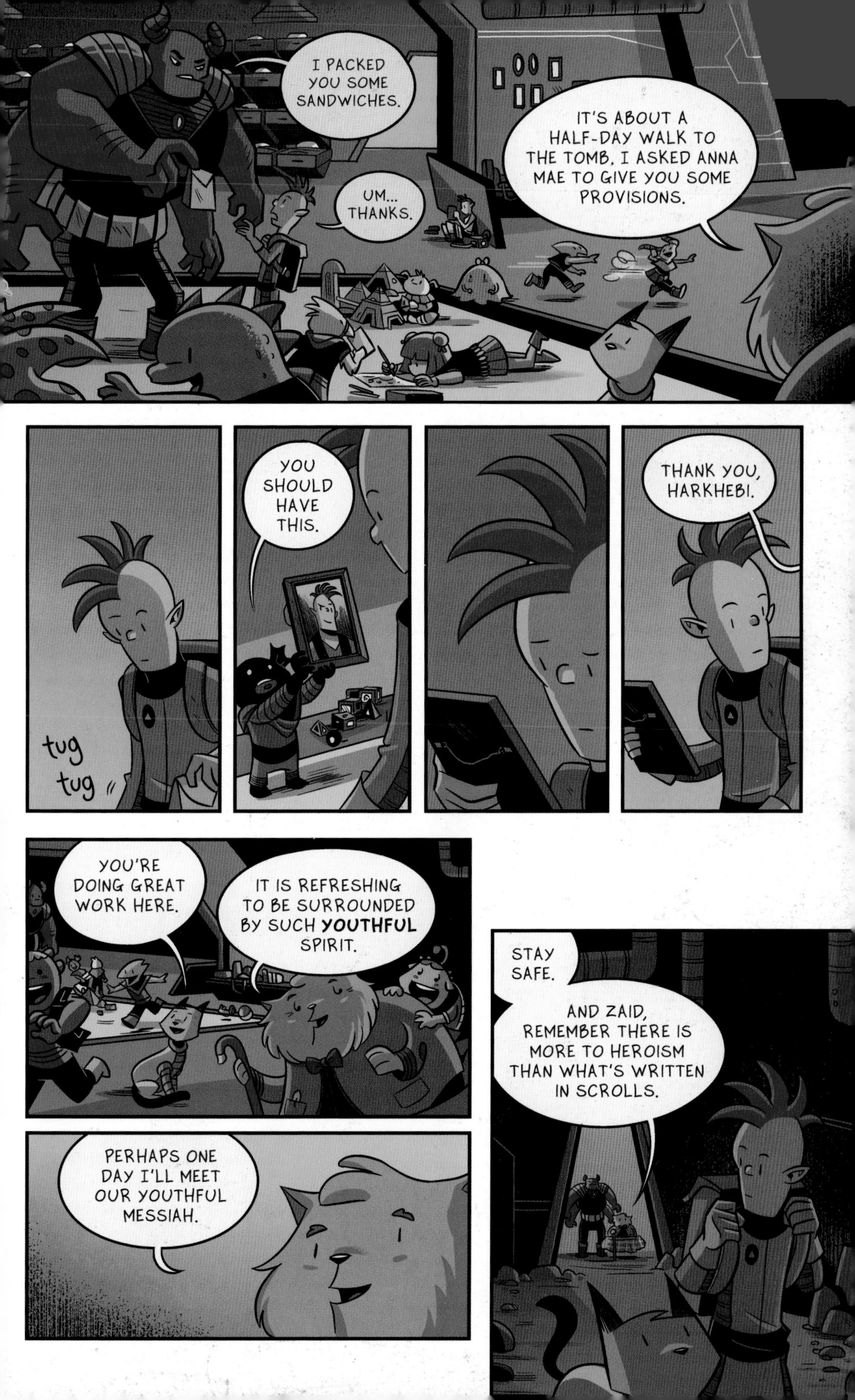
I PACKED YOU SOME SANDWICHES.
UM... THANKS.
IT'S ABOUT A HALF-DAY WALK TO THE TOMB. I ASKED ANNA MAE TO GIVE YOU SOME PROVISIONS.
tug tug
YOU SHOULD HAVE THIS.
THANK YOU, HARKHEBI.
YOU'RE DOING GREAT WORK HERE.
IT IS REFRESHING TO BE SURROUNDED BY SUCH YOUTHFUL SPIRIT.
PERHAPS ONE DAY I'LL MEET OUR YOUTHFUL MESSIAH.
STAY SAFE.
AND ZAID, REMEMBER THERE IS MORE TO HEROISM THAN WHAT'S WRITTEN IN SCROLLS.

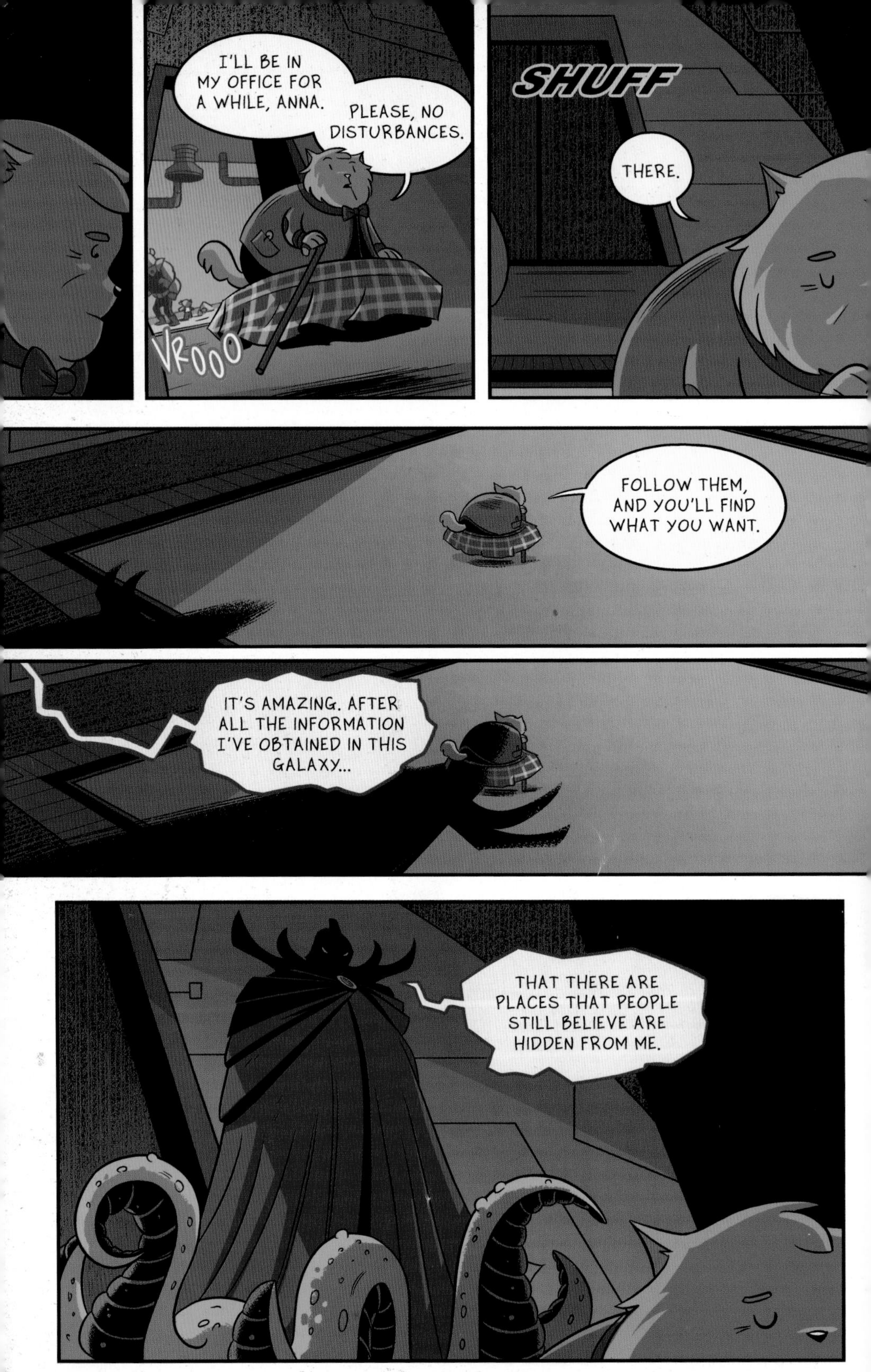

I'LL BE IN MY OFFICE FOR A WHILE, ANNA.
PLEASE, NO DISTURBANCES.
VROOO
SHUFF
THERE.
FOLLOW THEM, AND YOU'LL FIND WHAT YOU WANT.
IT'S AMAZING. AFTER ALL THE INFORMATION I'VE OBTAINED IN THIS GALAXY...
THAT THERE ARE PLACES THAT PEOPLE STILL BELIEVE ARE HIDDEN FROM ME.

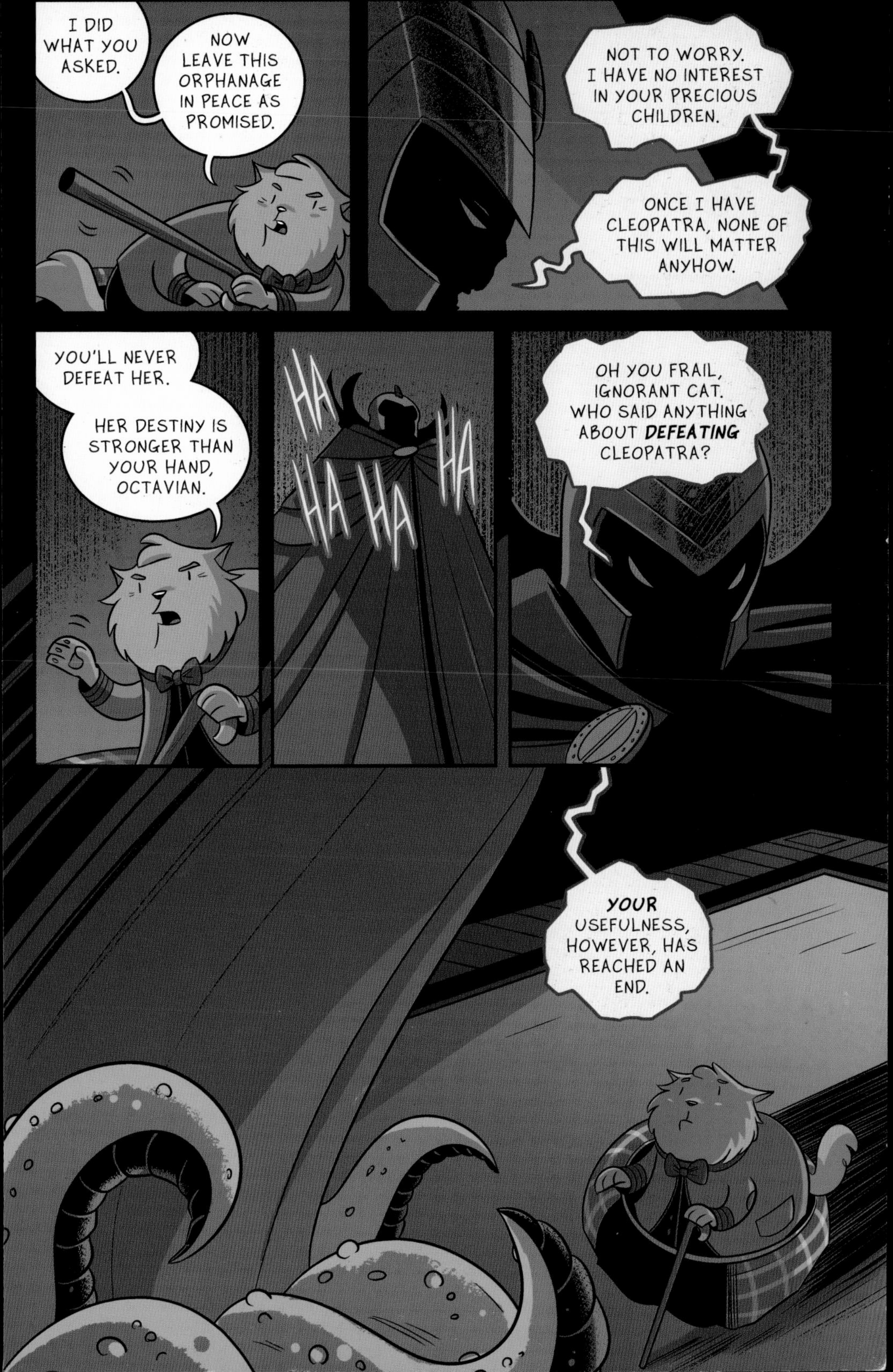
I DID WHAT YOU ASKED.
NOW LEAVE THIS ORPHANAGE IN PEACE AS PROMISED.
NOT TO WORRY. I HAVE NO INTEREST IN YOUR PRECIOUS CHILDREN.
ONCE I HAVE CLEOPATRA, NONE OF THIS WILL MATTER ANYHOW.
YOU'LL NEVER DEFEAT HER.
HER DESTINY IS STRONGER THAN YOUR HAND, OCTAVIAN.
HA HA HA HA HA HA
OH YOU FRAIL, IGNORANT CAT. WHO SAID ANYTHING ABOUT **DEFEATING** CLEOPATRA?
YOUR USEFULNESS, HOWEVER, HAS REACHED AN END.

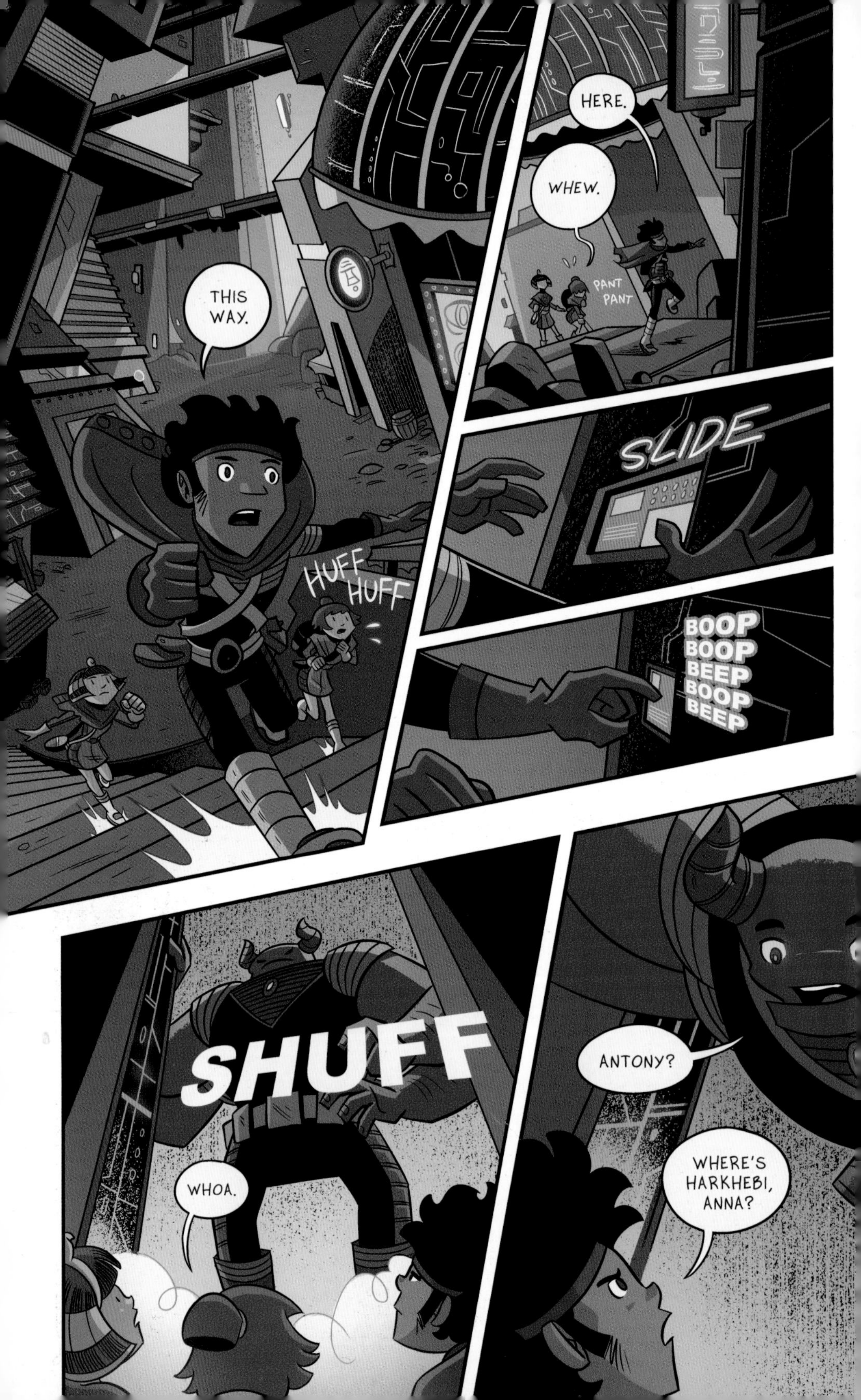
THIS WAY.
HUFF HUFF
HERE.
WHEW.
PANT PANT
SLIDE
BOOP BOOP BEEP BOOP BEEP
SHUFF
WHOA.
ANTONY?
WHERE'S HARKHEBI, ANNA?

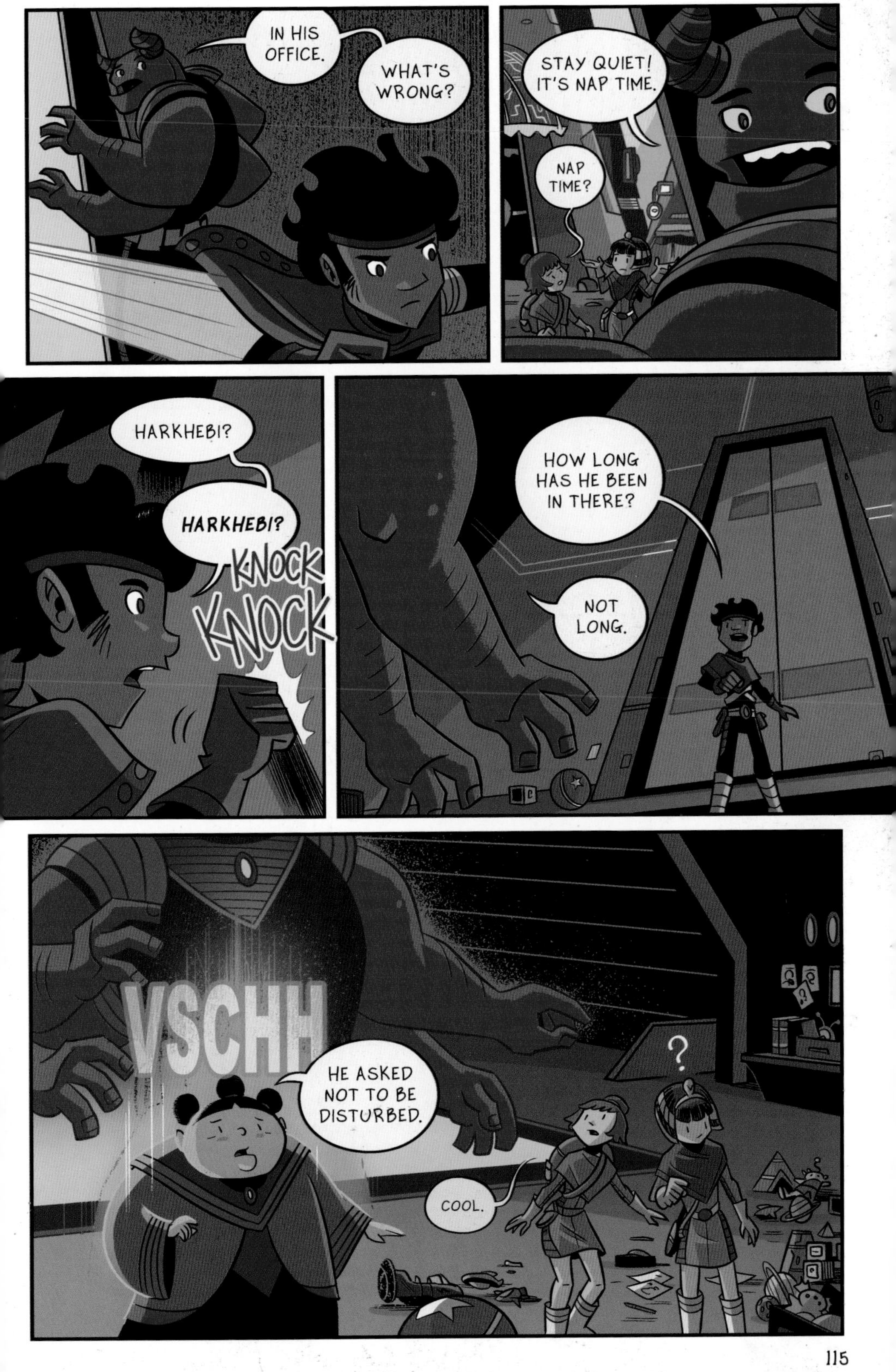
IN HIS OFFICE.
WHAT'S WRONG?
STAY QUIET! IT'S NAP TIME.
NAP TIME?
HARKHEBI?
HARKHEBI?
KNOCK KNOCK
HOW LONG HAS HE BEEN IN THERE?
NOT LONG.
VSCHH
HE ASKED NOT TO BE DISTURBED.
?
COOL.

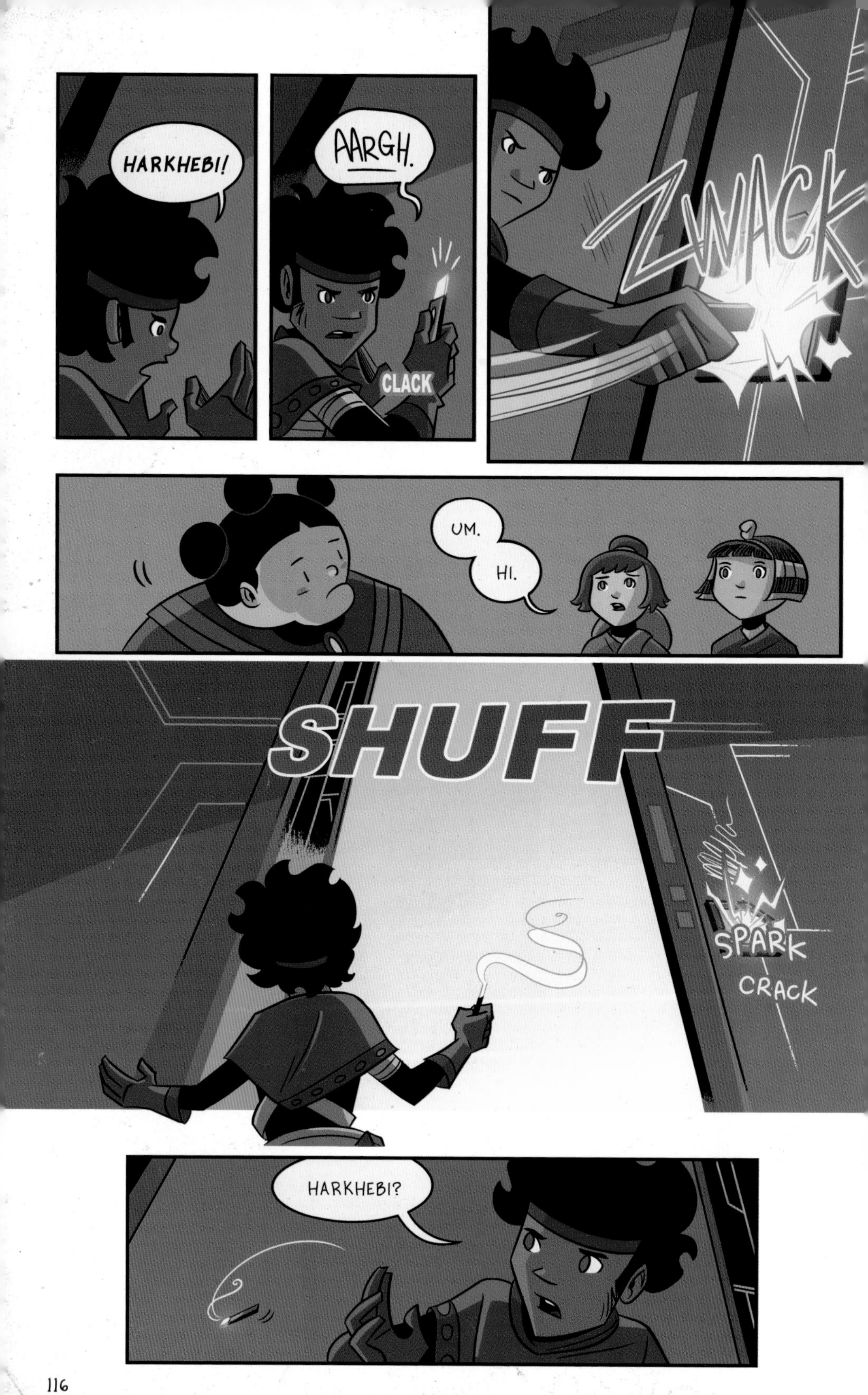
HARKHEBI!
AARGH.
CLACK
ZWACK
UM.
HI.
SHUFF
SPARK
CRACK
HARKHEBI?

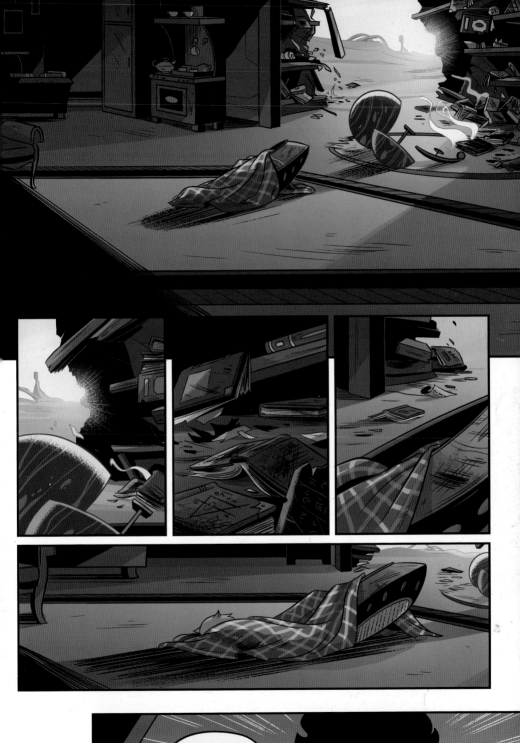

HARKHEBI!

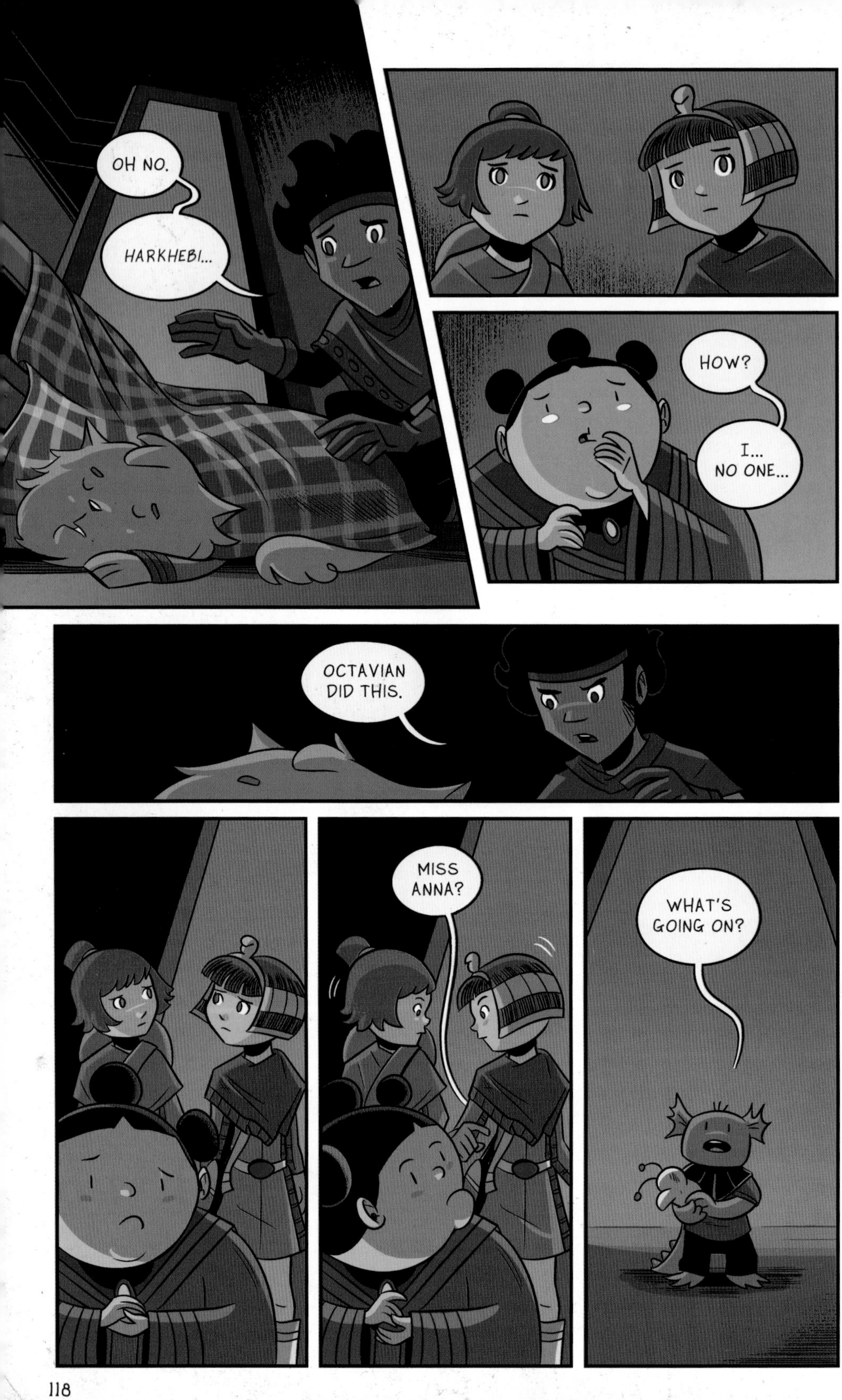
OH NO.
HARKHEBI...
HOW?
I... NO ONE...
OCTAVIAN DID THIS.
MISS ANNA?
WHAT'S GOING ON?

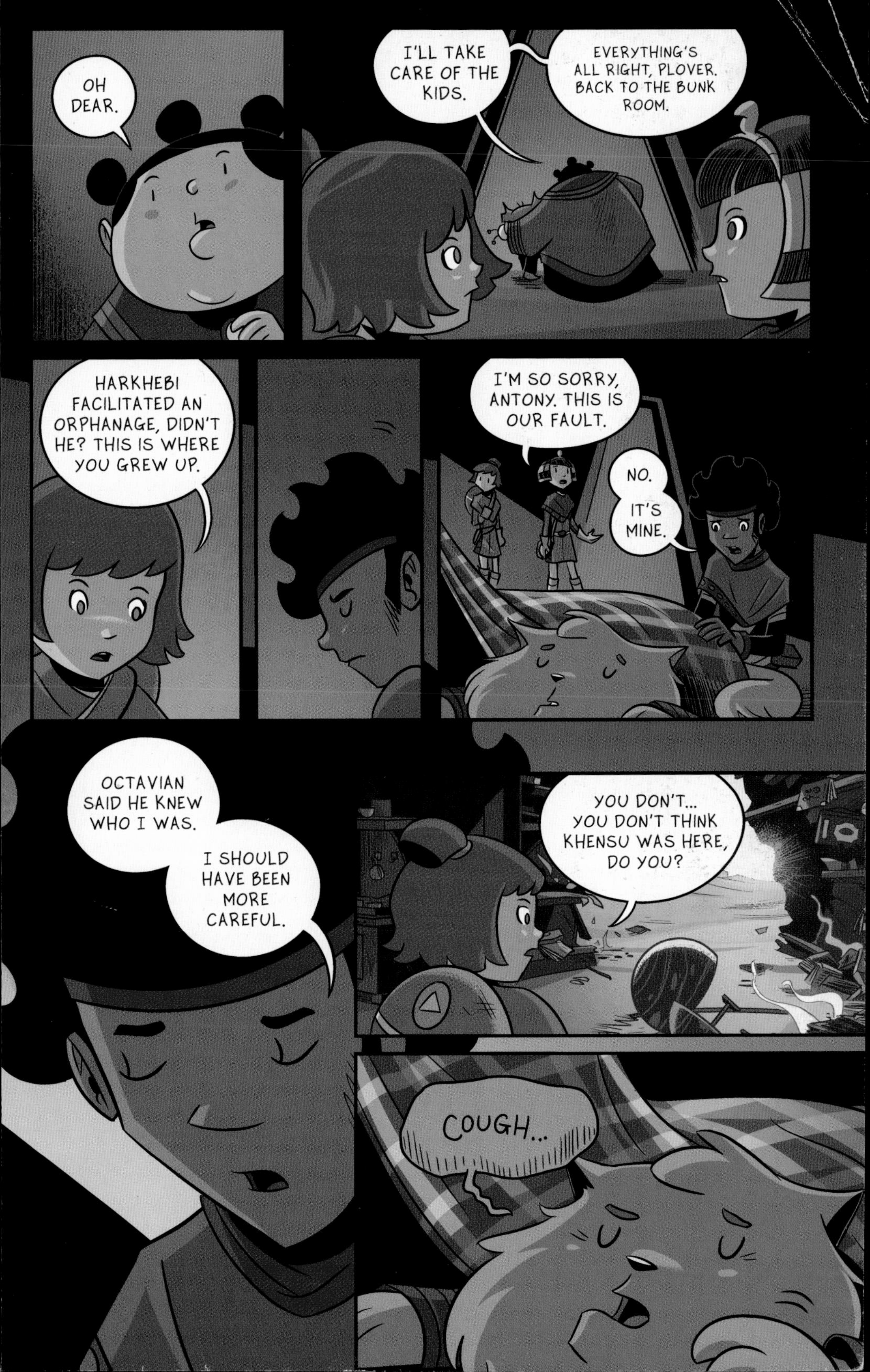
OH DEAR.
I'LL TAKE CARE OF THE KIDS.
EVERYTHING'S ALL RIGHT, PLOVER. BACK TO THE BUNK ROOM.
HARKHEBI FACILITATED AN ORPHANAGE, DIDN'T HE? THIS IS WHERE YOU GREW UP.
I'M SO SORRY, ANTONY. THIS IS OUR FAULT.
NO.
IT'S MINE.
OCTAVIAN SAID HE KNEW WHO I WAS.
I SHOULD HAVE BEEN MORE CAREFUL.
YOU DON'T... YOU DON'T THINK KHENSU WAS HERE, DO YOU?
COUGH...

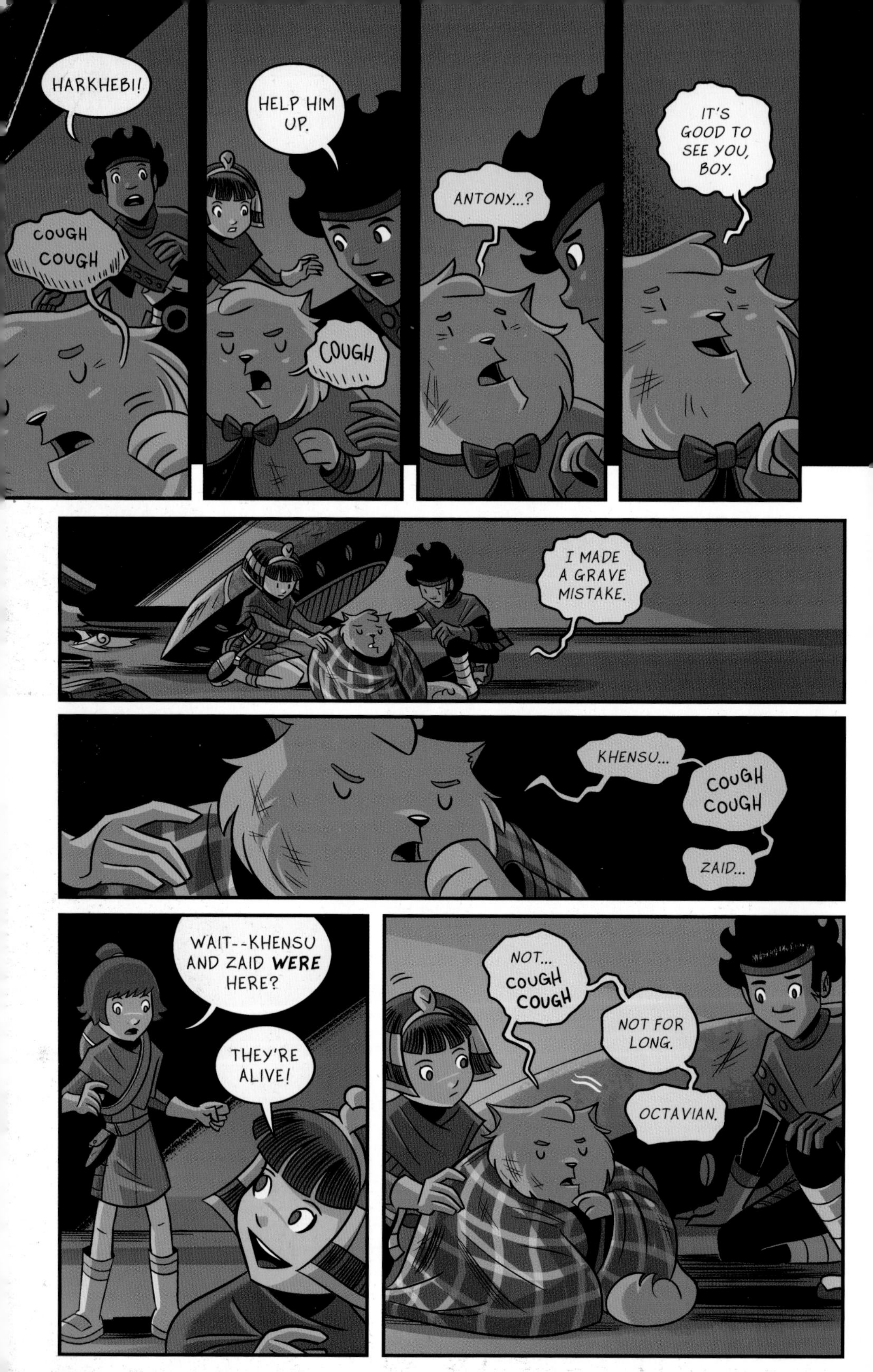
HARKHEBI!
COUGH COUGH
HELP HIM UP.
COUGH
ANTONY...?
IT'S GOOD TO SEE YOU, BOY.
I MADE A GRAVE MISTAKE.
KHENSU...
COUGH COUGH
ZAID...
WAIT--KHENSU AND ZAID **WERE** HERE?
THEY'RE ALIVE!
NOT...
COUGH **COUGH**
NOT FOR LONG.
OCTAVIAN.

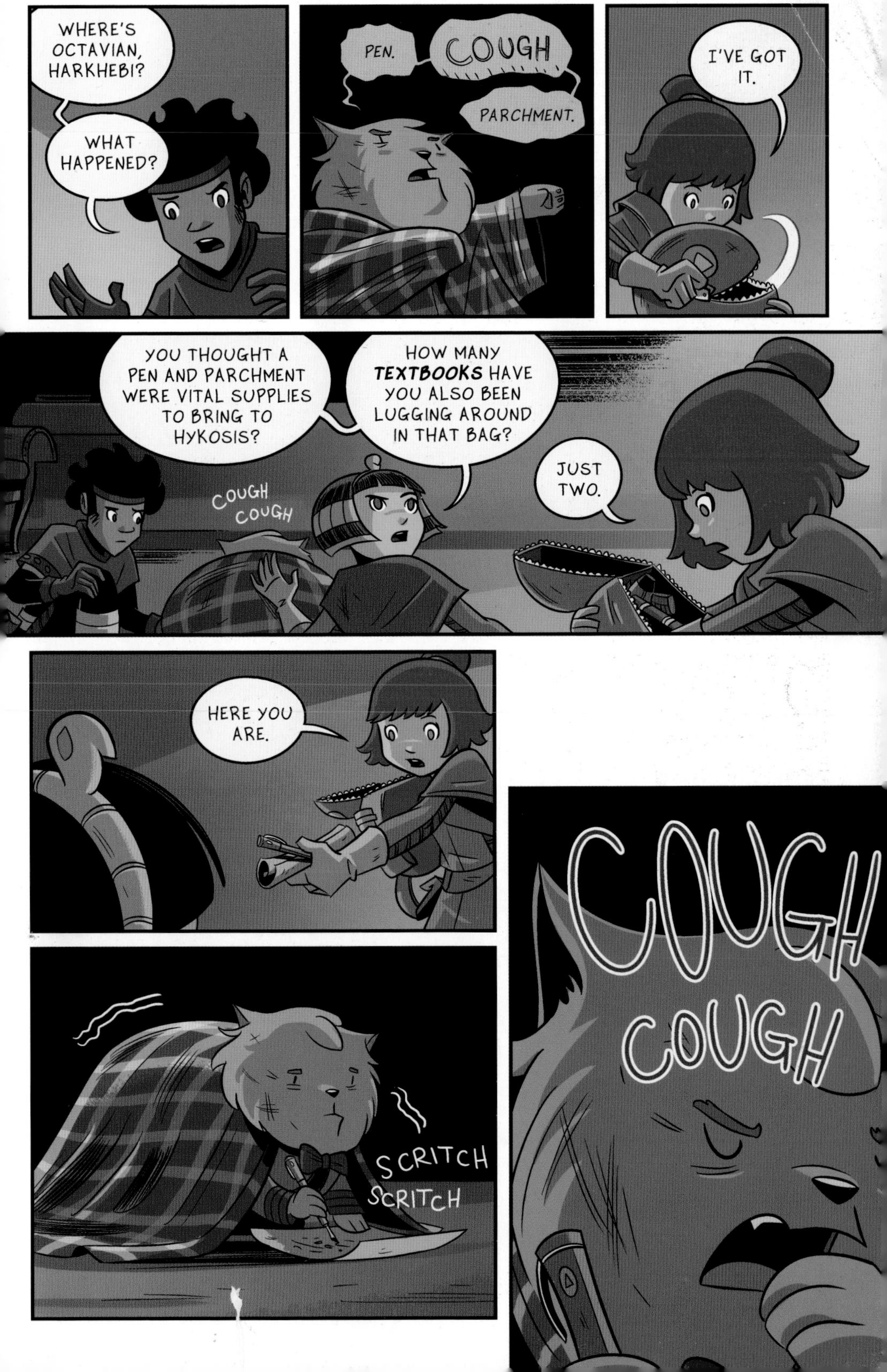
WHERE'S OCTAVIAN, HARKHEBI?
WHAT HAPPENED?
PEN.
COUGH
PARCHMENT.
I'VE GOT IT.
YOU THOUGHT A PEN AND PARCHMENT WERE VITAL SUPPLIES TO BRING TO HYKOSIS?
HOW MANY TEXTBOOKS HAVE YOU ALSO BEEN LUGGING AROUND IN THAT BAG?
COUGH COUGH
JUST TWO.
HERE YOU ARE.
SCRITCH
SCRITCH
COUGH
COUGH

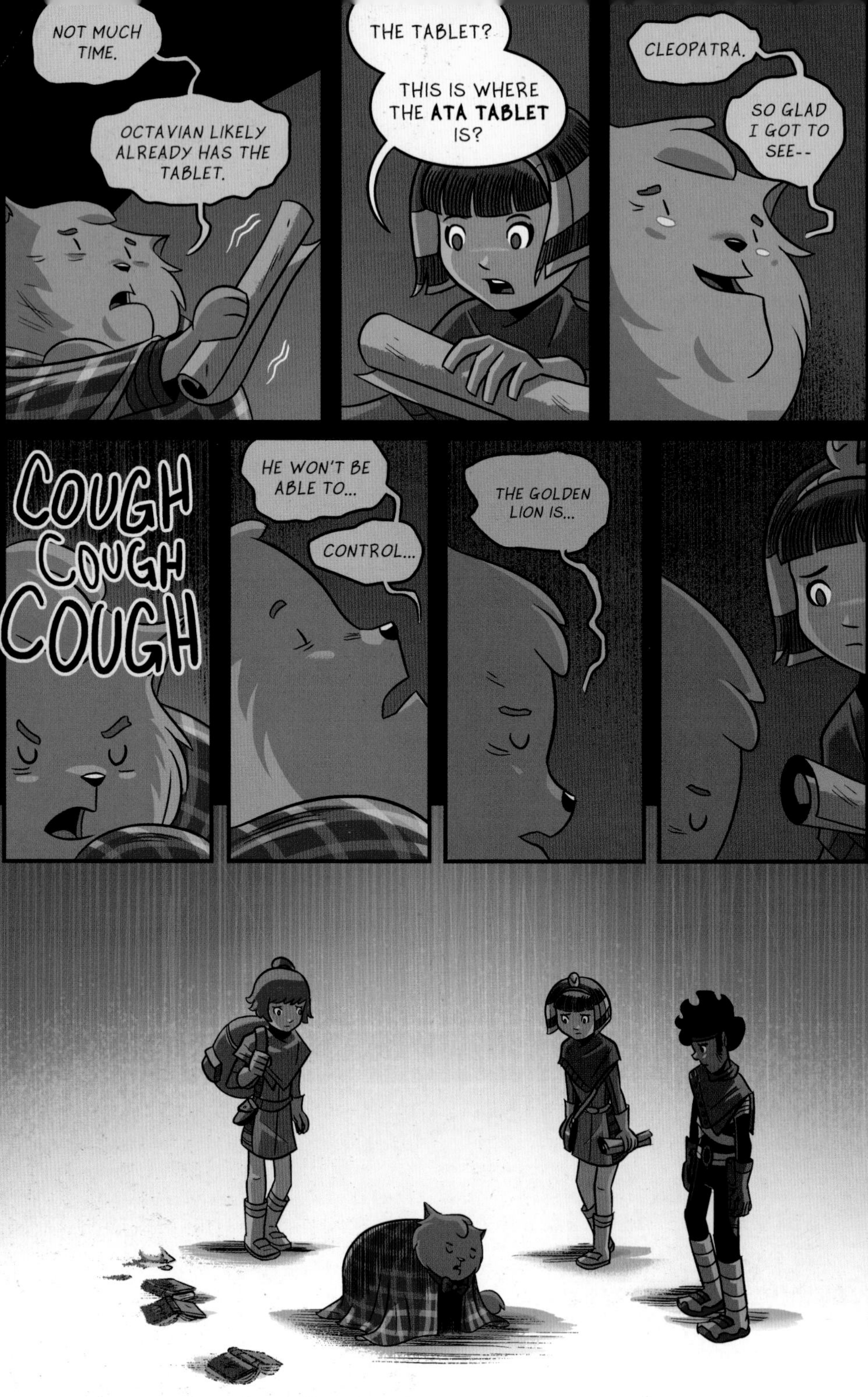
NOT MUCH TIME.
OCTAVIAN LIKELY ALREADY HAS THE TABLET.
THE TABLET?
THIS IS WHERE THE **ATA TABLET** IS?
CLEOPATRA.
SO GLAD I GOT TO SEE--
COUGH COUGH COUGH
HE WON'T BE ABLE TO...
CONTROL...
THE GOLDEN LION IS...

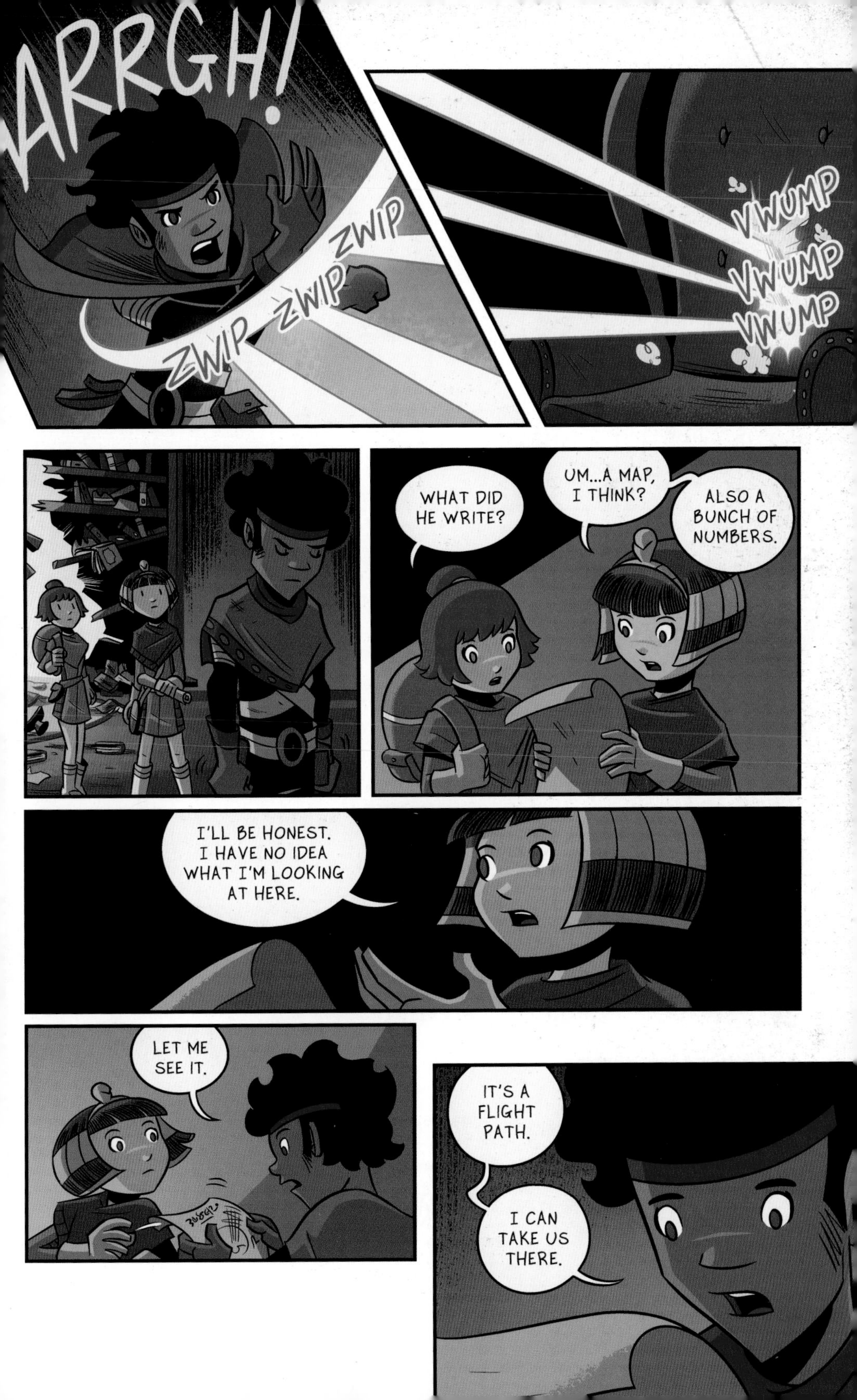
ARRGH!
ZWIP ZWIP ZWIP
VWUMP
VWUMP
VWUMP
WHAT DID HE WRITE?
UM...A MAP, I THINK?
ALSO A BUNCH OF NUMBERS.
I'LL BE HONEST. I HAVE NO IDEA WHAT I'M LOOKING AT HERE.
LET ME SEE IT.
IT'S A FLIGHT PATH.
I CAN TAKE US THERE.

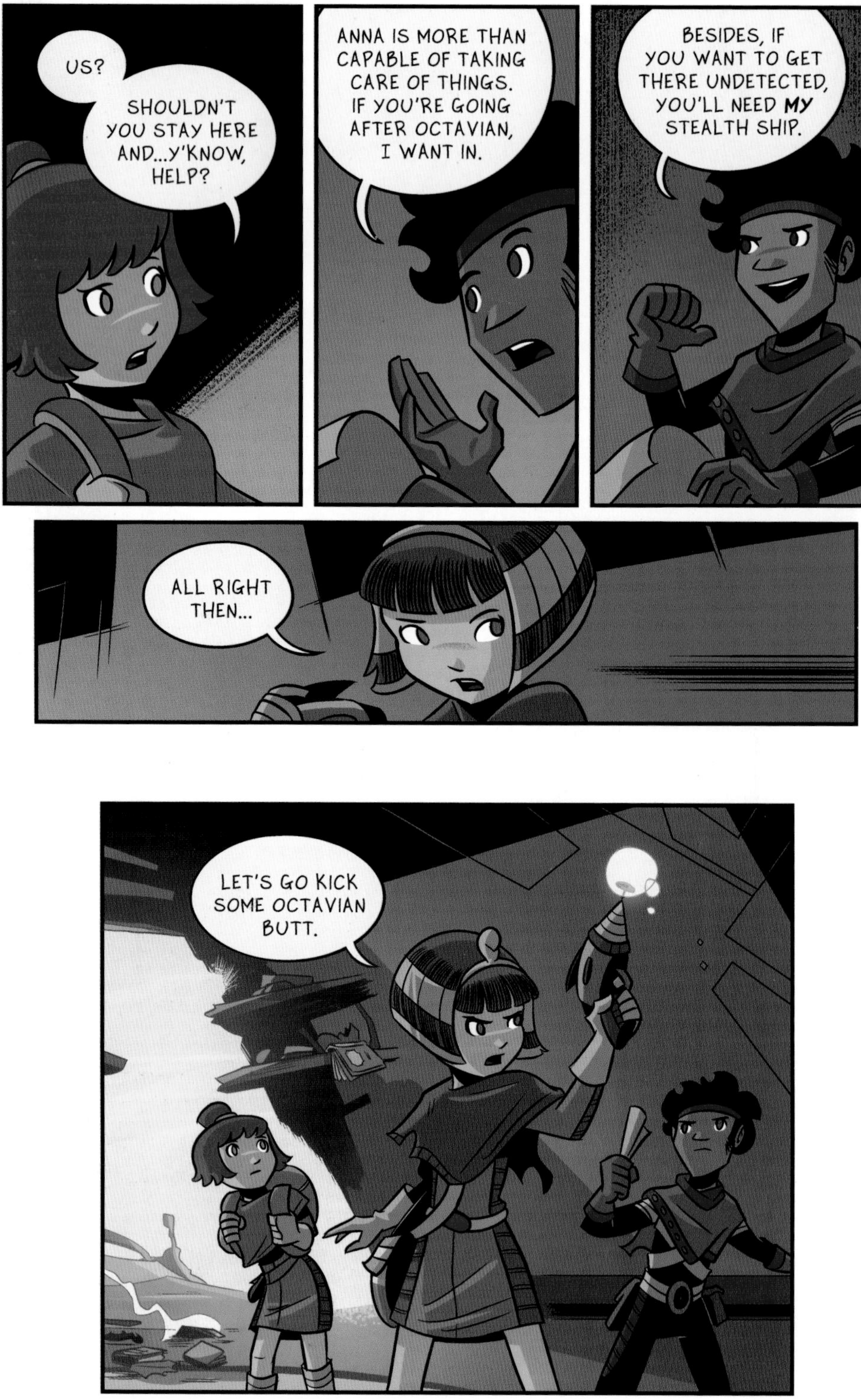
US?
SHOULDN'T YOU STAY HERE AND...Y'KNOW, HELP?
ANNA IS MORE THAN CAPABLE OF TAKING CARE OF THINGS. IF YOU'RE GOING AFTER OCTAVIAN, I WANT IN.
BESIDES, IF YOU WANT TO GET THERE UNDETECTED, YOU'LL NEED **MY** STEALTH SHIP.
ALL RIGHT THEN...
LET'S GO KICK SOME OCTAVIAN BUTT.

CHAPTER THREE

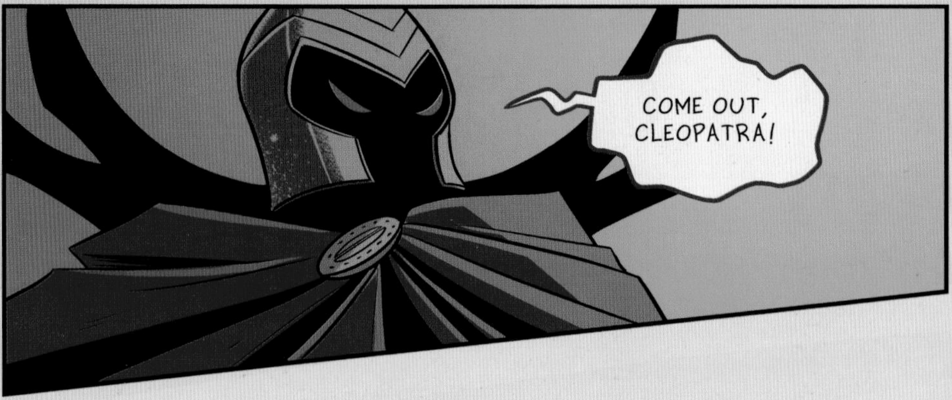
COME OUT, CLEOPATRA!

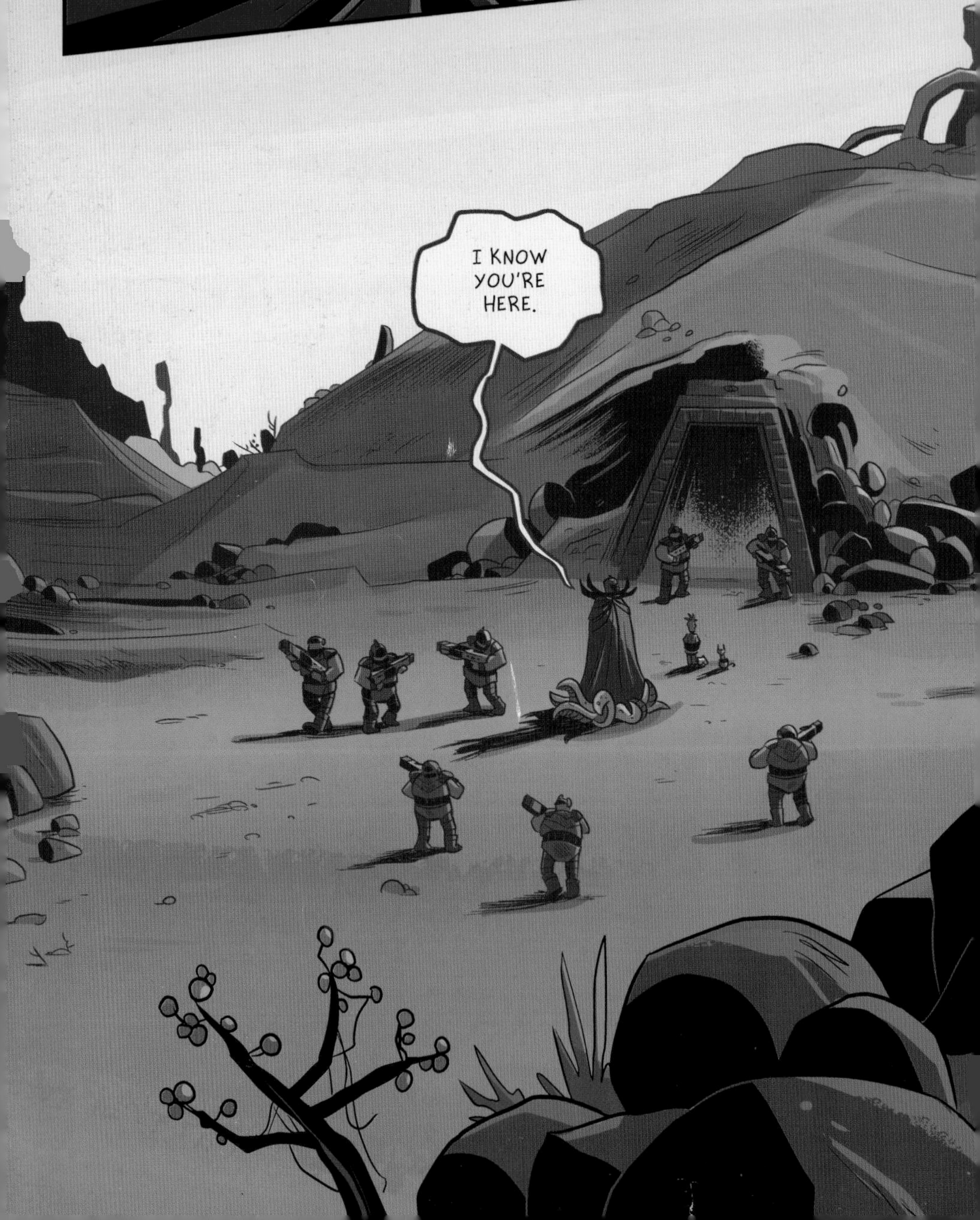
I KNOW YOU'RE HERE.

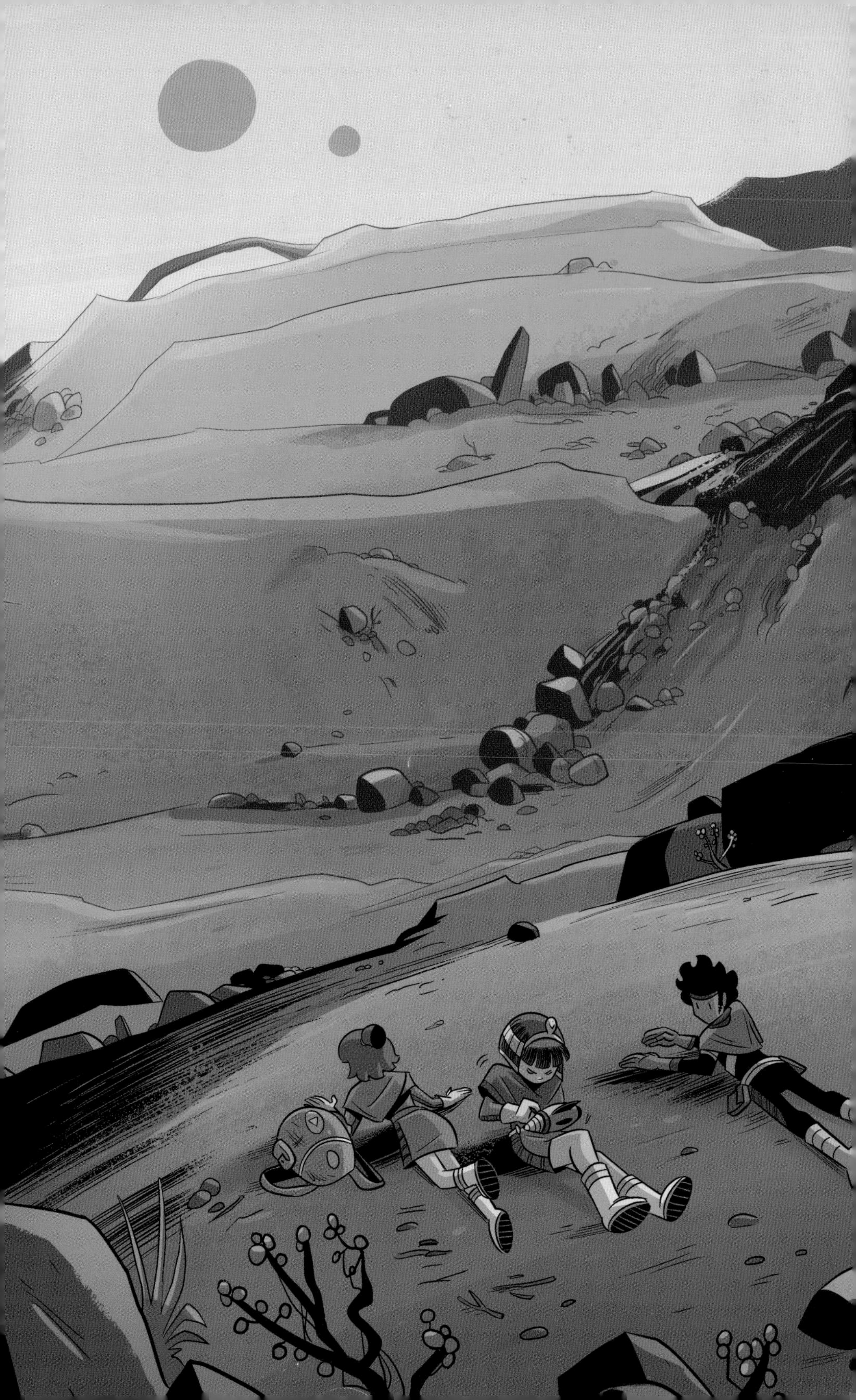

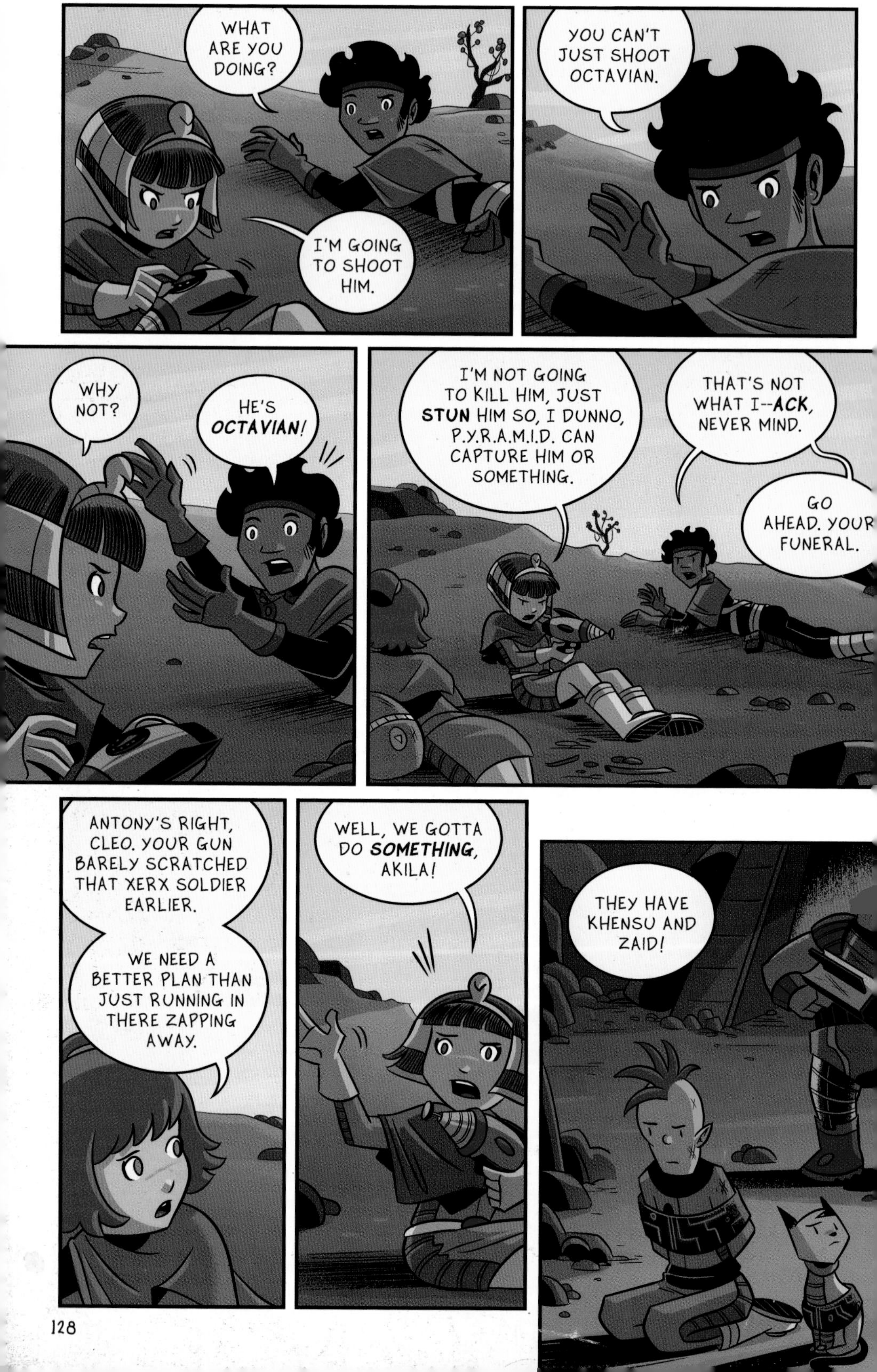
WHAT ARE YOU DOING?
I'M GOING TO SHOOT HIM.
YOU CAN'T JUST SHOOT OCTAVIAN.
WHY NOT?
HE'S OCTAVIAN!
I'M NOT GOING TO KILL HIM, JUST STUN HIM SO, I DUNNO, P.Y.R.A.M.I.D. CAN CAPTURE HIM OR SOMETHING.
THAT'S NOT WHAT I--ACK, NEVER MIND.
GO AHEAD. YOUR FUNERAL.
ANTONY'S RIGHT, CLEO. YOUR GUN BARELY SCRATCHED THAT XERX SOLDIER EARLIER.
WE NEED A BETTER PLAN THAN JUST RUNNING IN THERE ZAPPING AWAY.
WELL, WE GOTTA DO SOMETHING, AKILA!
THEY HAVE KHENSU AND ZAID!

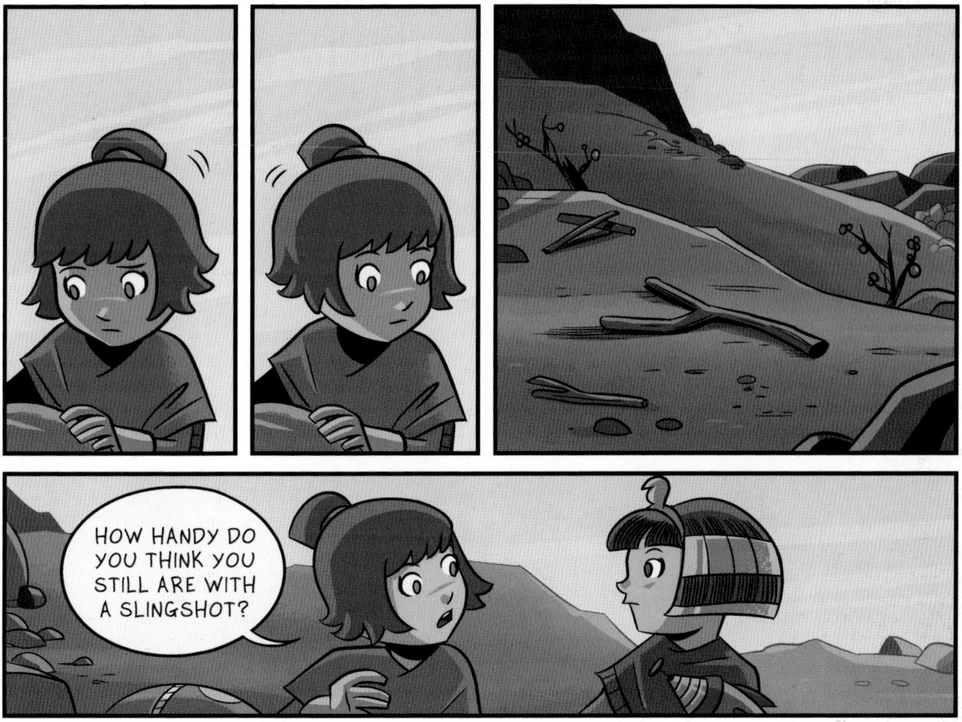
HOW HANDY DO YOU THINK YOU STILL ARE WITH A SLINGSHOT?

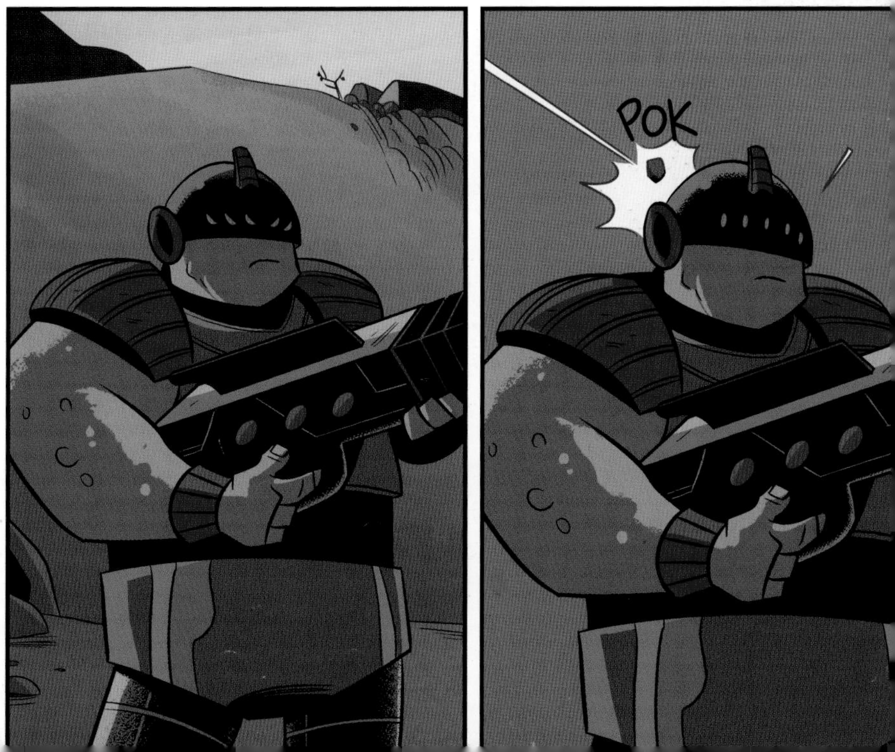
POK

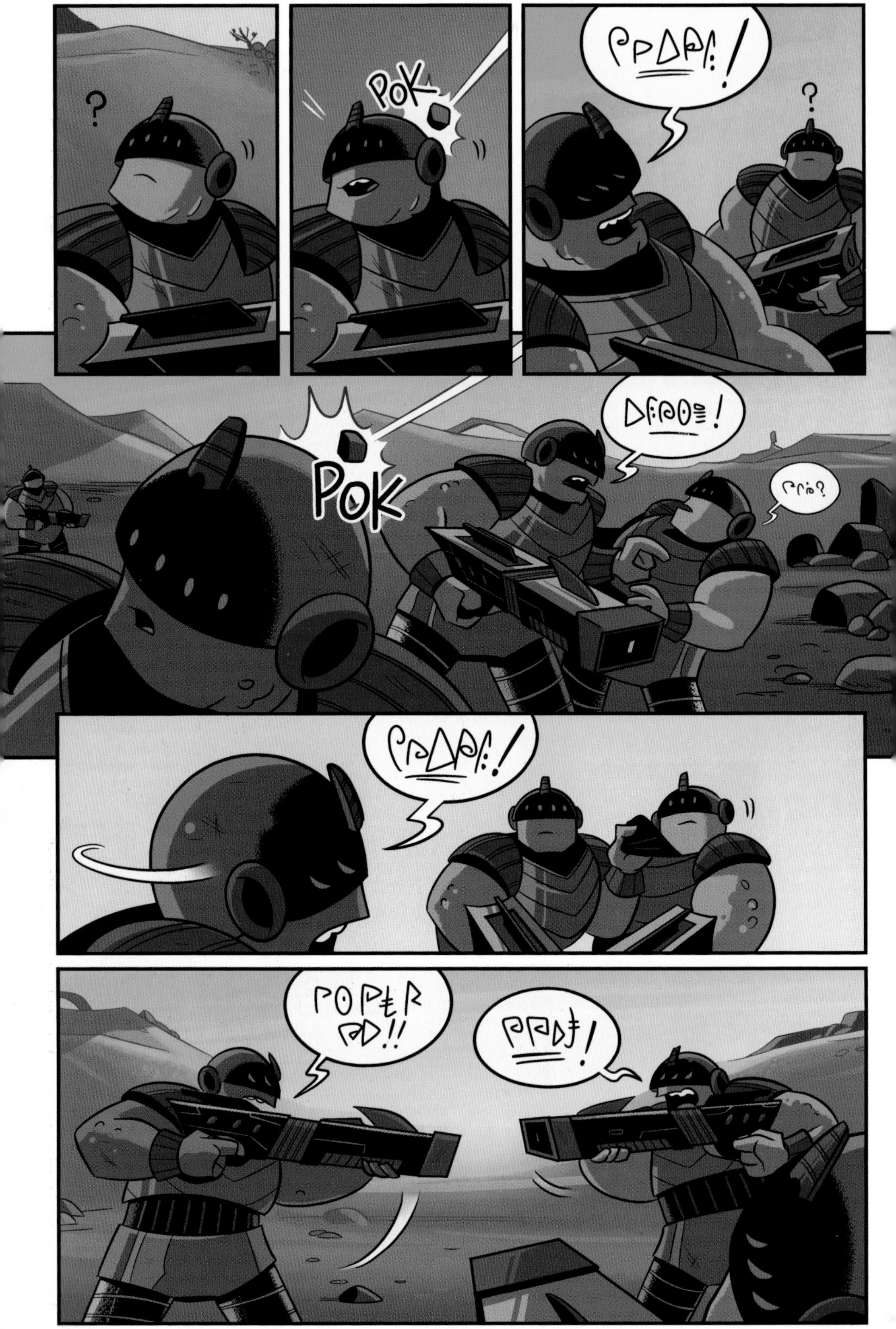
?
POK
?
POK

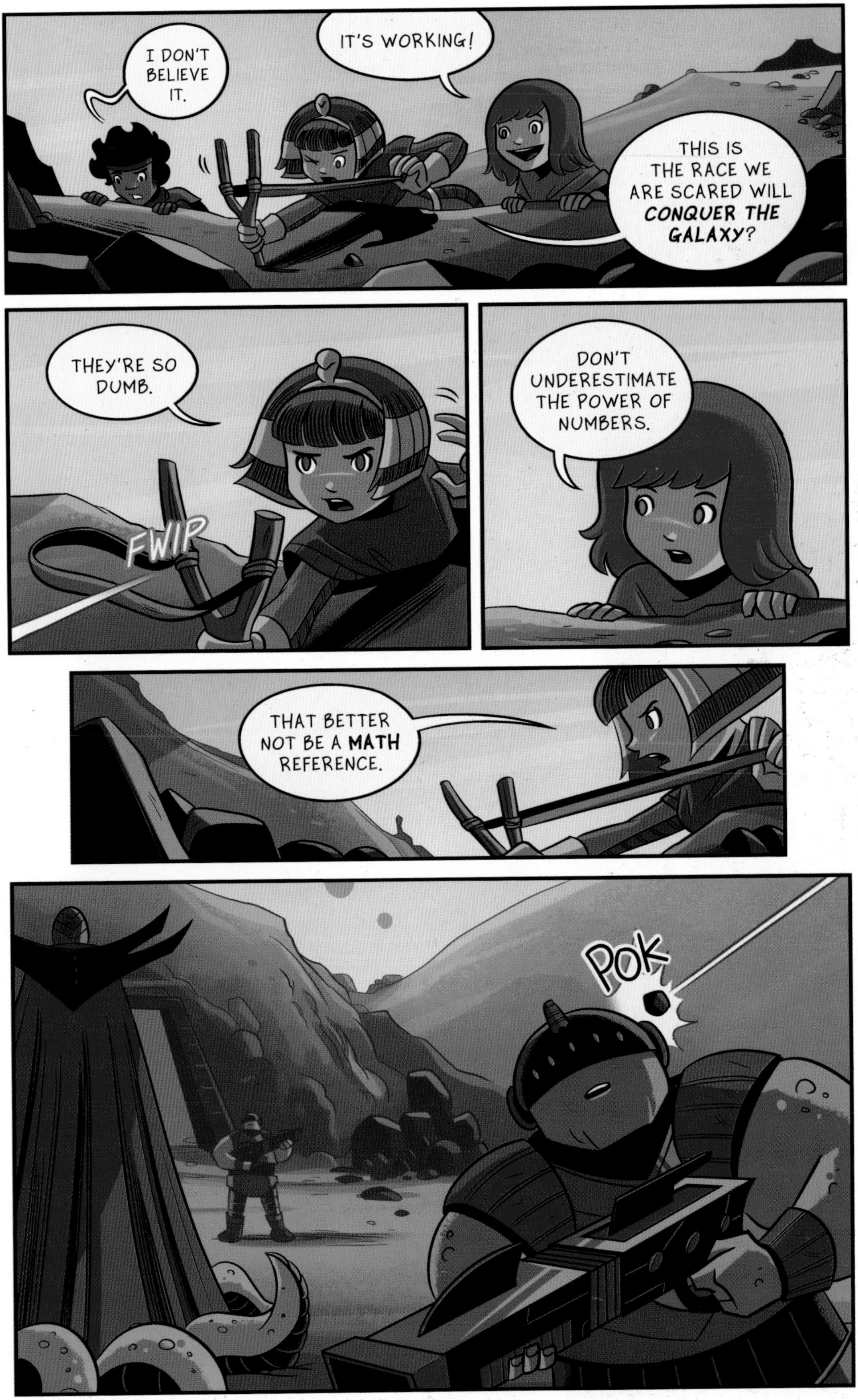
I DON'T BELIEVE IT.
IT'S WORKING!
THIS IS THE RACE WE ARE SCARED WILL **CONQUER THE GALAXY**?
THEY'RE SO DUMB.
FWIP
DON'T UNDERESTIMATE THE POWER OF NUMBERS.
THAT BETTER NOT BE A **MATH** REFERENCE.
POK

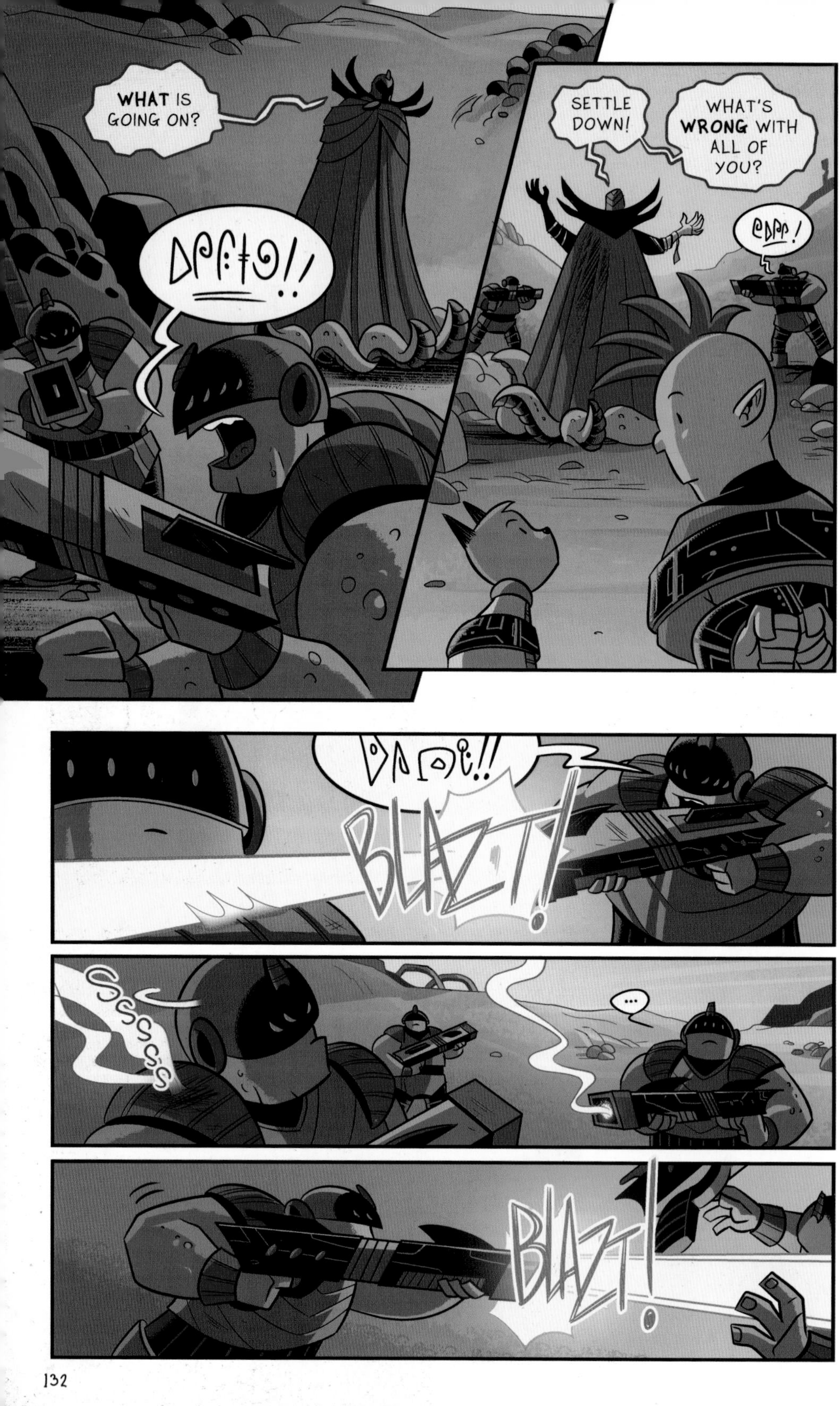
WHAT IS GOING ON?
SETTLE DOWN!
WHAT'S WRONG WITH ALL OF YOU?
BLAZT!
SSSSSS
...
BLAZT!

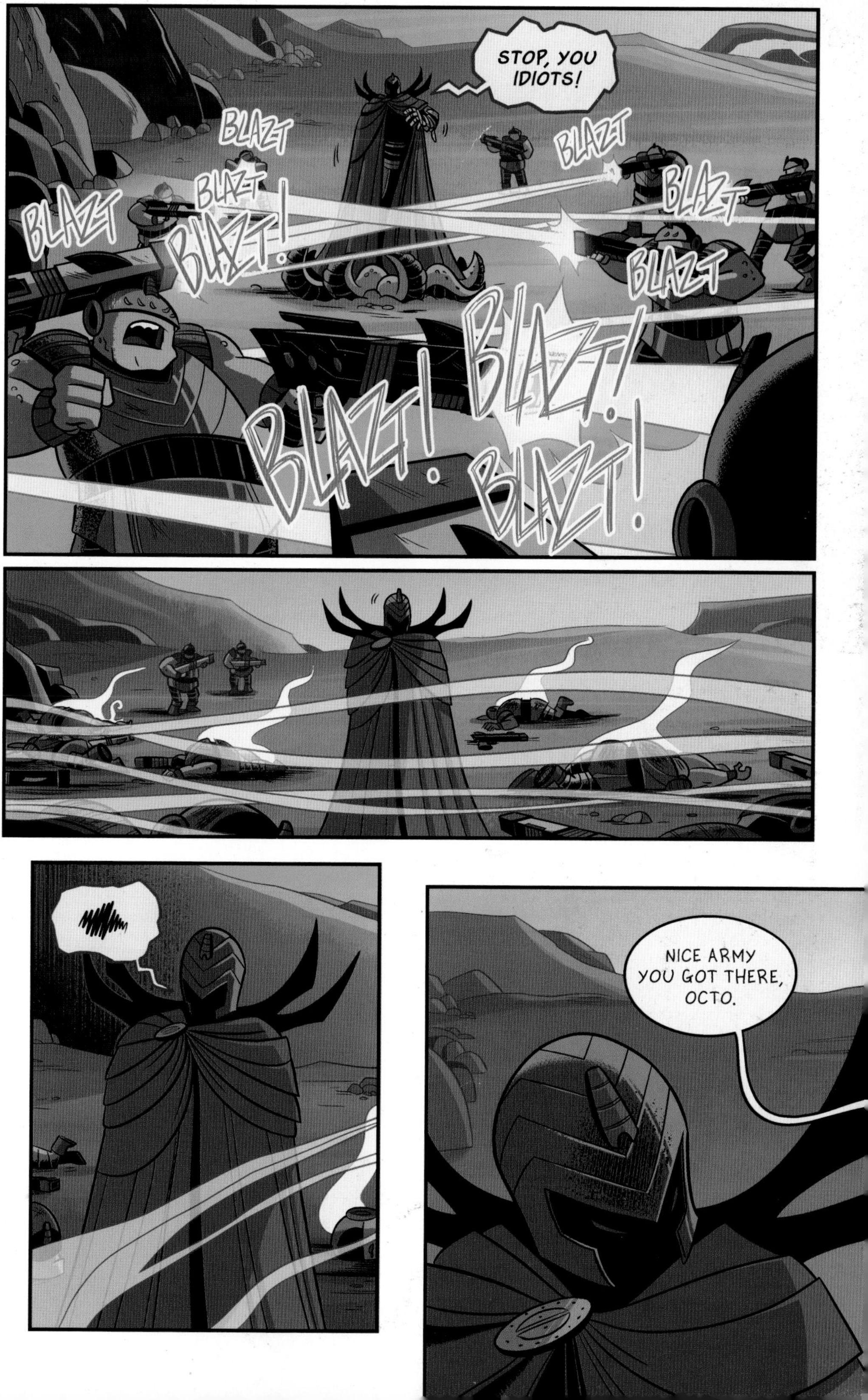
STOP, YOU IDIOTS!
BLAZT
BLAZT
BLAZT
BLAZT!
BLAZT
BLAZT
BLAZT
BLAZT! BLAZT! BLAZT!
NICE ARMY YOU GOT THERE, OCTO.

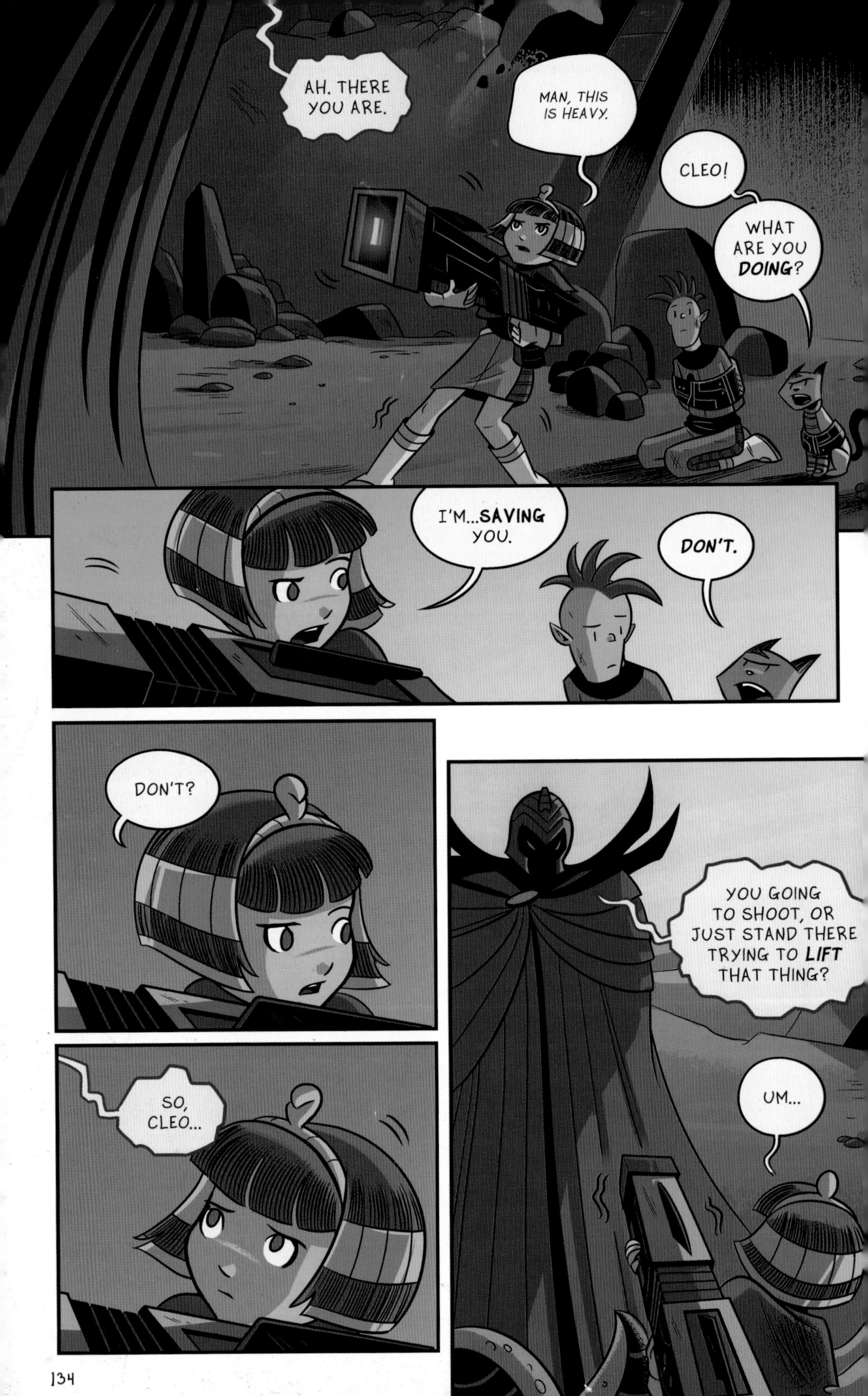
AH. THERE YOU ARE.
MAN, THIS IS HEAVY.
CLEO!
WHAT ARE YOU **DOING**?
I'M...**SAVING** YOU.
DON'T.
DON'T?
YOU GOING TO SHOOT, OR JUST STAND THERE TRYING TO **LIFT** THAT THING?
SO, CLEO...
UM...

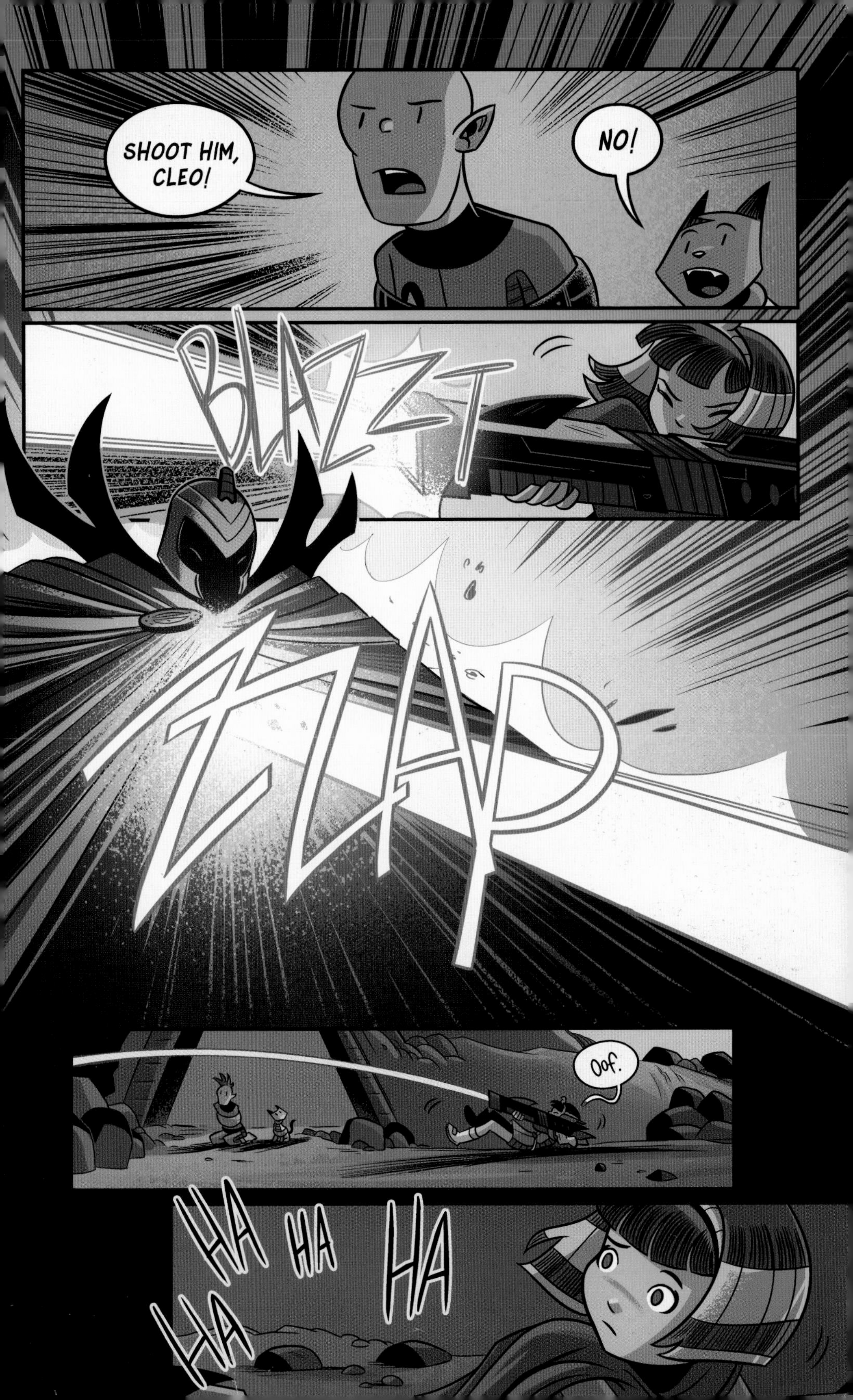
SHOOT HIM, CLEO!
NO!
BLAZZT
ZZAP
Oof.
HA HA HA HA

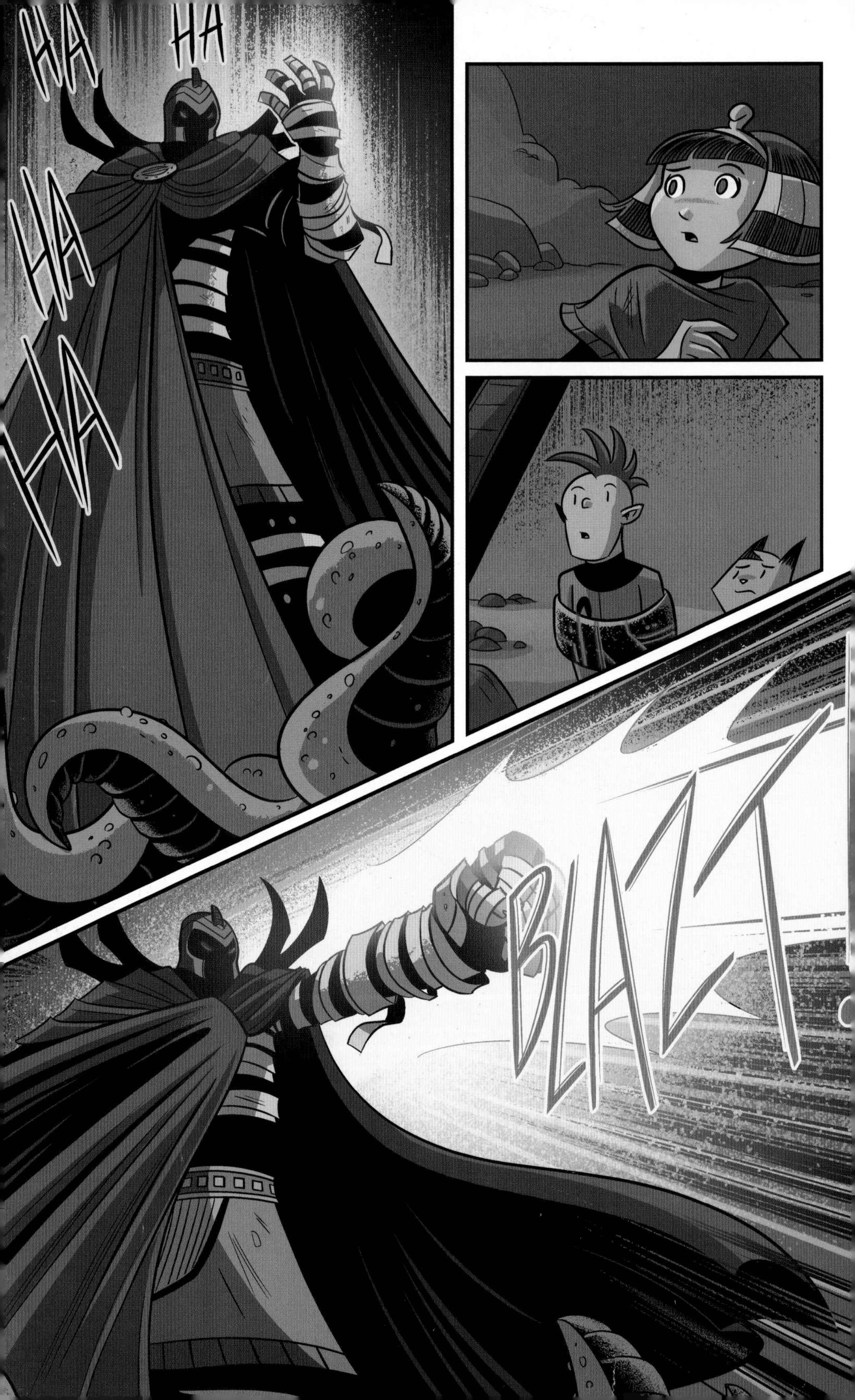
HA HA
HA
HA
BLAZT

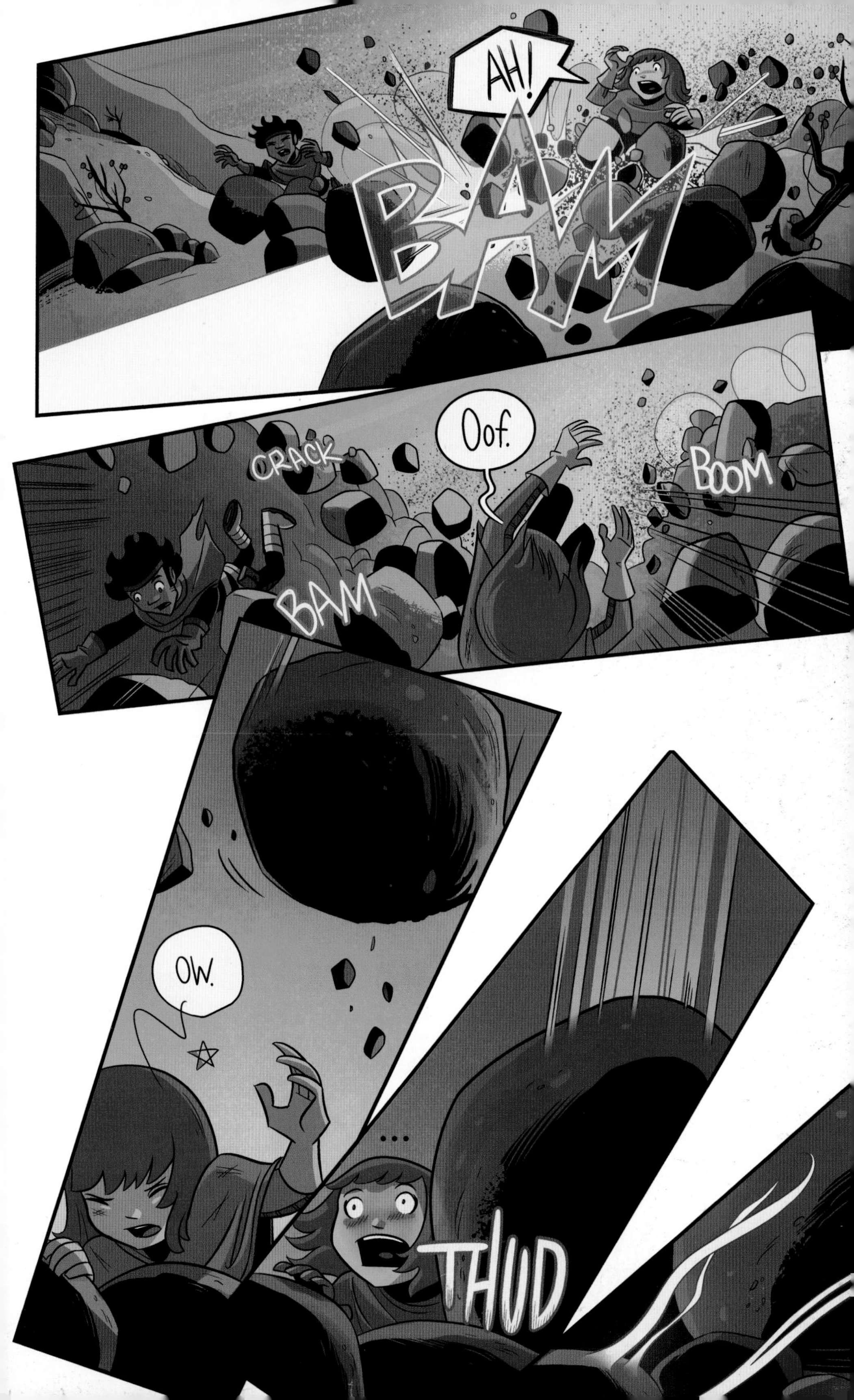
AH!
BAM
CRACK
Oof.
BOOM
BAM
OW.
...
THUD

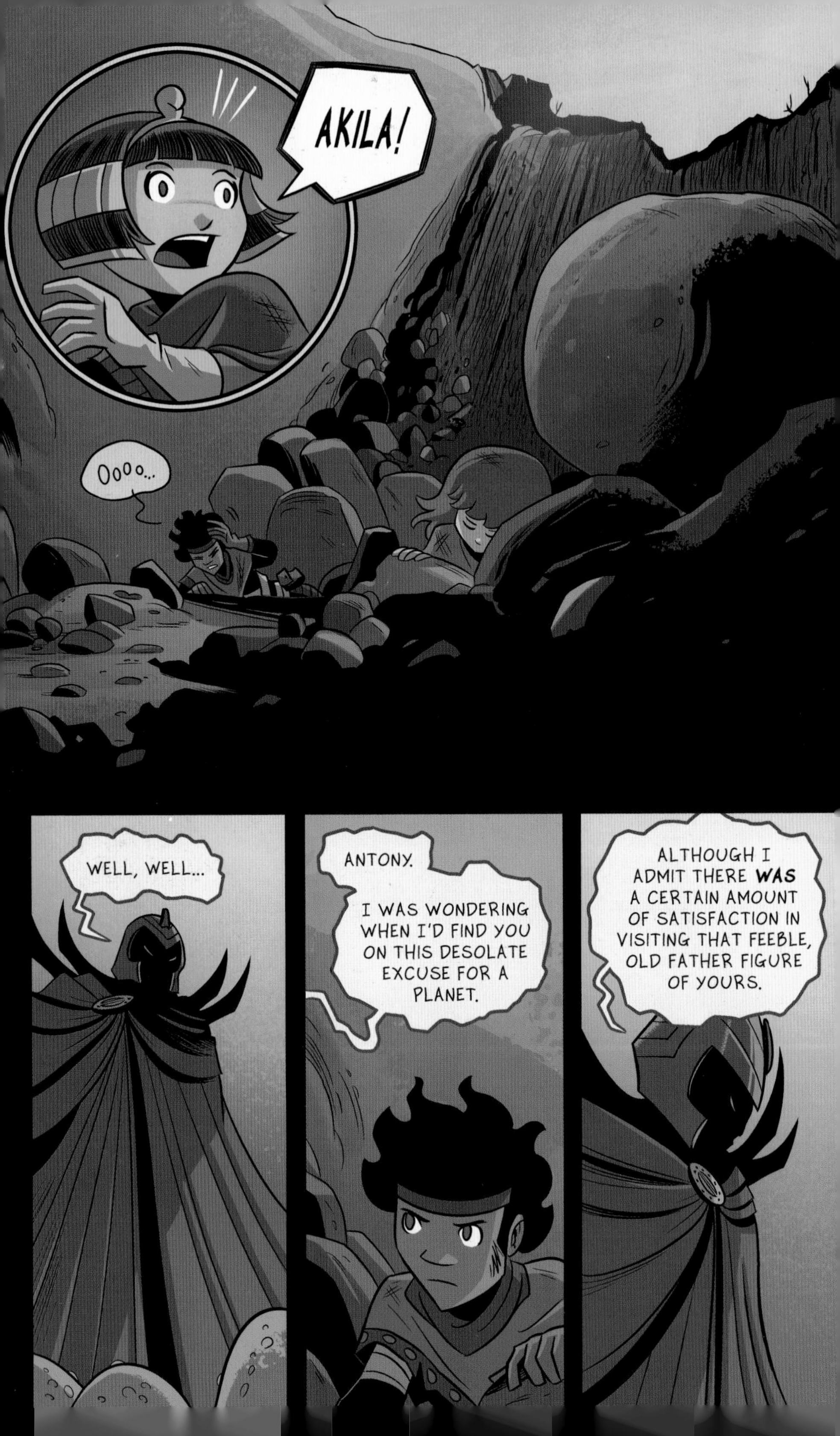
AKILA!
Oooo...
WELL, WELL...
ANTONY.
I WAS WONDERING WHEN I'D FIND YOU ON THIS DESOLATE EXCUSE FOR A PLANET.
ALTHOUGH I ADMIT THERE **WAS** A CERTAIN AMOUNT OF SATISFACTION IN VISITING THAT FEEBLE, OLD FATHER FIGURE OF YOURS.

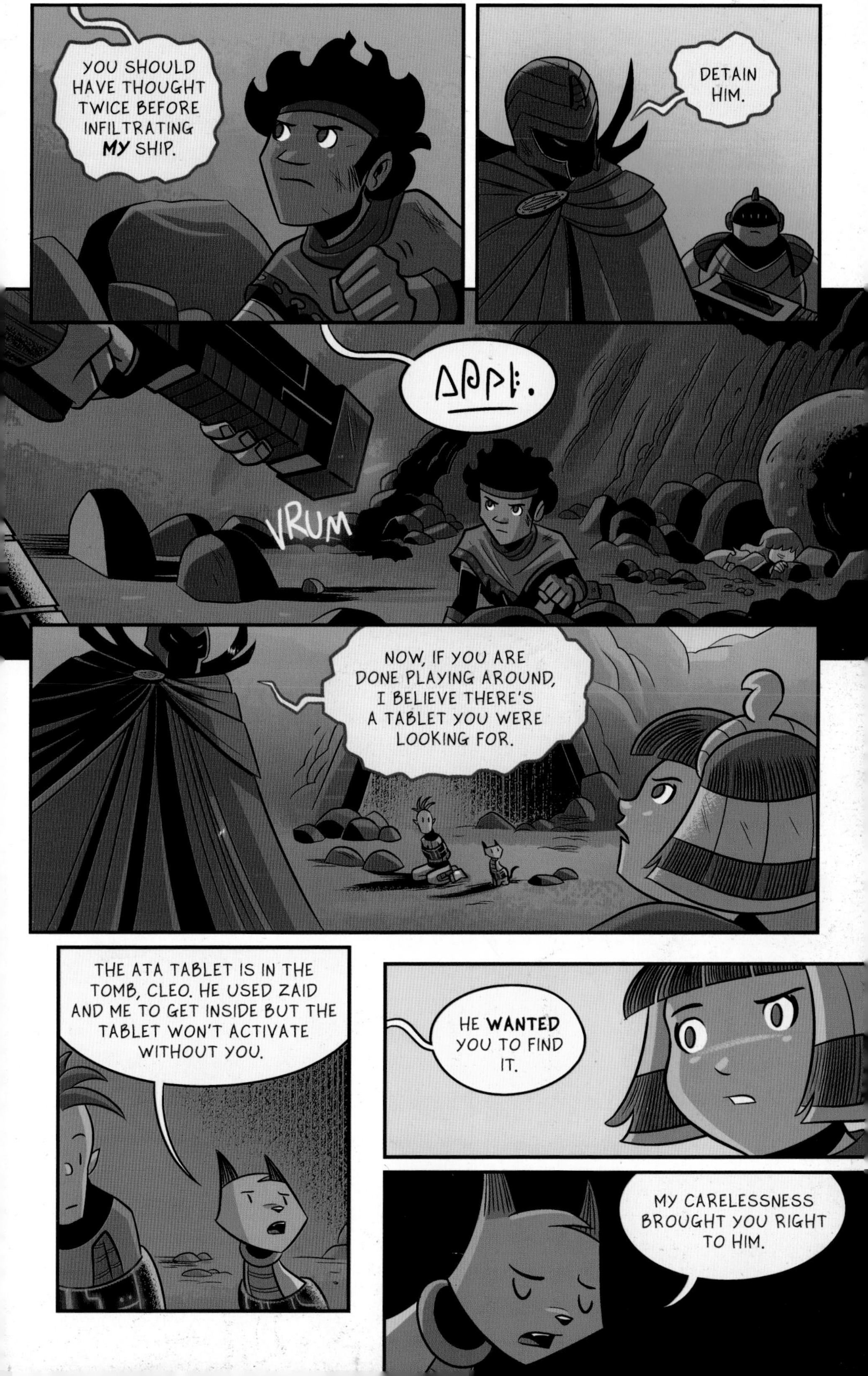
YOU SHOULD HAVE THOUGHT TWICE BEFORE INFILTRATING **MY** SHIP.
DETAIN HIM.
VRUM
NOW, IF YOU ARE DONE PLAYING AROUND, I BELIEVE THERE'S A TABLET YOU WERE LOOKING FOR.
THE ATA TABLET IS IN THE TOMB, CLEO. HE USED ZAID AND ME TO GET INSIDE BUT THE TABLET WON'T ACTIVATE WITHOUT YOU.
HE **WANTED** YOU TO FIND IT.
MY CARELESSNESS BROUGHT YOU RIGHT TO HIM.

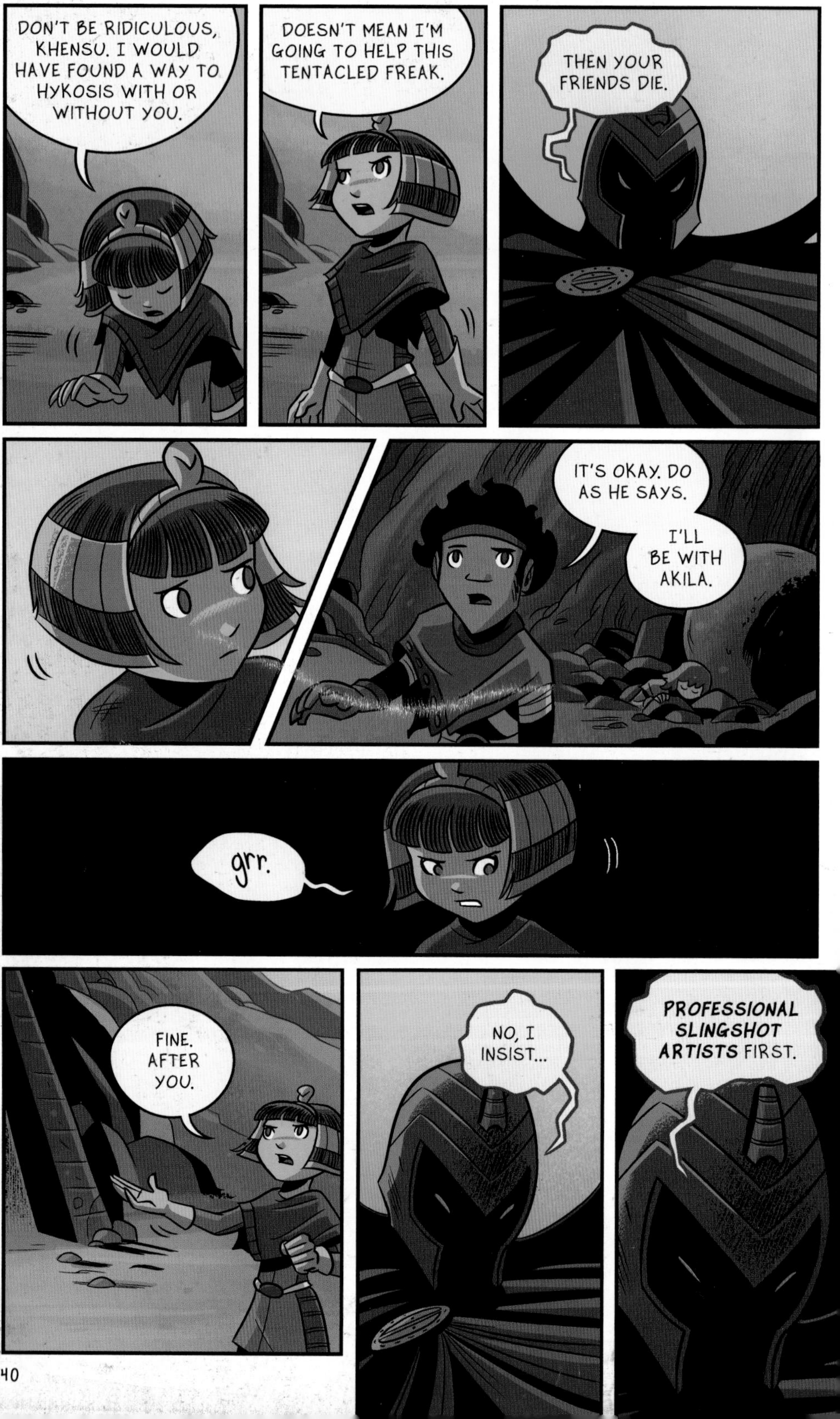
DON'T BE RIDICULOUS, KHENSU. I WOULD HAVE FOUND A WAY TO HYKOSIS WITH OR WITHOUT YOU.
DOESN'T MEAN I'M GOING TO HELP THIS TENTACLED FREAK.
THEN YOUR FRIENDS DIE.
IT'S OKAY. DO AS HE SAYS.
I'LL BE WITH AKILA.
grr.
FINE. AFTER YOU.
NO, I INSIST...
PROFESSIONAL SLINGSHOT ARTISTS FIRST.

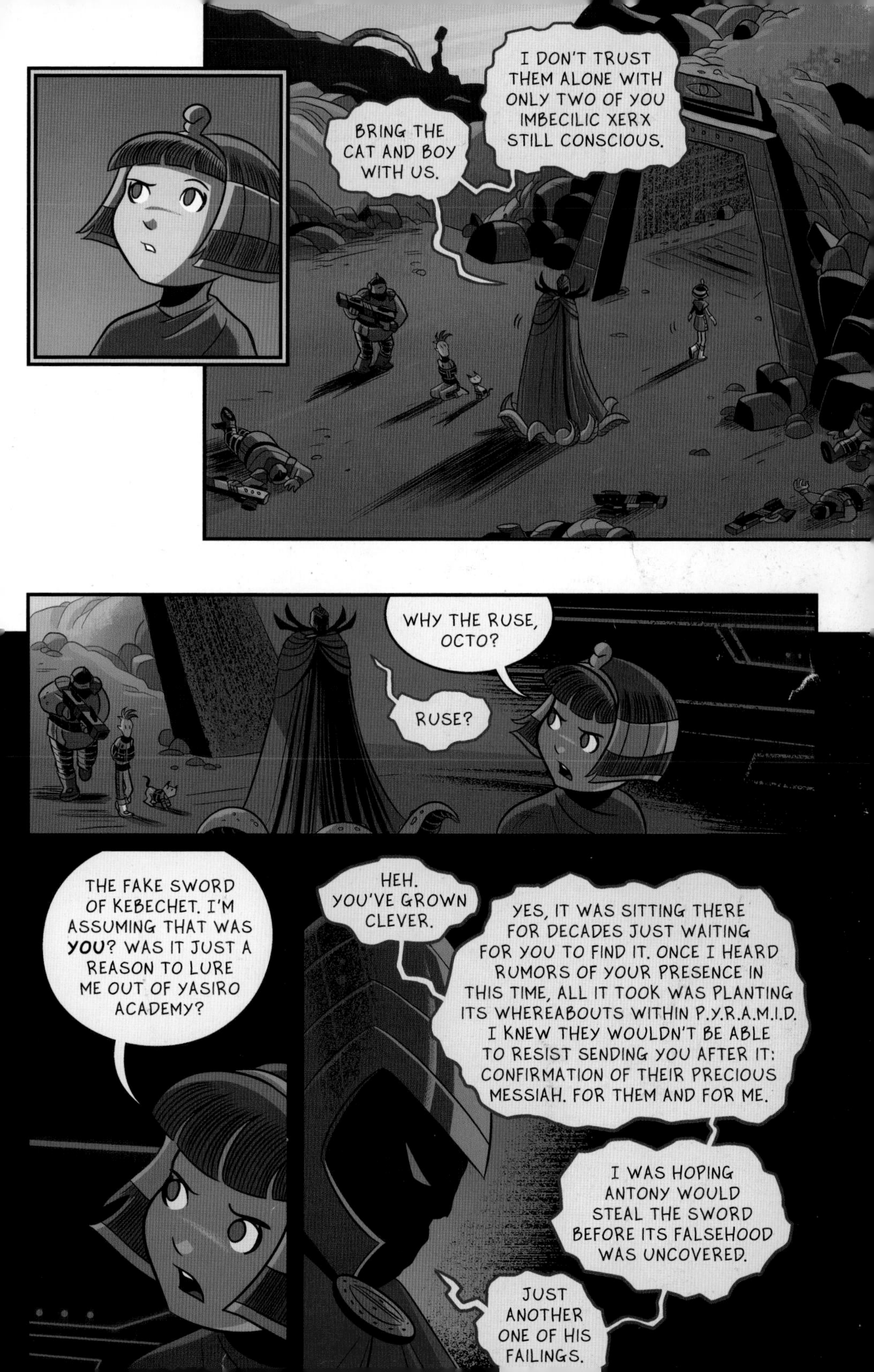
BRING THE CAT AND BOY WITH US.
I DON'T TRUST THEM ALONE WITH ONLY TWO OF YOU IMBECILIC XERX STILL CONSCIOUS.
WHY THE RUSE, OCTO?
RUSE?
THE FAKE SWORD OF KEBECHET. I'M ASSUMING THAT WAS **YOU**? WAS IT JUST A REASON TO LURE ME OUT OF YASIRO ACADEMY?
HEH. YOU'VE GROWN CLEVER.
YES, IT WAS SITTING THERE FOR DECADES JUST WAITING FOR YOU TO FIND IT. ONCE I HEARD RUMORS OF YOUR PRESENCE IN THIS TIME, ALL IT TOOK WAS PLANTING ITS WHEREABOUTS WITHIN P.Y.R.A.M.I.D. I KNEW THEY WOULDN'T BE ABLE TO RESIST SENDING YOU AFTER IT: CONFIRMATION OF THEIR PRECIOUS MESSIAH. FOR THEM AND FOR ME.
I WAS HOPING ANTONY WOULD STEAL THE SWORD BEFORE ITS FALSEHOOD WAS UNCOVERED.
JUST ANOTHER ONE OF HIS FAILINGS.

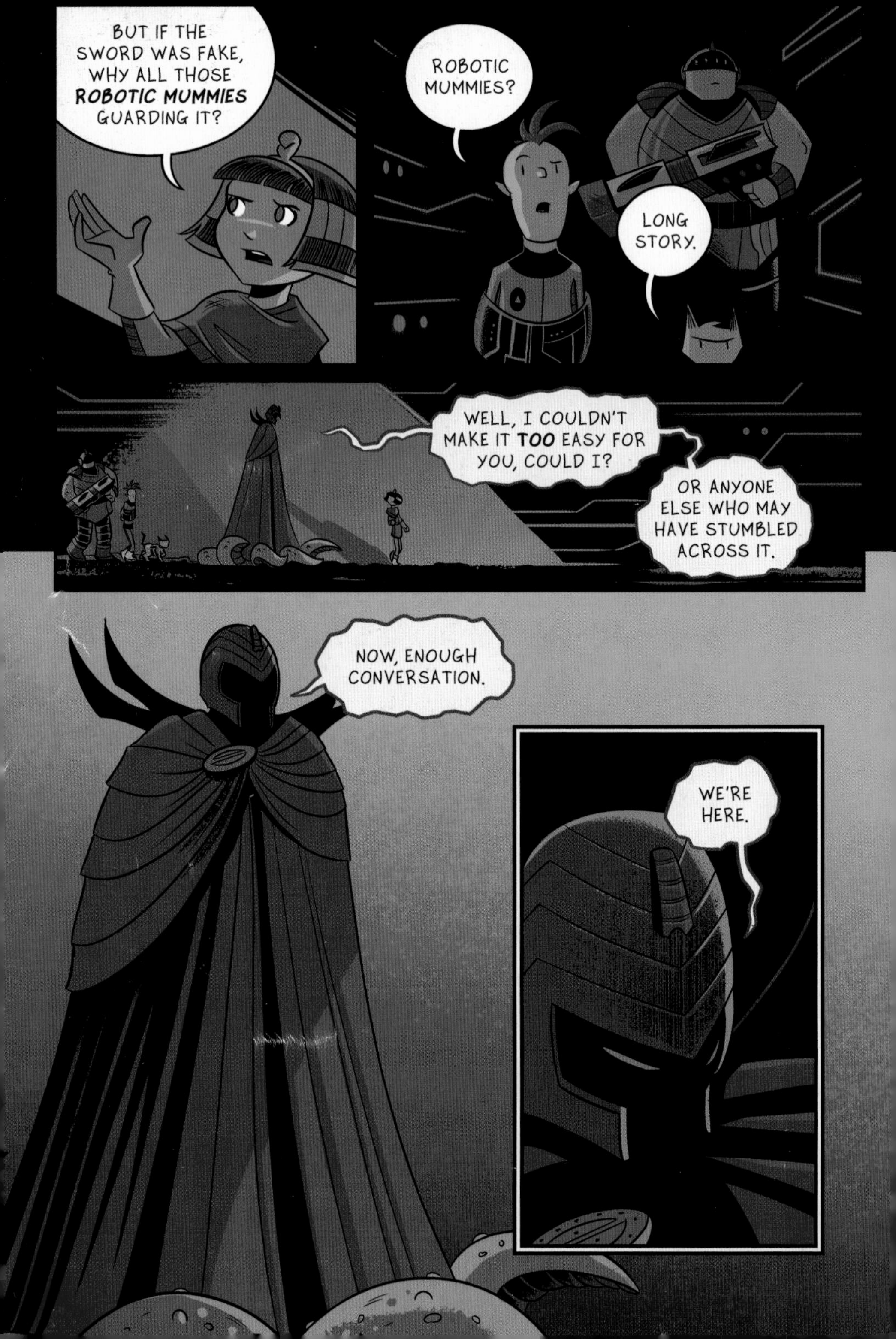
BUT IF THE SWORD WAS FAKE, WHY ALL THOSE **ROBOTIC MUMMIES** GUARDING IT?
ROBOTIC MUMMIES?
LONG STORY.
WELL, I COULDN'T MAKE IT **TOO** EASY FOR YOU, COULD I?
OR ANYONE ELSE WHO MAY HAVE STUMBLED ACROSS IT.
NOW, ENOUGH CONVERSATION.
WE'RE HERE.

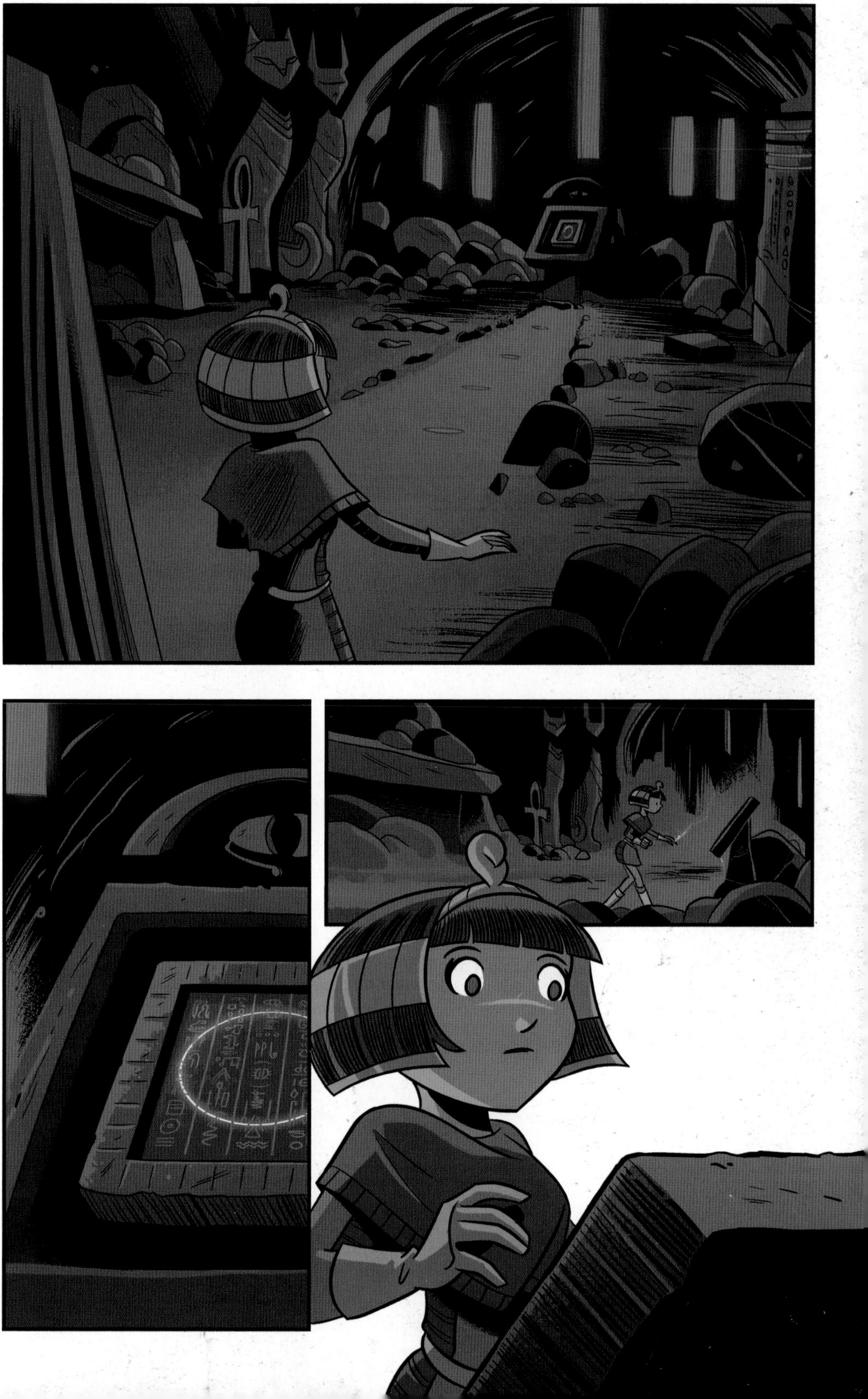

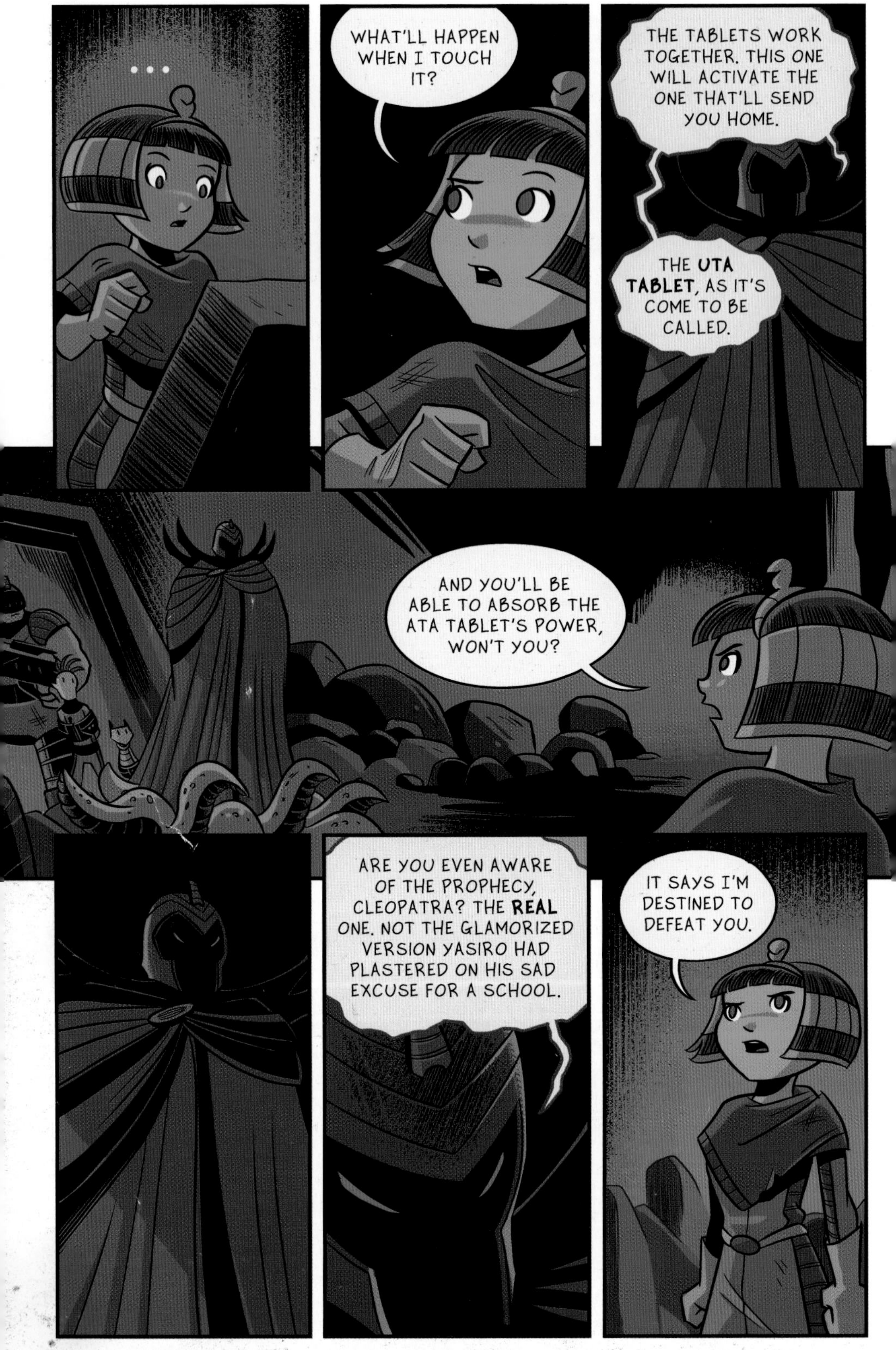
...
WHAT'LL HAPPEN WHEN I TOUCH IT?
THE TABLETS WORK TOGETHER. THIS ONE WILL ACTIVATE THE ONE THAT'LL SEND YOU HOME.
THE **UTA TABLET**, AS IT'S COME TO BE CALLED.
AND YOU'LL BE ABLE TO ABSORB THE ATA TABLET'S POWER, WON'T YOU?
ARE YOU EVEN AWARE OF THE PROPHECY, CLEOPATRA? THE **REAL** ONE. NOT THE GLAMORIZED VERSION YASIRO HAD PLASTERED ON HIS SAD EXCUSE FOR A SCHOOL.
IT SAYS I'M DESTINED TO DEFEAT YOU.

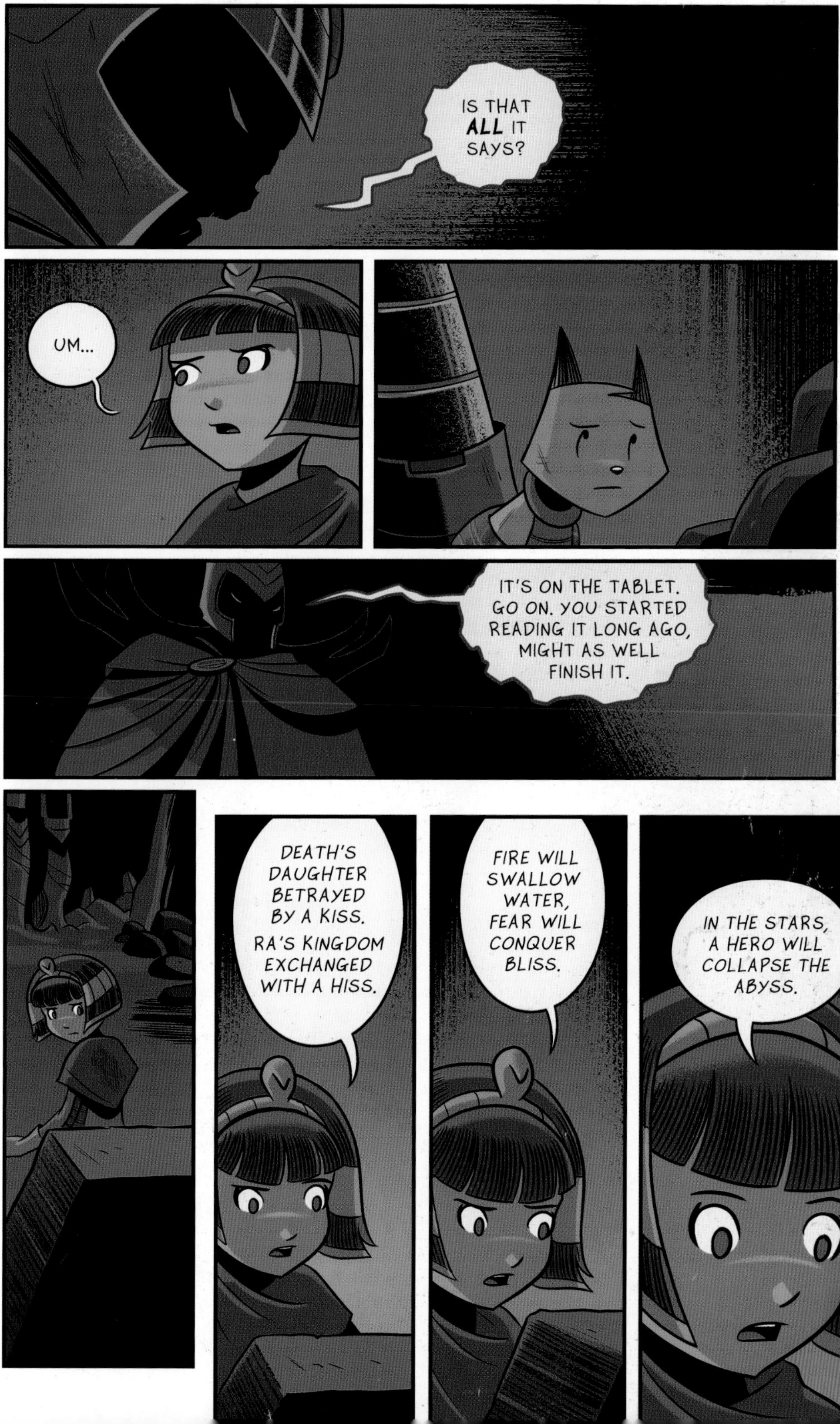
IS THAT ALL IT SAYS?
UM...
IT'S ON THE TABLET. GO ON. YOU STARTED READING IT LONG AGO, MIGHT AS WELL FINISH IT.
DEATH'S DAUGHTER BETRAYED BY A KISS.
RA'S KINGDOM EXCHANGED WITH A HISS.
FIRE WILL SWALLOW WATER, FEAR WILL CONQUER BLISS.
IN THE STARS, A HERO WILL COLLAPSE THE ABYSS.

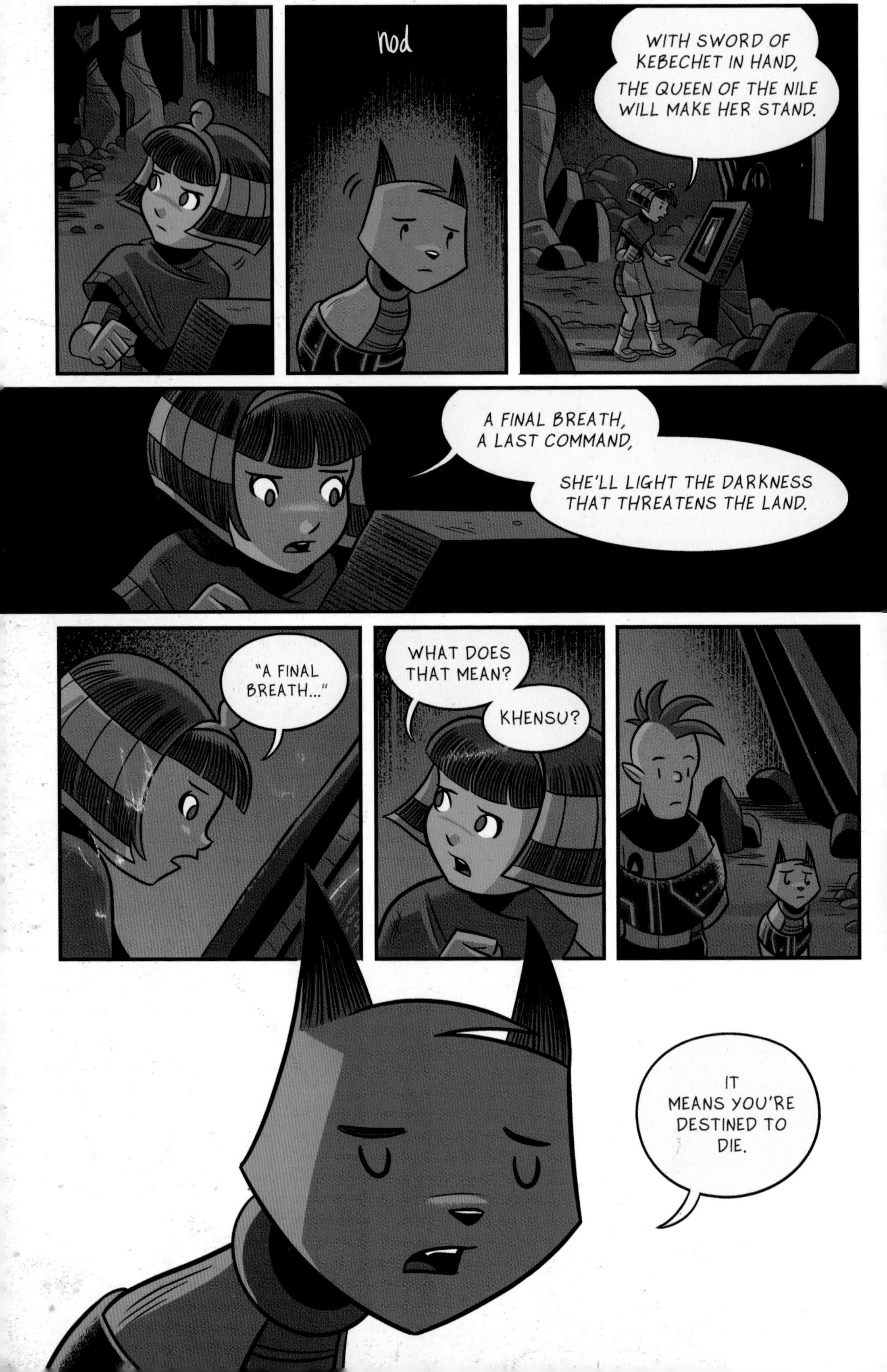
nod
WITH SWORD OF KEBECHET IN HAND,
THE QUEEN OF THE NILE WILL MAKE HER STAND.
A FINAL BREATH, A LAST COMMAND,
SHE'LL LIGHT THE DARKNESS THAT THREATENS THE LAND.
"A FINAL BREATH..."
WHAT DOES THAT MEAN?
KHENSU?
IT MEANS YOU'RE DESTINED TO DIE.

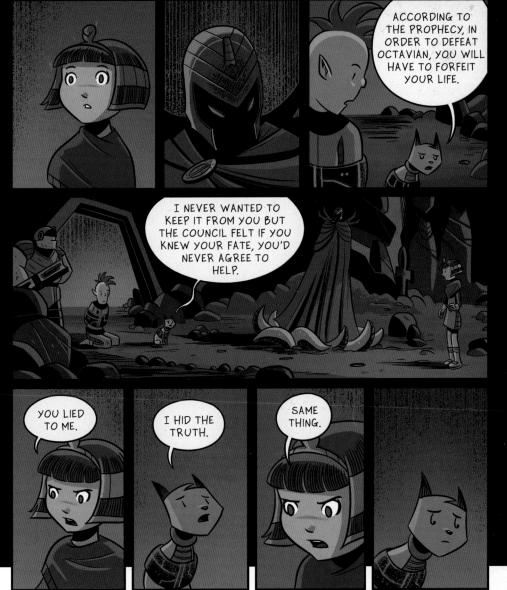

ACCORDING TO THE PROPHECY, IN ORDER TO DEFEAT OCTAVIAN, YOU WILL HAVE TO FORFEIT YOUR LIFE.

I NEVER WANTED TO KEEP IT FROM YOU BUT THE COUNCIL FELT IF YOU KNEW YOUR FATE, YOU'D NEVER AGREE TO HELP.

YOU LIED TO ME.

I HID THE TRUTH.

SAME THING.

ENOUGH.

TIME TO DECIDE, CLEOPATRA. DO YOU WANT TO DIE SAVING A PLACE YOU DON'T EVEN BELONG...

OR GO BACK HOME TO A KINGDOM YOU WERE BORN TO RULE?

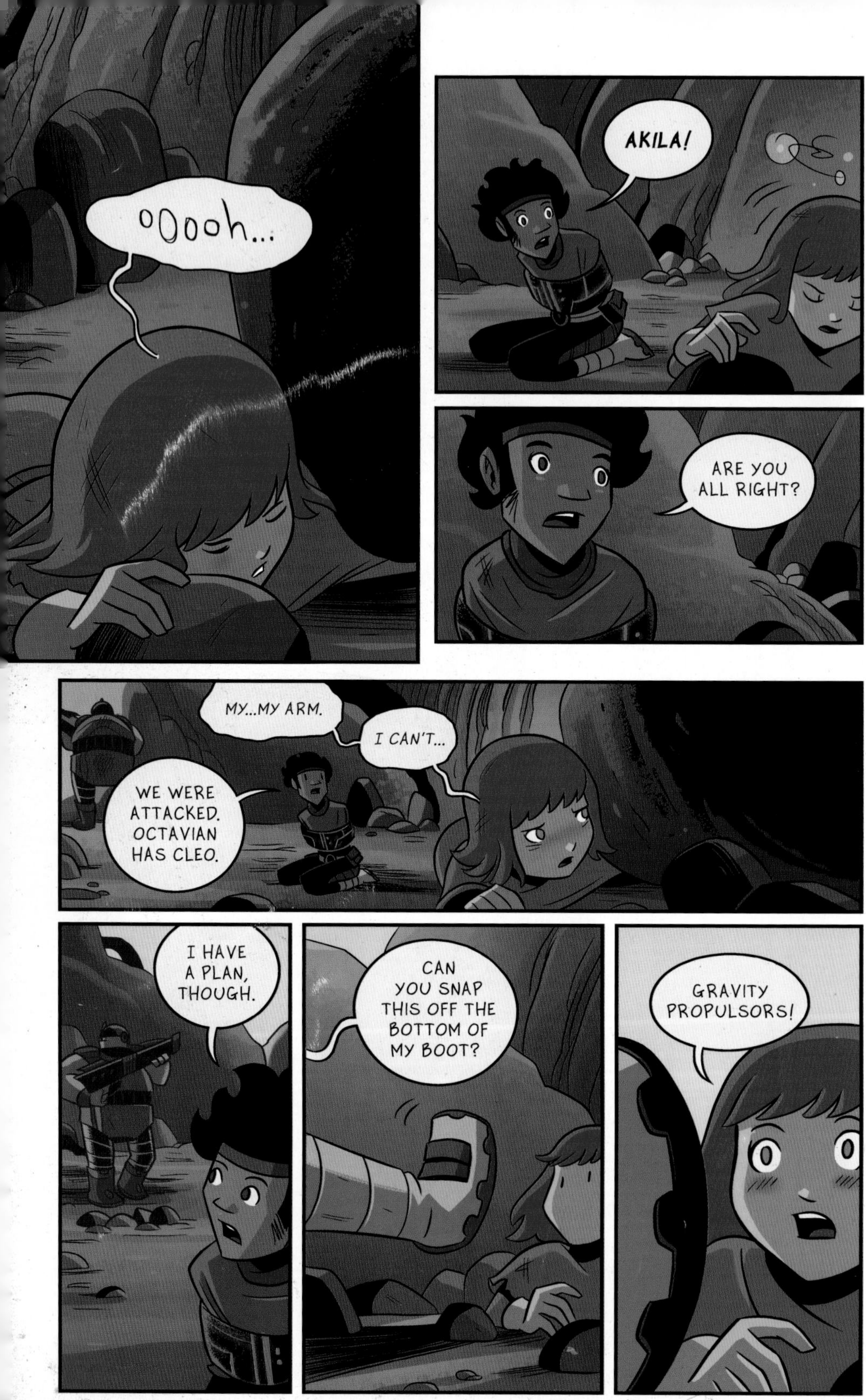
oOooh...
AKILA!
ARE YOU ALL RIGHT?
MY...MY ARM.
I CAN'T...
WE WERE ATTACKED. OCTAVIAN HAS CLEO.
I HAVE A PLAN, THOUGH.
CAN YOU SNAP THIS OFF THE BOTTOM OF MY BOOT?
GRAVITY PROPULSORS!

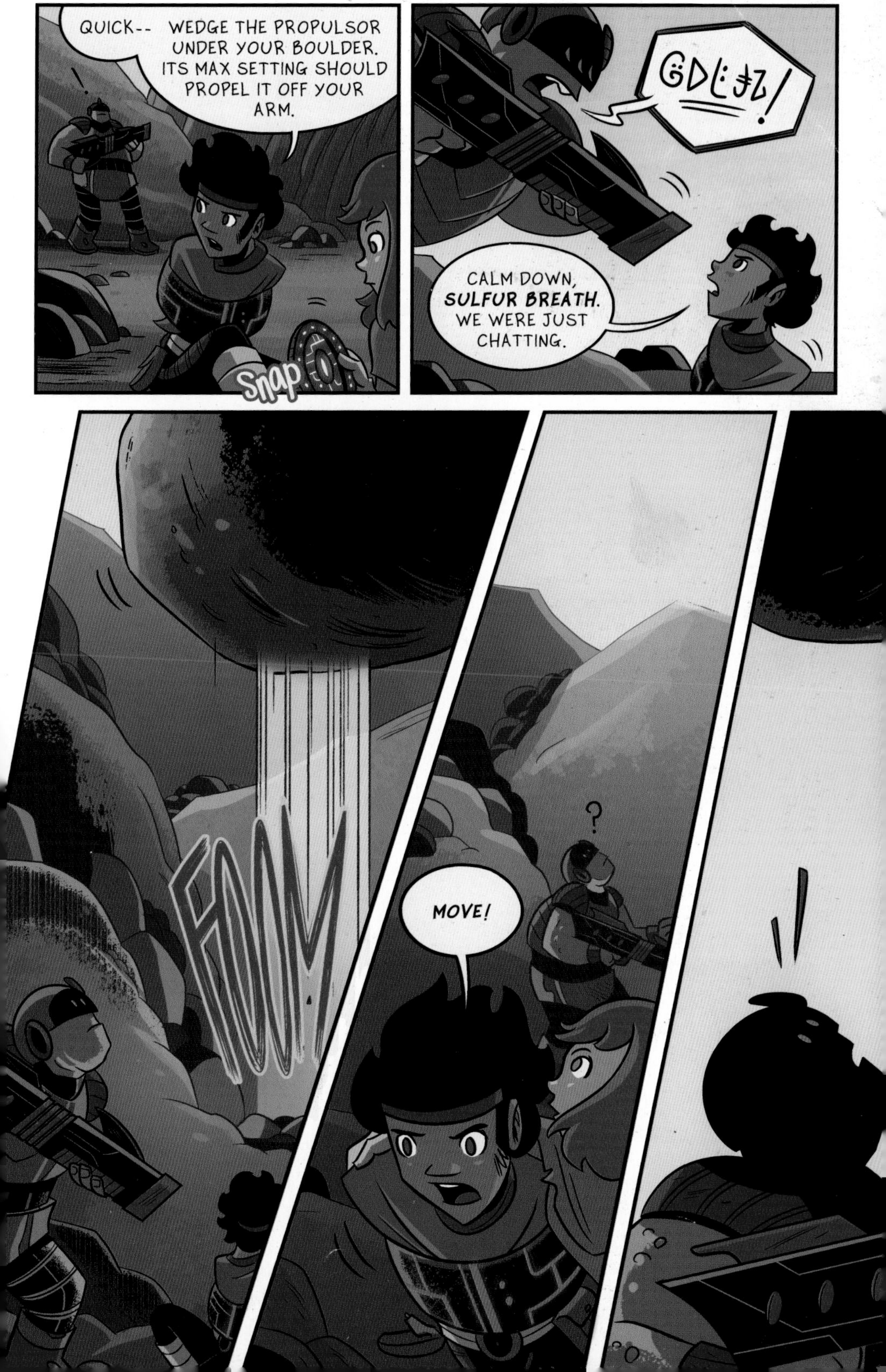
QUICK-- WEDGE THE PROPULSOR UNDER YOUR BOULDER. ITS MAX SETTING SHOULD PROPEL IT OFF YOUR ARM.
!
SNAP
CALM DOWN, **SULFUR BREATH.** WE WERE JUST CHATTING.
?
MOVE!

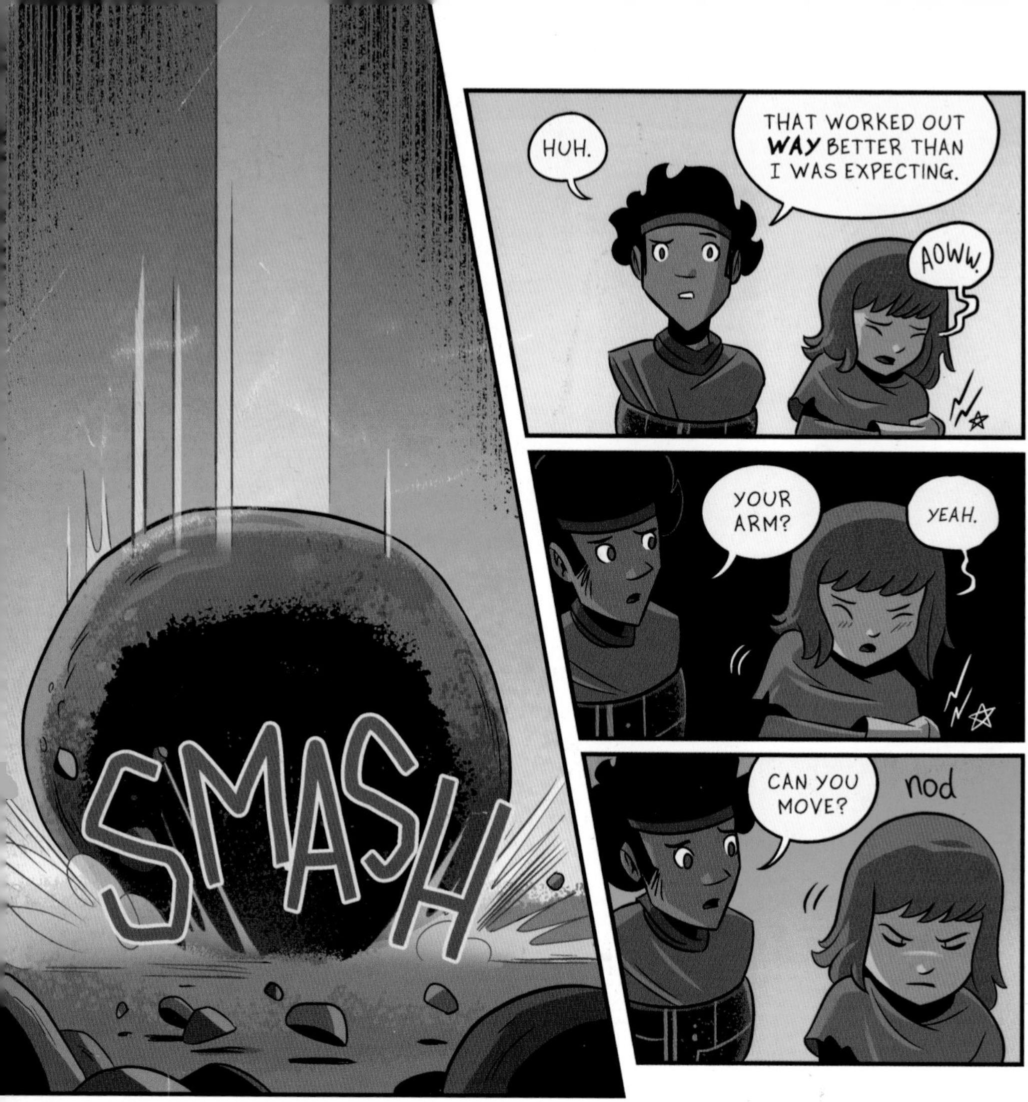
SMASH
HUH.
THAT WORKED OUT WAY BETTER THAN I WAS EXPECTING.
AOWW.
YOUR ARM?
YEAH.
CAN YOU MOVE?
nod

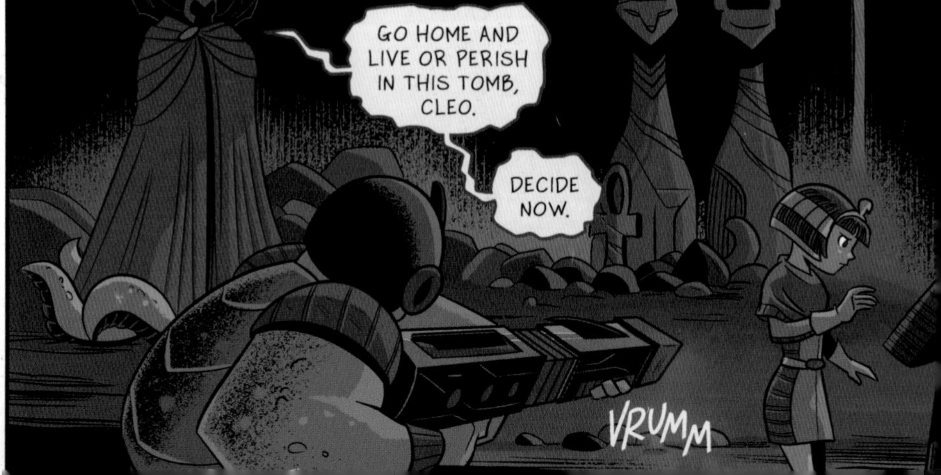
GO HOME AND LIVE OR PERISH IN THIS TOMB, CLEO.
DECIDE NOW.
VRUMM

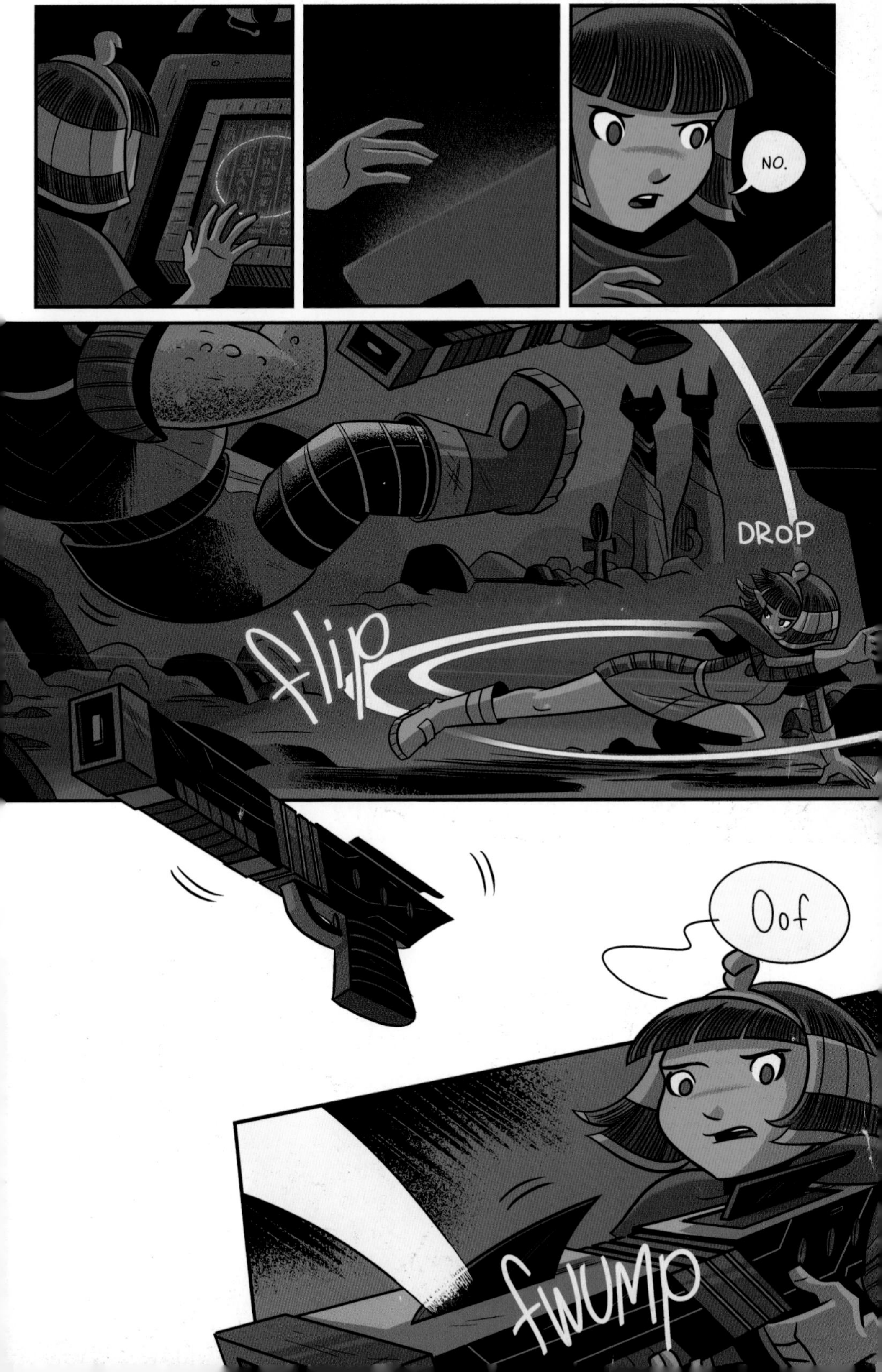
NO.
DROP
flip
Oof
fwump

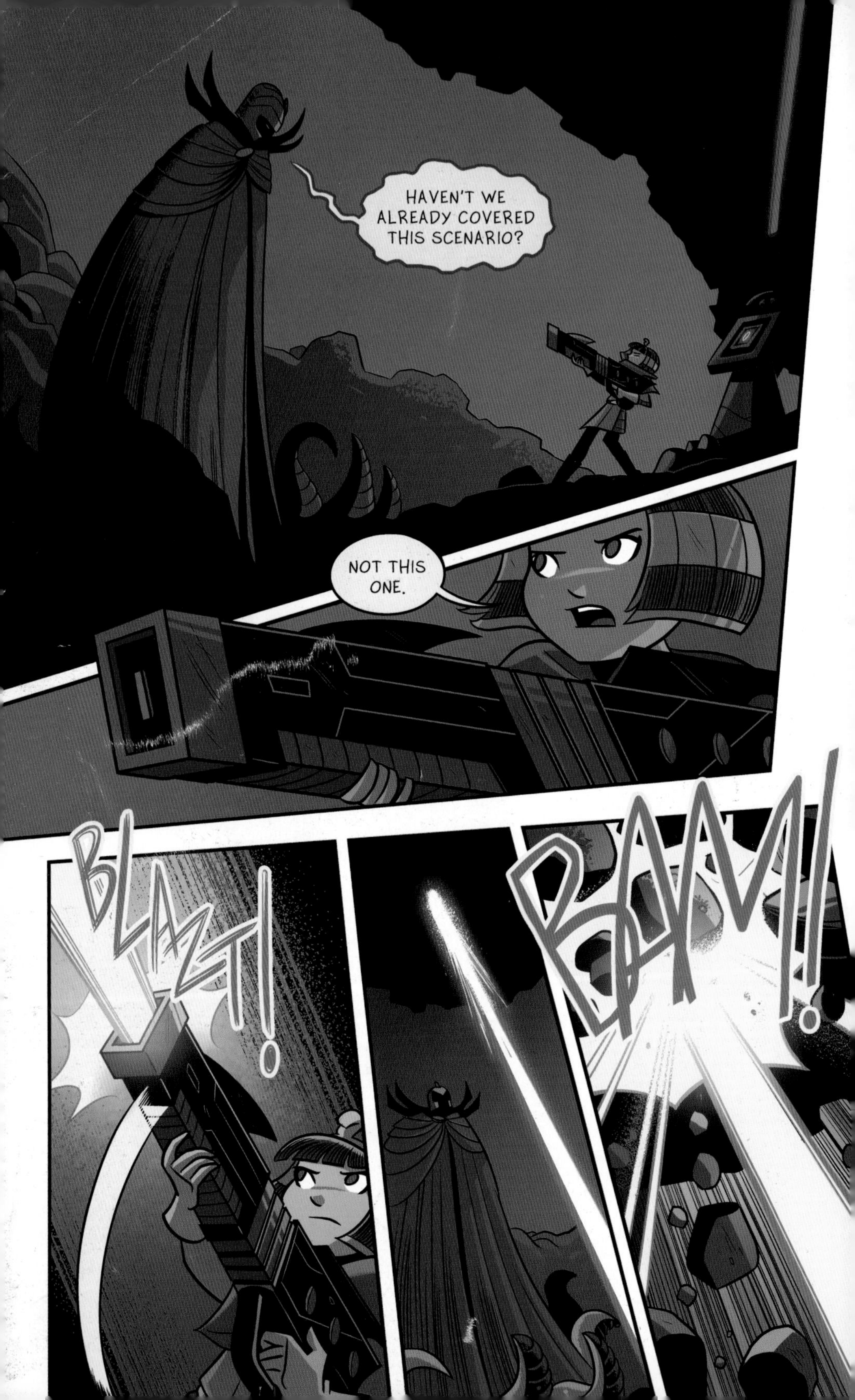
HAVEN'T WE ALREADY COVERED THIS SCENARIO?
NOT THIS ONE.
BLAZT!
BAM!!

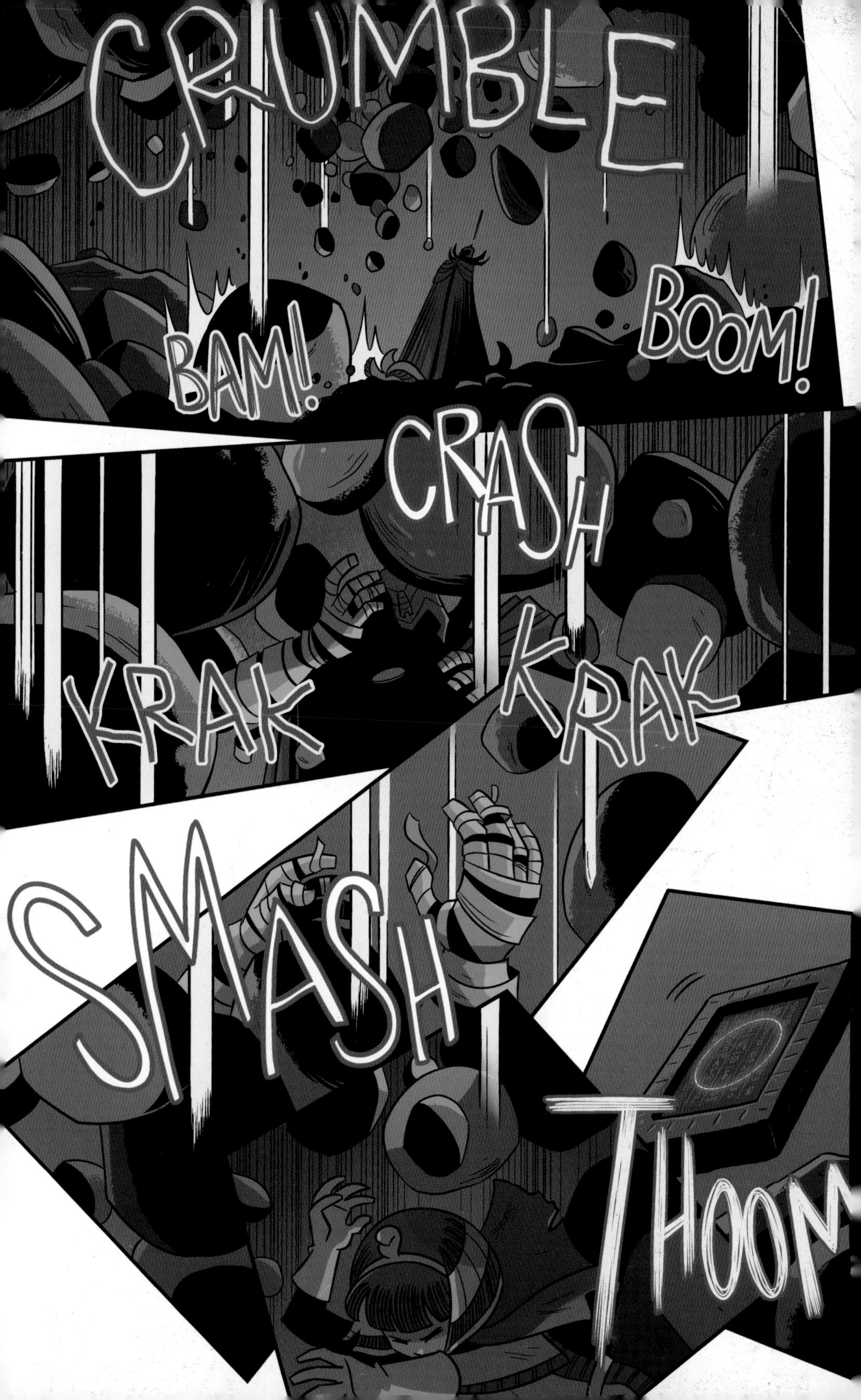
CRUMBLE
BAM!
BOOM!
CRASH
KRAK
KRAK
SMASH
THOOM

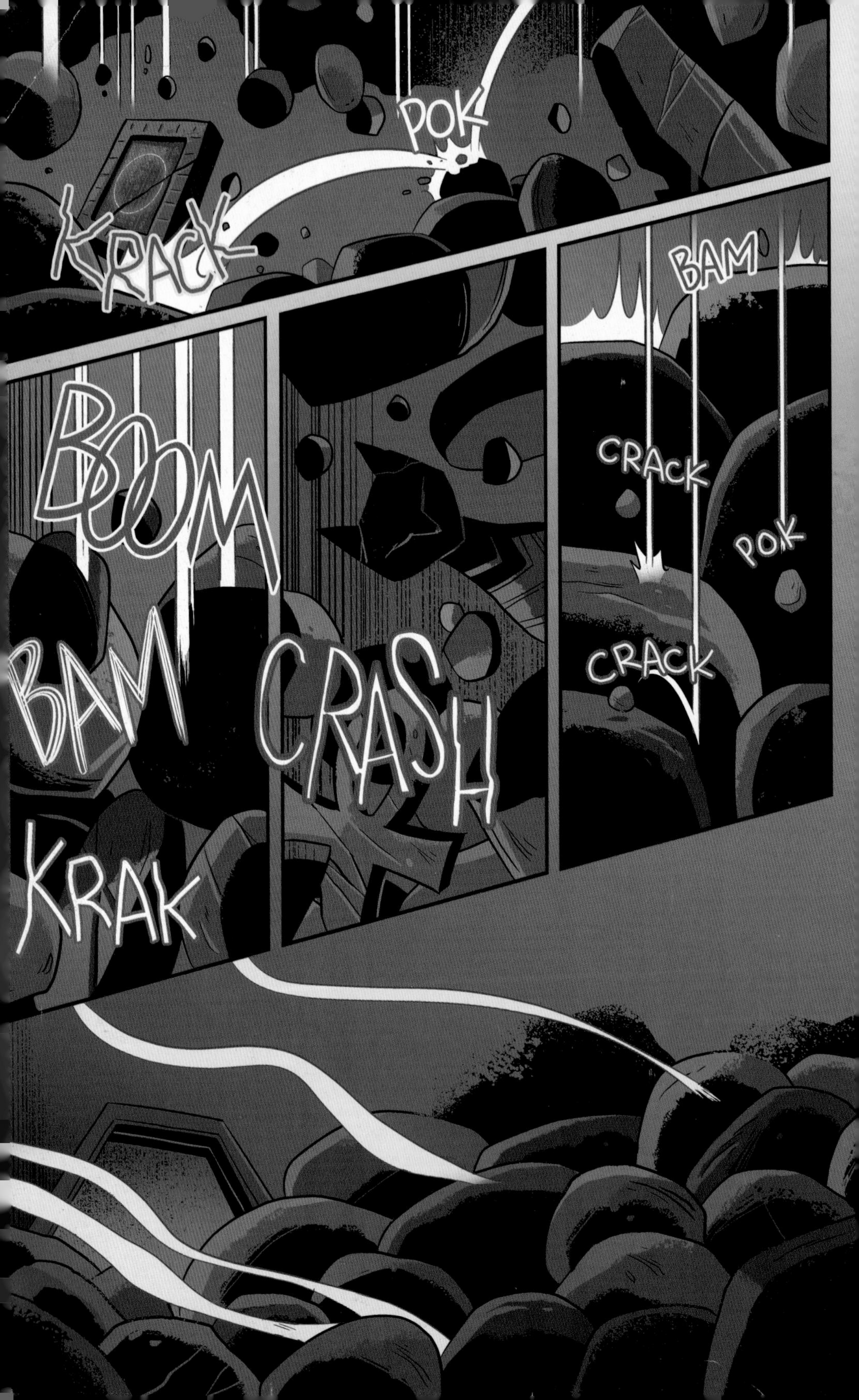
POK
KRACK
BAM
BOOM
BAM
KRAK
CRASH
CRACK
POK
CRACK

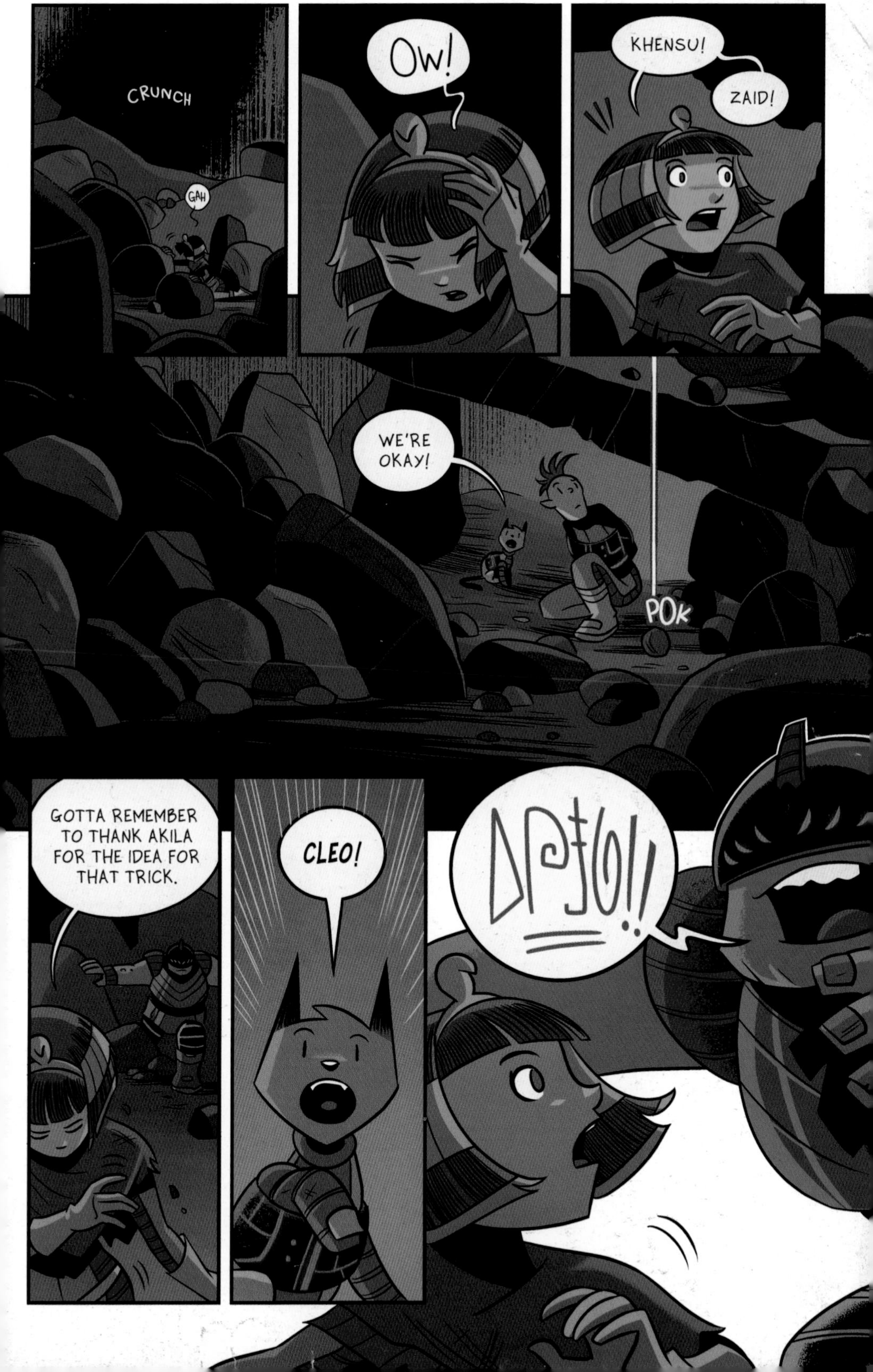
CRUNCH
GAH
OW!
KHENSU!
ZAID!
WE'RE OKAY!
POK
GOTTA REMEMBER TO THANK AKILA FOR THE IDEA FOR THAT TRICK.
CLEO!

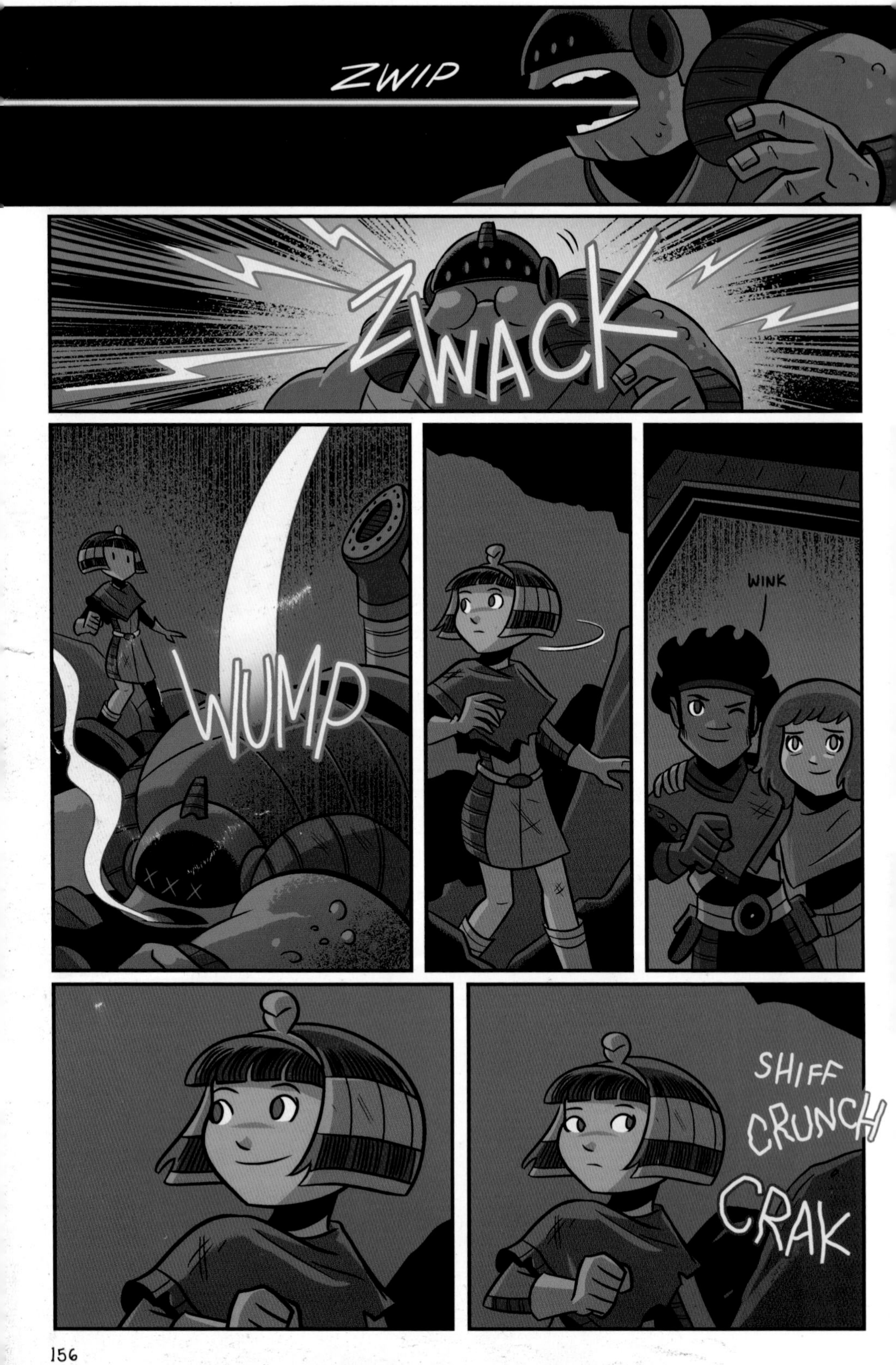
ZWIP
ZWACK
WUMP
WINK
SHIFF
CRUNCH
CRAK

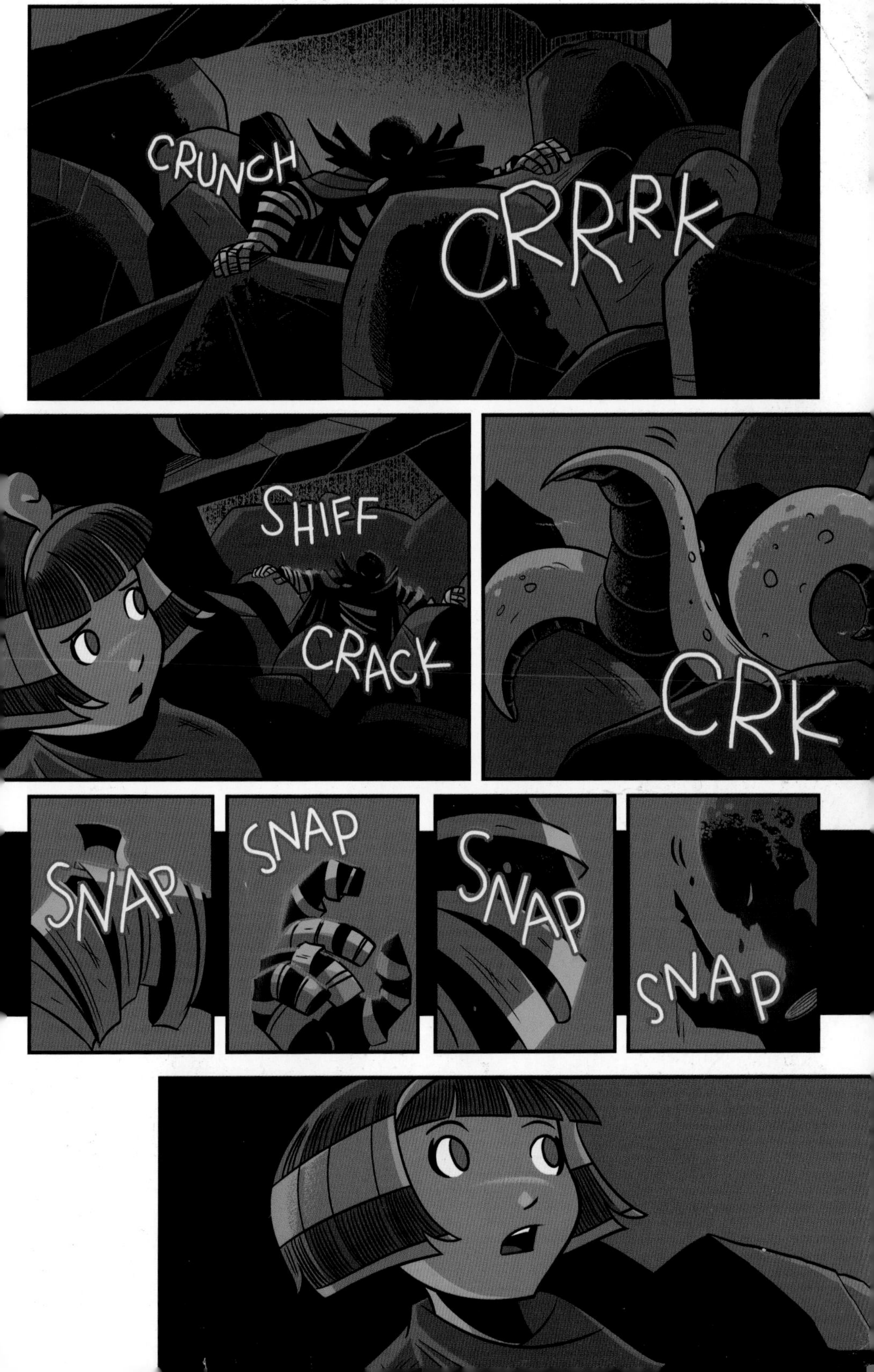
CRUNCH
CRRRK
SHIFF
CRACK
CRK
SNAP
SNAP
SNAP
SNAP

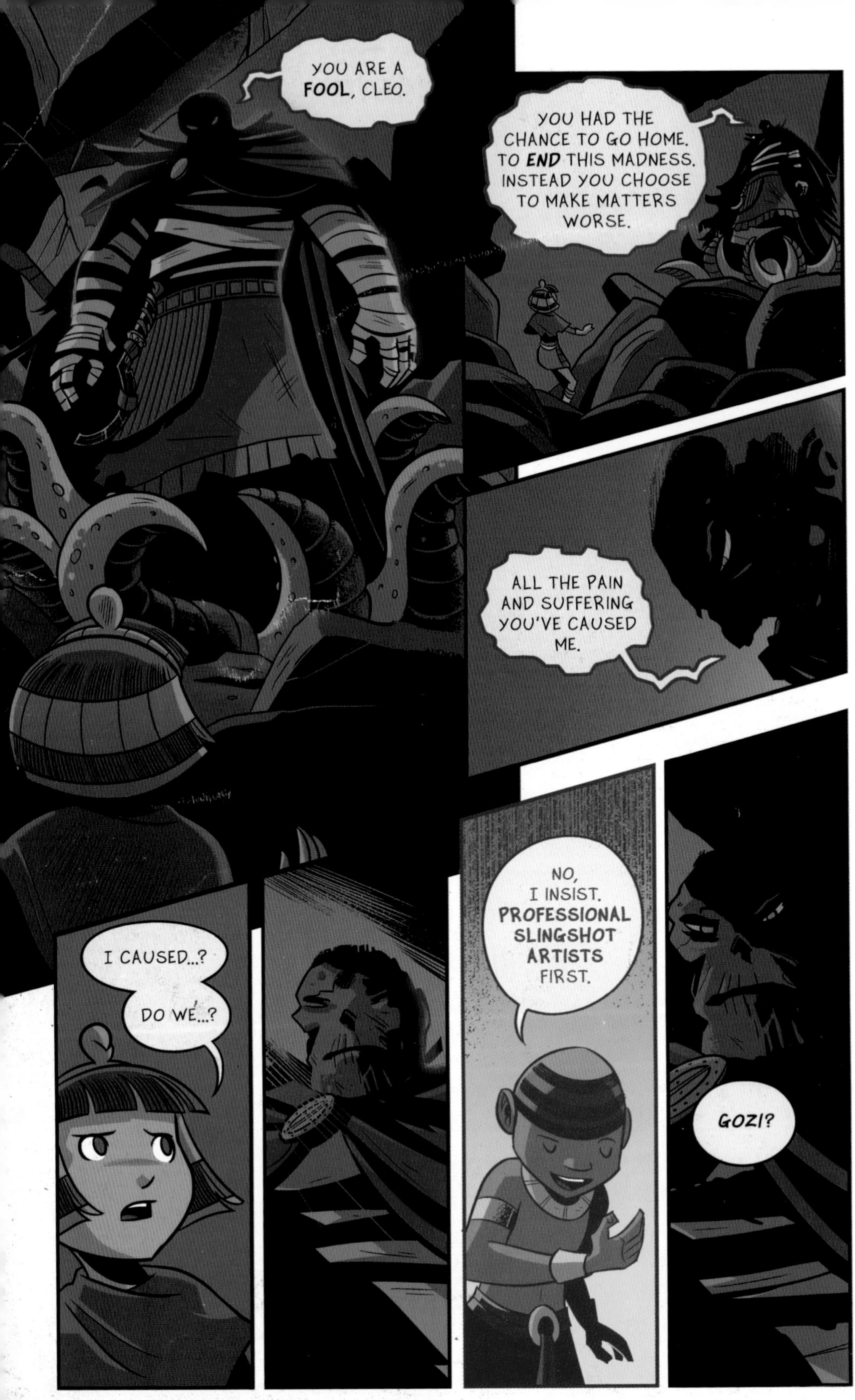
YOU ARE A FOOL, CLEO.
YOU HAD THE CHANCE TO GO HOME. TO END THIS MADNESS. INSTEAD YOU CHOOSE TO MAKE MATTERS WORSE.
ALL THE PAIN AND SUFFERING YOU'VE CAUSED ME.
I CAUSED...?
DO WE...?
NO, I INSIST. PROFESSIONAL SLINGSHOT ARTISTS FIRST.
GOZI?

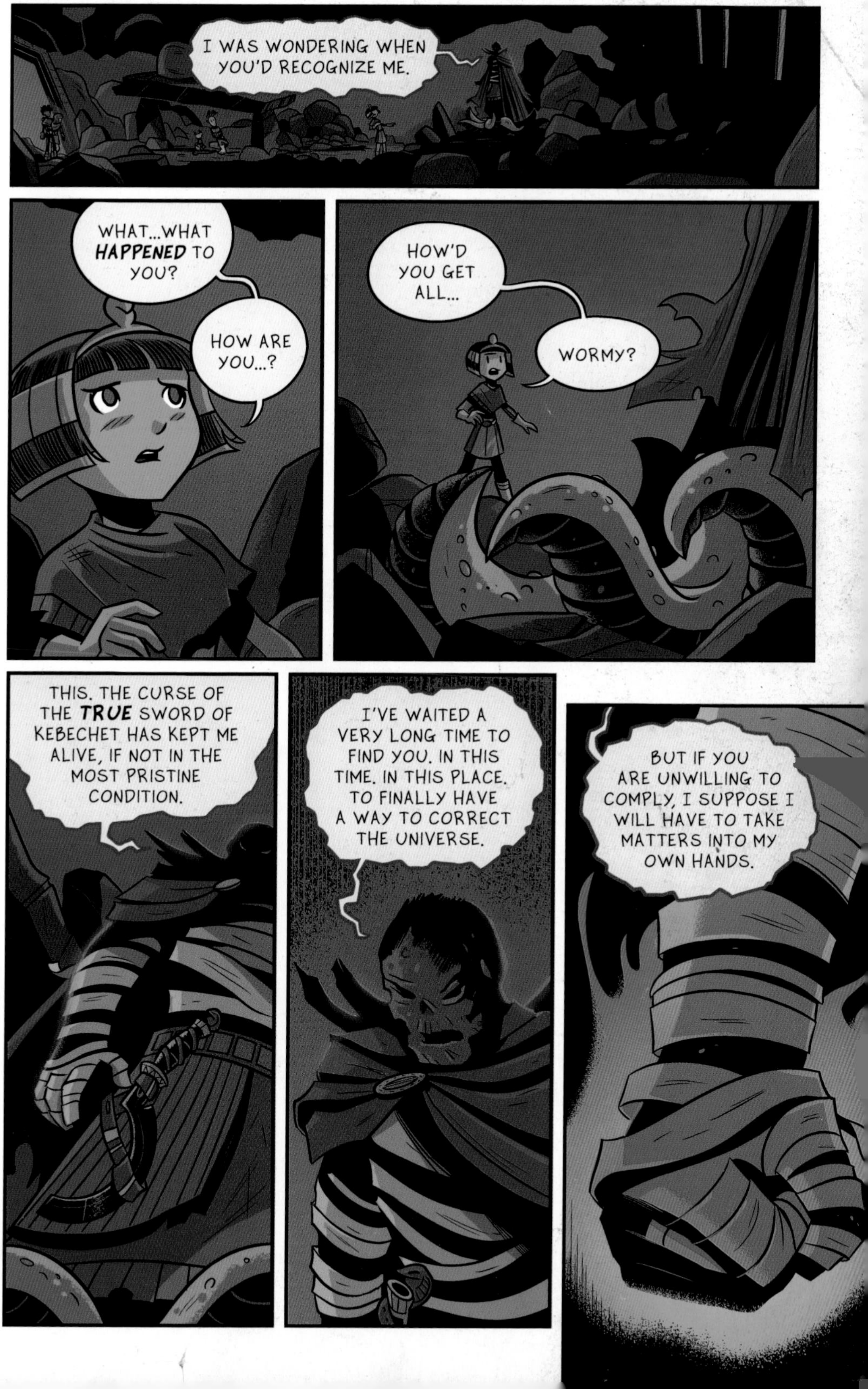
I WAS WONDERING WHEN YOU'D RECOGNIZE ME.
WHAT...WHAT **HAPPENED** TO YOU?
HOW ARE YOU...?
HOW'D YOU GET ALL...
WORMY?
THIS. THE CURSE OF THE **TRUE** SWORD OF KEBECHET HAS KEPT ME ALIVE, IF NOT IN THE MOST PRISTINE CONDITION.
I'VE WAITED A VERY LONG TIME TO FIND YOU. IN THIS TIME. IN THIS PLACE. TO FINALLY HAVE A WAY TO CORRECT THE UNIVERSE.
BUT IF YOU ARE UNWILLING TO COMPLY, I SUPPOSE I WILL HAVE TO TAKE MATTERS INTO MY OWN HANDS.

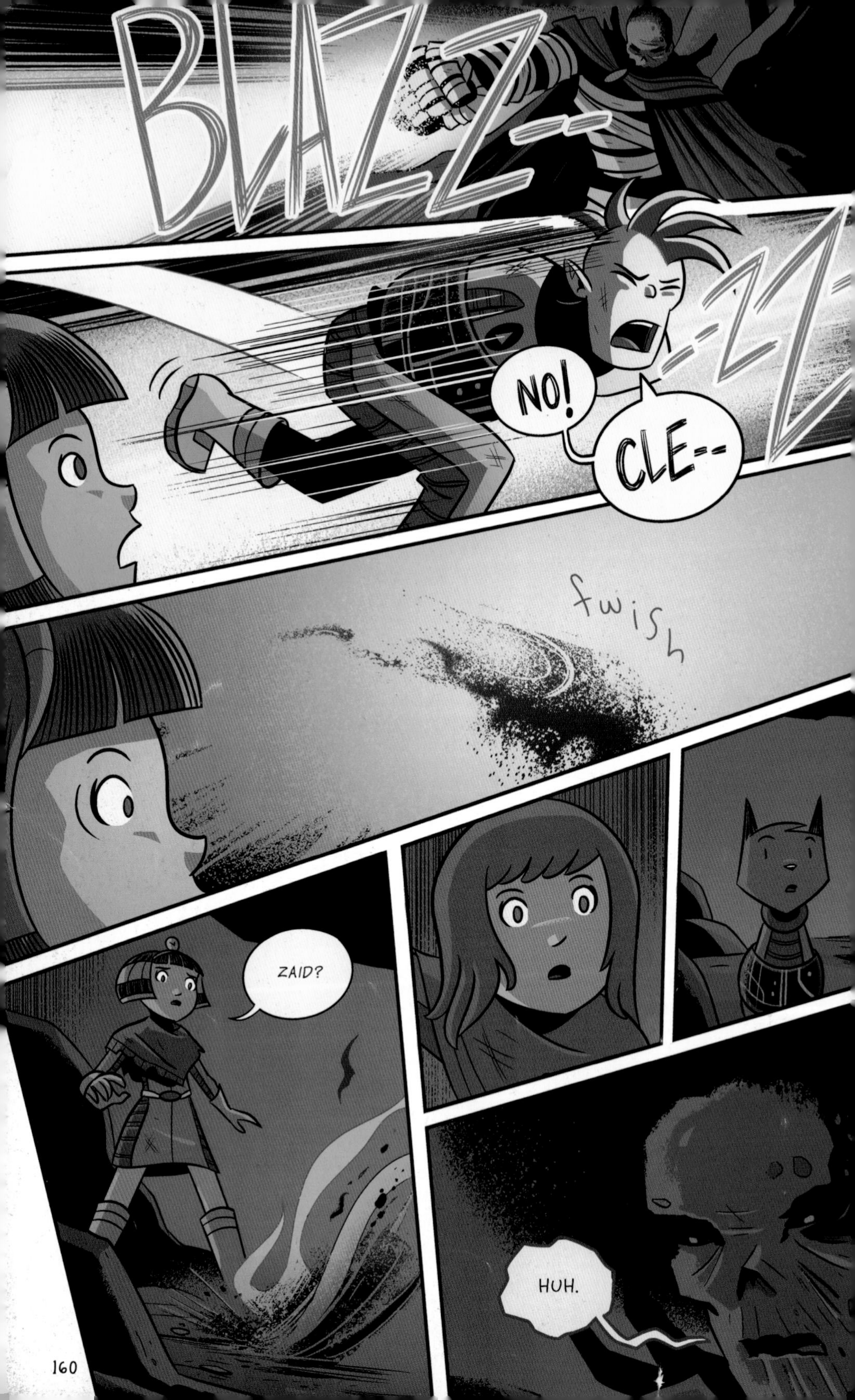
BLAZZ--
NO!
CLE--
ZZZ--
fwish
ZAID?
HUH.

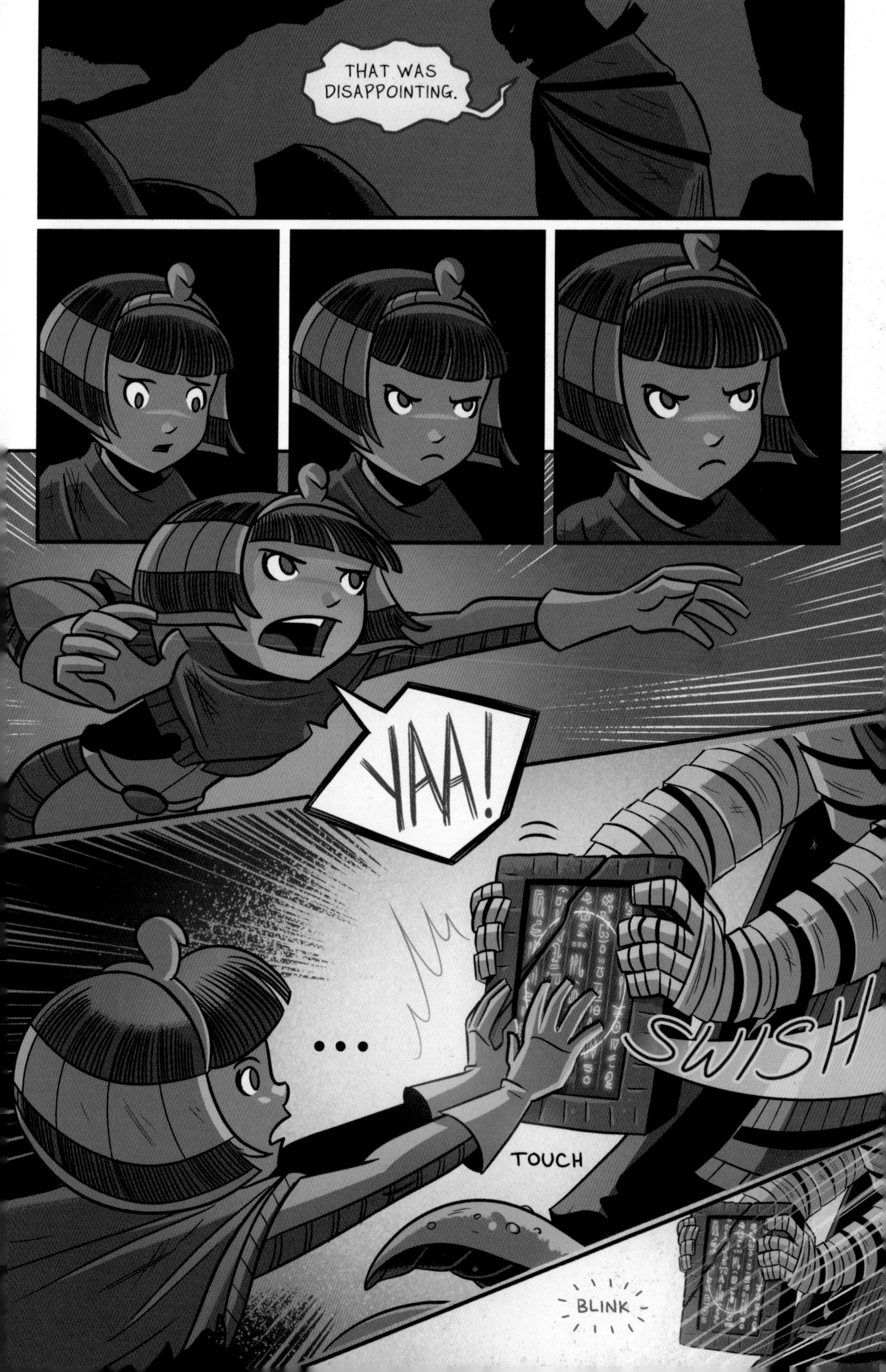
THAT WAS DISAPPOINTING.
YAAA!
...
SWISH
TOUCH
BLINK

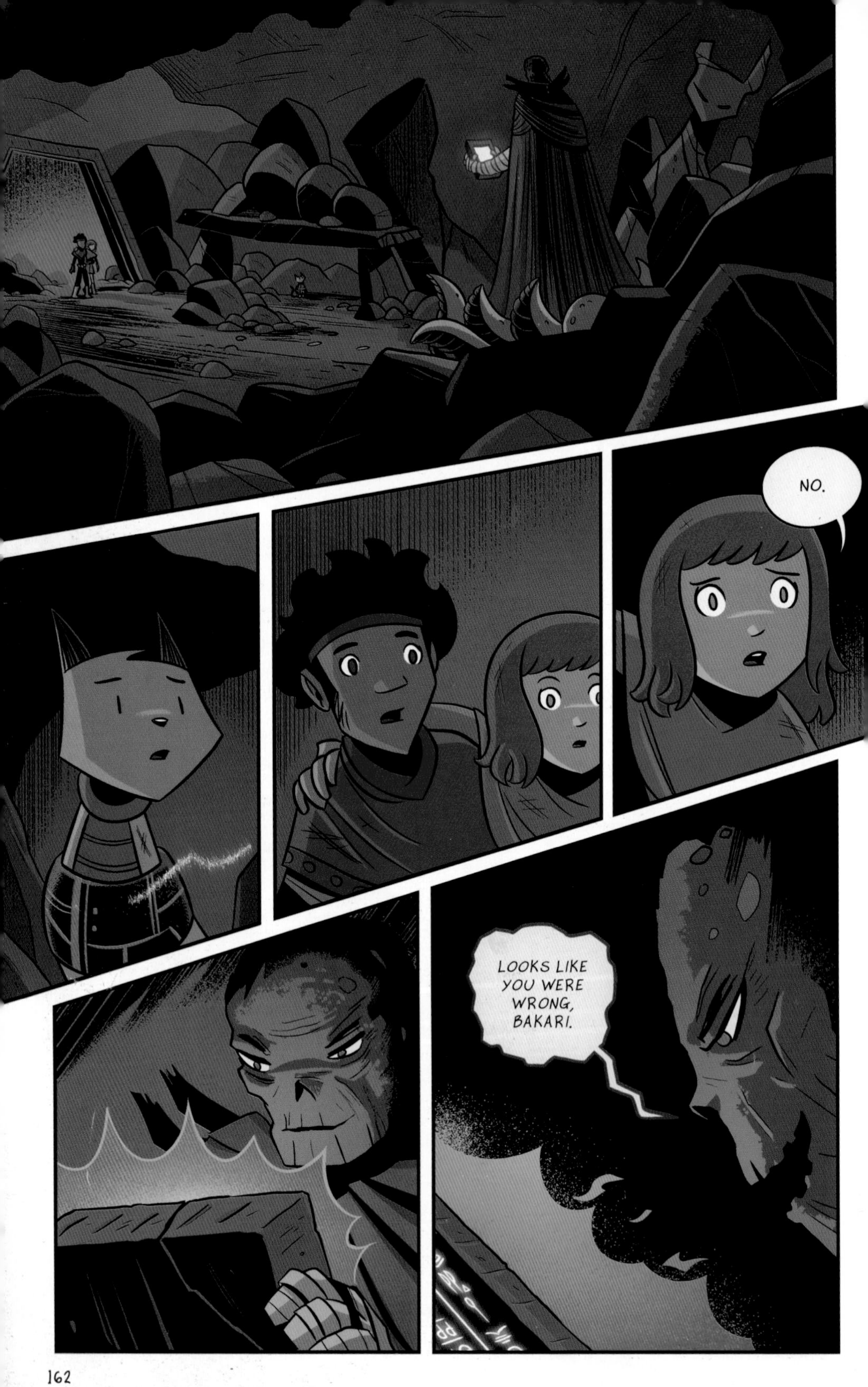
NO.
LOOKS LIKE YOU WERE WRONG, BAKARI.

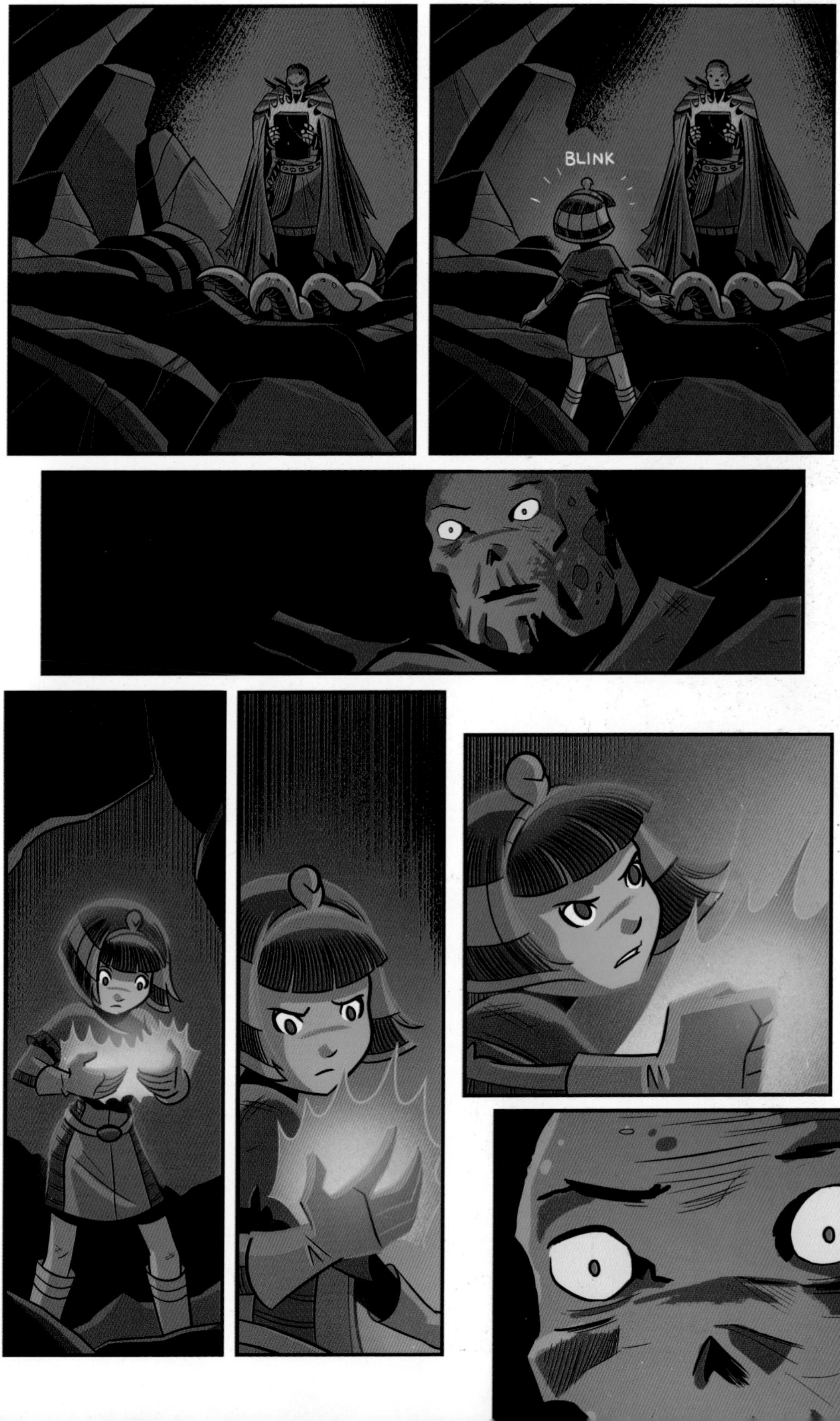
BLINK

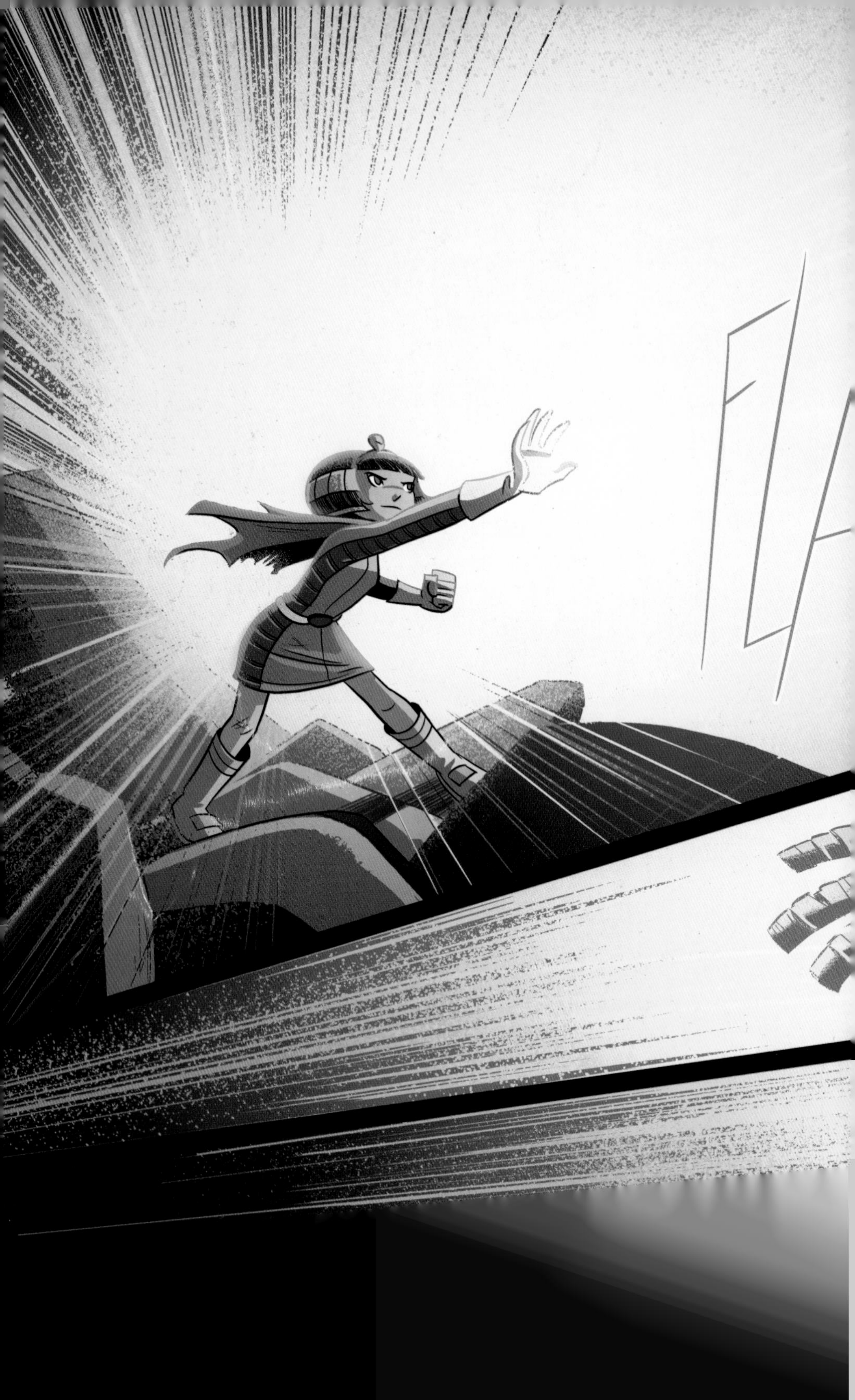

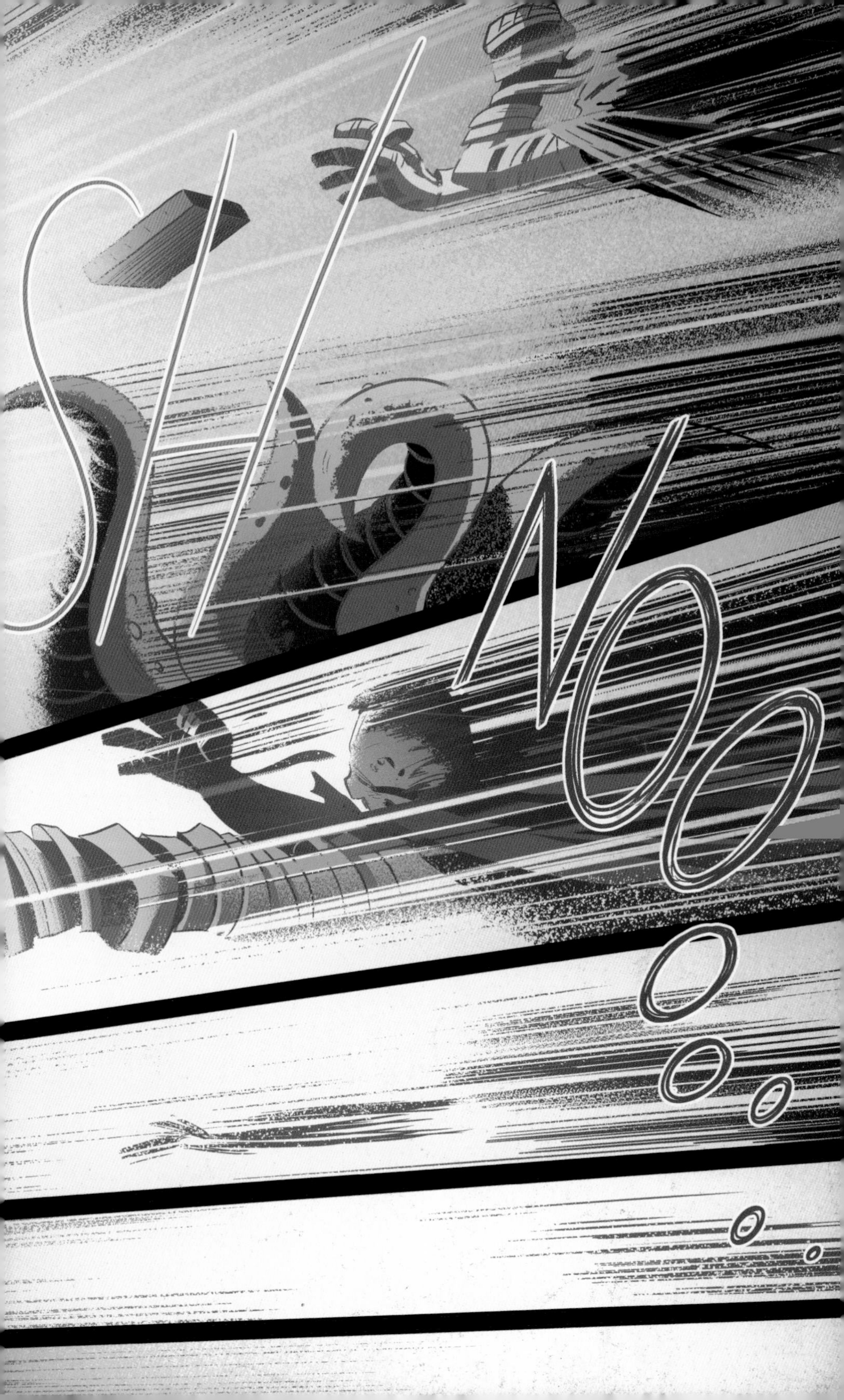
SHH
NOOOO

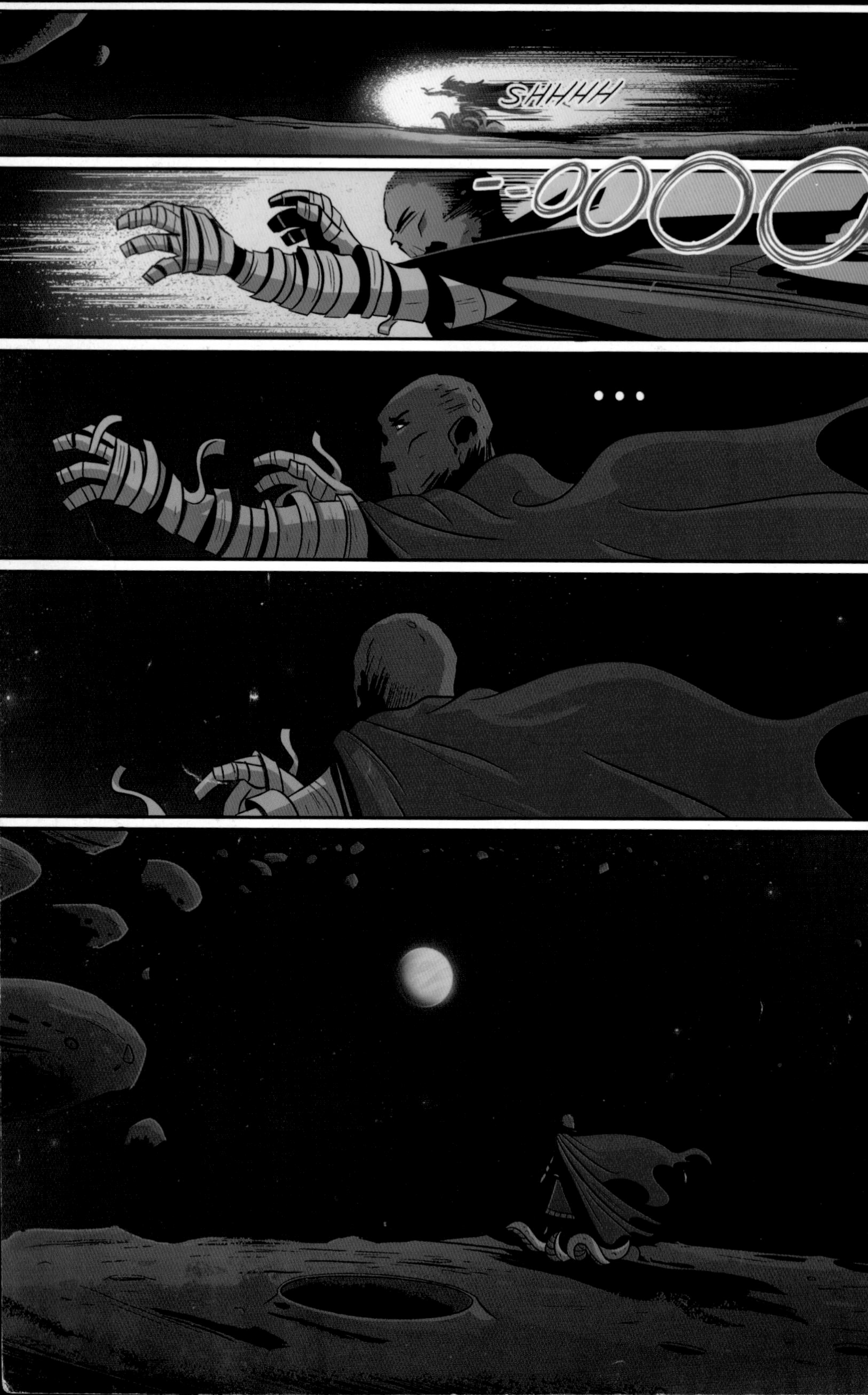
SHHHH
...

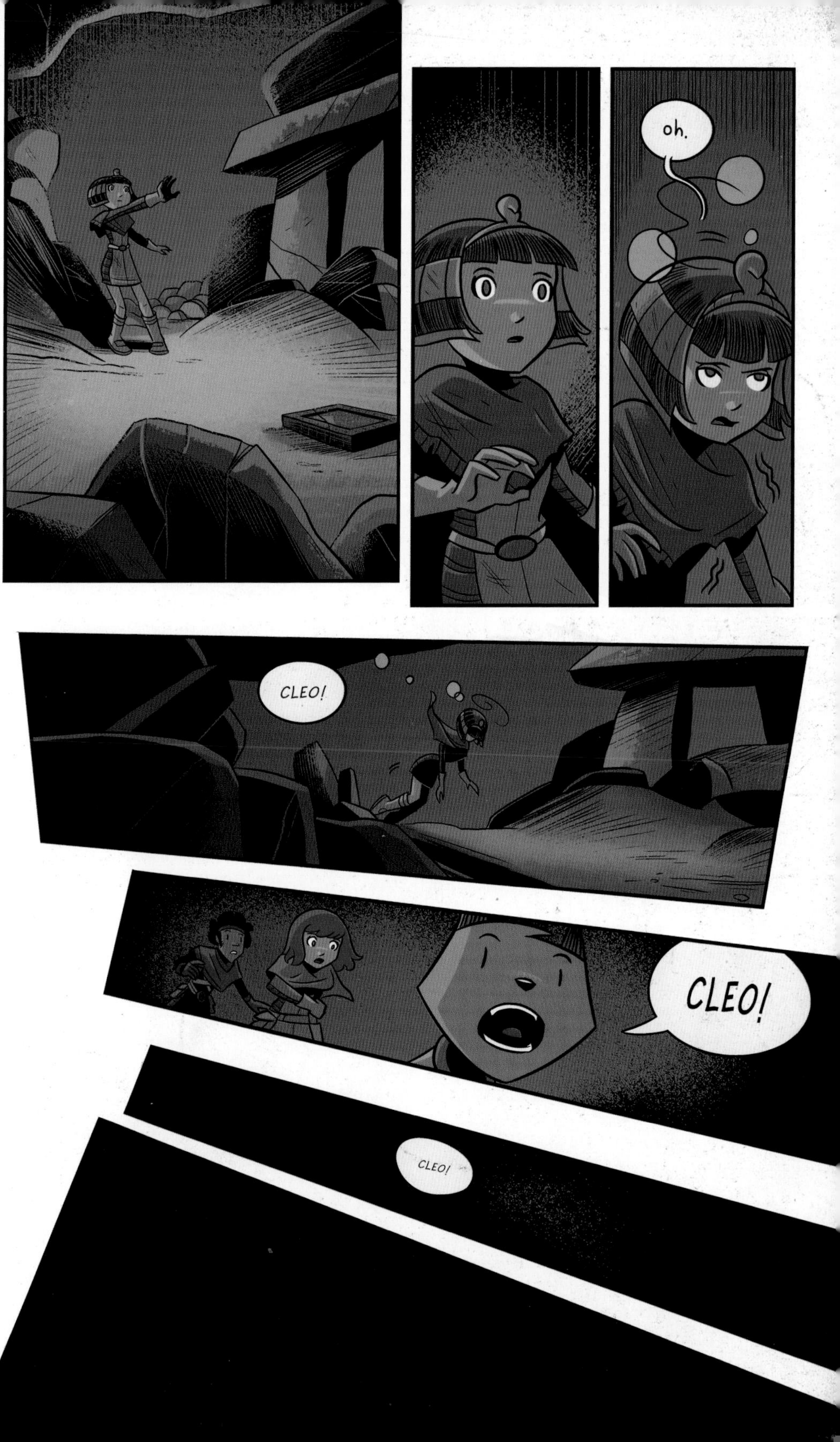
oh.
CLEO!
CLEO!
CLEO!

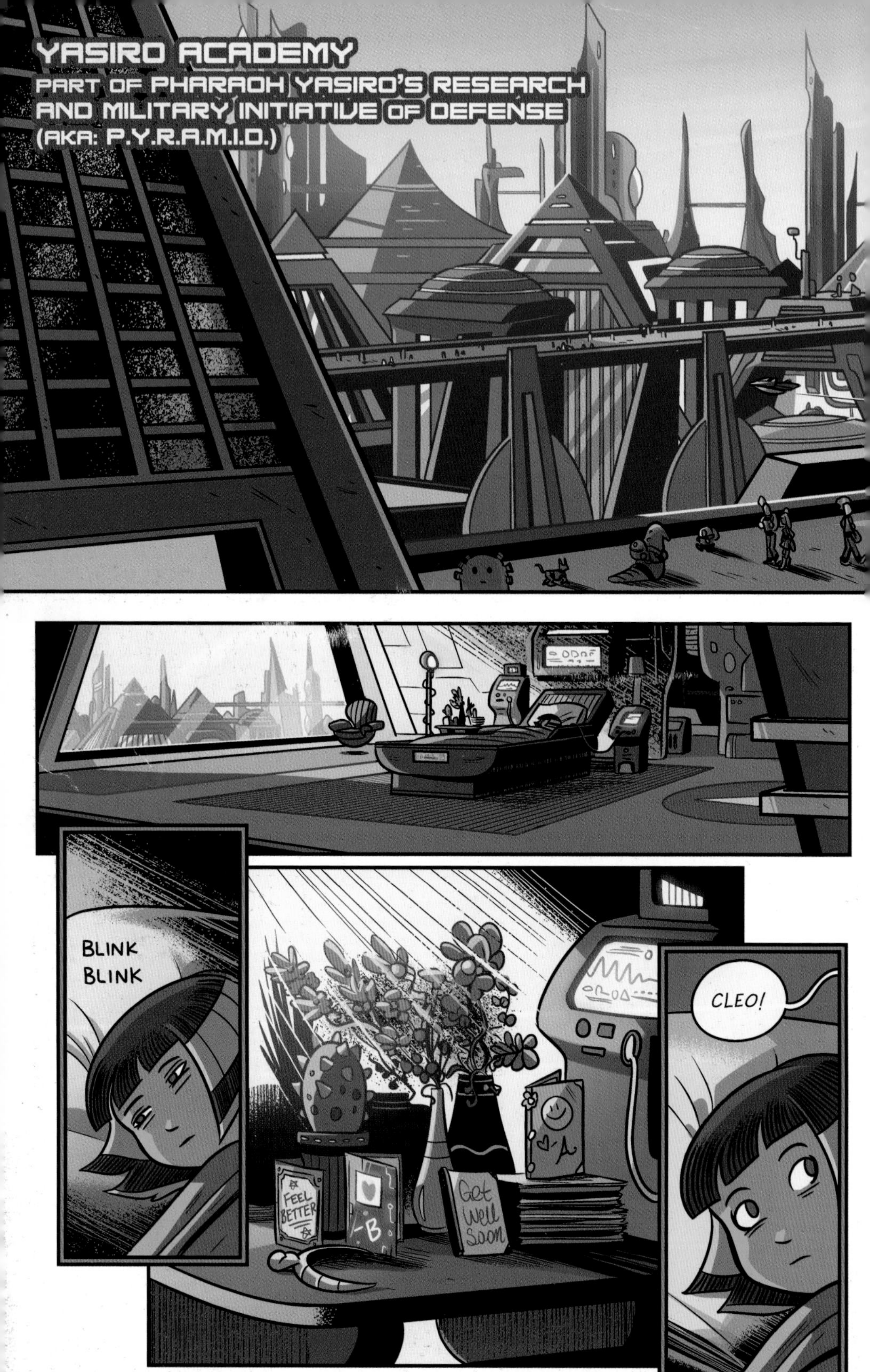
YASIRO ACADEMY
PART OF PHARAOH YASIRO'S RESEARCH AND MILITARY INITIATIVE OF DEFENSE (AKA: P.Y.R.A.M.I.D.)
BLINK BLINK
FEEL BETTER
-B
Get Well Soon
CLEO!

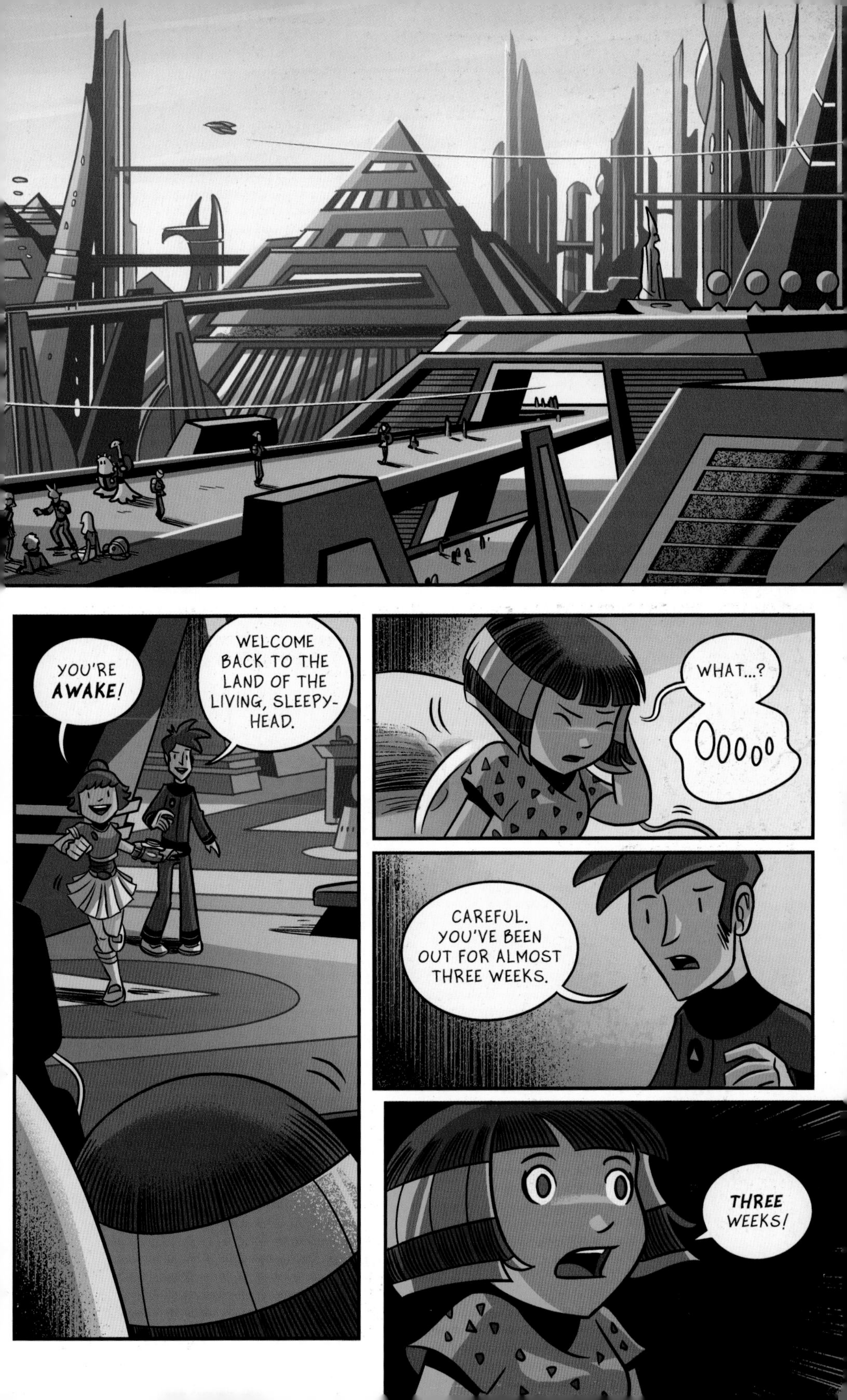
YOU'RE **AWAKE**!
WELCOME BACK TO THE LAND OF THE LIVING, SLEEPY-HEAD.
WHAT...?
Ooooo
CAREFUL. YOU'VE BEEN OUT FOR ALMOST THREE WEEKS.
THREE WEEKS!

HOW-- HOW DID I...

YOU DEFEATED *OCTAVIAN*, CLEO!

WELL, SORTA.

P.Y.R.A.M.I.D. SCOUTS REPORTED SPOTTING HIM AND HIS FLEET NEAR MENDESIA.

HE SEEMS TO HAVE LEFT THE AILUROS SYSTEM ALONE, THOUGH. FOR NOW, AT LEAST.

BRIAN MANAGED TO GET THE LOCATION BEACON ON OUR ESCAPE POD REPAIRED. P.Y.R.A.M.I.D. FOUND HIM, NOTICED ALL THOSE STUNNED XERX OUTSIDE THE TOMB, AND BROUGHT US BACK HERE. WELL, EXCEPT ANTONY. HE DISAPPEARED PRETTY MUCH AS SOON AS P.Y.R.A.M.I.D. ARRIVED.

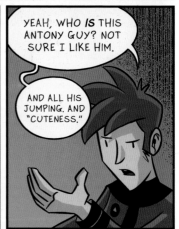

YEAH, WHO *IS* THIS ANTONY GUY? NOT SURE I LIKE HIM.

AND ALL HIS JUMPING. AND "CUTENESS."

SHUSH, BRIAN. ANTONY'S COOL.

HOW ARE YOU FEELING?

LIKE A CAVE COLLAPSED ON MY HEAD.

WHAT ABOUT ZAID?

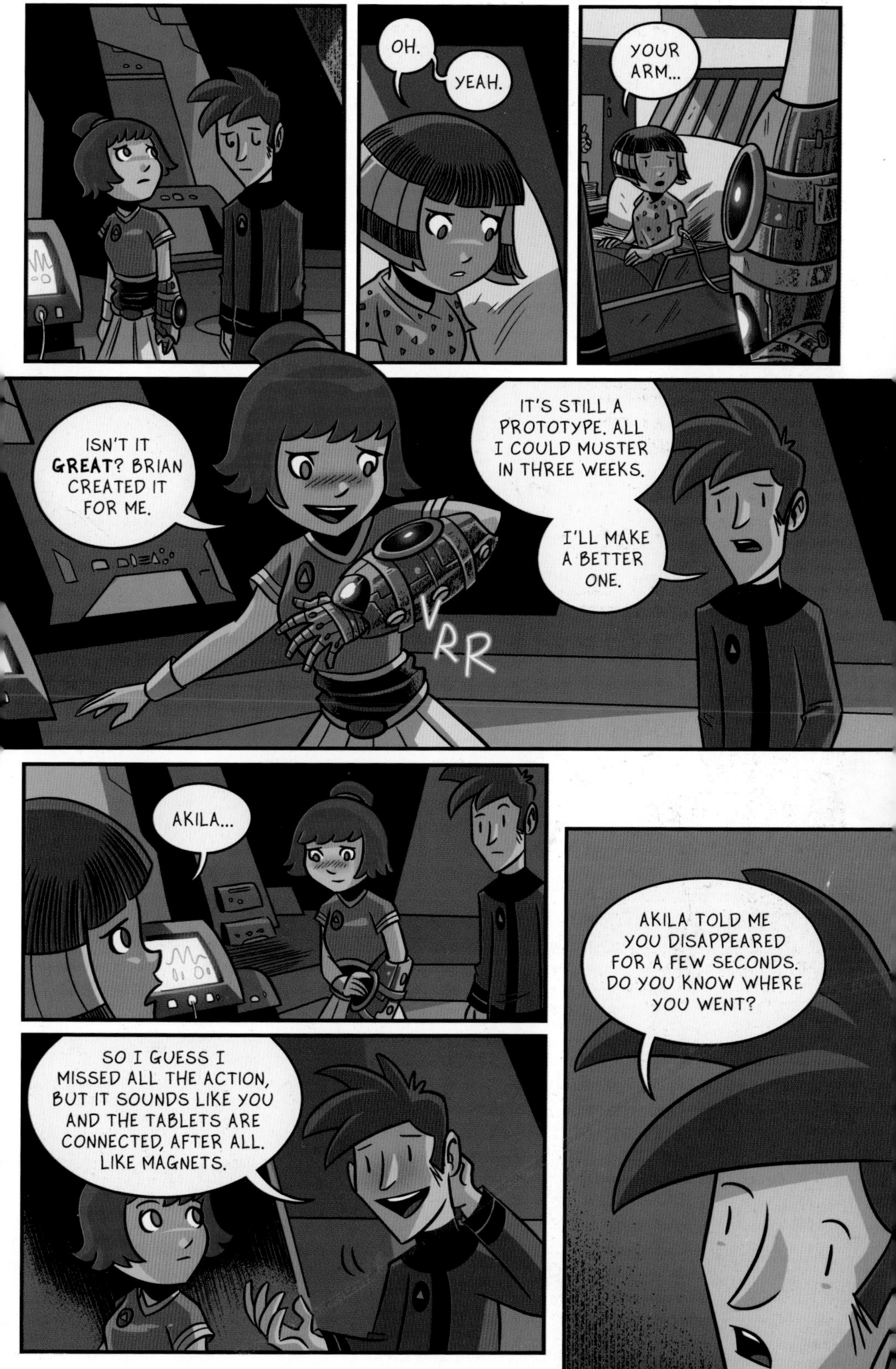
OH.
YEAH.
YOUR ARM...
ISN'T IT **GREAT**? BRIAN CREATED IT FOR ME.
IT'S STILL A PROTOTYPE. ALL I COULD MUSTER IN THREE WEEKS.
I'LL MAKE A BETTER ONE.
VRR
AKILA...
AKILA TOLD ME YOU DISAPPEARED FOR A FEW SECONDS. DO YOU KNOW WHERE YOU WENT?
SO I GUESS I MISSED ALL THE ACTION, BUT IT SOUNDS LIKE YOU AND THE TABLETS ARE CONNECTED, AFTER ALL. LIKE MAGNETS.

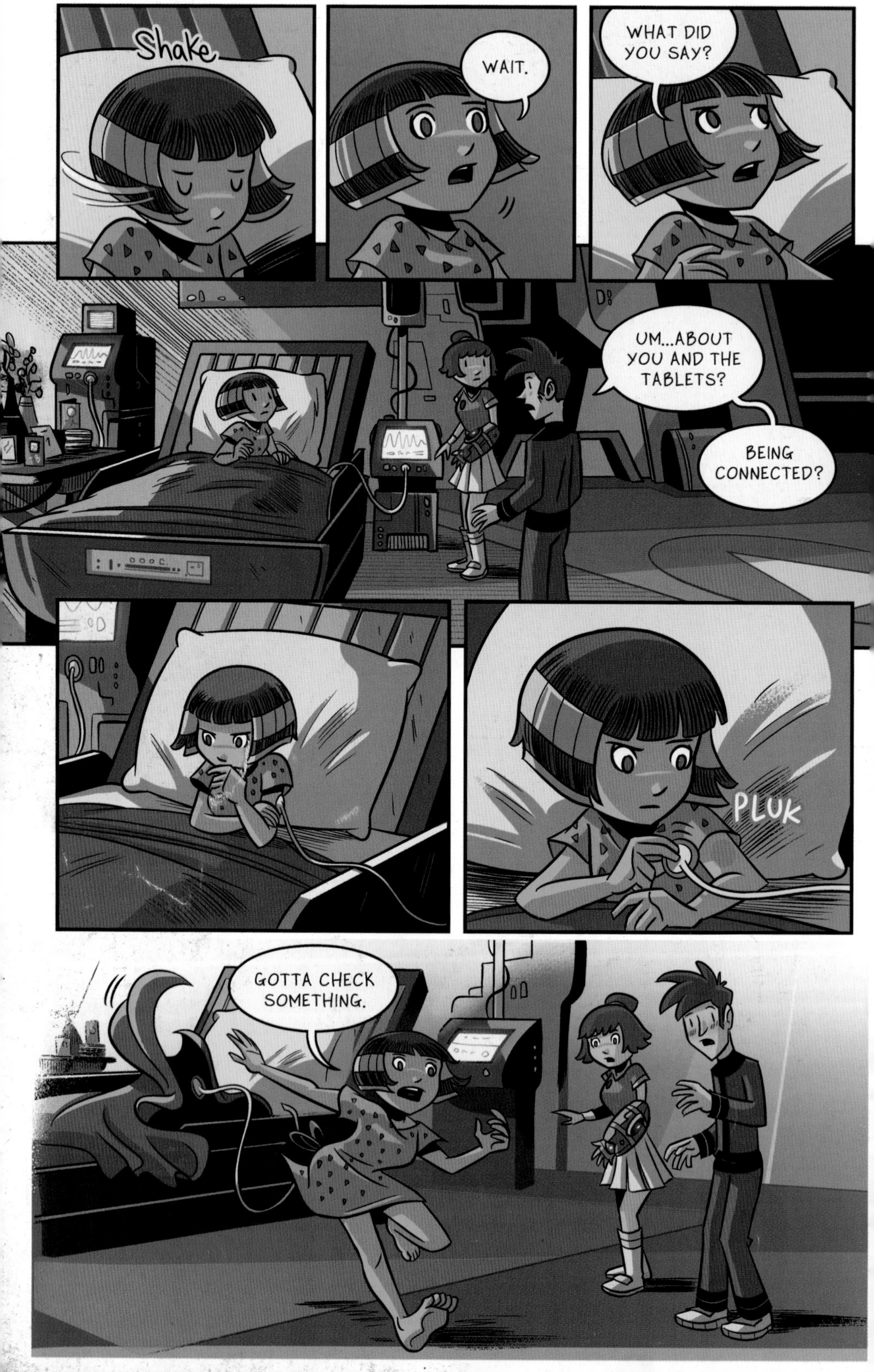
Shake
WAIT.
WHAT DID YOU SAY?
UM...ABOUT YOU AND THE TABLETS?
BEING CONNECTED?
PLUK
GOTTA CHECK SOMETHING.

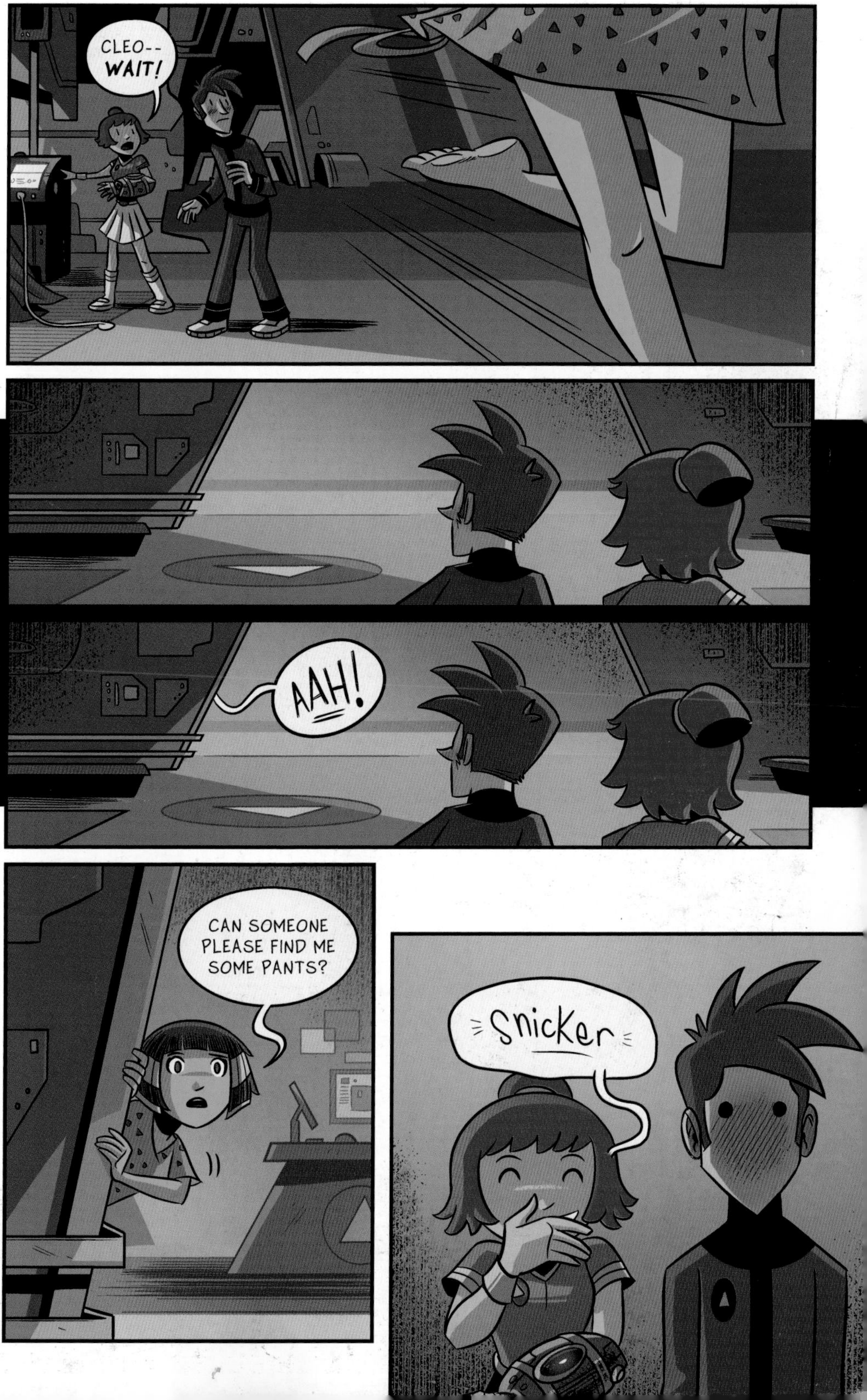
CLEO-- WAIT!
AAH!
CAN SOMEONE PLEASE FIND ME SOME PANTS?
Snicker

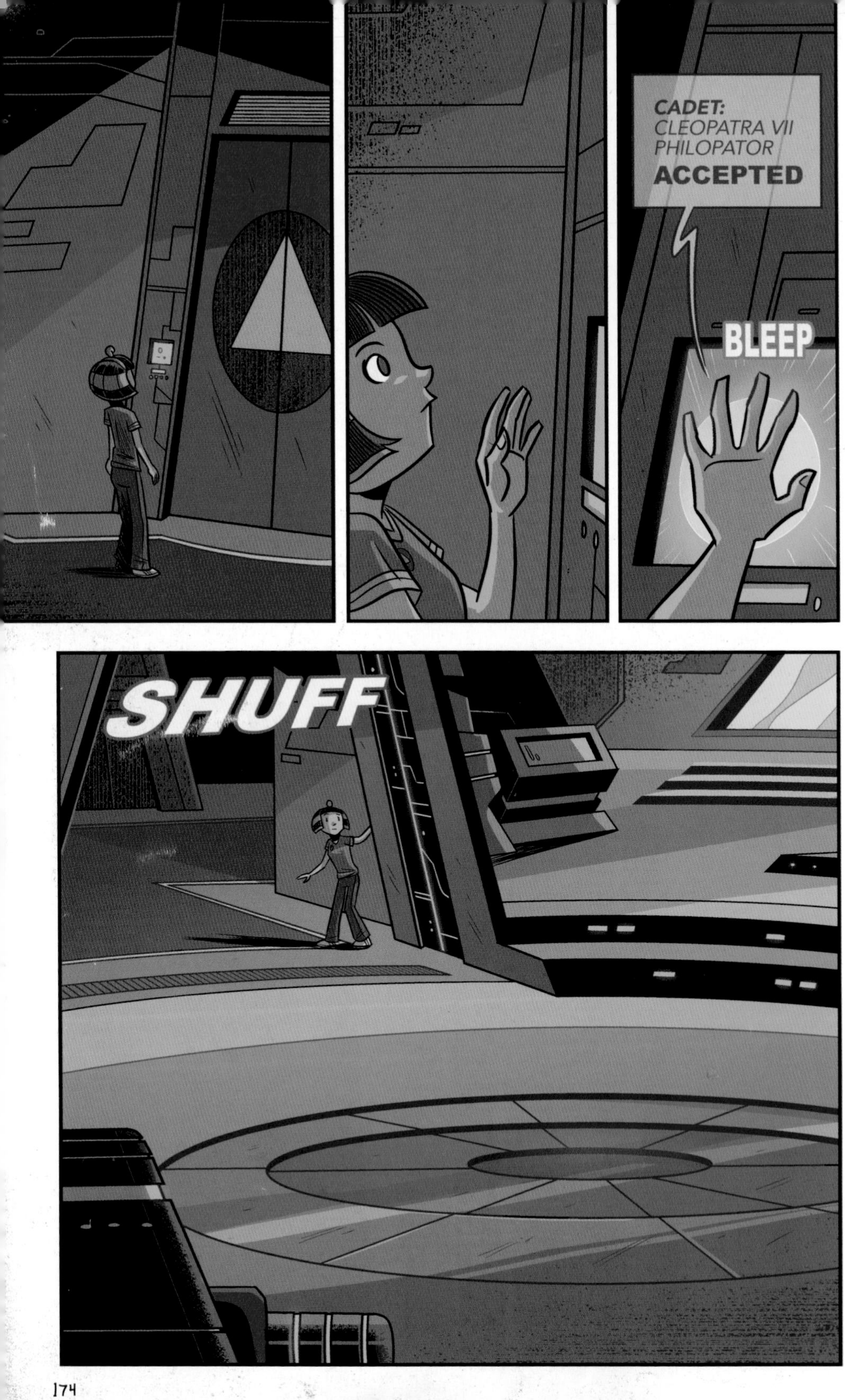
CADET:
CLEOPATRA VII
PHILOPATOR
ACCEPTED
BLEEP
SHUFF

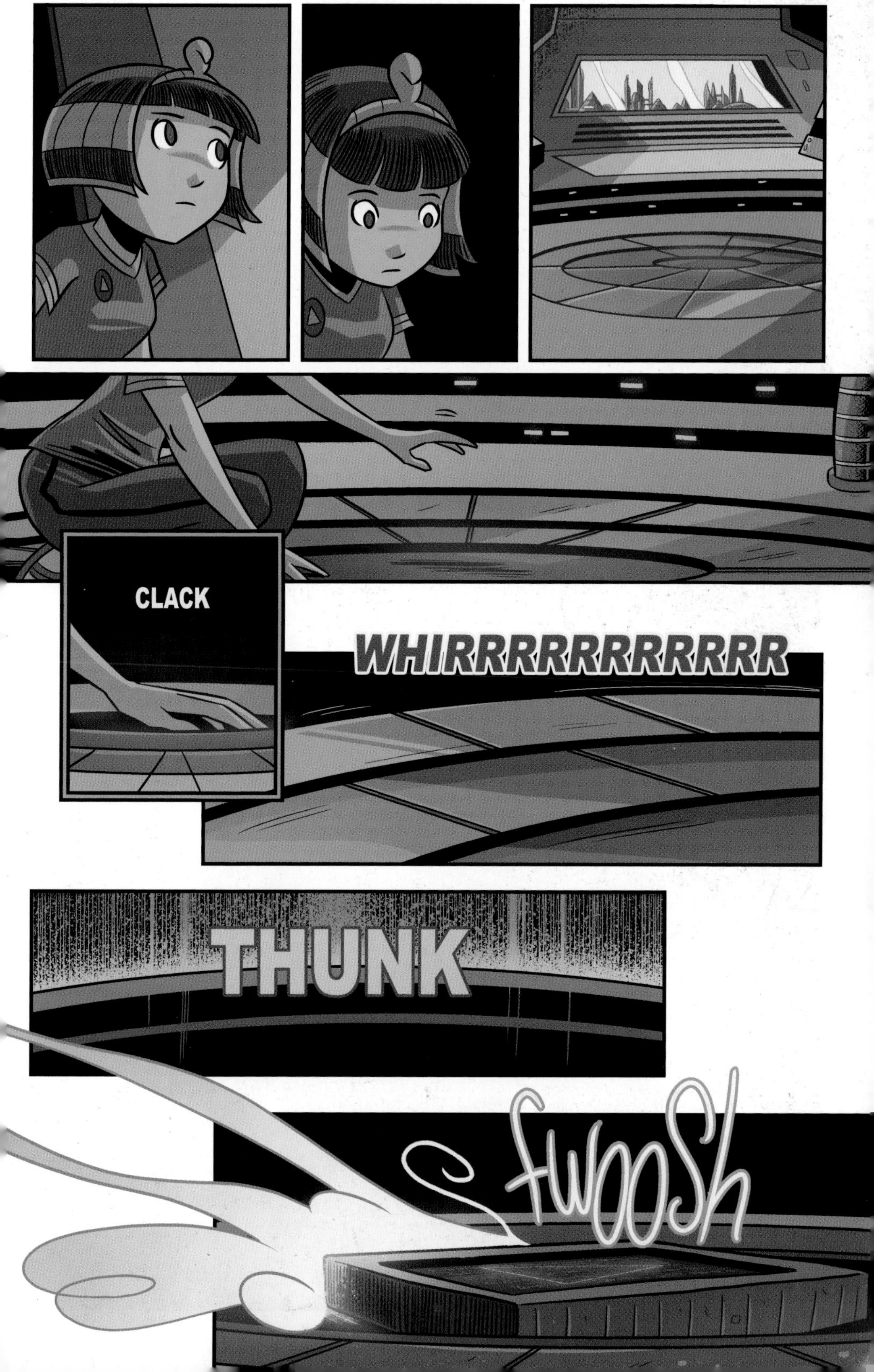
CLACK
WHIRRRRRRRRRRRR
THUNK
fwoosh

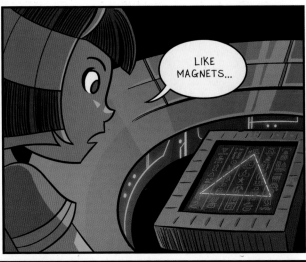

LIKE MAGNETS...

YASIRO HAD THE SCHOOL BUILT AROUND IT.

HE PREDICTED YOUR ARRIVAL WOULD BE LINKED TO THE UTA TABLET'S LOCATION. THAT'S HOW KHENSU KNEW TO BE IN THIS ROOM WHEN YOU APPEARED.

I FIGURED IT WAS ONLY A MATTER OF TIME BEFORE ITS PRESENCE PULLED YOU BACK HERE.

HE LIED TO ME. YOU **ALL** LIED TO ME. YOU HAD A WAY TO SEND ME BACK TO MY OWN TIME ALL ALONG.

NO, **YOU** HAD A WAY. WHEN I SAID THE POWER THAT SENT YOU HERE WAS NOT FROM US, THAT WAS THE TRUTH. THE TABLETS SEEM TO ACTIVATE BY YOUR TOUCH ALONE.

YOU REALLY ARE THE CHOSEN SAVIOR.

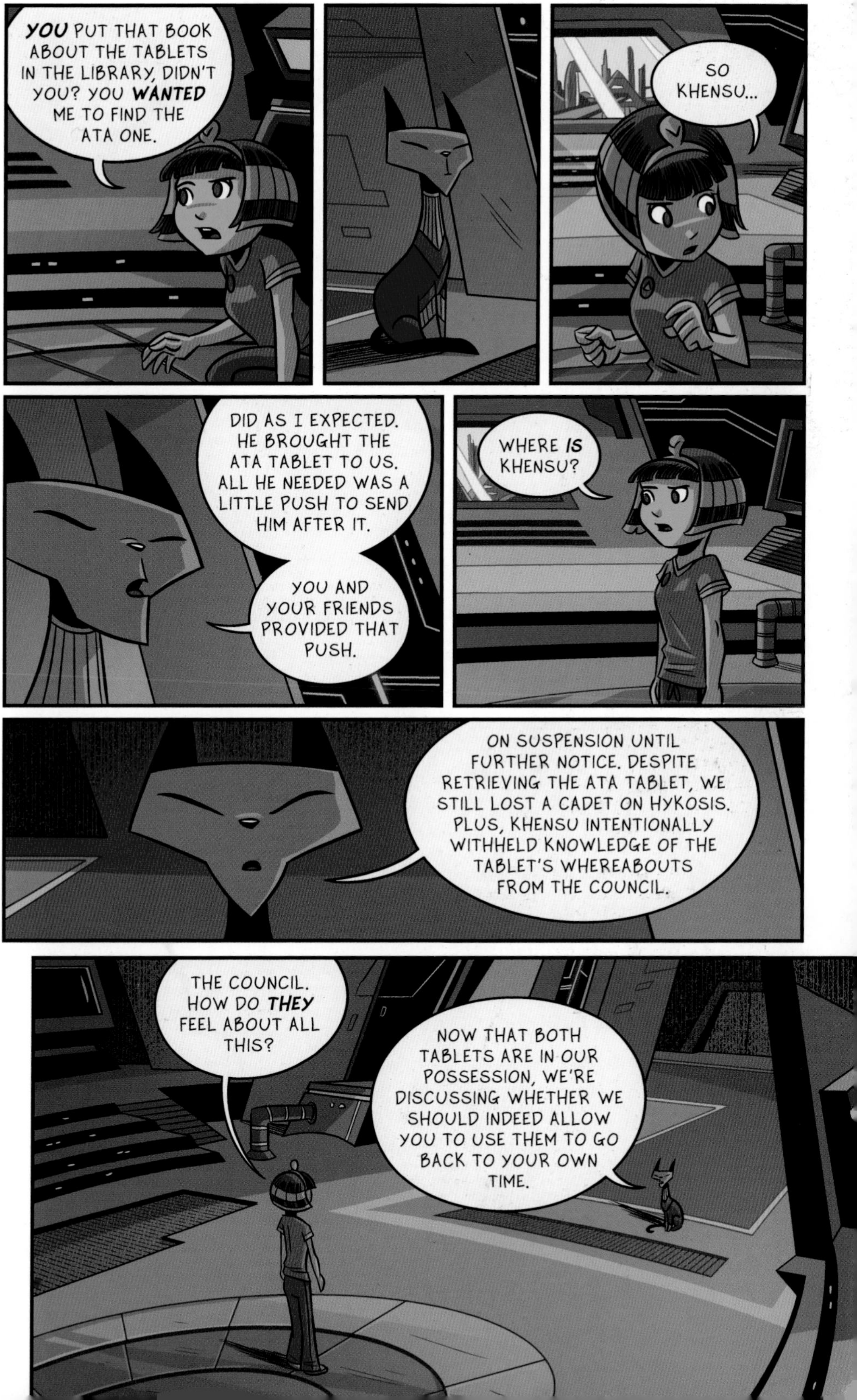
YOU PUT THAT BOOK ABOUT THE TABLETS IN THE LIBRARY, DIDN'T YOU? YOU WANTED ME TO FIND THE ATA ONE.
SO KHENSU...
DID AS I EXPECTED. HE BROUGHT THE ATA TABLET TO US. ALL HE NEEDED WAS A LITTLE PUSH TO SEND HIM AFTER IT.
YOU AND YOUR FRIENDS PROVIDED THAT PUSH.
WHERE IS KHENSU?
ON SUSPENSION UNTIL FURTHER NOTICE. DESPITE RETRIEVING THE ATA TABLET, WE STILL LOST A CADET ON HYKOSIS. PLUS, KHENSU INTENTIONALLY WITHHELD KNOWLEDGE OF THE TABLET'S WHEREABOUTS FROM THE COUNCIL.
THE COUNCIL. HOW DO THEY FEEL ABOUT ALL THIS?
NOW THAT BOTH TABLETS ARE IN OUR POSSESSION, WE'RE DISCUSSING WHETHER WE SHOULD INDEED ALLOW YOU TO USE THEM TO GO BACK TO YOUR OWN TIME.

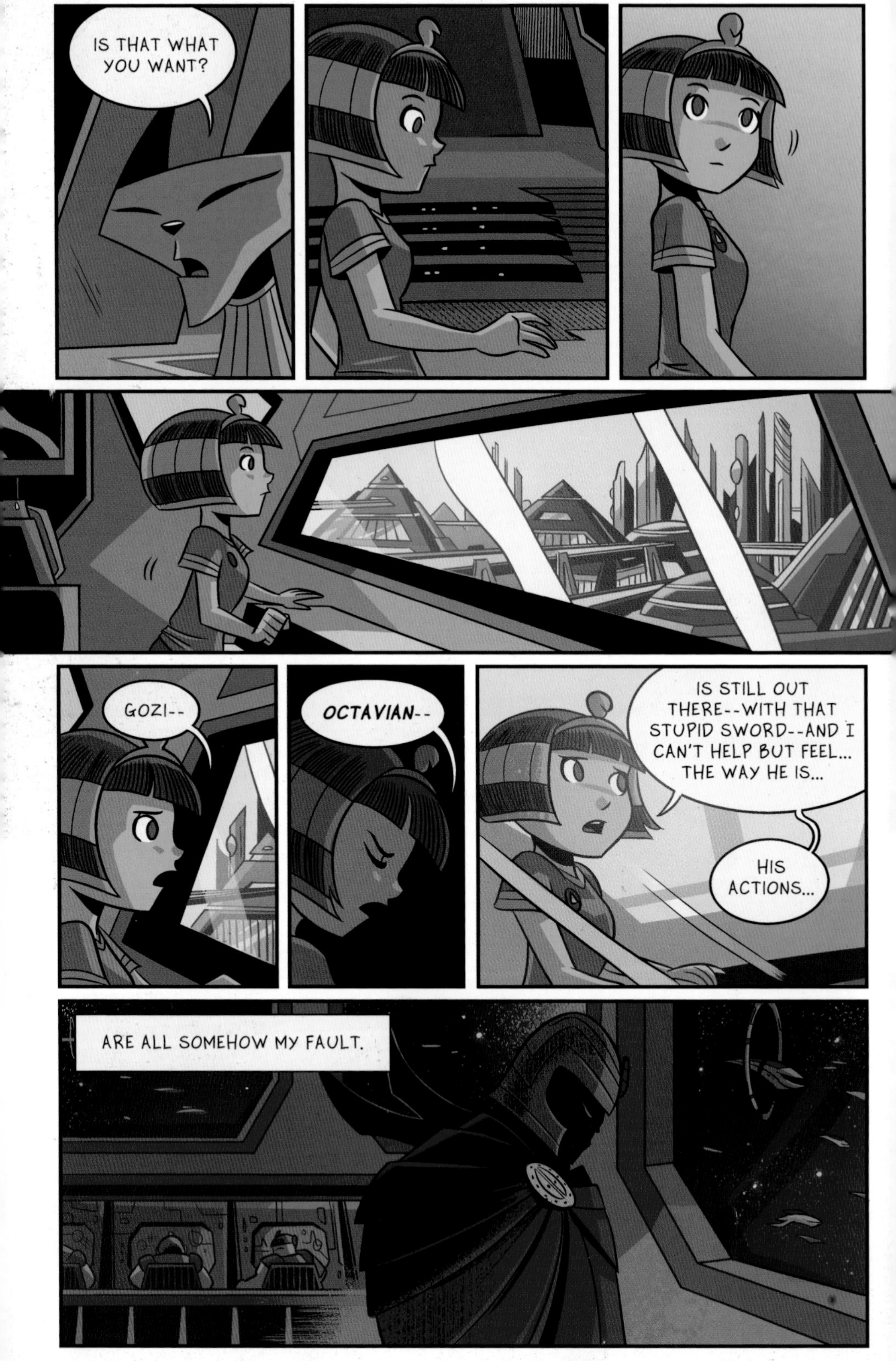
IS THAT WHAT YOU WANT?
GOZI--
OCTAVIAN--
IS STILL OUT THERE--WITH THAT STUPID SWORD--AND I CAN'T HELP BUT FEEL... THE WAY HE IS...
HIS ACTIONS...
ARE ALL SOMEHOW MY FAULT.

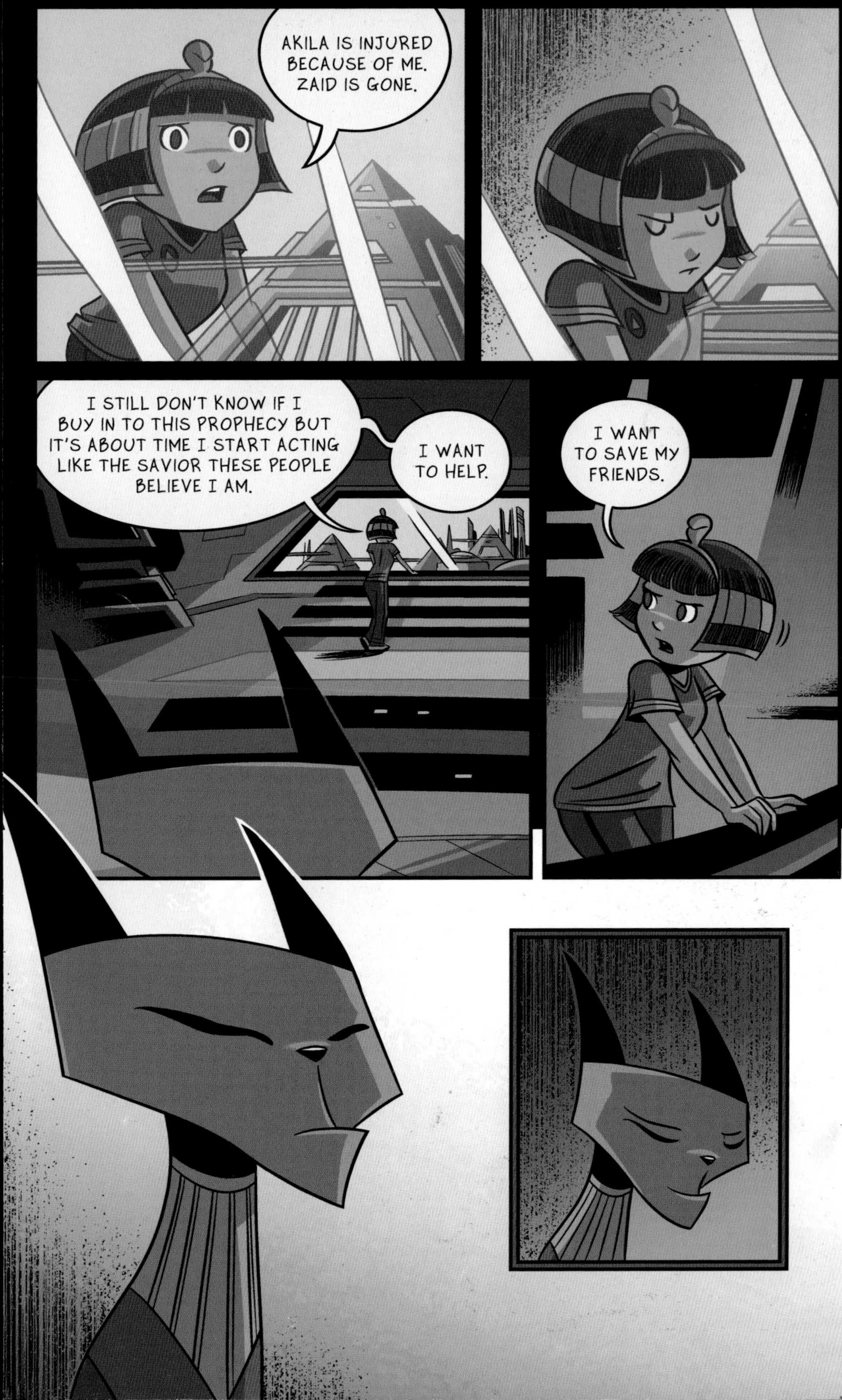
AKILA IS INJURED BECAUSE OF ME. ZAID IS GONE.
I STILL DON'T KNOW IF I BUY IN TO THIS PROPHECY BUT IT'S ABOUT TIME I START ACTING LIKE THE SAVIOR THESE PEOPLE BELIEVE I AM.
I WANT TO HELP.
I WANT TO SAVE MY FRIENDS.

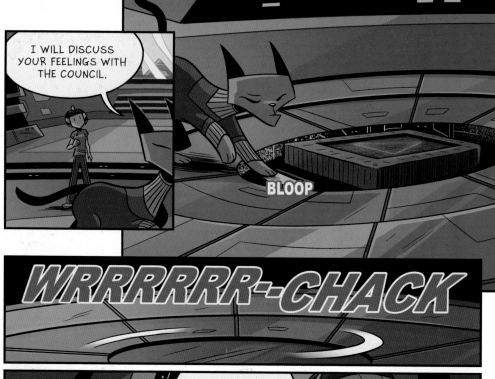

I WILL DISCUSS YOUR FEELINGS WITH THE COUNCIL.

BLOOP

WRRRRRR--CHACK

FOR NOW, I THINK IT'S BEST YOU GET SOME REST.

PHARAOH YOSIRA!

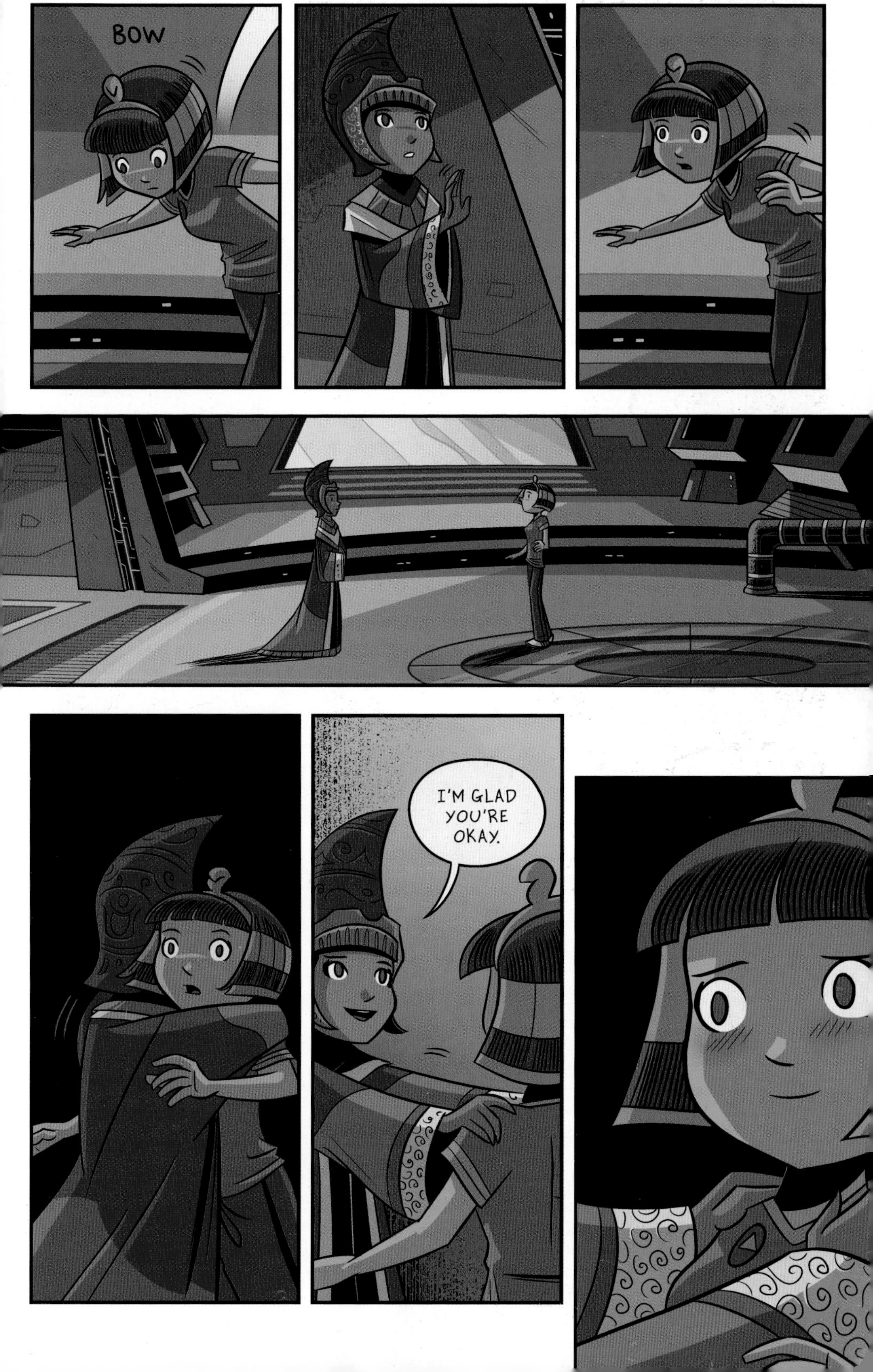
BOW
I'M GLAD YOU'RE OKAY.

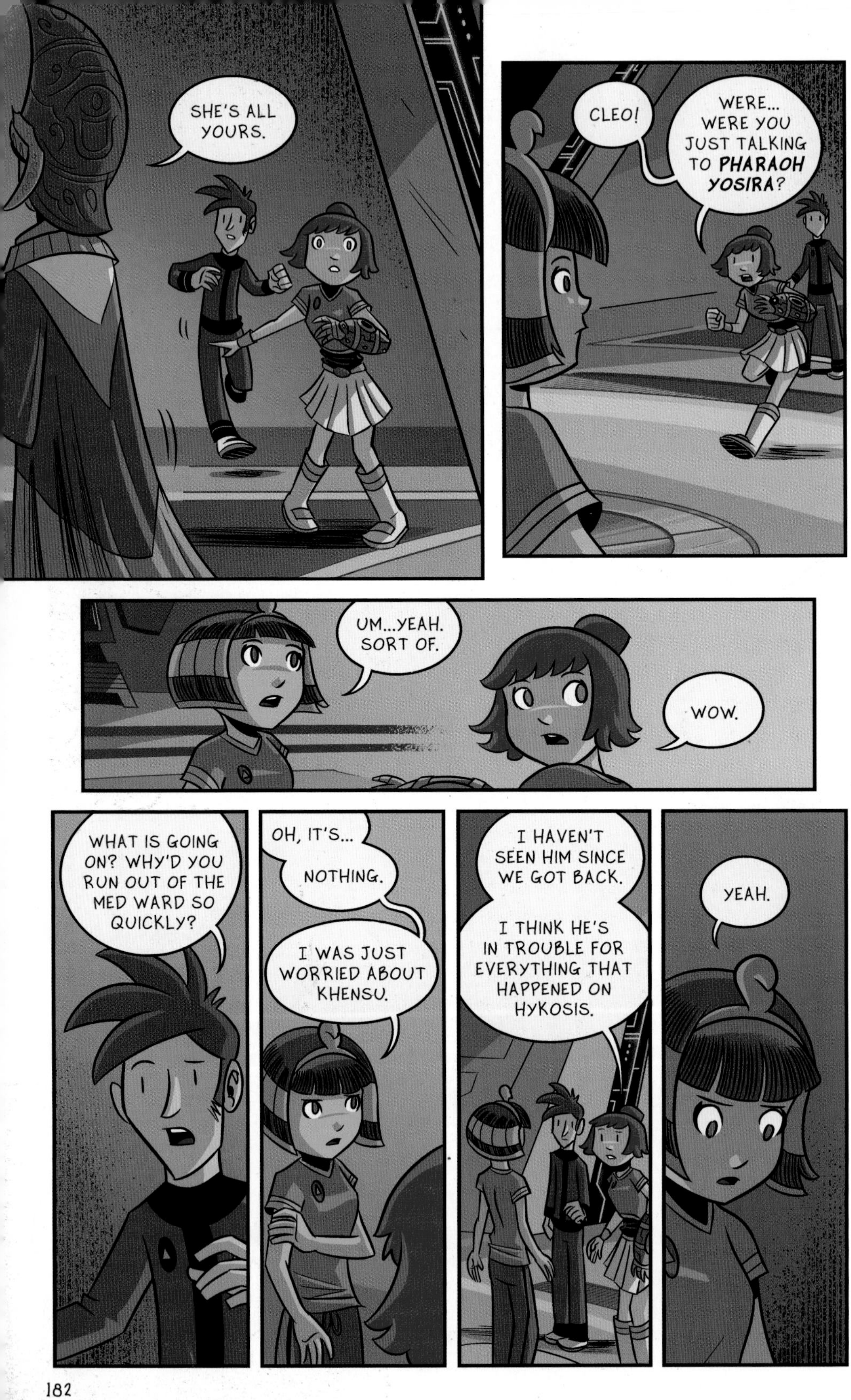
SHE'S ALL YOURS.
CLEO!
WERE... WERE YOU JUST TALKING TO **PHARAOH YOSIRA**?
UM...YEAH. SORT OF.
WOW.
WHAT IS GOING ON? WHY'D YOU RUN OUT OF THE MED WARD SO QUICKLY?
OH, IT'S...
NOTHING.
I WAS JUST WORRIED ABOUT KHENSU.
I HAVEN'T SEEN HIM SINCE WE GOT BACK.
I THINK HE'S IN TROUBLE FOR EVERYTHING THAT HAPPENED ON HYKOSIS.
YEAH.

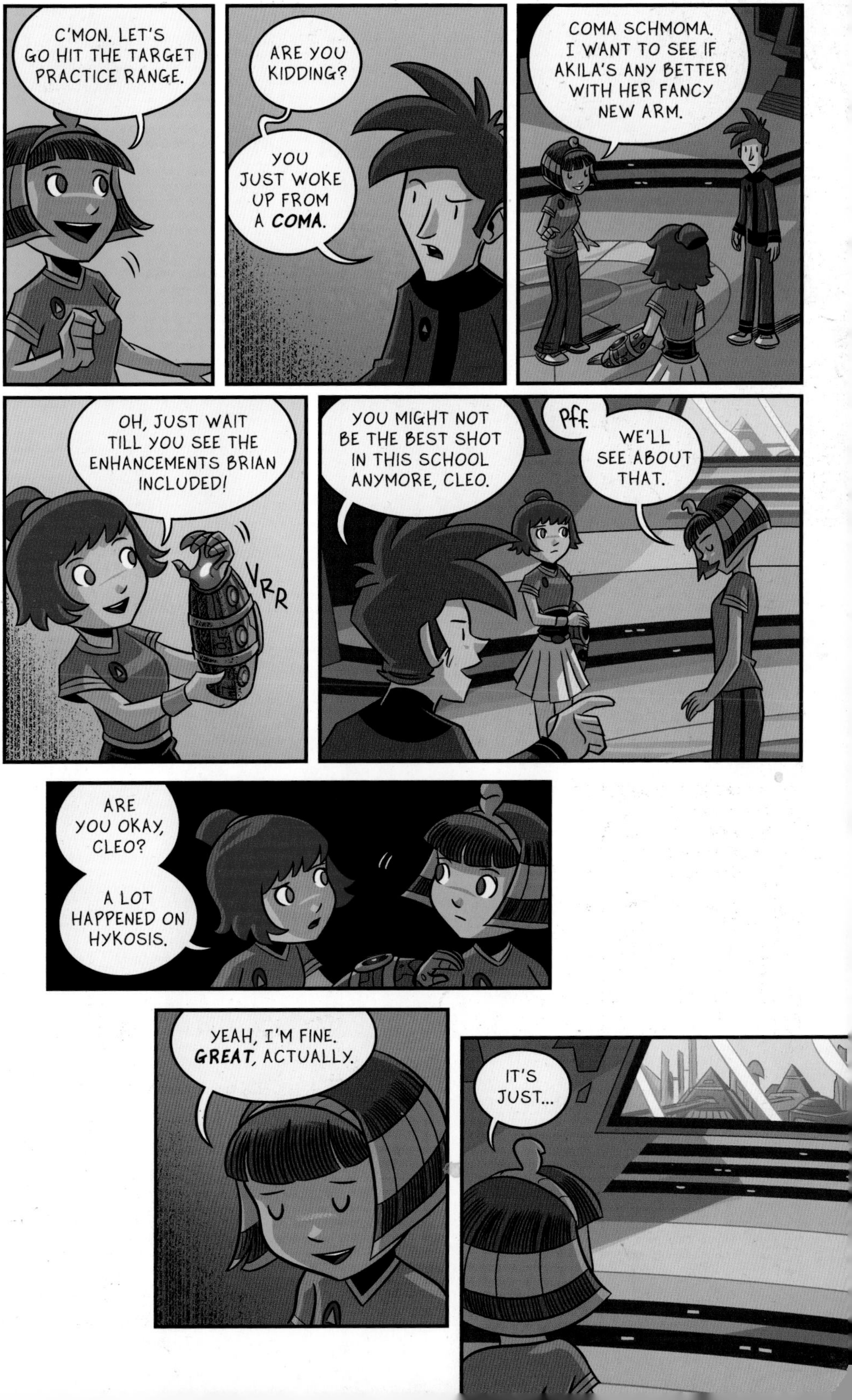
C'MON. LET'S GO HIT THE TARGET PRACTICE RANGE.
ARE YOU KIDDING?
YOU JUST WOKE UP FROM A **COMA**.
COMA SCHMOMA. I WANT TO SEE IF AKILA'S ANY BETTER WITH HER FANCY NEW ARM.
OH, JUST WAIT TILL YOU SEE THE ENHANCEMENTS BRIAN INCLUDED!
VRR
YOU MIGHT NOT BE THE BEST SHOT IN THIS SCHOOL ANYMORE, CLEO.
Pff.
WE'LL SEE ABOUT THAT.
ARE YOU OKAY, CLEO?
A LOT HAPPENED ON HYKOSIS.
YEAH, I'M FINE. **GREAT**, ACTUALLY.
IT'S JUST...

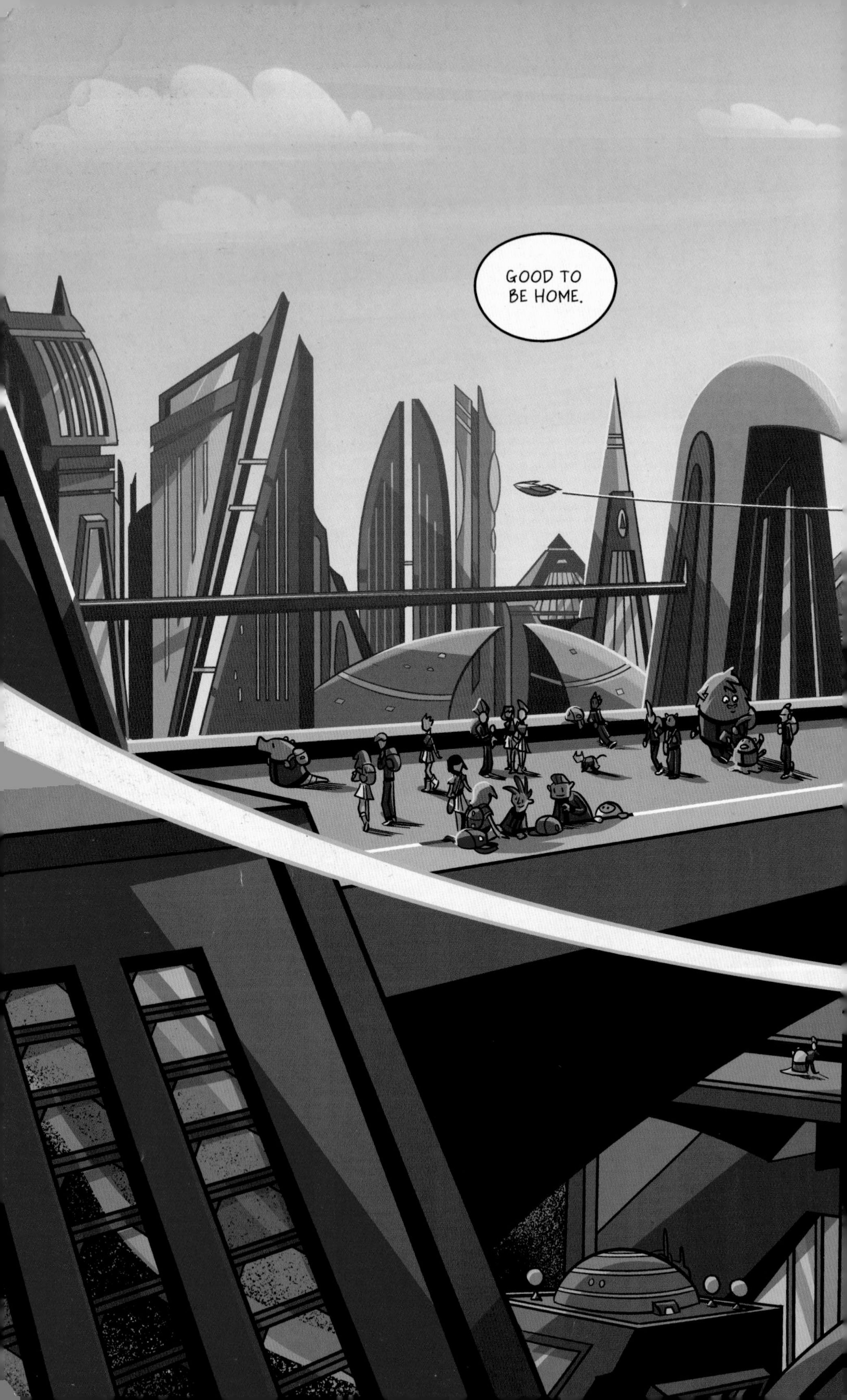
GOOD TO BE HOME.

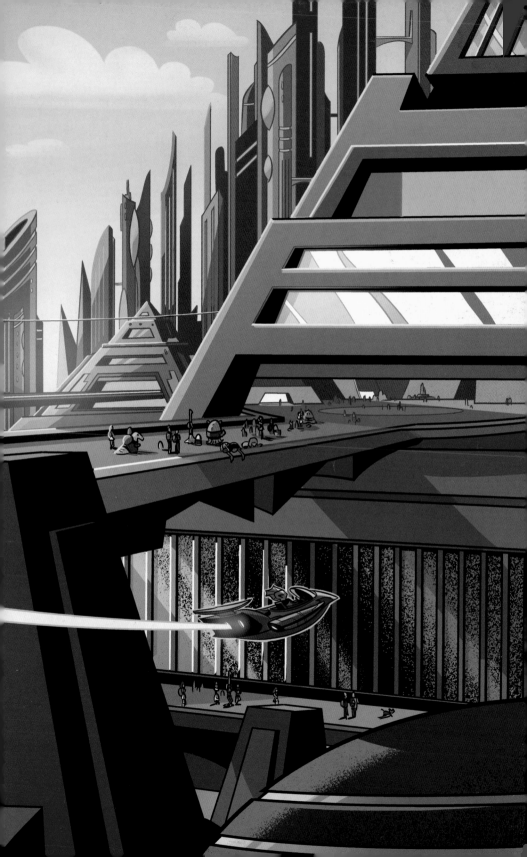

SPECIAL THANKS TO:

My incredibly supportive (and patient) family: Jen and Oliver and Orion Maihack, Sam and Barb Maihack, Brian and Jill Maeda, Patrick and Kim Tally, John and Darci Roberts, Chad and Jen Roberts, KeAli'i and Lindsey Rozet, Randy and Janice Meade, and everyone else I wish I had room to include here (there are so many of you now!).

My chill office companion, Misty. Your purring eased the stressful bits of this book. My attention-craving office companion, Ash. I still miss you.

The superheroic folks at Scholastic (including but not limited to): Cassandra Pelham, David Saylor, Phil Falco, Lizette Serrano, Sheila Marie Everett, Tracy van Straaten, Bess Braswell, Denise Anderson, and Ed Masessa.

My agent, Judy Hansen. Please don't ever leave me.

Christ, for the various paths You presented to me this year, giving me the freedom to choose which ones to take, and then preparing me for what I found along the way.

Google Images, for your endless array of cowboy hats.

EXTRA SPECIAL THANKS TO:

All of the teachers, librarians, booksellers, parents, and readers out there who have supported Cleopatra in Space thus far. YOU GUYS ARE AWESOME!

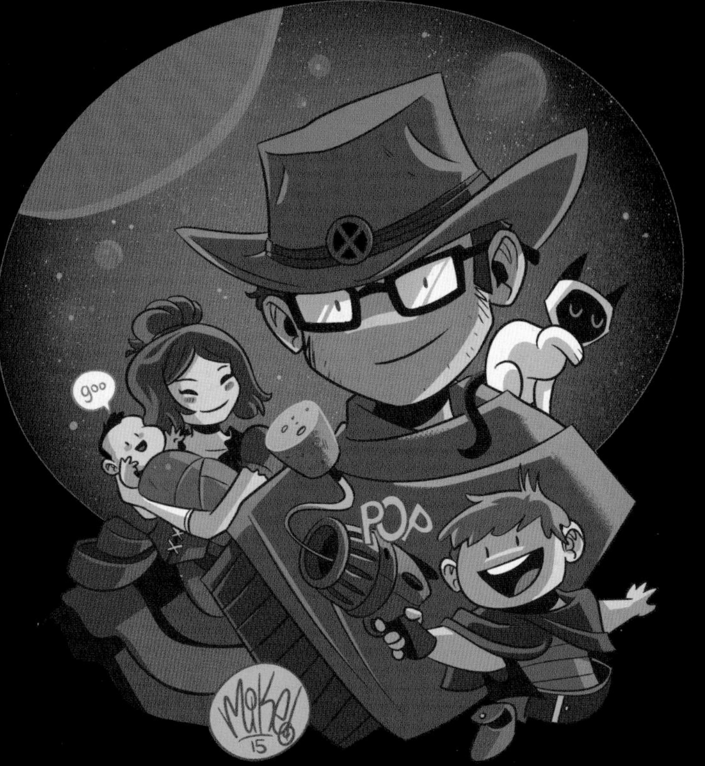
goo
POP

ABOUT THE AUTHOR

A graduate of the Columbus College of Art & Design, Mike Maihack spends his time, well, working on the Cleopatra in Space series. He is the creator of the popular webcomic *Cow & Buffalo* and has contributed to books like Sensation Comics Featuring Wonder Woman; *Parable*; *Jim Henson's The Storyteller*; Cow Boy; *Geeks, Girls, and Secret Identities*; and *Comic Book Tattoo*. *Cleopatra in Space: Secret of the Time Tablets* is Mike's third graphic novel, following *Target Practice*, which won a Florida Book Award, and *The Thief and the Sword*. He lives with his wife, two sons, and Siamese cat down in the humid depths of Lutz, Florida.

Visit Mike online at www.mikemaihack.com and follow him on Twitter at @mikemaihack.

ALSO BY MIKE MAIHACK

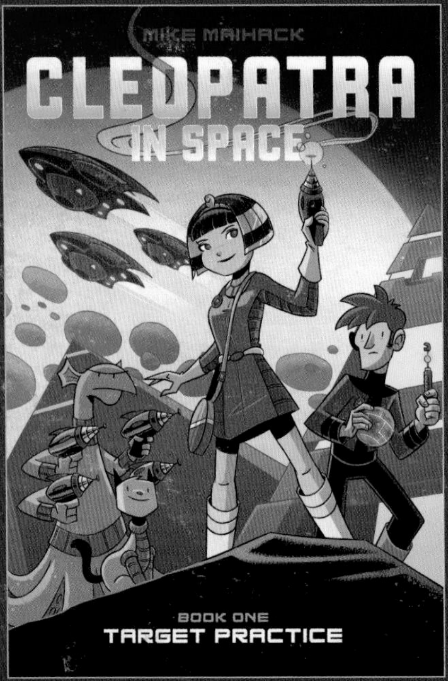
MIKE MAIHACK
CLEOPATRA
IN SPACE
BOOK ONE
TARGET PRACTICE

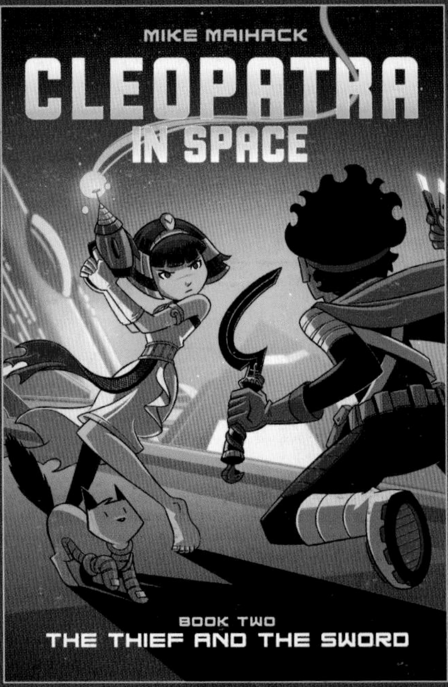
MIKE MAIHACK
CLEOPATRA
IN SPACE
BOOK TWO
THE THIEF AND THE SWORD